# Thinking Community Music

# Thinking Community Music

LEE HIGGINS

# OXFORD
UNIVERSITY PRESS

Oxford University Press is a department of the University of Oxford.
It furthers the University's objective of excellence in research, scholarship,
and education by publishing worldwide. Oxford is a registered trade mark of
Oxford University Press in the UK and in certain other countries.

Published in the United States of America by Oxford University Press
198 Madison Avenue, New York, NY 10016, United States of America.

© Oxford University Press 2024

All rights reserved. No part of this publication may be reproduced, stored in
a retrieval system, or transmitted, in any form or by any means, without the
prior permission in writing of Oxford University Press, or as expressly permitted
by law, by license or under terms agreed with the appropriate reprographics
rights organization. Inquiries concerning reproduction outside the scope of the
above should be sent to the Rights Department, Oxford University Press, at the
address above.

You must not circulate this work in any other form
and you must impose this same condition on any acquirer

Library of Congress Cataloging-in-Publication Data
Names: Higgins, Lee, 1964– author.
Title: Thinking community music / Lee Higgins.
Description: [1.] | New York : Oxford University Press, 2024. |
Includes bibliographical references and index.
Identifiers: LCCN 2024017243 (print) | LCCN 2024017244 (ebook) |
ISBN 9780190246990 (paperback) | ISBN 9780190246983 (hardback) |
ISBN 9780190247027 | ISBN 9780190247010 (epub)
Subjects: LCSH: Community music—History and criticism. | Music—Social aspects.
Classification: LCC ML3916 .H563 2024 (print) | LCC ML3916 (ebook) |
DDC 780.71—dc23/eng/20240416
LC record available at https://lccn.loc.gov/2024017243
LC ebook record available at https://lccn.loc.gov/2024017244

DOI: 10.1093/9780190247027.001.0001

Paperback printed by Marquis Book Printing, Canada
Hardback printed by Bridgeport National Bindery, Inc., United States of America

*For all those community musicians that
I have met and collaborated with along the way.
Your commitment to the work takes my breath away.*

# Contents

| | |
|---|---|
| *Figure List* | ix |
| *Acknowledgments* | xi |
| Arrival | 1 |
| 1. Intervention | 25 |
| 2. Hospitality | 39 |
| 3. Pedagogy | 62 |
| 4. Social Justice | 85 |
| 5. Inclusion and Excellence | 97 |
| 6. Music | 111 |
| 7. Research | 130 |
| 8. Becoming | 152 |
| Departure | 177 |
| *References* | 183 |
| *Index* | 207 |

# Figure List

| | |
|---|---|
| A.1. Community Music Assemblage | 14 |
| 3.1. Informal, Non-formal, Formal Continuum | 71 |
| 3.2. Music Making in a Youth Club | 72 |
| 3.3. School of Rock | 72 |
| 3.4. Rock 'n' Roll After-School Club for Girls | 74 |
| 3.5. Samba at FDA | 82 |
| 5.1. Inclusion as a Process | 106 |
| 5.2. Inclusion as the Outcome | 108 |
| 8.1. Community Music Assemblage | 176 |
| D.1. Concept Mind Map | 178 |

# Acknowledgments

Thank you to Norm, who kept the faith

A big thanks to those who were part of the ICCMs writing retreats and offered an ear to the various drafts, especially to Catherine and Sarah-Jane.

Daniel Stirrup for the illustrations.

To Dave, Brydie, Helen, and Jo thank you for giving time and offering constructive comments. Your suggestions really helped solidify the ideas. A special thanks to Roger for the care he gave and the insights – your critical eye has strengthened my work through the years of our friendship.

Thank you to those that contributed to the illustrations of practice: Wang Lin Lin, Fiona Chatwin, School of Rock, Esme Bridie, Dana Monteiro, Huib Schippers, Olcay Muslu, Andre de Quadros, Connect music project, Johnny Mekoa, Jo Gibson, Simon Glenister, and Charlie Keil.

Thanks to Meredith and the whole OUP team.

To my family, Holly, Esme, George, Stephen and Mum. Thanks for Being there.

Finally –to Michelle for her unwavering support - I love you always and look forward to our continuing journey together.

# Arrival

The genesis of this book began many years ago. I can clearly remember the initial conversation with the acquisitions editor for Oxford University Press (OUP), Norman Hirschy. We were at a conference in Cambridge, Massachusetts, and the year was 2013 (I particularly remember that week because the Boston Red Sox won the World Series, and the city went wild with excitement). Norm encouraged me to work on something that built upon my 2012 OUP publication, and the following year, I produced an outline and secured a contract for publication. Although that particular title was set for a different course, my overarching project has always dealt with similar questions. Consequently, the book you are reading has many similar overtones and features to the original proposal; however, the path to get here differs from the initially envisioned journey. *Thinking Community Music* has undoubtedly taken some time to arrive—I liken it to being in a holding pattern, waiting for the right time, looking for the approach lights to guide me toward the form through which I can land its ideas. As a "complete" text, this book is a "pulling together" of thoughts, writings, presentations, conference papers, and experiences from around 2010 until now. Some of the things I present have been previously published in different forms, while many of the ideas have only ever existed as notes for teaching seminars, conference presentations, and/or memories of the many conversations with colleagues, students, and practitioners over the years.

Kaleidoscopic in nature, the "chapters," or *think pieces* as I have called them, can be read in any order, although it is important to read "Arrival" first for context.[1] There are eight think pieces in all. Each contains several elements: (1) a critical question; (2) illustrations of practice: examples of work that ground the ideas through concrete explanations—these examples are embodiments of the ideals and idea to be discussed; (3) a provocation

---

[1] This idea is reminiscent of the metaphor used to describe Deleuze and Guattari's *A Thousand Plateaus*, that of a vinyl record (1988, p. xiii). *Kaleidoscope* is also an American heist drama where the episodes can be watched in any order.

*Thinking Community Music.* Lee Higgins, Oxford University Press. © Oxford University Press 2024.
DOI: 10.1093/9780190247027.003.0001

## 2 THINKING COMMUNITY MUSIC

and/or some theoretical exploration: ideals community musicians might strive for rather than statements of fact; (4) exploratory thoughts and reflection; and (5) closing remarks called "flight lines," a section that poses further questions and considers how things might connect rather than how things "are."

The central questions have been constructed as a response to issues and themes commonly arising through the wider discourse as I have experienced it. The eight guiding questions are:

1. *Is the notion of intervention apt for a growing global field?*
2. *What makes the idea of community music as an act of hospitality important?*
3. *Can community music have a pedagogy?*
4. *How might social justice be understood as a framework for community music practices?*
5. *How might notions of excellence and inclusion exist as a balanced pairing?*
6. *How might we understand the "music" in community music?*
7. *How might I do community music research?*
8. *How might community music become?*

Each think piece has been conceived as a self-contained jumping-off point, a moment of reflection and a springboard for discussion, an opportunity to extend the conversation into a larger arena, for example, a seminar, symposium, conference, pub discussion, or further research and publications. The end chapter is entitled "Departure" and takes the key ideas from each flight line and weaves them into five short statements. Labeled "constellations," each statement represents a particular perspective and suggests multiple connection points. Although "Departure" is the "final" section, it can be read at any point during the reading process and, therefore, can act as an opening for the think pieces, albeit through a different direction.

It is important to acknowledge that the ideas in this book have been written from my perspective and flow from the particular position from within the field that I am part of. This statement might sound rather obvious, but it feels necessary and is in keeping with the book's theoretical framework. The central driving force behind *Thinking Community Music* was to create something that encourages the practitioner-researcher in a journey of reflection with an overall aim to strengthen community music practices in all its diverse forms. I am aware that there continues to be some tensions regarding what might be described as the "academicization" of community music. I understand this to mean intellectually colonizing the practice through theory in a way divorced from the "doing" of community music. I know that my book *Community Music: In Theory and in Practice* is sometimes seen as instrumental in bringing this about. In light of this, it feels essential to underline that this book has been written to support current practices, as I understand them, and future iterations that have yet to be. Alongside this, community music can be a powerful critical lens through which to consider other music-making experiences. My aspirations would be that the ideas proposed here will be helpful to those working in music education, ethnomusicology, music therapy, and musicology, among other fields of practice that intersect with community music, such as social work.

The following section offers a broad contextual overview of community music from then until now, providing a historical map to help with orientation.

## Historical Map

From an ethnomusicological perspective, music is a distinctively human practice and a fundamental aspect of what makes humans different from other species (Blacking, 1973). The act of "musicking," as musicologist Christopher Small (1998) might term it, supports us in our understanding of who we are. Music can be a lifeline, a dynamic aspect of individuality, and a significant contributor to personal and group identity (MacDonald et al., 2002; Stokes, 1994). For people of all cultures around the world, music has been a vital form of expression and communication (Hesser & Bartleet, 2020). Community musicians often quote Article 27 in the Universal Declaration of Human Rights, which states that "everyone has the right to participate freely in the cultural life of the community, to enjoy the arts and to share in scientific advancement and its benefits."[2] From this

---

[2] https://www.un.org/en/about-us/universal-declaration-of-human-rights. Owen Kelly (2023) makes the point that these articles are rooted in a particular view of people as individuals and therefore reflective of a "post-Cartesian" view of European history in which nations consist of a state apparatus that oversees individuals who may, if they so wish, form communities or other types of groups. As such, this does not adhere to how people come to be as we are all, first and foremost, born into a community.

# 4 THINKING COMMUNITY MUSIC

perspective, effective community music processes can be understood as ethical responses to issues concerning social justice. As part of a broader musical ecosystem, community music has a vital role in developing active music making throughout the lifespan. It is important because it can propose critical questions about the role of music in society, its value, funding policies, and issues surrounding teaching and learning processes. As a musical practice that emphasizes people, participation, places, inclusivity, and diversity, there has been a growing program of scholarship and international projects. More recently there have been invaluable insights from cultural contexts from the Majority World and Indigenous populations, challenging and problematizing accepted approaches, priorities, and ideas within the field. The growth of scholarship and academic courses has also increased the number of people engaging in community music, and these new voices, agendas, and contexts point toward a field that is expanding and diversifying. To create a jumping-off point for the eight think pieces that follow, I will begin by offering a historical sketch (at least how I see it) of two key moments and describe why I think they are significant both in terms of the field and specifically for this book.[3]

## 1984: Establishing Practices

The year 1984 was a "key year" for community music (Joss, 1993). Two significant things happened: First, the Commission for Community Music Activity (CMA) was adopted as the seventh International Society of Music Education's (ISME) discrete working group.[4] Second, the Music Education Working Party (MEWP), organized and managed by what was then called the Arts Council of Great Britain, was inaugurated with a mission to forge a connection between the worlds of education, community, and music.[5] These two developments were of international importance in at least three ways: First, the MEWP provided validation and working opportunities

---

[3] It was brought to my attention during the review stage of this book that another key moment may be located around 2018, a time when the voices of First Nations musicians and those from what is sometimes described as the Global South began to have more prominence.

[4] https://www.isme.org/our-work/commissions/community-music-activity-commission-cma

[5] In Tim Joss's original statement, he highlights three significant things. The first was the appointment of an orchestral education manager to the London Sinfonietta and the first full-scale community residency by a British orchestra. I have narrowed these down to what I consider the most important two for the context of this book.

for musicians who had been previously engaged in the capacity of a music leader or facilitator outside of formal music education arenas. Although an initiative from England, the recommendations of the MEWP helped generate a new breed of music professional, initially named *music animateur or music development worker*, that has had influence beyond the country. These include musicians who have an aptitude toward socially engaged art, artistic citizenship, community cultural development, and more broadly those involved in community arts (Adams & Goldbard, 2001; Goldbard, 2006; Jeffers & Moriarty, 2017; Kelly, 1984; Matarasso, 1994; Naidus, 2009; Phillips et al., 2020) Elliott, Silverman & Bowman (2017).[6] Second, the CMA heralded a formal recognition from within music education that valuable musical experiences happen in places such as youth clubs, enclosed environments, and health settings and within local communities. The creation of the CMA provided a much-needed space to discuss and debate issues concerning what was framed as "community music activity." Musics from other cultures, such as Brazilian samba, steel pan playing from the Caribbean, Ghanian drumming, and Indonesian gamelan, as well as experimental music composition, free improvisation, and contemporary pop and rock music, were implicit in the discussions of the CMA from its inception. The biennal symposium it hosted became an environment that enabled those interested in participatory music making to reflect on their practices away from the day-to-day business of seeking work or running music workshops. These meetings were a rarefied space for musicians working within a freelance economy and an environment where those teaching within higher education interested in its activities could find out more. Early pioneers of the CMA, such as Einar Solbu, John Drummond, David Price, Tim Joss, Sallyann Goodall, Elizabeth Oebrle, and Kari Veblen, brought a variety of ideas surrounding practice and theory that created a healthy atmosphere of debate and discussion that went on to spawn several regional offshoots.[7] Finally, both the MEWP and the CMA gave credence to musics beyond the European classical canon, a style of music that had dominated formal music education in schools, conservatoires, and universities. Their existence provided legitimacy for those looking to shake up the music education system.

---

[6] For a discussion on the development of the music animateur in the United Kingdom see Higgins (2012b, pp. 46–49).

[7] For a presentation of its history up to 2007, see (McCarthy, 2008, pp. 49–61).

6 THINKING COMMUNITY MUSIC

Essential conceptual touchstones included:

- the ideas emulating from Paulo Freire's (1970/2002) account of critical pedagogy or liberatory education and his use of *conscientization* as a process of emancipation;
- Christopher Small's (1977) seminal book *Music Society Education* that challenged the elitism in the musical traditions of Western societies in contrast to the communal music making of other cultures and was a precursor to his notion of musicking (1987, 1998), a verb that emphasized the doing of music;
- John Blacking's (1973) collection of lectures entitled *How Musical Is Man?* built upon Alan Merriam's (1964) anthropological discussion surrounding the importance of music in the lives of human beings and later the work of Pat Campbell (1996), for example, the chapter "Music, Education, and Community in a Multicultural Society"; and
- Kari Veblen and Bengt Olsson's (2002) chapter "Community Music: Toward an International Overview," which was published in the second iteration of *The New Handbook of Research on Music Teaching and Learning.*

From sociological and ethnomusicological perspectives, both Small and Blacking had advocated a broader approach to music education, which resonated with those involved in community music in those early days. Underpinning these ideas was the concept of cultural democracy. As an idea, cultural democracy "revolves around the notion of plurality and around equality of access to the means of cultural production and distribution" (Kelly, 2023, p. 128). It is "an approach to arts and culture that actively engages everyone in deciding what counts as culture, where it happens, who makes it, and who experiences it" (64 Million Artists, 2018, p. 2). As part of a broader social discourse, cultural democracy's potency relies on its interactions with the cultural sphere and the economics and political domains, offering a shift away "from a view of culture as consisting of Great Works made by "artists" to a view of everyday creativity" (Kelly, 2023, p. 174). It is not, therefore, to be understood as just an argument for changes to centralized arts funding policies but as a central concept that drove community music at this time. As a key concept, the idea will feature prominently throughout this book.

Between 1984 and the time of writing, a rich array of work can be categorized under the banner of community music. This includes music projects, education and training developments, networks and national organizations, conferences, reports, evaluations, and research. There has been fascinating work from Singapore to South Africa, Israel to Ireland, Australia to Austria, the United States to the United Kingdom, all made possible by the many dedicated musicians, advocates, and policymakers committed to the larger project. So why begin by describing some of the consequences of what happened in the "key year" of 1984? Historically, this time was influential in establishing many things now associated with community music practice. I propose that the practice reached another milestone, another "key year," in its growth and development between 2012 and 2013, some 20 years after Tim Joss made the initial statement (see footnote 5). Before elaborating on this premise, please be mindful that I am aware that history is a fuzzy and inaccurate measure and always depends on who is telling the story and, therefore, controlling the narrative. My background, context, economic status, gender, and ethnicity are all part of my experience and thus shape my perspective. That said, I hope to offer a convincing reason for observing that 2012–2013 is an important milestone for the practice.

## 2012–2013: An Emergent Field

Between July 2012 and January 2013, a trio of scholarly works were published that directly addressed concerns about community music. In order of publication date, these included my *Community Music: In Theory and in Practice* (Higgins, 2012b), the first full-length work on the subject that investigated community music as an active intervention and offered a theoretical framework from which the activities could be described and analyzed. Next came a two-volume set, *The Oxford Handbook of Music Education*, edited by Gary McPherson and Graham Welch (2012a, 2012b). In volume two, and relevant to this discussion, is the dedicated section "Music in the Community." The section was edited by David Elliott, a North American music educator who has been an important figure in the history of community music scholarship, most noticeably through his influential philosophical framework commonly described as the paraxial approach to music education (Elliott, 1995, 2005).[8] Previously, with different editors in 1992 (Colwell, 1992) and 2002 (Colwell & Richardson, 2002), *The Oxford Handbook of Music Education* was the

[8] See Think Piece 6: Praxis.

8  THINKING COMMUNITY MUSIC

third incarnation of this type of tome; the others were published by Schirmer Books and Oxford University Press, respectfully. Although different in many ways, *The Oxford Handbook of Music Education* became the first to include a dedicated section on community music activity. The 2002 edition included the chapter "Community Music: Toward an International Overview" by Kari Veblen and Bengt Olsson (2002) and was placed within the section "Social and Cultural Contexts." Veblen and Olsson's chapter was isolated in terms of being the only text that directly discussed the concerns of the community musician and was influential in laying out a broad groundwork at the time. The 2012 handbook includes seven chapters and a commentary from the section editor covering topics such as social capital (Jones & Langston, 2012), social justice (Silverman, 2012), at-risk youth (Cohen et al., 2012), and migration and community (Phelan, 2012).[9] The final publication in this trio appeared in early 2013 and was entitled *Community Music Today* (Veblen et al., 2013). A confessed "labor of love," this book was an edited collection guided by the music educator and community music researcher Kari Veblen. The tome featured a collection of 20 essays and, according to Veblen's introduction, "illuminates the work of community music workers who improvise and reinvent themselves and their vision in order to lead through music and other expressive media and attempt to answer the perennial equation 'What is Community Music?'" (Veblen et al., 2013, p. 1). With over 50 contributors, each intent on sharing their stories and contextual perspectives, *Community Music Today* threads the many ways of community music into a tapestry of voices from across the globe. As a collection of community music moments, what is striking is a general resistance toward any sense of homogeneity, a refusal to ground community music in any one definitive statement. In addition to these texts, the *International Journal of Community Music* (IJCM) deserves mention because, during this time, it moved into its sixth year of commercial publication and had doubled its institutional circulation since its inception in 2008 (see Think Piece 7). Between 2012 and 2013, the journal published 43 articles and project reports responding to issues surrounding work connected to disability, well-being, technology, recreation, lifelong learning, service learning, homelessness, and positive aging.[10] In short, it was during these years that a critical mass of published scholarship provided

---

[9] A multivolume paperback has since been released. The community music section is contained in volume 4, entitled *Special Needs, Community Music, and Adult Learning* (McPherson & Welch, 2018).

[10] See the journal's webpage: https://www.intellectbooks.com/international-journal-of-community-music

the "practical" enterprise of community music, a body of scholarship and research that had not previously been available.

Crucial to my reasoning that this period can be understood as significant is the framing of community music as a practical enterprise, which is why I place the word in quotation marks above. Over the years that I have been involved in community music, it has been my experience that many of those working in this domain actively resist the notion of theoretically thinking about the work.[11] Vehemently describing activities as "practical" has been used by some to separate practice from theory, creating what I see as a false opposition. In saying this, there are some very good reasons this might be so. Most people who describe themselves as community musicians do not have regular full-time employment, tending to operate as freelancers within the self-employed economy; it is far more common to find community musicians holding a portfolio career, a series of short contracts, part-time work, and one-off engagements. This means community musicians are always seeking and occupied-in, pursuing the next gig or contractual arrangement. For many reasons, such as lost earnings, previous bookings, and individual costs, freelance employment arrangements do not lend themselves easily to the "luxury" of going to conferences to discuss the whys and wherefores of the work. Although a generalization, those who attend seminars, symposia, and conferences are, by and large, professors and lecturers working in higher education. This fact can underscore the sense that those "philosophizing" about the work are disconnected from the practical doing of what they purport to discuss. Describing the work in terms of the practical also speaks to the grassroots nature of community music and its associated processes of engagement.[12] Working collaboratively with people in ways that seek coauthorship can be "messy"; it is challenging work that often takes place in complex contexts and with limited resources. As a practice that has its history in the social activist movements of the late 1960s and 1970s, a call to action in a fight against the privileged few having access to "cultural" activities, it is understandable that musicians who were drawn to its vision were fixed on getting things done, in providing a solution for change rather than sitting around thinking about it.

These may be broad-brush generalizations but nevertheless do speak to my experience. By way of a personal story, when I was halfway through my PhD research, around 2003, I had several comments and accusations that

---

[11] See also Brown et al. (2014) and McKay and Higham (2012).

[12] This is what I perceive Dave Camlin (2023) is referring to when he states that "CM is a practical activity" within his philosophical text (p. 29).

10 THINKING COMMUNITY MUSIC

challenged the very need to engage with community music conceptually. In one instance, someone suggested that my time would be much better served running musical activities rather than "navel gazing"! That said, a good number of inspirational people have understood that theory and practice are interdependent and, if embraced together, can and do provide a powerful combination through which arguments about the work can be made.

What of the publications that appeared between 2012 and 2013? How can they be understood as signaling a significant moment in the development and growth of community music? I propose that after this date, community music could be recognized and named as a "field of practice." This means that (1) its practical imperative, a honed set of skills and approaches, and (2) a growing articulation of its processes and underlying dispositions brought forth through research and scholarship were now being more readily acknowledged as being intrinsically linked. The combination of research and scholarship in reciprocal exchange with the practical business of making music with people meant that community music could be considered a *field* of practice.[13] The scholarly dimension to the "practical" work supports and enriches its claims and prominence.

Straddling both periods and important to the historical story has been the growth of community music training and education, particularly from the university sector. I have accounted for this from around 1990 to 2012 in previous writing (Higgins, 2012b, pp. 86–91). Since then, there has been continued interest in supporting courses within institutes of higher education in countries such as Australia,[14] Canada,[15] Germany,[16] Greece,[17] Ireland,[18] Italy,[19] Israel,[20] New Zealand,[21] Norway,[22] Portugal,[23] South Africa,[24] the

---

[13] Drawing upon ideas outlined by sociologist Pierre Bourdieu, a field is a "social space" through which interactions, transactions, and events occur (Thomson, 2008, pp. 67–81).

[14] Griffith University; University of Melbourne; University of Sydney.

[15] Wilfrid Laurier has led the charge in Canada, hosting both graduate and undergraduate programs, including a PhD.

[16] Hochschule Dusseldorf (music/social work/community); Katholische University Eichstatt-Ingolstadt (inclusive pedagogy/community music).

[17] The University of Macedonia

[18] The Irish World Academy of Music and Dance, based at the University of Limerick, has hosted an MA in Community Music since around 1999.

[19] Free University of Bozen-Bolzano; University of Florence IUL.

[20] The Academic College Levinsky-Wingate has an ongoing commitment to community music training.

[21] University of Otago; University of Canterbury.

[22] Western Norway University of Applied Sciences

[23] Universidada Nova de Lisboa: See Graça and Rodrigues (2021).

[24] University of the Witwatersrand, Johannesburg; Stellenbosch University.

ARRIVAL    11

United Kingdom,[25] and the United States.[26] Interestingly, at the time of writing, there are 80 universities listed throughout 28 different countries on the International Directory of Music and Music Education Institutions[27] that state "community music training" as one of the features of their provision. In synergy to this, there has also been a proliferation of online activity, significantly increasing throughout the pandemic years (2019–2020), which has attracted regular and diverse audiences; these include the ISME CMA,[28] the Community Music Learning platform,[29] and events[30] hosted by the International Centre of Community Music. Courses and programs have come and gone, reflective of difficult economic times for the higher education sector and changing political agendas. However, globally, community music now has a much stronger representation throughout those universities and conservatoires engaging in music and music education.

## A Field of Practice

My characterization of community musicians' resistance toward conceptualizations has faded over the years, albeit still prominent in some quarters as I continue to experience. I would reason that the growth of national networks; the intensification of discussions surrounding community music, specifically at both national and international events and conferences; the increase of learning and research opportunities in schools of music and universities; and a steady flow of scholarly writing have nourished the practice to the extent that those working within it are much more open to developing theoretical and conceptual frameworks, or at least engaging in the possibility that they may be necessary. From the perspective of my argument that 2012–2013 was a significant milestone, a continuing flow of publications has provided a tangible collection that deals directly with the concerns of community music and confidently critiques and celebrates it as a diverse,

---

[25] The University of York was the first university to establish a graduate program when Bruce Cole became a teaching fellow in community music in 1986. Commitments to the ideas behind community music are embedded within many music programs throughout the country. Named programs appear less frequently, often operating within a fixed time period.

[26] The University of Southern California; New York University; the University of Massachusetts-Lowell; and the University of Miami.

[27] https://idmmei.org/

[28] https://www.youtube.com/playlist?list=PLo9fAQF9pvoc3ZAw4OLllZ2MNfZuXxtpl

[29] https://www.youtube.com/c/communitymusiclearning/videos

[30] https://www.youtube.com/c/internationalcentreforcommunitymusic

12 THINKING COMMUNITY MUSIC

vibrant, and valuable aspect of musical doing. These texts have created more expansive opportunities for more people to understand the terrain with all its unevenness, potholes, and rich green pastures. Many of these texts have supported the think pieces that follow.

However, there continues to be some confusion regarding the meaning of the term *community music*. Although I want community music, in the broadest sense, to influence what I say, I am specific in how I operationalize the term in this book. I have previously described community music in the following three ways: (1) music of the community, with an emphasis on the music of a particular (cultural, ethnic) community and the musical content and the relationship between the music makers and the music; (2) communal music making, where the emphasis is on people and place and the shared music-making experience; and (3) an active intervention between a music leader, educator, or facilitator and those participants who choose to work with them (Higgins, 2012b, pp. 3–5).[31] It is with the third perspective, as an active intervention, that I think community music is chiefly concerned. Why? Because it reflects the intention of the community musician toward creating and/or working for spaces that engage people in participatory musical doing from a perspective that is rooted within cultural democracy. It is interesting to note that "defining" the term *community music* was a prerequisite for the editor I worked with on *Community Music: In Theory and in Practice*. Those statements were not in the first draft of the manuscript. I had been resistant to any sense of definitional statements in fear that grounding the term would be seen as a violation of the community music project. I wanted to leave the concept open to individual interpretations. It was put to me by my editor that it would be very difficult to defend allocating resources to publish a book in a little-known area if one could not have clarity regarding the subject. After a good number of emails defending my position, it was made clear that a "definition" was needed or the proposed publication could not proceed. I made the adjustment with some degree of resistance. However, in retrospect, the right call was made and has, I think, benefited the subsequent growth of scholarship because, like it or not (and I know some do not like it), it has created some clearer waters through which to understand community music as a discrete field and provided a "definition" interested parties "outside" the immediate terrain can respond to. Although

---

[31] Huib Schippers (2018a) distinguishes three slightly different characteristics: (1) organic, (2) intervention, and (3) institutionalized (pp. 24–29).

ARRIVAL 13

I still use this characterization of community music, it has its problems, and this is explored in Think Piece 1. As a subsidiary thought, I want to acknowledge that I am conscious that my work has been influential on the discourse and as such has, in some ways, shaped how the work has been discussed and categorized. The process of writing this book has been an opportunity to reflect upon how my voice and perspective have evolved within the context of the broader dialogue. Of course, I would like the ideas to influence the field. However, I must emphasize that the book structure has been designed to encourage open dialogue rather than dictating a limited perspective.

The shift toward an established field of practice was a critical moment for those who believed community music should not continue as a peripheral and inconsequential activity on the margins of music more generally. There is no intention here to turn my back on the metaphor of the community musicians as "boundary walkers," an idea that I have used in the past, but instead to mark the boundaries they walk, remaining mindful that boundaries are fluid and subject to periodic adjustment.[32] The arrival of the three texts in 2012–2013 and the subsequent advance of community music scholarship since has reinforced the practice and has, I believe, created greater opportunity for practitioners to be part of ongoing discussions surrounding the importance of music in our society. Scholarship has enabled community musicians to be part of a wider discourse.

Folding the scholarship inward and between an already established practice has expanded community music's visibility. Building from a figure that appeared in a previous text (Higgins & Willingham, 2017, p. 172), Figure A.1 remaps this drawing, visually reflecting community music's kaleidoscopic form.[33] A full exploration of this visual representation is explored in Think Piece 8.

Whether we like it or not, scholarship and research have a habit of validating practical concerns, albeit through a particular perspective and within domains such as educational institutes and governmental organizations. In short, the advance of community music scholarship has reinforced a notion of what constitutes the practice and, I would argue, created greater opportunities for community music practitioners to be part of the wider discussion.

---

[32] A phrase first used in *Case Studies and Issues in Community Music* (Kushner et al., 2001).

[33] Other fields could be inserted alongside those I have chosen. I encourage experimenting with other domains, for example, social work, which is particularly prevalent as an intersecting area in countries such as Germany and Switzerland.

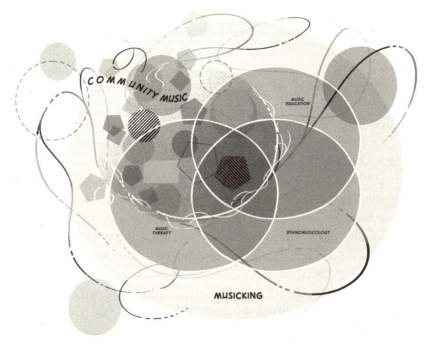

**Figure A.1** Community music assemblage.

## Theoretical Lens

The theoretical concepts employed throughout this book resonate with what could be broadly described as poststructuralism,[34] a diverse body of thought cumulating in the late 20th century and responding to the events of phenomenology[35] and structuralism.[36] I particularly respond to ideas flowing from Jacques Derrida, Gilles Deleuze, and Felix Guattari, with Gianni Vattimo

---

[34] As a response to structuralism, which flourished most widely from the 1950s to the 1970s, poststructuralism offered a critique of the human subject, historicism, meaning, and philosophy. It supported the idea that "reality" is purely a discursive phenomenon, a product of codes, conventions, languages, and signifying systems. See the following for an introduction: Belsey (2002), Sarup (1993), and Cutting (2011).

[35] The philosophical study founded in the early 20th century considered the structures of the experience of self. Thinkers within this tradition include Edmund Husserl (1859–1938), Maurice Merleau-Ponty (1908–1961), and Martin Heidegger (1889–1976).

[36] Beginning with linguistics and the work of Ferdinand de Saussure (1857–1913), structuralism sought to imply that elements of human culture can be understood through their relationship to a broader structural organization. Working within anthropology, Claude Lévi-Strauss (1908–2009) was influential in promoting structuralism.

playing an important supporting role. This theoretical grounding reflects previous work and, as such, maintains an internal consistency, not only here but also across my "project" as a whole. As a kaleidoscopic work, each think piece has a certain independence. In some instances, I use extensive footnotes to elaborate upon the philosophical import and see these not as marginal pieces of information but rather in play with the "main" text.

Why have these theoretical tools been selected in front of others? I have found that Derrida, Deleuze/Guattari, and Vattimo provide thought systems and expressive language that help me articulate how I have experienced community music as a practitioner, participant, and scholar. From my perspective, the themes they explored resonate with community music connecting deeply to people, participation, places, equality, and diversity. Their ideas have also been influential in the development of feminist theory, queer theory, and critical race theory, areas of discourse that have been fertile ground for understanding community music.

The style of the book has each "chapter" operating as an independent provocation, meaning that the concepts utilized are revealed and explained within the individual sections using footnotes to elaborate and give a wider context to the philosophical ideas. This section provides context not given within the think pieces, primarily offering some introductory biographical notes and some broad-brush strokes regarding each thinker's project. The final paragraphs point toward some similarities and differences between Derrida and Deleuze to provide a rationale as to why these philosophical projects might occupy the same space.

In my previous work, ideas attributed to Jacques Derrida have been paramount. Algerian born and of Jewish descent, Derrida (1930–2004) followed Friedrich Nietzsche and Martin Heidegger in elaborating a critique of Western metaphysics, arguing that philosophers throughout history have been able to impose various systems of thought by ignoring and suppressing the destructive effects of language. Initially following a strategy of closely reading canonical philosophical texts, Derrida developed a reputation for his gesture of "deconstruction," a purposeful "strategy" that calls into question ideas and beliefs that legitimize institutional forms of knowledge. As a strategy of thinking, deconstruction might be explained through three gestures:

1. Establish the stable field and note its *construction*.
2. Destabilize the field by inversion—*deconstruction*.

16  THINKING COMMUNITY MUSIC

3. Reinstate the field with an awareness of the continuing possibility of destabilization—*reconstruction.*[37]

Using previously articulated concepts and ideas as sites of dislocation, Derrida foregrounds the incompleteness, blind spots, and fault lines always already at work in any given text, insisting that "[deconstruction] is not *neutral. It intervenes*" (1981b, p. 93). Derrida's (1976, p. 158) often misunderstood quotation "*there is nothing outside of the text*" does not mean what is written in a book but rather, as he affirms, "life in general" (Payne & Schad, 2004, p. 27). In other words, like those working in community music, he is concerned with context, "that there are only contexts, that nothing *exists* outside context" (Derrida, 1988a, p. 152). Derrida's (1997b) preoccupation with disjunction leads him to insist on heterogeneity, on "what prevents unity from closing upon itself, from being closed up" (p. 13). Like those working within community music, Derrida's work has an ethical demand alongside this; his analysis of any given text flows from within that which he is exploring: "Deconstruction is not a method or some tool that you apply to something from the outside. Deconstruction is something which happens and which happens inside" (Derrida 1997b p. 9). Following this lead, my theoretical ideas have flowed from my experience as a community music practitioner and are, therefore, intrinsically tied to active music making with people.

As philosopher Simon Critchley (2005)[38] remarked, "A vital measure of the influence of a thinking on a discipline is the extent to which they transform its customs, protocols and practices in a way that makes it difficult to conceive how things were done before they appeared on the scene" (p. 25). Derrida is one of these thinkers who had significant influence over a whole generation of philosophers and was hugely impactful across many diverse disciplines that extended far beyond the early influence within literary studies in the 1970s and 1980s (Apter et al., 2005). As Critchley notes, "It is difficult to think of a philosopher who has exerted more influence over the whole spread of humanistic study and social sciences" (p. 27).[39] Derrida's work continues to be extensively engaged with books like *Derrida: Negotiating the Legacy*

---

[37] Notably, Derrida (1991) said he did not care for the term *deconstruction.*
[38] Critchley was particularly important for highlighting the ethical aspect of Derrida's work (see Critchley, 2014).
[39] Critchley notes that the only other comparable figure would be Michel Foucault.

ARRIVAL    17

(Fagan et al., 2007), helping a meta-understanding of the work's impact, while the journal *Derrida Today* offers regular focused discussions on contemporary debates surrounding the ongoing relevance of Derrida's work to politics, society, and global affairs.[40]

Gilles Deleuze (1925–1995) was a contemporary with Derrida and shared specific synergies, such as inhabiting canonical texts to challenge and transform the thought in question and thinking from the repression of the history of philosophy. Like Derrida, Deleuze was schooled in the history of Western philosophy in France and wanted to shake free from what he understood as its conformity. Alongside his collaborator Felix Guattari (1930–1992), Deleuze characterizes philosophy as "the art of forming, inventing, and fabricating concepts" (Deleuze & Guattari, 1994, p. 2). Concepts are understood as fragmentary wholes, "a matter of articulation, of cutting and cross cutting" (p. 16). Deleuze sought to revolt against what he saw as thinking awash with the state's official language. He sees that those who maintain this position are the "public professors," who are gainfully employed "to conform to the dominant meanings and to the requirements of the established order" (Deleuze & Parnet, 2002, p. 13). As a revolutionary in this respect, Deleuze's project challenges the "discourse of sovereign judgment," its stable subjectivity legislated by "good" sense, of rocklike identity, "universal truth, and (white male) justice" (Massumi, 1992, p. 1).

Poststructural thinking more generally challenged the possibility that there are foundational knowledges, and Deleuze saw this as a cause for "celebration and liberation," asking us "to grasp this opportunity, to accept the challenge to *transform life*" (Colebrook, 2002, p. 2) and think about how to open up new regions for living (May, 2005). Although other poststructural thinkers of the day sought to free thinking from the grip of structures and forces that produce and reproduce conformity—for example, Michel Foucault's genealogical account of a contingent human history and Derrida's relentless challenge to the metaphysic of presence—Deleuze's project differs because it embraces an ontology[41] that is generally rejected by the likes of

---

[40] See https://www.euppublishing.com/loi/drt.

[41] To clarify this, ontology has two distinct camps: (1) Analytic tradition, the study of what there is, a study of the beings of which the universe is constituted. Analytic philosophers seek to account for the nature and existence of those beings and the relationship between them. (2) Continental thought, the study of being (or Being). First, continental philosophers generally reject scientism, the view that the natural sciences are the best or most accurate way of understanding all phenomena. Both ask about the nature of what there is, but both have different inflections to the process of asking. Poststructural thinkers reject the analytic account of ontology.

# 18 THINKING COMMUNITY MUSIC

Foucault and Derrida.[42] You could say Deleuze agreed with Derrida's diagnosis but not with the cure. For Deleuze and Guattari, concepts are there to move us beyond our everyday experiences toward the thinking of new possibilities. In pursuing productive connections, "concepts are creative or active rather than representative, descriptive, or simplifying" (Parr, 2005, p. 51).[43] Deleuze asks us to question some of our entrenched understandings of experience, reality, and thinking, and the implication of encountering Deleuze can produce what film theorist Reidar Due (2007) calls "a *revolution in the mind, a fundamental change in how we think*" (p. 1). Deleuze resonates with my experiences as a community musician because I have always thought that community music practices have the potential to ask difficult questions regarding ways music is taught and learned. Deleuze can indeed be difficult to read; new terms and concepts cannot be easily defined as individual ideas make sense only in their relation to the whole. This is undoubtedly a challenge to the usual ways we engage in ideas and consequently demands that we think about things differently. Community music can provide some challenging pathways through which to engage in debates concerning music teaching and learning, and Deleuzian orientation can be helpful in this respect.

For Deleuze, a "materialist"[44] and "monist,"[45] everything is physical, and thinking is always connected. He is interested in exploring how things change over time. Deleuze claims that value in living needs to be found within ourselves. To reach our full potential, we must fully express our power rather than rely on judgments emphasizing nonempirical, transcendent standards. From my community music experiences, these general notions resonate with its history and diverse contemporary expression. Identifying a zone through which difference might emerge, Deleuze emphasizes thought rather than knowledge. Thought is, therefore, an act of problematization and, in resonance with community music, serves to stress practical action, consequently offering us

---

[42] Foucault rejects any ontology of human beings, any account of the ultimate nature of human beings, while Derrida rejects any sense of fixed terms that attempt to fix ontological description.

[43] The concept has "no *reference*: it is self referential" (Deleuze & Guattari, 1994, p. 22) and, as such, is not employed as a way to use experiences to deduct abstract ideas for categorizing phenomena.

[44] In contrast to idealism, a branch of philosophy that prioritizes ideas, values, and goals over concrete realities, materialism holds that matter is the fundamental substance in nature, including mental states and consciousness, and is the result of material interactions. Deleuze's materialism derived predominately from Baruch Spinoza (1632–1677), Henri Bergson (1859–1941), Gottfried Wilhelm von Leibniz (1646–1716), and Friedrich Nietzsche (1844–1900).

[45] Although there are various types of monism, the thing that binds them together is the attribution to oneness or singleness to a concept. For Deleuze, a concept is understood in terms of singularity; philosophy's task is to arrange these into assemblages that constitute multiplicities. See Schift (2019).

ARRIVAL    19

a radically different way to approach living. From a Deleuzian position, we need not conform. If, as political philosopher Todd May suggests (2005), our lives are to be interesting ones, "capable of new feelings, new pleasures, new thoughts and experiences, we must not conform" (p. 25). The issue, therefore, becomes not, is it true?, but rather, does it work? What new thoughts does it make possible to think (Massumi, 1992, p. 8)? These sentiments seem in line with the growth and development of community music.

In his eulogy for Deleuze, Derrida (2001) wrote that he felt "a nearly total affinity" between his work and that of Deleuze, particularly pinpointing both thinkers' profound interest in a difference that refuses to be reducible to dialectical opposition and contradiction (Derrida, Brault, & Naas, 2001, p. 192). Derrida says that the "very obvious distances, in what I would call— lacking any better term—the 'gesture,' the 'strategy,' the 'manner' of writing, of speaking, of reading perhaps" (p. 192). This suggests that Derrida saw a strategic or methodological difference rather than anything else. Larger divergencies can, however, be pointed to. American philosopher Daniel Smith (2003) puts it simply as different trajectories through Heidegger: Derrida's interest in transcendence and Deleuze's orientation in immanence. Derrida's notion of difference is essentially postphenomenological and ethical in character.[46] Deleuze's difference is, on the other hand, material and forceful. There are a good number of texts that explore the synergies and divergence between these two thinkers, in some instances suggesting the difference is slight, while others reveal a larger chasm (Bearn, 2000; Cisney, 2018; Kuiken, 2005; Patton & Protevi, 2003). Of course, it depends on the lines of inquiry you pursue; in this book, both philosophers present workable, practical, and valuable ideas to start radical conversations regarding community music practices. From my perspective, the core of their philosophies are written in hope, as Deleuze and Guattari (1994) espouse "as to summon forth, a new earth, a new people" (p. 99). They are dreams, but dreams worth dreaming.

## Overview

What follows are eight think pieces, each independent provocations but always in play with each other. This means they can be read in any order, the

---

[46] For a sustained argument surrounding an ethical reading of deconstruction see Critchley (2014).

20   THINKING COMMUNITY MUSIC

ideas and concepts cross-pollinating, offering slightly different perspectives depending on where you start.

## Intervention

Describing community music as an "active intervention" has become a common way to articulate the distinctive nature of its activities. This think piece sets out to consider the meaning of intervention and its association with community music practices and asks: *Is the notion of intervention apt for a growing global field?* In dialogue with cultural democracy, I outline positive and negative interpretations of the term *intervention*, seeking to prompt community musicians to take a reflexive view of their own cultural legacy and current practices. Exploring the term *intervention* provides community musicians an opportunity to recalibrate the language used, leading to an enhanced understanding of what community music does, what it can be, and what it is.

## Hospitality

Since the book *Community Music: In Theory and Practice* (Higgins, 2012b), the idea of community music as an "act of hospitality" has become part of the lexicon associated with the practice. This think piece deepens this notion by asking, *What makes the idea of community music as an act of hospitality important?* After recapping the previous argument, hospitality is articulated as a conceptual pivot central to the human experience that can be understood as a cultural and social imperative in constructing relationships and fueling a need for belonging. By placing the host/guest relationship as central to the human experience, I consider the first moments of contact between community musicians and potential music participants through ideas on the *stranger*, the *threshold*, and the *place*—a discussion on the limits of hospitality grounds the idea within contemporary global tensions. Rethinking community through the lens of hospitality presents an opportunity to think critically about the processes of negotiating the boundaries between our dreams and the differing realities we reside in. As an act of hospitality, the notion of community presents us with the potential to say "yes," an opportunity to be welcoming alongside a promise that is genuinely inclusive and without discrimination. As a cultural imperative of our time, hospitality is not exclusive to first encounters; it is a productive mindset that retains the notion of that original communication and can be applied to the everyday.

## Pedagogy

This think piece poses the question: *Can community music have a pedagogy?* By considering the historical roots of nonformal learning, I tease out the key features and explore how these ideas have been utilized within community music practices. Considering facilitation as the central strategy, I explore a continuum that includes both informal and formal learning. Distinctive traits of facilitation are described, and illustrations of practice help illuminate the mechanisms community musicians use within their work. Each example is plotted on a diagram shaped like mixing desks that aid understanding. In conclusion, it is noted that as the field expands, its contribution to the musical ecosystem becomes more influential. To continue and increase its influence within these larger conversations, is it time for community musicians to shake off an entrenched sense of being in opposition to "traditional," "formal" ways of engaging people in music? If the approaches to practice offer repeatable and commonly used processes, is it time to consider these collective traits and name the approach in terms of community music pedagogy?

## Social Justice

Community musicians focus on creating environments where, through musical interaction, individuals and communities can take charge of their self-expression and shape their futures. In this sense, community musicians set out as agents of change, often under the auspices of what might be described as a framework of social justice. Exploring ideas associated with a promise of justice, this think piece asks, *How might social justice be understood as a framework for community music practice?* Engaging in Derrida's invitation to return to the question of justice, I work toward

## 22 THINKING COMMUNITY MUSIC

an idea of "hospitable music making," an open embrace toward those who wish to participate in active music making and those who just might. Seeking to spark conversation, I encourage discussion regarding the necessity of community music as a vital field in these challenging and turbulent times.

### Inclusion and Excellence

When music participants work with musicians, they are typically in groups co-constructing the types of music to be created and identifying specific tasks and goals, emphasizing learning within the participants' life context. With musicians working alongside people to actively identify their learning needs, the concept of inclusion has been at the heart of this approach. Responding to the question, *How might notions of inclusion and excellence exist as a balanced pairing?*, this think piece draws upon a collaborative research project with music educator Jennie Henley. Examples of inclusion and excellence are illustrated through two examples of practice, and through a discussion, I explore whether excellence is better articulated as a process and inclusion better expressed as an outcome of this process. Following this, the flight line amplifies the ideas before encouraging some reflective thought, indicating that those working in the field might find a greater nuance in their language and their doing.

### Music

In this think piece I ask, *How might we understand the "music" in community music?* The question seeks to address possible ways that those working in the field might describe the "music," or "musics," being made by the participants they work with and, to some extent, why it might be deemed valuable. Using three "critical incidents" as concrete examples, I explore three philosophical lines of inquiry: David Elliott and Marissa Silverman's praxis, Derrida's always-already, and Deleuze's expression. Although there is some consideration of the intersections between these three ideas, the purpose of the chapter is to present a conceptual offering through which to spark thought and discussion.

## Research

The purpose of this think piece is to evoke research approaches resonating with community music's ethos and practice. After contextualizing questions that have driven my project, I engage with the figure of the margin and present some ideas of how this may be useful when considering community music research. Following this, I use my tenure as the editor of the *International Journal of Community Music* as a case to explore Gianni Vattimo's notion of weak thought, suggesting ways those in positions of power might model community music's ethos for the next generation of scholars. Through two illustrations of practice, I discuss representations of community music practice within two different research frames and ask, *How might I do community music research?*

## Becoming

In this think piece I ask, *How might community music become?* This provocation encourages those involved in community music practice to reflect upon its status, both within its own terms of reference and within the broader parameters of music making, teaching, and learning. The question is open and exploratory, containing a "might" rather than an "ought" or a "should," and thus points toward opportunities to explore its challenge either as an individual practitioner or collaboratively as a group, as an ensemble, at a conference, at a symposium, or as part of an academic course. It is a chance to wonder or imagine community music's future regarding impact, policy, pedagogy, musicking, and research. In part, it is an extension of questions regarding definition. Moving in, though, and between Deleuzian concepts, the chapter explores the idea that community music is a multiplicity, an assemblage that seeks relational connections and an endless potential configuration.

## Departure

As the final chapter of *Thinking Community Music*, the ideas emerging from the eight think pieces are brought together. Using the key themes that are

## 24 THINKING COMMUNITY MUSIC

displayed visually in a mind map, this short chapter offers five statements reflective of possible ways to think about community music. Each statement contains ideas drawn from the eight think pieces, and each individual idea has a location so readers can pinpoint where to find the expanded descriptions. As a constellation of concepts, community music is finally understood as hospitable music making, a relational music practice vibrating to the tune of the politics of cultural democracy and responding to contemporary and historical forms of cultural and social inequality.

# 1

# Intervention

## "Left Behind" Children in Taikang

*Wang LinLin is a musician who studied at the China Conservatory in Beijing. During her time away from Taikang County, located in the Henan province in central China, Wang LinLin spent time reflecting on her good fortune in having parents who have been able to support her throughout her education and training as both a professional musician and music therapist. Studying music full time at most of the world's universities or conservatoires requires privileges that are often linked to a person's history—for example, economic means, such as financial investments that stretch back to the first private lesson; opportunity, such as having access to a quality music education and/or a music education that meets specific "standards" or expectations; and support, affirmation from family and friends who nurture and protect physically, emotionally, and spiritually.*

*Wang LinLin's reason for appreciating her current situation is set against the context of where she spent her formative years. Taikang County, with its 23 townships and 700+ villages, is one of many examples of how the economic disparities between China's rural communities and the rapid growth of urban wealth have severely affected community life. Brought about through a widening gulf between those who have and those who have not, parents are forced to leave their children while they go to the large cities for a stable income. This situation has resulted in many children being left in places where they are looked after and schooled until they are around 9 or 10 years of age. Many rural children are sent to Taikang because, in some cases, schools can provide room and board from birth. The staff who work there are also able to take responsibility for the children's safety; however, this can result in not allowing the children out during the days they are in attendance. During the time at the school, the children see their parents once, maybe twice a year. For many children, achieving their professional ambitions seems an impossible task. Wang LinLin evaluates her narrative against this background and feels that she has been blessed with good fortune and wishes to give back to the community she loves dearly.*

*Thinking Community Music.* Lee Higgins, Oxford University Press. © Oxford University Press 2024.
DOI: 10.1093/9780190247027.003.0002

*Working with music in Taikang County, Wang LinLin creates environments where children can express their feelings through rhythm and song. Simple rhythmic games enable the children to add their own words and lyrics, and traditional Chinese songs provide a sense of unison. Through music making, Wang LinLin cultivates trust between herself and the children. There is an openness to the possibility of change, a sense of humanity, and a sense of the "just," what philosopher Emmanuel Levinas might describe as a humanism of, and for, the Other. Speaking through an interpreter, she admits that there is a "numbness" among the children: "They don't know their parents' love," Wang LinLin laments, "but the songs we sing provide opportunities for emotional release." Through her interventions with the children "as individual and precious human beings," Wang LinLin evokes friendship and gives them a particular type of permission to express their inner thoughts. Her actions reflect Jacques Derrida's notion that justice is a vocation, an affirmative step toward another human being (see Think Piece 4). The children will initially say, "I'm not angry that my parents are gone because I know they are making a better life for me." After a time of music making, some of the children reveal that they miss their parents and ask, "Why did they leave me here?" A sense of the unjust drives Wang LinLin's work: Why are these children left alone? This situation the children find themselves in does not seem fair for the parents, for the children, or for China's society. In the future, Wang LinLin wants to make the musicians and music students studying in Beijing aware of this situation. Wang LinLin is convinced that if she can somehow showcase her work to those privileged and studying in the city, they too will be empathetically touched and inspired to head to the rural villages as community musicians.*

This think piece sets out to consider the concept of *intervention* and its association with community music practices. Over recent years, describing community music as an "active intervention" has become a common way to articulate its distinctive nature (see "Arrival": A Field of Practice). When distinguishing his three key contexts for the practice, music educator Huib Schippers (2018) notes that community music as an intervention "is by far the most documented type of community music," adding that "it may also be the most elusive because of its sheer diversity and scope" (p. 26). As the field expands globally, is now the time to reassess the use of the term *intervention*? What are the implications when using this word, and is the notion of intervention apt for a growing global field? I begin by offering some thoughts on how the term may have initially found an association with community music.

Following this, I sketch out some common daily usage of the term, then fold in some thoughts and ideas from practitioners. In flight lines, I offer some reflections and encourage those in the field to critically explore the term as an opportunity to recalibrate the language and understanding of what community music does, what it can be, and what it is.[1]

## Context

In the United Kingdom, the interventionist approach to community music is linked to the community arts scene that flourished during the counterculture era of the 1960s and 1970s. Within this era, a time of considerable social upheaval in the form of anti-government and anti-establishment protests, social issues became the subject of art making. As a distinctive strand from that movement, community music shared the goals of community arts through activism, challenging repressive and hierarchical social norms, and commitment to personal growth and notions of empowerment. Following those working during this time, there were desires to address issues of access and inclusion in social and musical-cultural contexts by asking questions such as: Who in society has access to music? Who makes and plays music? Who decides what is "good" music and what is not? Community music activity also grew in response to shifts in government policy concerning education curriculum, to changes in expectations and delivery requirements of publicly funded arts organizations, and to the needs and agendas of formal service providers such as government agencies and nongovernmental organizations in areas of health, education, and social services (Brown et al., 2014; Doeser, 2014). It is this latter set of relationships in particular that inform the contemporary activities of community musicians (Bartleet & Higgins, 2018b; Veblen et al., 2013; Willingham, 2021).

The contention that music-making experiences have the potential to influence and/or bring about positive and beneficial change in both individual and collective terms has its roots in antiquity (Horden, 2000). It is today widely supported by scholars working across multiple disciplines, including music therapy (Ansdell & Denora, 2016; Stige, 2012; Stige et al., 2010), music psychology (MacDonald et al., 2012), music education (McFerran et al.,

---

[1] The spine of this piece was a provocation offered to a group of people working in and around community music. See https://learn.rcm.ac.uk/courses/1240/pages/lh-perspectives

2019; Váradi, 2022), and ethnomusicology (Barz & Cohen, 2011; Koen, 2008; Pettan & Titon, 2015), that music has a positive impact concerning health and well-being and can be an enhancement of individual capacities. Music as a social outcome and its relationship with creating a positive social environment and helping with the maintenance of traditional cultures have been of scholarly interest in areas such as community development (DeQuadros & Dorstewitz, 2011), international development (Bolger, 2012), and peacebuilding alongside conflict resolution (Bergh, 2010; Sweers, 2015). This array of intentions and goals can also be observed in music programs initiated in places of extreme human needs, such as communities at war or in recovery from violent conflict (Howell, 2015, 2018), and in the range of ways that many of the world's cultures employ music as a tool for healing (Gouk, 2000). Similarly, there are notable historical antecedents for using shared music to create a sense of empowered communal spirit, social bonds, and cohesion. These include employing music to mobilize large numbers of people to a common political cause or ideal (Hebert & Kertz-Welzel, 2016). Ethnomusicologist Thomas Turino (2008) cites the role of mass singing in the youth rallies of Nazi Germany and the U.S. civil rights movement as two examples of music used for the mobilization of the masses. While the ideologies underpinning those two movements were strongly contrasting, both effectively utilized the sense of shared unity, purpose, and courage that mass singing could generate toward their respective political aims.

The notion of music making as an intervention can be understood as an instrumentalization of music's potential to transform lives for the "better." This might be understood as music making is "good" and enriches your overall life experience. This sentiment has a history that can be traced back to several key moments; for example, the Industrial Revolution saw not only the advent of large-scale changes to employment and emphasis on small family units but also the introduction of industry-sponsored workers' choirs and musical groups, precursors to many of today's community choirs and brass bands. Ensembles such as these were understood as providing productive, pleasurable, and self-improving pastimes for workers, who might otherwise spend too much time drinking in local public houses and potentially getting caught up in revolutionary action. Furthermore, there was a belief that music could improve the morals of both singers and listeners (McGuire, 2009). This idea also informed the work of many religious missionaries, traveling into new territories as part of colonial expansion and using shared music making to facilitate union with God, to inspire feelings of unity and community cohesion, and as a mechanism through which the colonized or proselytized could be "improved" and "civilized" (Willson, 2011).

Contemporary community music practices are strongly informed by a history of social action, as well as by a set of beliefs and a growing evidence base about the potential of shared music making to bring about positive and beneficial individual and collective change. This is why, as community artist François Matarasso (2019) explains, the notion of instrumentalization does not reflect the intent of those engaged in community arts: "the accusation of instrumentalizing art has been flung at community artists, as a way of discrediting their work and its challenge to dominant practice" (n.p.). I would concur that instrumentalization does not reflect the intent of those engaged in community music. As musicians who choose to work creatively alongside people, the notion of instrumentalization is rooted in an aesthetic ideal that objectifies music as having a possibility of existing independently (Bowman, 1998). The growth of what has become known as an interventionist approach to community music may partly be because its history has collided with the contemporary needs of social service provision. Consequently, the growth of the intervention model, if that is what it is, has driven the subsequent rise in importance and professionalization of the role of the community musician. However, in some cases, it may have compromised it politically.

## Common Usage

With its origin set around the 1580s, the etymology of the word *intervene* derives from the Latin *intervenire*, meaning "to come between": *inter*, a prefix meaning between, among, in the midst of, together, coupled with the word *venire*, meaning "to come."[2] Commonly used to describe a mediation, a coming between disputing people or groups, the term *intervention* evokes taking part in something to prevent or alter a result or course of events. Often associated with a sense of force, such as intervening in the affairs of another country, the term is used to describe someone or something intentionally becoming involved in a problematic situation to improve it or prevent it from worsening. Intervention is then the act of intervening.

Many examples of intervention have a negative connotation. Wars in, for example, Vietnam, Iraq, and Afghanistan all attract significant criticism

---

[2] https://dictionary.cambridge.org/dictionary/english/intervene

surrounding the idea of intervention (Bhatia, 2003; Smith, 1996; Yoon, 1997). The American intervention in Korea has frequently sparked protests, especially over how it is portrayed in film (Goldstein, 2014). Other quotes attributed to various leading figures demonstrate this. Consider Vladimir Putin's suggestion that "it's alarming that military intervention in internal conflicts in foreign countries has become commonplace for the United States."[3] Samantha Powers, an Irish-born American diplomat, notes, "Historical hypocrites have themselves carried out the very human rights abuses that they suddenly decide warrant intervention elsewhere."[4] Pointing toward colonialism, a course of action closely connected to notions of intervention, Haile Selassie, an Ethiopian statesman and former emperor, reminded fellow Ethiopians, "Above all, we must avoid the pitfalls of tribalism. If we are divided among ourselves on tribal lines, we open our doors to foreign intervention and its potentially harmful consequences."[5] Along similar lines, political activist Noam Chomsky states, "The former colonies, in Latin America in particular, have a better chance than ever before to overcome centuries of subjugation, violence and foreign intervention, which they have so far survived as dependencies with islands of luxury in a sea of misery."[6] Certainly, the actions made under the term have had damaging consequences to many peoples and is particularly associated with colonization in countries such as Australia, Aotearoa New Zealand, and Canada, where the idea of intervention has many complex undertones.[7]

The concept of intervention does, however, have positive connotations, for example, its usage in descriptions surrounding preventative approaches in both health and education; COVID-19 is a standout example of modern times.[8] American democratic politician Lucille Roybal-Allard highlights this, noting, "Newborn screening is a public health intervention that involves a simple blood test used to identify many life-threatening genetic illnesses before any symptoms begin." As a champion for young families, she describes the

---

[3] Quote appears in an opinion piece written by Putin for the New York Times in 2013. See https://www.nytimes.com/2013/09/12/opinion/putin-plea-for-caution-from-russia-on-syria.html?hp&_r=0

[4] https://www.brainyquote.com/authors/samantha_power.

[5] https://www.brainyquote.com/authors/haile_selassie

[6] https://www.brainyquote.com/authors/noam_chomsky

[7] See Amnesty International for discussions and ongoing campaigns surrounding human rights associated with these issues.

[8] For example, see https://www.cochranelibrary.com/cdsr/doi/10.1002/14651858.CD013769/full; https://systematicreviewsjournal.biomedcentral.com/articles/10.1186/s13643-020-01371-0; https://www.frontiersin.org/articles/10.3389/fpubh.2020.604089/full.

Head Start program,[9] a service that provides early childhood education, health, and nutrition to low-income children and their families, in the following way: "I have long been a supporter of the Head Start program because each and every year I witness the dramatic positive impact that early intervention services have on children's lives in my congressional district."[10] Autism spokeswoman and scientist Temple Grandin underlines this sentiment: "A treatment method or an educational method that will work for one child may not work for another child. The one common denominator for all of the young children is that early intervention does work, and it seems to improve the prognosis."[11] As a final example, Maajid Nawaz, British politician and founder of Quilliam,[12] a counterextremism think tank, says, "The British state already invests in early intervention campaigns in drug abuse and sexual health. Challenging extremism should be no less of a priority."[13] As is clear from these examples, the word intervention and the actions that have been carried out under its banner have a complex and diverse history which requires an understanding of the context to gauge whether it can be deemed as a good thing or not. The next section locates the word within community music practice and theory.

## Reflections

As part of a discussion thread, Kirstin Anderson,[14] a musician working within the criminal justice system, asks, What are the implications for using the word *intervention*? She says within a collaborative research group chat, "The word [intervention] implies that one group has power over another, there is someone intervening in another's affairs. If organizations and/or individuals see themselves as working in collaboration with a community, then I think the word is limiting." Kirstin suggests that the term may restrict the ability to engage different types of groups, especially, she says, "those groups who have started to disrupt the (sometimes) elitist grip on access to the arts for themselves." From this standpoint, community agency would be diminished. Following criminologist Yvonne Jewkes,[15] Kirstin states,

---

[9] https://www.acf.hhs.gov/ohs
[10] https://www.brainyquote.com/authors/lucille_roybalallard
[11] https://www.brainyquote.com/authors/temple_grandin
[12] https://www.quilliaminternational.com/
[13] https://www.brainyquote.com/authors/maajid_nawaz
[14] See Anderson and Willingham (2020).
[15] https://prisonarchitecturedesign.com/

## 32 THINKING COMMUNITY MUSIC

"Change the language and it will change the culture." There is a sense here that people have a strong connection to words. How, for example, do people in prisons, communities, and schools feel about taking part in an "intervention"? What does that term make them think of? Have "we" asked them?'

I have always acknowledged that my articulation that community music is an active intervention between music facilitators and participants is (1) grounded in my history as a U.K. practitioner and (2) the expression of practice that interests me most. As a fulcrum, the notion of intervention has helped focus my arguments and conceptual propositions. However, with the exponential growth of community music as a field of practice and scholarship, it now seems responsible to interrogate this idea more fully. In the introduction of the *Oxford Handbook of Community Music*, Brydie Leigh Bartleet and I reflected upon this point:

> We have been asking ourselves deeply critical questions about this definition and the impact it has had on the field. . . . [W]e have questioned whether the prevailing notion of community music as an active intervention still accurately reflects the contemporary manifestations of the field. We have asked ourselves whether there is a better term to use, and if so, what it would be. (Bartleet & Higgins, 2018a, p. 15)

At the time, Brydie and I thought that the term *intervention* potentially still encapsulated many community music practices worldwide and reflected the intentions to "interrupt" particular situations, such as socially inequitable and unjust systems or politically repressive contexts, and bring about positive social change. As Schippers explains:

> Based on an expressed or perceived need, one or more music practices are developed with or for the community to restore existing practices or to introduce new ones. These initiatives usually have a short to medium-term lifespan due to their brief availability of personnel, organizational structure, and (mostly external) funding sources. (Schippers, 2018, p. 24)

In conversation with practitioners, one respondent candidly said:

> It's a word I use when I am speaking to people, describing what we do and it's a word we use a lot when we fill in funding applications. I've never really thought about its meaning in any great depth, it's just a word I know,

it seems to fit what I mean however that might be because everyone else is using it too, and that we all think we mean the same thing. In doing so now, I've come to the conclusion that it needs much more thought and interrogation, as in its current understanding, it means something that doesn't sit too well with what I aim to do in my practice.... I'm now not sure how I feel about it, bearing in mind the things we proclaim our practice to be built on.

This statement speaks to a growing need to reflect on the intentions behind the term and critically examine where power, agency, and self-determination reside.

Other practitioners I talked with were concerned that the term reflected a deficit-based perspective. A deficit-based perspective attributes failures such as lack of achievement, learning, or success in gaining employment to a personal lack of effort or deficiency in the individual rather than to failures or limitations of the education and training system or to prevalent socioeconomic trends (Wallace, 2009). One musician admitted that:

In my early practice, I equated it [interventions] with people (usually privileged/with power) deciding what other people (usually disadvantaged/subjugated) need. And reflecting on my role as a community music facilitator, I question the extent to which I may be the former in this equation and what that might mean for approaches to practice.

Those working within an intercultural context could enable a rethinking of the idea from the standpoint of decolonization. Talking from an Australian context, Bartleet and Carfoot (2016) state, "[It is] important to avoid discourses of social justice that privilege outsider perceptions of need over the demands of the communities themselves" (p. 346). Aotearoa New Zealand music educator Te Oti Rakena identifies tension in intervention through consideration of "Western models of community music" with non-Western communities. Rakena (2018) states, "To participate in community music-making for Māori and Pacific Island students is to participate in the traditions of the [European settlers'] culture of power" (p. 82). Musician and educator Dave Camlin (2020) suggests that because *intervention* is an active verb, somebody has to be the person doing the intervening; consequently, there is always a risk of objectifying the participants you are working with and, as such, becoming part of the very problem community musicians say they wish to overcome. Responding to public education scholar Gert Biesta

(2004, 2006), Camlin draws upon the notion of the "rational community," rational agents who speak an everyday discourse as representatives of the community. Although community music interventions are taken from good intentions, the actions might be understood as complicit in maintaining the cultural dominance of those in power—more often than not, the "rational community." Camlin worries that even if it is born out of good intention, "this process of 'othering' is one of the ways in which 'rational community' maintains its hegemonic grip on the means of cultural production" (Camlin, 2023, p. 117). From Biesta's perspective, the rational community can maintain their influence, which can result in exclusionary practices. This is problematic if we consider the central tenets of community music and their historic location; it is the very thing community music has sought to address, a practice rooted in the concept of cultural democracy.

Central to the concept of community music as an intervention has been the concept of cultural democracy, a process by which the power to decide cultural creativity lies within each person[16] and thus cocreates multiple versions of what culture is (Graves, 2005; Jeffers & Moriarty, 2017; Kelly, 2023). Cultural democracy contrasts the democratization of culture, which is far more in tune with the deficit model—in short, "taking great art to the people" (Wilson et al., 2017, p. 23). There has been plenty of work to address the inequalities of cultural participation (Elliott et al., 2017; Hunter et al., 2016; Wilson et al., 2017), and Camlin, for one, welcomes these initiatives but alerts us to the possibility that the ideas can be highjacked by those in control of cultural policy, which in turn might lead to furthering culture inequalities. Despite these concerns, Camlin (2020) concludes that "paradoxically, and despite my misgivings about the term, music as an intervention might provide one such means of emancipation from the deadlock of cultural orthodoxy, providing an alternative social reality to the one experienced in the everyday lives of citizens" (n.p.).[17] In a personal communication, Camlin fine-tunes this thought, saying that intervention can potentially be positive when it disrupts people's relationship with the orthodoxy of the neoliberal consensus by providing people with different ways of being in relationship with fellow human beings.

In previous work, I rethought cultural democracy by placing the idea within the structure of the unpredictable future and the promise of the

---

[16] For podcast conversations, see https://miaaw.net/.

[17] Camlin (2016) explores this further by following Jacques Rancière and exploring the idea of "dissensus."

unforeseeable, "a structure of openness to the future," readjusting each day in relation to the flux of daily living (Higgins, 2012b, p. 169). As a "dream" toward that which will never fully arrive, the figure of a "cultural democracy to-come" would be, as U.K. community musician Jo Gibson (2020) describes, something to work toward within any interventionist music practice. Acknowledging the problematics, Gibson reconciles these within the "cultural democracy to-come" figure, noting that when participants and community musicians "invent new music together, there is the coming of something new, something different from before. To work towards this is to engage in dialogue, listening to the other through presence in the encounter" (p. 29).[18] Gibson further outlines how, as a practitioner, she attempts to reconcile such dilemmas by asking more questions from the funder alongside the participants to cultivate togetherness and enact critical practice through listening and reflection.

Nelson Mandela was reported to say that "intervention only works when the people concerned seem to be keen for peace."[19] This suggestion has at its heart a call for dialogue and open conversation between any two parties where intervention is a possibility. From this departure point, where an agreement or knowledge of the intervening process is understood, the word *intervention* is operationalized in the work of community musicians. That said, does this reflect the situation on the ground, or is this an ideal, a story of an imagined narrative community musicians tell themselves and those who fund their projects?

The above examples highlight how intervening is commonly understood as a "coming between." From the perspective of community music, I would like to advocate for a far more reciprocal understanding, one that is closer to what I perceive as being at the heart of Mandela's declaration that places both parties as being in consultation with a recognition of the power imbalances. This speaks to the theoretical character of community music as an act of hospitality, a way to describe the relationship between music facilitator and participant that is structured through an ethical experience where the aim is that the first move is always through the participants' call to attend a music-making event (see Think Piece 2). This cyclical structure of call and welcome, evoking both decision and responsibility, offers a far more complex

---

[18] In an interview, literary theorist Jean-Michel Rabaté underlines the relevance of Derrida's "democracy to come," arguing that he sought a democracy "that would be open to the ethical values of hospitality" (Greaney, 2021, p. 102).

[19] https://www.brainyquote.com/authors/nelson_mandela

36 THINKING COMMUNITY MUSIC

and nuanced understanding of the term that allows for considerations of power, control, and privilege to be critiqued and unpacked within the musical exchange. Of course, in practice, who gets to attend, how, and why are complicated matters. Coercive participation can also be at play, so understanding the complexity helps harness a nuanced understanding.

As part of the community music lexicon, the noun *intervention* can sit quite comfortably alongside others often associated with its practice—each having roots with the Latin *venire*, "to come." For example, the notion of *invention* is vital for the practice of improvisation, a significant approach to music making used by community music facilitators. Invention is the coming of something new, something to come that is different from what has come before. Invention speaks to discovery, exploring, and finding out, setting a course for *adventurous* journeys. Community music happenings are often phrased in terms of *events*, which is related to *venire*. French philosopher Jean-François Lyotard describes events as occurrences of something important that call for new modes of experience and different forms of judgment (Malpas, 2003). They are occurrences that disrupt pre-existing frames or contexts, giving an opportunity to the possible emergence of new voices (Lyotard, 1991). From Lyotard's perspective, art and literature are exemplary locations through which events happen, potentially generating circumstances after which nothing will be the same again (Readings, 1991).

Intervention,
  Invention,
    Adventure,
      Event

are all concepts that signal the arrival of the unexpected. As a cluster, they all have semantic associations with the word *welcome*, an idea connected to the facilitation process. *Welcome* is a word derived from the Old English *wilcuma*, a kindly greeting,[20] one whose coming is in accord with another's will, from *willa*, meaning pleasure, desire, or choice, and *cuma*, meaning "guest," related to *cumin*, "to come."[21]

---

[20] https://www.etymonline.com/search?q=Welcome
[21] https://www.etymonline.com/search?q=come

## Flight Lines

Community music from within the United Kingdom grew through the community arts movement in the 1970s, a politicized, socially engaged movement that looked to disrupt the elitist grip on access to art. With cultural democracy as a conceptual driver, music interventions were employed as means of creating openings for active musical doing and, in so doing, to provoke debates surrounding access, inclusion, and participation; challenging repressive and hierarchical social norms; and a commitment to personal growth and empowerment. The strongest work took place through invitation, where artists stepped into communities and worked alongside people to produce new music that expressed local identity. As a consequencet these types of collborative experiences offered the possibility of deep community connectionsns that enabled participants to amplify their collective thoughts on issues affecting them such as poverty, crime, education and environment, among many other things. Following Brazilian educator Paulo Freire (1970/2002), community musicians like Wang LinLin sought to "empower" those they worked with and provide opportunities for transformative educational moments.[22] As a form of thoughtful disruption, intervention denotes an encounter with "newness," a perspective that seeks to create situations where new events innovate and interrupt the present toward moments of futural transformation (Bhabha, 1994). Put this way, maybe the issue is not so much the process of intervention but rather the structures behind it.

Although there might be a danger that those who intervene are seen as an all-knowing other, community music as an intervention includes leading workshops, facilitating discussions, and supporting groups in their musical endeavors. These conscious and deliberate strategies seek to enable people to find self-expression through musical means. Using procedural concepts rooted in nonformal learning (see Think Piece 3), community musicians emphasize negotiation through collaboration, and thus, learning takes place through a "bottom-up" rather than "top-down" approach. When I described community music as an active intervention, I did so from this inheritance. The use of the word was as an intention to "interrupt" particular situations, such as social and political disadvantage, and bring about social change. It was not used in terms of "helping" someone, nor from a deficit perspective.

---

[22] For a discussion on how terms such as *empowerment* and *transformation* have been used in the discourse of community music see Humphrey (2023).

However, my thoughts flow from a position both European and of privilege. Since the global growth of community music, subsequent analysis, mainly from Canada, Australia, and Aotearoa New Zealand, has alerted the field to the problematics of the term and that it needs to undergo adequate interrogation. In Australia, for example, the term *intervention* is associated with a highly controversial and problematic political package of changes to welfare provisions, law enforcement, land tenure, and other measures such as allegations of child sexual abuse and neglect (Bartleet & Higgins, 2018a). Many may argue that musical interventions are needed more than ever in such circumstances, while others suggest that the work that changes people's lives is not an intervention as much as an "awakening," drawing out something that is already latent within. However, community music facilitators are challenged to ask themselves (1) on whose terms this musical activity is happening, (2) whether those are appropriate to the cultural context in which they are operating, and (3) whether the intervention is acting as another colonizing endeavor or promoting a more positive sense of self-determination for participants (Ashley & Lines, 2016; Rakena, 2018). In a personal communication, one community musician mentioned: "If we are the right people to 'intervene,' what qualifies us to be able to do this? Is it because we think we can? Is it because we've been trained to do so? Are we imposing what 'we' want to do and the way 'we' want to do it?" If the meaning of intervention denotes an action or process that interferes with a situation or scenario, does the word limit a broader understanding of the work community musicians do? We might also reflect upon the idea of an intervention as a catalyst for change, and as such, are catalyzing agents open for change also?

As a global phenomenon, community music has now become more nuanced. The questions arising from this think piece, which are complex and many, prompt community musicians to take a reflexive view of their own cultural legacy and their current work. Exploring the term *intervention* provides those in the field an opportunity to recalibrate the language and understanding of what community music does, what it can be, and what it is. It is a good time to determine what intervention does, and what the intentions behind it are, and critically examine where the power, agency, and self-determination reside.

# 2

# Hospitality

## Villa Musica

*Villa Musica is a community music center located in San Diego, California. Inspired by a desire to forge opportunities for lifelong musical learning, Fiona Chatwin established the center as a nonprofit corporation in 2005. As a vibrant place where people come together to take music lessons, play in an ensemble, or participate in a workshop, the center fulfills the need for inclusive and accessible musical interactions for those who wish to take part. Striving for a balance among formal, nonformal, and informal music making, Villa Musica offers a wide range of possibilities, including individual lessons, group classes for children, group classes for adults, music therapy, and community ensembles and workshops. Surviving on funding from many individual donors, the center strives to develop future stable relationships with funding foundations to sustain and expand its programs. By becoming the focal point for community music education in the area, Villa Musica has become a place where teachers and students can meet and experience the joys of making music together, forming meaningful relationships both within the center and outside. Through the development of this school, Fiona has created an open and hospitable space where instruments can be put in the hands of children who may not have had the opportunity to play before. This may be because parents need more financial capital or are unaware that music learning could be an option.*[1]

For most of us, finding others with whom we can have an engaging and meaningful encounter is essential to our existence. Whether committing to a partnership, stopping at a neighbor's for coffee, meeting friends in a local bar, or hosting a dinner party, finding ways to negotiate successful and happy relationships is a lifelong pursuit. As a practice, community music has always been concerned with relationships in terms of the individual, the group, and the wider connections between those in the community. Its intentional

---

[1] See http://www.villamusica.org/. Thanks to Steven Dziekonski, who brought Villa Musica to my attention. See Snow (2013, pp. 93–111) for more information.

*Thinking Community Music.* Lee Higgins, Oxford University Press. © Oxford University Press 2024.
DOI: 10.1093/9780190247027.003.0003

orientation toward participation has meant that matters concerning how to engage with others have been paramount in developing its ethos and pedagogy. In basic terms, how you speak to people, greet them, and respond to their questions and idiosyncrasies are all vital ingredients in any participatory music encounter. Previously, I have explored the concept of community as it relates to the larger concept of community music (Higgins, 2007a, 2012a, 2012b). I have presented the argument in the following way:

*Community music practices have an emphasis toward people, participation, places, inclusivity, and diversity.*

*A traditional notion of community can be at odds with community music practices.*

*Community is a complex and contested idea open to many interpretations.*

*Reflective of contemporary perspectives maintaining that communities are not static or bounded but rather organic and plural, the phrase "community without unity" becomes a useful starting point. In this formulation, "without" designates an openness, a community of possibilities rather than a limited gathering.*

*As an articulation of the importance of diversity in communal relationships, this idea suggests that community is as much about struggle as it is about unity.*

*This is important because, as an approach to music making, community music has always been concerned with the messy and difficult business of relationships, whether in youth clubs, prisons, hospitals, daycare centers, or education institutions.*

*Responding to these ideas and drawing from the work of philosophers such as Jacques Derrida, Emmanuel Levinas, and John Caputo, community, conceived as an "act of hospitality," runs deeply through the practice of community music.*

*Beginning with a call to be worked with, potential music participants await a welcoming invitation to begin the process of music making.*

*The welcome can be understood as an ethical gesture, an open invitation to build a relationship with another person.*

*The music facilitator is prompted to say "yes" to ensure the exchange becomes a collaborative encounter.*

HOSPITALITY 41

*The simple act of saying "yes" is vital because it requires a conscious decision and, in so doing, provides the opportunity for unconditional acceptance, a welcome without reservation. It suggests that new and interesting things can happen by reaching out beyond what may be thought possible.*

*It is very much entwined with the daily conditional realities community musicians face, including restrictions such as limited time, resources, and money, plus larger social issues such as privilege and social inequalities.*

*Hospitality also alerts us to the imbalances of power within human relationships. From a quick glance into its etymology, we can see that its Latin roots are common to both the words* host *and* hostile.

*Community musicians have to negotiate this two-sided coin as they facilitate music making. On one side, there are aspirations to relinquish control, ensuring creative ownership and a sense of equality, while on the other, music facilitators are in positions of power and, as such, have responsibilities.*

*Central to any act of hospitality is the interaction between the host and the guest, or in the case of community music, the music facilitator and the participant.*

*The social construct inherent in this type of relationship is the root of any civilized society. It is an important idea because, as a relational practice, the concept of hospitality is vital in every socially interactive musical experience, regardless of context.*

*Community music as an act of hospitality reminds those involved in the practice that an open invitation, given with full knowledge of the tensions and challenges inherent within such a gesture, can result in an experience of connectivity that can produce lasting impressions on both community musicians and participants.*[2]

Rooted deep within our ancient cultures, hospitality as an idea is as old as recorded human history and is tied to this fundamental human need to be with others. Considering the first moments of contact between community musicians and potential music participants, the call, the welcome, and the "yes" inherent in any act of hospitality are poetic spaces for listening and dialogue that may lead to effective and meaningful music-making experiences.

[2] You can view an animation that outlines the key point of the argument and can be found on YouTube (https://www.youtube.com/watch?v=H9EVR7GCaxI).

## 42  THINKING COMMUNITY MUSIC

These gestures will always be at risk of imperfection and failure, and this is to be celebrated, not plastered over and ignored. Building from previous work, this think piece provokes the question: *What makes the idea of community music as an act of hospitality important?* I intend to deepen my initial argument that community music can be seen as an act of hospitality by providing examples of how hospitality has been a conceptual pivot central to the human experience, a cultural and social imperative in the construction of relationships fueling a need for belonging. During the flight lines, questions are raised regarding the tensions when using this semantically ambiguous term.[3]

## The Call, the Welcome, and the "Yes"

Through an etymological analysis of the terms *community* and *hospitality*, the idea of "community" within community music is best understood through the concept of hospitality, as initially articulated by Jacques Derrida (1999; 2000b; 2001). I propose that hospitality encompasses the central characteristics of community music practice, broadly understood as people, participation, places, inclusivity, and diversity. I do not argue that hospitality should replace the term *community*, but that hospitality evokes the meaning of community in the work of community musicians. From this perspective, I propose that *community*, conceived as an "act of hospitality," runs deeply through the practice of community music. Through reimagining the word *community* as *hospitality*, there is a foregrounding of the key characteristics of community music, a sharpening of the traits that make it a distinctive field of practice. The argument can be summarized in the following way.

Beginning with a *call* and/or an openness to be worked with collaboratively rather than worked on, potential music participants look toward a welcoming gesture from community musicians to begin engaging in or furthering meaningful music-making experiences. The following three bullet points capture the encounter from the perspective of hosting a music workshop and describe an ongoing cyclical structure:

- The participants decide to attend music-making activities and meet the community musician.
- The participants are ready to make and create music and expect to do so.

[3] Some of the following text is a reworking from Higgins (2020b).

HOSPITALITY  43

- The community musician is open and ready to work with the participants to enable a meaningful music-making experience.

Similarly, the structure can reflect situations when the community musician is understood as a guest:

- Through invitation, the community musician attends existing music-making activities and meets the group.
- The group is ready to make and create music alongside the community musician.
- The group is open and ready to work with the community musician to enable a meaningful music-making experience.

This structure sets up and ignites a learning experience that is active rather than passive. It describes an act of hospitality that can break down boundaries, cultures of suspicion, individualism, and isolation. Hospitality is the act of making time for another person and a beckoning invitation to the other to become included and resonates strongly with Irving Goh's (2020) analysis of the prepositional.

Through careful consideration of the "to" as mobilized in Levinas's "face to face," Derrida's "to-come," Irigaray's "I Love to you," and Nancy's "being-to," Goh's elicitations underscore the idea of co-opting an open hospitality in advance of arrival.[4] As an "experience of freedom," the act of being open to a call, a readiness to embrace any potential participants in the music-making space, emphasizes the prepositional and, as Goh suggests, generates movement that leads us to others. The movement toward should be understood as something other than just a linear gesture. There is always space for one and the other, opportunities to separate, leave, or retreat to the self.

The "being-to" gives way to the *welcome* inherent within a hospitable action. This act can be understood as an ethical gesture, an open invitation to build a relationship with another person. This idea draws upon the work of the Lithuanian/French philosopher Emmanuel Levinas (2006). Levinas would describe this as a humanism of the other, according to which being-for-the-other takes precedence over being-for-itself. This type of hospitality suggests unconditional acceptance, a welcome without reservation, without a previous assessment of what might happen and who the other is. Unconditional hospitality, as mobilized within the context of community

---

[4] For an exploration of love in the context of community music, see Bartleet (2019).

## 44   THINKING COMMUNITY MUSIC

music, is not a transcendental idea, one toward which we should aspire even though it is inaccessible. In the context used here, unconditionality breaks from the Kantian notion that describes something unconditional as an absolute or an archetypal instance given to itself. Therefore, unconditionality is accepted as residing at the very origin of the seminal concepts that give the West its history, politics, and culture. Therefore, the unconditional is always entwined with what is conditional and must be recalled to rethink and transform commonly accepted ideas and concepts. In the context of community music, this is an unlimited display of goodwill toward a potential music participant. Although this description may sound idealistic, it is not to be conceived this way but rather taken as a suggestion that by reaching out beyond what may be thought possible, new and interesting things can happen. In this sense, the gesture of the welcome is entwined with the conditional realities community musicians face daily, including things such as time, resources, and money.

As an attempt to create accessible music-making environments, the work of the community musician is often described as inclusive (see Think Piece 5). There is a thinking toward unconditionality (full inclusivity) but a working reality that demands conditionality (exclusivity). These two positions are not opposed but rather braided together, creating productive tensions. In this sense, the unconditional breaks from the Kantian idea of an absolute[5] and rather links it intrinsically to an unforeseeable future. Unconditional hospitality, therefore, embraces a future that will surprise and shatter predetermined horizons, implying a disruption toward that which is stable, fixed, and comfortable.

Hospitality is a word translated from the term *philoxenia*, "love of the stranger," from New Testament Greek.[6] A glance into the etymology of the word *hospitality* reveals that its Latin root *hostis* is common to both the words *host* and *hostile*. These two English words appear opposites, but their relationship can be revealed upon careful inspection.[7] Consider this

---

[5] See Kant (1998).

[6] See Wrobleski (2012).

[7] From the Latin *hostis*, meaning both guest and enemy. See Dufourmantelle (2013). Other related terms include *Hostille*, meaning to treat equably one to the other—to compensate and pay in return; *hostimentem*, to compensate; and *hostelle*, meaning sacrificial victim. It also includes the hostage and the despotic, the master/host. Building from Marcel Mauss's (1924/1990) observation that *hoses*, meaning between guests, is a contraction of *hosti-pet*, meaning guest-master, Derrida coins the neologism "hostipitality," which makes audible the tension and thus uncovers the aporia. Derrida's hostipitality is put to work in a deconstruction of Kant's (1903) proposition that "the rights of men, as citizens of the world, shall be limited to conditions of universal hospitality" (p. 137). Kevin O'Gorman (2007) suggests that all modern words associated with hospitality are evolved from the same hypothetical Proto-Indo-European root *ghos-ti*, meaning "stranger, guest, host: properly someone with whom one has reciprocal duties of hospitality."

thought experiment: You have organized a dinner party for your friends and family in your home. As the host, you welcome everybody "unconditionally," introducing them to each other and trying to make them feel at home. You offer them drinks and a meal and cultivate simulating conversation among the group. To your friends and family, you have been a great host, warm, welcoming, generous, and giving. Although unstated, it was always clear that this was *your* party, you were running the show, and you were indeed in "control" of this event. As the host, you placed certain conditions upon the event: You put away the wine when you thought people had had enough, the downstairs sitting room was out of bounds because of the new carpets, and you were not initially pleased when someone swapped your favorite vinyl for music you didn't much care for on Spotify as it stood to ruin the ambience you had tried so hard to create. To take it a step further, somebody had asked if they could have your recipe for the soup you had served, and you insisted it was a secret handed down to you by your grandmother.

To some extent, your party laid an initial claim to be hospitable. You were welcoming, went to a great deal of trouble and expense, and invited people you did not really know or particularly care for because you genuinely wanted to widen your friendship circles and build bridges. But there was undeniable hostility in your hosting: not too much drinking, no one was getting that soup recipe, and in one case, you only invited a family member because you thought you should. As it happens, the party went very well, and had you not had a heart toward the unconditional, genuine openness and welcome for a variety of guests, the event would not have taken place. Your thoughts toward a welcome without reservation, the initial act of hospitality, enabled you to push forward with the planning, the invitations, and the final celebration.

This type of scenario can be mapped across any number of situations. Within a community music context, for example, facilitators often imagine a time when more people would be able to participate than their current context allows. Everyday conditions such as time, resources, and money often prevent this type of "dream" from happening. The motivation behind Villa Musica to put instruments into the hands of those who have yet to have previous opportunities is a desire for something that is probably not attainable in the way its founder, Fiona Chatwin, strives for. However, Fiona's passion for equitable music provision has generated the project and provided the spark for things to happen. As I have illustrated, the unconditional, as described here, is not sovereign and absolute but is rather intrinsically linked to the conditional. The tensions between the two are significant features in the work of community musicians. For example, a community musician may have prepared an improvisation workshop. The session's content is planned for 12 young people who have been excluded from school. Although the morning's activities have been carefully considered in recognition of the type of participant the community musician expects to work with, there is an acknowledgment that things can always take an unexpected turn and often does. The changes in participant dynamics can be linked to social issues pertaining to the young people's behavior, for instance, unstable living situations or mental health issues. Meticulously planned music workshops can be equally disrupted through ordinary weekly events. This might include an encounter with a recently discovered music idea through the latest recording or a recent experience at a live music concert. Either or both might impact the community musician's planned "future," and as such, they will need to augment their mapped trajectory, making way for alternative possibilities. In this context, being attuned to unconditional hospitality means that one is prepared to embrace a future that will surely surprise and shatter predetermined horizons. It therefore follows that the hospitable "community" within the work of the community musician should not subscribe to an idealistic community, understood as a desire for that which has no imperfections, as this would be a utopian dream existing as a sovereign lament. This would betray the realities of the community musician whose work should be a response—and indeed a responsibility to—the messy world of human agency. Like the example of Villa Musica, the musician's openness toward the unconditional ignites a mindset that enables the event to move forward, reflecting the central tenets of community music, participation, inclusion, and diversity, and thus impacts those who are involved, which includes both the participants and those who support them.

## As Old as Recorded Human History

Central to any act of hospitality is the interaction between the host and the guest. The social construct embroiled in this relationship can be understood as the root of any society. For example, consider the parable of the Good Samaritan and its contemporary meaning of one who helps a stranger.[8]

---

[8] Gospel of Luke (10:25–37).

HOSPITALITY    47

Earlier still is the Greek notion of Xenia, the generosity and courtesy shown to those who are far from home, found in the articulation of Homer's (2003) travels in *The Odyssey*. Iconic paintings depict these ideas, such as *Jupiter and Mercurius in the House of Philemon and Baucis*,[9] which tells the story of how the Greek god Zeus and his son Hermes test a village's practice of hospitality, rewarding those who were hospitable, namely Philemon and Baucis, and punishing their neighbors who did not welcome their presence. The relationship between hosts and guests also lies at the very basis of the Islamic ethical system, which sees hospitality as potentially leading to "ennobling and transformative moments" and may even evolve into "a restorative energy crucial for the survival of the human race" (Reynolds, 2010, p. 184).[10] These historical accounts can be seen as a "sacred obligation" to accommodate guests and protect the stranger (Lynch et al., 2011, p. 4).

From a macro perspective, hospitality has played a vital role in developing human societies, a catalyst used to facilitate all human activities (O'Gorman, 2007). From research on expressions of hospitality found in ancient and classical texts and society, Keven O'Gorman (2007), professor in management and business history, suggests five dimensions of hospitality, which include honorable tradition, fundamental to human existence, stratified, diversified, and central to human endeavor. Hospitality can be seen as initially concerned with the protection of others. Old Testament verses such as Leviticus 19:33–34 reflect this notion, while a more contemporary example is staged in Lars von Trier's film *Dogville* (2003). Both stories stress hospitality as a primary and vital feature of human existence, dealing with primordial human needs such as food, drink, security, and shelter. Maybe the most ubiquitous representation of hospitality in the Western world is through images of the tourist industry, a multifaceted practice that represents "a host's cordial reception, welcome and entertainment of guests or strangers of diverse social backgrounds and cultures" (Morrison & O'Gorman, 2008, p. 218)—for example, servers standing and smiling politely while offering a plate of hors d'oeuvres at the beginning of a wedding feast or glossy tourist brochures and websites parading exotic pictures of hotels in various locations. Although emulating from a business, leisure, and tourism perspective, Morrison and O'Gorman (2008) provide a framework for a pluralistic and critical analytical

[9] *Jupiter and Mercurius in the House of Philemon and Baucis* (1630–1633) by the workshop of Rubens.
[10] See also Kahaleel (2017).

## 48 THINKING COMMUNITY MUSIC

tool underlined through contemporary tourist research. Work in this area has led to an effective means of exploring and understanding our society.[11] Everyday examples of hospitable signage include the notifications we encounter in shopping malls, such as the international symbol of access[12] and the baby changing sign, both of which mark an accessible and friendly territory. The pineapple fruit has been associated with the return of ships from extended voyages and is often seen as an international symbol of hospitality.

Within the field of critical hospitality and tourism, Lynch et al. (2011) suggest two dominant themes that drive discussions surrounding hospitality: (1) as a means of social control and (2) as a form of social and economic exchange. Travelers regularly encounter both ideas through the multilingual signs that are posted as greetings upon arrival at an international airport. With translations of the word *welcome* into myriad different languages, including bienvenido, willkommen, добро пожаловать, 欢迎, and ترحيب, passengers are greeted into Toronto, Los Angeles, Beijing, and Manchester. The international airport is, however, a place that reminds us that the term *hospitality* houses tensions between the welcome and hostility. In these instances, the host, or national government, is dominant, "imposing their sense of order upon the other" and thus reinforcing notions of inclusion and exclusion (Sheringham & Daruwalla, 2007, p. 36). As travelers attempt to traverse an immigration process to cross international lines, their passports and visas reinforce that their status is one of a guest and, as such, they will be leaving at some time. Although in a very different context, the tensions inherent in the host/guest relationship explored in the party example above might be recalled regarding the border control queue. The officers at these terminals are gatekeepers for the host country and, from my experience, can be either welcoming or downright hostile, challenging your reason for being in their country and sometimes marching you off to another room for interrogation. In moments like these, the smiling cardboard faces or large-screen displays that voice a multitude of different welcomes seem somewhat inauthentic.

Following Derrida (2000b) and Levinas (1969), hospitality is viewed as a foundation of culture and ethics and, therefore, an intrinsic part of the human

---

[11] See the journal *Hospitality and Society*: www.intellectbooks.com/hospitality-society.

[12] Disability activists advocate against using the traditional international symbol of access since it displays passivity and focuses more on the wheelchair than the person. Sara Hendren of the Accessible Icon project has designed a new icon, which displays an active, engaged image focusing on the person. See https://accessibleicon.org/.

condition: "Not only is there a culture of hospitality, but there is no culture that is not also a culture of hospitality. All cultures compete in this regard and present themselves as more hospitable than the others. Hospitality—this is culture itself" (Derrida, 2002b, p. 361). Here, hospitality is fashioned into an ethical-political framework through which the realities of living in and among diverse populations can be understood. Taking as his starting point the person-to-person encounters, Levinas suggests that hospitality is the original impulse; it is the concept "that precipitates any association with others"[13] (Dikeç et al., 2009, p. 6). Hospitality has a contemporary social significance because it is embedded in the social and cultural processes humans regularly engage in. Anthropological studies such as those by Matei Candea and Giovanni da Col (2012) reveal that hospitality is deep and wide within human societies. Studies with the Native Americans (Morgan, 1881/2012), the Inuit (Boas, 1887), the Balinese (Geertz, 1975), the Jordanian Bedouin (Shryock, 2009), and the sherpas of Nepal (Ortner, 1978) present a dizzying range of social and cultural contexts through which acts of hospitality take place. In an article originally published in 1977, social anthropologist Julian Pitt-Rivers (2012) excavates evidence from ritual customs, habitual practices, and poetry to demonstrate how the logic of hospitality has been ubiquitous throughout human interactions. He concludes, "The law of hospitality is founded upon ambivalence. It imposes order through an appeal to the sacred, makes the unknown knowable, and replaces conflict with reciprocal honor. It does not eliminate the conflict altogether but places it in abeyance and prohibits its expression" (p. 513). As a concept that touches upon crucial anthropological problematics, namely identity, difference, belonging, and politics, hospitality is foundational to human life.

Stressing the importance of hospitality to all our existence, feminist philosopher Irina Aristarkhova (2012a, 2012b) tells us that the foundation of hospitality is located within the maternal relationship, an exemplar of gifts and generosity. Through her interrogation of the way Levinas and Derrida position and idealize the feminine as central to hospitality, Aristarkhova seeks to reclaim the idea as a tool for feminist critique and argues that hospitality needs to accent the maternal relation to more accurately account for "its potential to enable a different ethics to others, including the mothers whose

[13] This is in direct response to Kant's proposed instituting of a single global set of laws of hospitality, which would guarantee the security of those moving across nation-state borders. From Levinas's perspective, Kant overlooks the individual face-to-face encounters for the mass movement of people across territories.

work as hosts has been systematically denied in conventional discourses of hospitality" (Aristarkhova, 2012b, p. 177). Conjuring up the image of the Khôra, first described by Plato in the Timateus as the mother and receptacle of all,[14] Aristarkhova calls for the reintroduction of the maternal to account for the mother, as it brings together questions of space, matter, and generation. Building upon this perspective, French philosopher Anne Dufourmantelle's (2013) analysis pushes deeply into how hospitality is vital in an understanding of who we are in relation to others and how hospitality might be considered as a precondition of life.[15]

The feminist critique surrounding relational philosophies suggests that traditional understandings of hospitality situate men and women differently. This has been readdressed from within a hospitality framework, which helps expand the depth of care ethics (Hamington, 2010; Held, 2006; Noddings, 1984; Sander-Staudt, 2010; Taylor et al., 1995). This is underscored through Derrida's work inasmuch as he neglects the feminine by focusing on the abstract concept and never really reflects on the embodied necessity of relational interactions. Levinas's positioning is also problematic as the feminine in his discussions suggests that women are more naturally hospitable than men (Diprose, 2009; Haggerty, 2010). As ethicist Maurice Hamington (2010) notes, "A feminist theory of hospitality can influence the evolving definition of this ancient practice, but more importantly, it can inform policies and practices that have for too long devalued the work of caring" (p. 34). Thus, in a world where people and nations desperately need to improve relations, perhaps feminist hospitality, Hamington notes, can positively contribute to peace processes. Therefore, we need to work harder to build sustainable and peaceful relationships, and the notion of hospitality can emerge as a critical concept in the quest.

The multidisciplinary interest in the concept of hospitality suggests that its importance is a sign of the current times, a concept and experience that reflects our human need for belonging and relationships as we move through the 21st century: How should we treat each other? How should we welcome those we invite? How should we welcome those who knock at our door to visit us? In a society where violence, the harm we do to ourselves and others, appears to be ever more present, there seems to be an increasing need to think and act in ways that might limit such altercations. As a vital concept

---

[14] See Plato (1977).
[15] See also Dufourmantelle's YouTube lecture of 2011 (http://www.youtube.com/watch?v=vWWR pMu_l3E).

in our contemporary era of global migration and globalized social life, hospitality is a figure of openness, but while, from one perspective, the world may be more borderless, it is not necessarily more hospitable (Cheah, 2013; Lashley et al., 2007; Moiz & Gibson, 2012). The impact of globalization also creates a stratification of those who can access a particular type of international hospitality and those who are locked into immobility through economic circumstances (Dikeç et al., 2009). If hospitality is part of the current *zeitgeist*, what are the key themes, and how might they help us understand the "community" in community music?

## The Stranger

I have tried to make the case that the host/guest relationship is a social construct recognized as the root of any society. One consequence might be that the world calls upon us to continually strive to improve our capacity to responsibly respond to others.[16] Understanding the notion of the "stranger" is important in realizing this. Dictionary definitions broadly suggest that a stranger is a person with whom one has had no personal acquaintance, a newcomer in a place or locality, an outsider, a person who is unacquainted with or unaccustomed to something, or a person who is not a member of the family, group, or community.[17] A history of the stranger can be tracked through phenomenological investigation. Phenomenology, a concrete analysis of our existential life-world, is a return to the "things themselves," an attempt to understand both animate and inanimate objects (Moran, 2000). Inaugurated by Edmond Husserl (1973) and flowing through Levinas (1987), Derrida (2000b), Ricoeur (1992), and Merleau-Ponty (1962), phenomenology places the human encounter with the stranger as a paramount concern.[18]

New and consequently "strange" participants wishing to get involved in musicking can cause scheduling, resource, space, instrument, or financial difficulties for those running community music activities. However, as recorded in our most ancient texts, the notion of the stranger is there to

---

[16] Anthropologists and evolutionary psychologists such as Robin Dunbar (2021David Graeber (Graeber & Wengrow, 2021), and Jared Diamond (2014) offer some fascinating insights into the development of humanity and how we form, maintain, and conceive different relationships.

[17] http://dictionary.reference.com/browse/stranger

[18] For a brief overview of the synergies and disconnects between these thinkers regarding phenomenology, see Kearney and Semonovitch (2011). For a more in-depth analysis, see Moran (2000).

challenge us and test our moral fiber, resolve, and ability to deal with disruption. Sociologist George Simmel (1950) notes that the unity of nearness and remoteness involved in every human relation is organized through the stranger and thus should not be thought of in terms of here today and gone tomorrow. Accordingly, the stranger is a "potential wanderer" who has not as yet overcome the freedom of coming and going: "He [*sic*] is fixed within a particular spatial group . . . [and] his [*sic*] position in this group is determined, essentially by the fact that he [*sic*] has not belonged to it from the beginning, that he [*sic*] imports qualities into it, which do not and cannot stem from the group itself" (p. 402).

Although used interchangeably at times, the idea of the stranger can be brought into sharper focus by considering the term in conjunction with ideas about the "other" and the "foreigner." According to philosophers Richard Kearney and Kascha Semonovitic (2011), "It is a hinge that conceals and reveals, pointing outward and inward at the same time" (p. 5). In this sense, the foreigner is the stranger we see, and the other is the stranger we do not see. As an illustration, consider the following: On January 1, 2014, the transitional controls on free movement between Bulgaria and Romania and seven other member states of the European Union ended. From that date, Bulgarians and Romanians were free to live and work in the United Kingdom, among other countries. Before the controls were lifted, there was a lively debate in the United Kingdom about how many Bulgarians and Romanians would come seeking a place to live and work. With the debate and propaganda ensuing, those from Bulgaria and Romania were seen as *others*. They were a set of people that many of the British public had not encountered before. As *strangers*, they were unseen and unknown. After January 1, those who decided to exercise their right to come to the United Kingdom became foreigners in many people's eyes. They were still strangers but were now visible, if not in person, then certainly through the media as the whys and wherefores of immigration and the European Union's regulations were discussed across the news channels. Issues like this have been amplified since—for example, Brexit (de Zavala et al., 2017), refugees from Afghanistan (Parent, 2022) and those fleeing from the Ukrainian war (Polońska-Kimunguyi, 2022).

How are potential music participants acknowledged when they "knock at our door"? What type of *stranger* are they? Were they invited, or were they visitors? How community musicians interact in those initial few moments can become vital in the musical experience of the participant, both in that moment and in the longer term. Of course, for many of those working in community music, the participants are not strangers in a traditional sense; they may have been in the "samba" ensemble for a long time, they may have come up through the ranks of previous music pathways, or they may have been family or friends. Author Tahar Ben Jelloun suggests that acts of hospitality involve "an action (a welcome), an attitude (the opening of oneself to the face of another and the opening of one's door and the offering of the space of one's house to a stranger), and a principle (disinterestedness)" (quoted in Lynch et al., 2011, p. 11). As community musicians and hosts of the space through which we work, how the participants are spoken to, the attitude displayed toward them, and the level of obligation or self-interest displayed can determine whether or not the potential participant crosses the threshold and, as such, walks toward the musical experiences on offer. This initial interaction is not necessarily exclusive to first encounters but can be applied daily, becoming a productive mindset that retains the notion of the original communication.

So, what of the line that initially separates the host from the guest or the community musician from the participant? How can we think of the boundary or the threshold, and what limits do they suggest?

## Threshold and Boundaries

As the sill of a doorway, a frame that divides, or a boundary that marks, a threshold designates a crossing between two areas. In the context of community music, strangers come to the classroom; they visit the youth club and decide to attend a music event in a prison, daycare center, hospital, or university department. Would-be participants stand on the edge, whether at a door, a gate, or a reception. These thresholds, defined by their edges, are openings onto hospitality and can signal a chance of a welcome or not; doors can be opened, shut, left ajar, or removed. As frames offering passages, the boundaries structured by the edge are, in principle, porous and allow for a traversal across it in modes of two-way traffic (Casey, 2011). Once someone crosses the threshold, they affect the very experience of the thresholdfor themselves, the other participants, and those facilitating the musical doing.

## 54 THINKING COMMUNITY MUSIC

Although a potential act of hospitality is a chance to say "yes," it should not be the case that those leading musical activities forego discernment or *phronesis*, a practical wisdom as outlined by Aristotle in *Nicomachean Ethics* (2000).[19] Each potential participant approaching the community musician provokes a special kind of phenomenological attention and thus raises issues surrounding how one judges the risk facing us at any given threshold. This puts the music facilitator in a position to ask how to assess the potential of hostility within any act of hospitality. To respond to this type of dilemma, Kearney and Semonovitic (2011) recall Heidegger's "poetics"[20]—a productive act beholden to something beyond itself—which reflects deep within Derrida's (2000b) statement that "an act of hospitality can only be poetic" (p. 2). Following this, an affirmative "yes" to a potential music participant from a community musician might be considered a poetic action and creative activity.

Education consultant David Price offers an analysis of how being open through technological means shifts the focus to how best to learn rather than how we should teach. In the closing chapter of his book, Price (2013) states that as a concept, open means that "we can work this out for ourselves, level the playing field, share what we know, trust in our creativity, have fun doing it, and we'll let you know when we need help" (p. 215). In many ways, hospitality lies at the heart of his ideas, but I would argue that things can never be absolutely open as this would be irresponsible; pure openness is not always appropriate as it denies the integrity of the musical space and those who reside in it: "For the sake of hospitality itself, there must be limits to hospitality" (Wrobleski, 2012, p. xi). Hospitality is critical to be open, but, as theologian Jessica Wrobleski (2012) points out, this is shaped by the need to discern limits in the tensions between giving and receiving, safety and risk, solitude and community. In other words, hospitality, as described here, moves forward with a spirit of openness and the recognition that there can be a lack of responsibility without boundaries or limits. Acts of hospitality must enact limits while minimizing violence to those who look like they might be excluded. Put another way, "Hoping for unconditional hospitality is a way of ensuring that conditional hospitality does not become too conditional" Dooley, 1999, p. 169).

---

[19] See Thomas Regelski (1998) for a detailed analysis of an Aristotelian basis of praxis for music education.

[20] See Heidegger (2001).

## Place

Whether explicitly or implicitly, encounters between self and others tend to be conceived in a language that defines place. Examples include openness and closure, inclusion and exclusion, and border patrolling and boundary crossing, each communicating hospitable moments in specific locations. Our encounters with each other consist "in giving place to another and, as such, occur[] as part of a relationship between an implaced person and a displaced person" (Treanor, 2011, p. 50). Put another way, "Place becomes a mean to map the negotiated level of hospitality between host and guest" (Sheringham & Daruwalla, 2007, pp. 42–43). It is hard to imagine hospitality without displacement as "the 'stranger' who might be welcomed or turned away is most often characterized as one who has been spatially mobilized or displaced" (Dikeç et al., 2009, p. 4). Inclusion and, subsequently, exclusion are at the core of hospitality: "The metaphorical symbolization of hospitality with the host welcoming of an 'other' (guest) across thresholds signifying inclusion, equivalence among groups, and reaffirms insiders as socially similar; implicit is the converse of exclusion of unwelcome 'others' on the outside" (Lashley et al., 2007, p. 175). In music making, we might think of a new viola player to the community orchestra, a professional Zydeco band setting up for a gig, a class of elementary children about to sing a new song, or a first-time piano student turning up at a studio. In each example, those involved must cross a threshold into an unfamiliar space and contend with how the host—conductor, bar owner, or teacher—negotiates their initial encounter. A well-placed and genuine welcome might make those who receive it feel like the new place is a "home away from home," setting up a favorable situation where the wish is to repeat the experience.

## Bridge

As articulated here, hospitality is separate from duty. From a school music education perspective, school music students have a right to music teaching within a statutory education system. Therefore, music educators have a duty to teach their students. From the perspective of duty, the educative exchange is economic rather than hospitable. In other words, the music classroom or community music workshop door is open under obligation, and the potential music participant is admitted under tight conditions. As philosopher

## 56    THINKING COMMUNITY MUSIC

Brian Treanor (2011) explains, "Even the most unregulated point of entry, with the absence of any conditions of admittance, falls well short of hospitality" (p. 50).[21] Openness is necessary but not sufficient because hospitality requires a welcome set forth to make those it is directed to feel part of the context they are working in. To quote Derrida at length:

> For there to be hospitality, there must be a door. But if there is a door, there is no longer hospitality. There is no hospitable house. There is no house without doors and windows. But as soon as there are a door and windows, it means that someone has the key to them and consequently controls the conditions of hospitality. There must be a threshold. But if there is a threshold, there is no longer hospitality. This is the difference, the gap, between the hospitality of invitation and the hospitality of visitation. In visitation, there is no door. Anyone can come at any time and can come in without needing a key for the door. There are no customs checks with a visitation. But there are customs and police checks with an invitation. Hospitality thus becomes the threshold or the door. (Derrida, 2000a, p. 14)

For example, leaving the workshop door ajar is a rule or condition of hospitality. In this literal or metaphorical action, there is an invitation, an offer of hospitality toward those we know are due to arrive. Nevertheless, what of those participants we cannot see, potential musicians, waiting in the wings or hiding in the shadows? What of the strangers who wish to participate but have not received a direct invitation? What about the potential visitors who might "pop their heads in" to see what is happening or those for whom crossing the threshold needs to be done on their terms initially? There are many reasons these scenarios could be so: Perhaps there have been past experiences that have made people wary, cautious, or frightened, and previous music encounters that have caused one to tread carefully.

The idea of unconditional hospitality must drive democratic thinking; it should be something that worries us, haunts our actions, and helps shape

---

[21] Derrida's unconditional hospitality "takes on the aura of a moral imperative" (Dikeç et al., 2009, p. 3). Might we say that music educators have a moral imperative to respond to those who ask to be included and those who potentially might? From Nancy Snow's (2010) perspective, hospitality should be considered a virtue for three reasons: it is other regarding, helps us to live well, and contributes to the flourishing of those around us.

our decisions. Rather than hospitality being merely a shelter, hospitality should evoke visitations and invitations. Professor of rhetoric Pheng Cheah (2013) suggests, "The imperative 'to open (up) to' thus arises from the fact that the world itself has opened up and become open such that it can and should receive every single human being" (p. 57). As a cornerstone of hospitality, place, as described above, is locally conceived and rich in distinctive content. From this perspective, hospitality is always temporal, meaning invitations occur in time. An example might be that a choral group arrives at a designated stop ready to learn a new song. Visitations, on the other hand, might be said to give time, an example being a new tenor voice turning up and being keen to take part and thus impacting the rehearsal in such a way that the preplanned rehearsal takes a slightly different shape. As Levinas (1987) describes, "I do not define the other by the future, but the future by the other" (p. 82).

As I have tried to show, hospitality is as old as recorded human history and is tied to notions of the stranger, thresholds, and place. If humanity and belonging to a world are mutually defining terms, then blurring the edges between inside and outside hospitality "interrupts the distention between the one who gives and the one who takes, the one who is the host and the one who is hosted" (Friese, 2009, p. 64). Historian and political philosopher Hannah Arendt (1958) argues that the human right to hospitality is a right to be received by others and a fundamental duty to receive others. However, connected to the notion of giving and receiving, hospitable transactions constantly threaten to collapse and pose the possibility that we could be dispossessed of our belongings or freedom. As an act of possible reversal, this may put us in a position to ask for a hospitable response from those who once asked it of us. This is a scary thought that is infected with the sort of battles for domination and power articulated by Michel Foucault (1980). There is, though, a chance to act "authentically" through acts of hospitality, an opportunity to make a difference in someone's life. If inauthentic hospitality is mechanical and routine—what is described within the tourist industry as McDonaldized systems where qualitative matters are de-emphasized from consideration and where matters of efficiency and predictability rate above genuine relationships (Ritzer, 2004)—then authentic hospitality is personal and direct to the stranger creating meaningful relationships that might set up ongoing and sustainable experiences.

The idea of openness has the potential to disrupt what is familiar to us and thus offer the possibility for alternative pathways that are not held back by a predetermined future. As a deconstruction of the at-home, this unsettles our human power of world making by pointing to a constitutive vulnerability to the other as a stranger. Whether host or guest, community musician or participant, music teacher or student, two bodies meeting can induce an act of hospitality and thus lead toward transformative processes. In these moments, it may be unclear who is to make the first move, and during this crucial stage, the result might end up as a welcome or violent struggle. As a concept and action so central to our existence, hospitality precedes ideas such as democracy, praxis, and aesthetics, all central notions of music education philosophy. Concerning ourselves with music teaching and learning within the framework of hospitality provides an opportunity to examine the primordial exchange that ignites musical transactions: The call, the welcome, and the "yes" all take place at a threshold, and the significance of the encounter determines whether people cross into the musicking space or not. In creating Villa Musica, Fiona Chatwin responded to what she understood was a call from the local community—to start an inclusive community music place. The wide variety of possible musical offerings is encased in an open space that is inviting to both those accustomed to this type of thing and those not. Fiona's ambition to provide meaningful music-making opportunities is ignited through her optimism and her desire to say "yes," we can make this happen; together, we might just be able to get everybody making music.

## The Limits of Hospitality

We might consider the "yes" as the "spirit of hospitality" (Wrobleski, 2012). In the context of this think piece, I am constantly referring to a position of openness, an unconditional notion of hospitality while always mindful of the conditional things that impact any welcoming gesture. As a hope or heart toward absolute inclusivity, thinking from the perspective of a spirit of hospitality may help a positive confrontation of its limits and, consequently, help community musicians work more effectively within such a paradoxical concept.

The conditions of hospitality may be thought of in two distinct ways: First, echoing the examples above, conditions are placed upon the participants by the facilitator. These are necessary; for example, a community choir might not be able to accommodate someone who turns up with a drum and no desire to sing. This might seem somewhat extreme, but these situations test our notions of what it means to be hospitable. A more familiar but often necessary course of action is creating an agreed-upon way of working together—sometimes referred to as a "group contract" and collaboratively negotiated together. This can take the shape of a group agreeing on a set of conditions through which they will operate—for example, respecting individual contributions, no abusive language, listening, and respecting each other's points of view. The welcome initially given to the participants by the facilitator can, therefore, be withdrawn if conditions of the "contract" are not adhered to. Second, conditions may entail characteristics that make something possible. A space to work in, a good collection of instruments, and economic support to ensure sustainable practice might be an example of this. These are conditions for the possibility of community music events and are prerequisites for the practice. These "conditions of life" shape the limits of how facilitators can demonstrate hospitality in the first instance. The two are linked and together reveal a tension through which any community music as an act of hospitality must negotiate. This is reflective of much broader philosophical debates surrounding the arrival of migrants and the tension of ethical requirements to host the stranger on the one hand and, on the other, the political and legal limitations that restrict such a demand (Friese, 2009). It is also resonant with accounts that outline limits to hospitality within specific contexts such as in Poland, the United States, and Europe; Syrians in Lebanon; and the "European refugee crisis" (Khaleel, 2017; Kitlinski, 2022; Thorleifsson, 2016; Kyriakidou, 2021).

As dreamers, community musicians have a passion for the impossible and think in terms of the unconditional hope for an "emergence of something different" (Caputo, 1997b, p. 23), an inclusive environment that brings people together through music. Having this type of "hope" ensures that the inevitability of the conditions outlined above does not become too fixed or restrictive and remains flexible. A complete openness, a total unconditional musical space, can enable negotiation of the tensions inherent in any act of hospitality. In short, there is a balance to be had between a heart toward unconditional hospitality and the limiting conditions that make any welcoming gesture possible. Conditions exist as a direct challenge to the desires and rhetoric community musicians espouse, but always thinking in, around, and

60 THINKING COMMUNITY MUSIC

through the spirit of hospitality might provide a positive concept through which to act in the here and now while remaining open to the possibility of something different.

## Flight Lines

Hospitality has played a vital role in the development of human societies and has been a catalyst in facilitating all human activities. Rethinking community through its lens gives those invested in community music practices an opportunity to think critically about the processes of negotiating the boundaries between their dreams and the different realities in which we all reside. Saying "yes" and thinking in open, nonexclusive ways require considered decision-making processes. The consequence of our decisions and the utterances that follow are our promises to each other. These promises and the actions they incur are ours to own; they signify our responsibilities to those in our immediate vicinity, family, friends, and work colleagues, as well as those within the broader sphere of human connection, the wider communities we interact with, those within our country, and those we coexist with across the planet. This hospitable welcome is vital to every social interaction and in every context. As an idea and an action, hospitality is a complex and evocative concept conjuring up ideas and images that are both diverse and far-reaching. Traversing the braided knots incumbent on hospitality's weaving of unconditional and conditional realities gives us an opportunity to challenge behaviors that are exclusive and discriminatory while insisting that any decisions taken are made responsibly.

As an act of hospitality, the notion of community presents us with the potential to say "yes," an opportunity to be welcoming alongside a genuinely inclusive promise, without discrimination, and open. Since being proposed in connection to community music, it has taken hold in the lexicon associated with the field (Balsnes, 2016; Davis, 2011; DeVito & Bingham, 2014; Doherty, 2022; Howell, 2013; Phelan, 2012; Salvador et al., 2021; Sullivan, 2017; Urie et al., 2019; Vougioukalou et al., 2019; West & Cremata, 2016). Hospitality is a linguistically and semantically ambiguous term, so can hospitality be trusted by those willing to be hosted? Given that any hospitable music environment is regulated by conditions imposed by the facilitator, are the participants subjected to disempowerment? Is there a way to reduce the facilitators' authority, liberating the participants from a sense of dependence? Or is the facilitator equally disempowered, always having to suspend a sense of authority?[22] Hospitality's lack of one definition may provide an opportunity for conversation. As an act of hospitality, how might community music continue to speak to, about, and for current and potential participants?

[22] These questions have been adapted from Fusi (2012).

# 3

# Pedagogy

## Music Making in a Youth Club

*Caroline works within an inner-city youth service in Liverpool, United Kingdom. As a local musician, she is known to youth workers in the area. Caroline was invited into one of the local council's youth centers to discuss the possibility of supporting some of its young people in their musical development. This request occurred through a discussion between the youth workers and those who attend and use the center. It was of particular interest to a group of young males trying to form a cohesive rock band but needing help to organize themselves. There were many reasons creating an active music-making ensemble was important for the youth in the group. Many of their reasons went beyond those of a musical nature, as those in the ensemble wanted a reprieve from instability at home, getting in trouble with the police, difficulty forming healthy relationships, and lack of confidence brought about by low self-esteem.*

*The club that the boys attended was an after-school facility that stayed open until around 10 p.m. Young people between ages 12 and 19 meet at the center, where there are spaces to sit and chat and regular opportunities to participate in various trips, sports, and art activities. During the opening times, adult youth workers are on hand to give advice and offer instruction at the young people's request. Working in ways described as "informal," the youth workers know the local context and are aware of the issues and pressures surrounding the young people.[1] As with most youth, there has always been a great interest in music among those who attend. Some of those who attend the center own guitars, drums, and keyboards and play them with varying levels of expertise. To harness this interest, and in consultation with the young people, the youth workers hired Caroline, a skilled and experienced local musician who regularly worked as a music facilitator in and around the city. With the help of a seeding grant, the center purchased a basic backline, drum kit, a couple of guitar amps and guitars, a small PA system, microphones, and a keyboard.*

---

[1] For a discussion on informal education, see Jeffs and Smith (2005).

*Thinking Community Music.* Lee Higgins, Oxford University Press. © Oxford University Press 2024.
DOI: 10.1093/9780190247027.003.0004

*This money enabled them to employ Caroline to facilitate their twice-weekly music club. During this time, Caroline guided the young people in their musical performance by helping with instrumental technique, arrangements, and constructive criticism of the group's original material and the cover numbers they had chosen to perform. Her role was not passive but highly engaged, and Caroline was constantly aware of the shifting group dynamics through regular conversation with youth workers and heeding their advice.*

*The music club has been popular over and beyond the initial request, and the center is beginning to see an overspill of its activities into the other weekday evenings. An independent peer mentoring network is now taking place between those with instrumental skills and those who wish to learn. Almost every night, you can witness peer teaching, a young musician teaching someone else a new lick, chord sequence, or vocal line.[2] Although there is growing confidence among the young people, Caroline's weekly presence is still treasured and appreciated. She is seen as an essential and stable influence in facilitating musical learning and as someone with insightful knowledge of the participants.*

Aiysha runs DJ workshops in a local youth club, Sarah facilitates a singing rehearsal for the Third Age Choir at a day center, Davey conducts the LGBTQ+ chorus at his college, and Benjamin leads a drum ensemble in a community center. These four community musicians work in different locations, with different people, and with different musical styles, but what binds them together is twofold: They work outside of traditional structures associated with music in schools, and they all work with an approach to active music participation that might be described in terms of "nonformal learning." Acting as a facilitator for musical engagement, community musicians have resisted the suggestion that their approach can be aligned to a particular "method" or is an example of "teaching." Within the field, there has been a suspicion of both terms: *method* because it suggests a fixed process usually ordered in sequential steps, and *teaching* because of its association with statuary schooling and set curricula. The purpose of this think piece is to consider whether community musicians might explicitly describe their approach as a "pedagogy." In this context, the term *pedagogy* would refer to a set of approaches, beliefs, and theories generally utilized within music-making activities or events said to be community music. This thought is sparked through an engagement

---

[2] For discussions on peer mentoring and music education, see Baker and Krout (2012), Green (2008), Lebler (2008), and Goodrich (2007).

in the many case studies that populate the literature, for example, in the *International Journal of Community Music*[3] (from 2007 onward), Sounding Board[4] (1992 onward), and the conference papers from the International Society for Music Education's Commission for Community Music Activity[5] (from 1990 onward) plus the many experiences I have had both running community music projects and talking to and witnessing practice internationally. From my experience, distinctive characteristics constitute the ways in which community musicians work. Suppose this is the case, and these traits are identifiable and repeatable. It might then be advantageous for the field to explicitly describe its approaches to practice in terms of the underlying concepts and features inherent within nonformal learning: contextual, flexible, and person centered. By considering the historical roots of nonformal learning, I will tease out its key features and explore how these ideas have been utilized within the wider field of music education and within community music particularly. Facilitation is the central strategy for engaging participants in learning that is designated as non-formal.[6]

So following this, I describe the distinctive traits of facilitation and offer examples to help illuminate nonformal processes to bring us closer to an understanding of how community musicians work and the mechanisms they use, and I pose the question: *Can community music have a pedagogy?*

## Nonformal Learning

Initially an "alternative" approach to formal "education" within developing countries, nonformal learning, or education as it was then articulated, gained interest from those who felt that formal education systems alone could not respond to the challenges of modern society. These included cultural, social, economic, and political changes, such as ideas connected to globalization, government decentralization, and growing democratization. Coming to prominence around the late 1960s with the work of Philip Coombs (1968),[7] nonformal education continued its growth through the

---

[3] https://www.intellectbooks.com/international-journal-of-community-music
[4] https://www.soundsense.org/
[5] https://isme-commissions.weebly.com/
[6] Extracts have been taken from a previously published chapter (Higgins, 2016).
[7] Coombs was a program director for education at the Ford Foundation and was later appointed by John F. Kennedy as the first assistant secretary of state for education and culture in the United States.

PEDAGOGY 65

1970s within the context of development, "the idea that deliberate action can be undertaken to change society in chosen directions considered desirable" (Rogers, 2004, p. 13). Although the term *nonformal education* had been used prior to the 1970s, it was Coombs who claimed the first systematic study of it, laying down several definitional frameworks, the most refined of which states that nonformal education is "simply any organized activity with educational purposes carried on outside the highly structured framework of formal education systems as they exist today" (Coombs & Ahmed, 1974, p. 233). Through a commissioned report for the International Council of Educational Development and funded by the World Bank, Coombs and Ahmed (1974) discuss how nonformal education increased the skills and productivity of farmers, artisans, craftsmen, and small entrepreneurs across 22 countries, including Tanzania, Mexico, Nigeria, and India. Underscoring that education is a lifelong process, Coombs and Ahmed demonstrated that nonformal education has the freedom and latitude to serve a wide range of people and situations. In contrast to those who equate education to schooling, they supported a "functional" view of education rather than a structural and institutional view (Coombs & Ahmed, 1974, p. 232). Education was an essential tool toward self-governance and practical action, and four characteristics came to be associated with it: (1) relevance to the needs of disadvantaged groups, (2) concern with specific categories of person, (3) a focus on clearly defined purposes, and (4) flexibility in organization and methods.[8] This was further clarified by World Bank economist John Simmons (1980), who suggests that nonformal education is "organized learning outside the traditional school and university curriculum" (p. 2). Those who work as nonformal educators are engaged in diverse and contextualized small-scale education activities centered on local specific problems determined by the participants rather than a preset curriculum (Gillespie, 2010; Mualuko, 2008; Sakya, 2001). The educational activities are often linked with community groups, thus making them highly contextualized and participatory. Characterized as educational enterprises that are embedded in planned activities and contain a vital learning element (sometimes described as semistructured learning), organizations such as the U.S. Peace Corps use nonformal education methods to further its goals in enabling people to develop the capacity to improve their own lives (Peace Corps, 2004).[9]

[8] www.infed.org
[9] For an example of a Peace Corps music project, see Erika Eckstrom (2008).

## 66 THINKING COMMUNITY MUSIC

As part of the lifelong learning discourse, nonformal education professionals searched for terminology covering alternative educational programs, especially for marginalized, excluded, and/or subordinated populations (Otero et al., 2005). The emphasis on this approach to enabling new skills, values, and knowledge is reflected at the turn of the millennium in the Council of Europe's recommendation that nonformal education should be recognized as essential in lifelong learning processes and youth policy (Council of Europe, 2011). In tune with technological advances, the Council of Europe extended their discussion to include e-learning environments for young people within nonformal contexts (Lopez, 2012). The report from the Organisation for Economic Co-operation and Development[10] (OECD; Werquin, 2010) highlights the "human capital" benefits of recognizing and making visible nonformal education. Benefits include economic, educational, social, and psychological boosts, as well as opportunities to improve equality and sustainability. Following this, Madhu Singh (2015), from the UNESCO Institute for Lifelong Learning, explores the recognition, validation, and accreditation of the outcomes of nonformal and informal learning to affect governmental policy regarding the status of nonformal education in terms of qualifications, equivalencies, and credits and the acknowledgment of the value of skills and competencies in the labor market or for academic entry or progression. Whereas this example points toward a global interest in nonformal learning, the work of the OECD could be said to reflect a neoliberal human capital agenda. If understood from this framework, it would be understood as mobilizing ideas in ways that rub against the central tenets of community music, for example, inclusion (see Think Piece 5) and cultural democracy (see Think Piece 1). Gert Biesta (2015;) critiques what he calls "the powerful roles of transnational organizations" (Biesta et al, 2020, p. 457), such as the OECD and UNESCO, acknowledging that their policies can negatively intersect with teacher education reform. Concerned about the economies driving this work, Biesta calls for an investigation regarding how policies of this sort can be resisted and recontextualized. In synergy with the historical roots of community music, there is a wonder as to where the locally based networks of educators and schools experimenting with bottom-up teacher education reform are emerging.

As an educational process, nonformal learning often takes place outside the established formal education system and is highly contextualized,

---

[10] The OECD was founded in 1961 with 18 member states, plus the United States and Canada. It is now listed as having 38 member states (https://www.oecd.org).

PEDAGOGY 67

intending to serve identifiable learning goals, and is based on a series of learning opportunities that are tailor-made and adapted to the needs of the learner group. Schemes of work are flexible and, as such, signify that the structure is nonlinear and thus resists top-down curriculum. Nonformal learning has been characterized, somewhat simply, as "learning by doing" depending strongly on reflection ("in" and "on" action) and fostered by a leader in the field who acts as a mentor, facilitating experience into knowledge, skills, attitudes, values, and convictions (Colardyn, 2001; Rogers, 2004).[11] Resonant to critical educational thinkers of the time, such as Paulo Freire (1970/2002), Malcolm Knowles (Knowles et al, 2011), Carl Rogers (1983), Ronald Dore (1997), David Kolb (1983), and Stephen Brookfield (1986), nonformal educators emphasize a bottom-up rather than top-down approach to teaching and stress inclusivity and participation, encouragement of a personalized learning experience, and an understanding that the work can have an impact beyond the content area itself.

If formal ways of learning are categorized as curriculum based, leading toward some certification, and placed within education and training institutions, nonformal learning can be understood as an alternative born out of insufficiencies within and criticism of the formal educational system (Torres, 2001). Notably, the initial development of nonformal learning resonates with the growth of community music, both taking place during the politically charged late 1960s and early 1970s. Both challenged established educational pathways and emphasized active participation, cultural equality, diversity, and transformation with the hope that it could lead to change through expression as a means of emancipation.

## School of Rock

*Nonformal musical approaches are predominantly rooted in group-based activities focusing on performing, listening, composing, and improvising. Learners are encouraged to have significant input in the learning, meaning the material is often co-constructed. An excellent example of this is a project called School of Rock,[12] which highlights young people's musical needs within*

---

[11] See also *The Encyclopaedia of Informal Education* (https://www.infed.org).
[12] Although the project title reflects the franchise (https://www.schoolofrock.com/), this project is not connected with this program.

68 THINKING COMMUNITY MUSIC

*a particular community. Operating with a twice-yearly project run by a village youth project, its mission has been to support and enable young people to achieve their full and unique potential emotionally, socially, morally, and spiritually.*[13] *Described as a club for "budding musicians," young people receive individual tuition for their chosen instrument for the first few weeks, then form bands and rehearse for a performance.*[14] *As an after-school program, the School of Rock has three components: First, the young people have individual lessons on instruments of their choice, guitars, bass, drums, keyboards, or vocals. The instrumental tutors are a mixture of professional and trainee facilitators drawn from either a local pool of working musicians or recipients of past projects. The situation is complex, as the tutors must deal with a range of skills, from beginners upward, and teach in rooms spread across the youth center and church hall. Instrumental instruction is more akin to facilitation and nonformal strategies than formal one-to-one instrumental teaching. Second, after 6 weeks of engagement in instrumental learning, everybody is placed in an ensemble and has 6 weeks to rehearse two or three songs. Finally, and with the guidance of the music facilitators, the groups perform several gigs for an audience. Sometimes, the venues can be prestigious and include an entire sound rig and lights. As well as providing a fun and engaging learning experience for those young people who desired to "have a go," the facilitative approaches used in the project have created opportunities for others to explore their music further. In 2015, 23 Fake Street was one such band that benefited from the project. They started as a group of mates, and their involvement with the project has helped consolidate their friendship and musical ambition.*[15] *Although years have passed since they started at the youth club, some band members continue to support the School of Rock project through the music development program, a training initiative that educates participants to become peer mentors and, eventually, music tutors.*

## Nonformal Learning and Music

To close the gap between two musical worlds, that of students' musical culture outside school and that of the classroom, music educator Lucy

---

[13] https://www.facebook.com/thebankVYP
[14] https://stm-upton.org.uk/children-and-youth/youth/
[15] https://www.getintothis.co.uk/2015/10/introducing-23-fake-street/

Green (2005) sought to recognize the informal learning practices of popular musicians and adopt these as a teaching and learning strategy within school classrooms. Until the publication of Green's *Music, Informal Learning and the School: A New Classroom Pedagogy* in 2008, formal music learning dominated the music education research agenda (Veblen, 2012). Since then, this pattern has begun to change, with informal music teaching and learning becoming a fertile ground for discussion, debate, and research within music education research (Carroll, 2020; Creech et al., 2020; Folkestad, 2005, 2006; Green, 2008; Hess, 2020;; Jenkins, 2011; Lonie & Dickens, 2015; Ng, 2020; O'Flynn, 2006; Rodriguez, 2009; Smith, 2013; Söderman & Folkestad, 2004; Westerlund, 2006; Wright & Kanellopoulos, 2010; Wright et al., 2016). Following Green (2014), formal music learning refers to types of institutions and types of practice. Broadly reflecting a top-down curriculum formation involving explicit teaching and assessment strategies, Western classical music has been historically linked to formal music learning. However, introducing other musical styles and genres into schools, universities, and conservatoires has meant practices such as jazz, pop, and rock and music from traditions across the world are also formally taught.

Discourses surrounding nonformal music learning have steadily risen since 2004 (Juan-Morera et al., 2022). Themes explored include person-centered and peer learning; inclusivity; facilitation; valuing learners' musical interests; the recognition that music making can contribute to young people's overall social, educational, and personal development; the interconnections between in-school and out-of-school musical interests and experiences; and the contribution that nonformal learning has to a lifelong musical journey. Examples can be found in the work of Abigail D'Amore (2009) and her analysis of approaches employed by musicians working in the Musical Futures project; Nina Kors (2007) and Peter Mak (2007; Mak et al., 2007) through their research with Rineke Smilde (2008) and the Lifelong Learning Lectorate in the Netherlands; On Nei Annie Mok (2011), who recognizes the lack of discussion surrounding the term *nonformal* and attempts to bridge the gap by introducing the concept and providing examples from both Japanese and Chinese musical transmission; Jo Saunders and Graham Welch's (2012) investigation into Youth Music Action Zones in England; Kari Veblen (2012) in her discussion of lifelong learning; Phil Mullen and Kathryn Deane (2018) in their consideration of working with young people in challenging circumstances; an Indonesian team investigating teaching strategies connected to COVID-19 and online education (Liu et al., 2022; Maragani et al., 2019); and the Ethno Research project's exploration into folk music residential gatherings in over 30 countries (Gibson et al., 2022).

A concise description of the three learning positions can be articulated as follows:

- *Formal music learning* occurs in education and training institutions, leading to qualifications recognized by relevant national authorities. Formalized learning is structured according to educational arrangements such as curriculum qualifications and teaching-learning requirements.
- *Nonformal learning* is learning in addition to or alternative to formal learning. In some cases, it is also more flexibly structured according to educational and training arrangements. It usually occurs in community-based settings, in the workplace, and through the activities of civil society organizations.
- *Informal learning* is learning that occurs in daily life, in the family, in the workplace, in communities, and through the interests and activities of individuals.[16]

Educational thinkers have long argued that the concepts of formal, nonformal, and informal learning cannot be understood as discrete, isolated, and unconnected from each other but instead exist on a continuum (Eraut, 2004; Sawchuk, 2009; Straka, 2005). If we consider formal and informal musical learning as either end of a continuum, then it is reasonable to locate nonformal music learning as sitting somewhere between the two. Organized approaches such as Musical Futures[17] (Hallam et al., 2015) and Modern Band[18] (Powell, 2021) look toward such a continuum as fertile ground for new music learning possibilities. Both examples are predominately predicated upon popular music and emphasize ear-based learning but are associated with the formal setting of a school. Adapting an idea proposed by Zürcher (2010), Figure 3.1 presents a continuum as a mixing desk, with informal learning at one end of the x-axis and formal learning at the other.

---

[16] Adapted from Singh (2015).
[17] https://www.musicalfutures.org/about/
[18] https://musicwill.org/

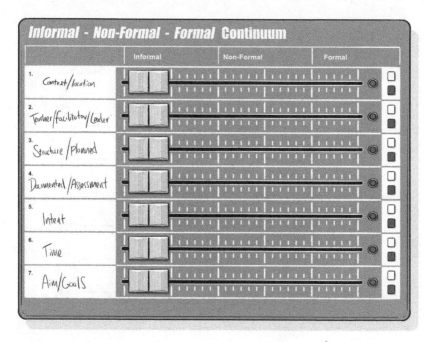

**Figure 3.1** Informal, non-formal, formal continuum.
See also Zürcher (2010).

Categories associated with planning a music workshop are presented on the y-axis.

Figures 3.2 and 3.3 visualize the two illustrations of practice presented so far.

From a big-picture perspective, the interaction of formal, nonformal, and informal learning contexts and processes is vital in promoting lifelong music learning (Bugos, 2017; Mantie, 2012; Smilde, 2021). If we consider musical learning as a dynamic interaction of a multiphased process that changes the emphasis from (1) independent learning in informal settings during early childhood to (2) formalized learning during the school years followed later by (3) nonformalized interactions occurring in community settings, then recognition that community musicians often move in and between both formal and nonformal approaches may benefit its development. To deepen an understanding of nonformal music learning in practice, the following illustration moves toward a discussion on facilitation.

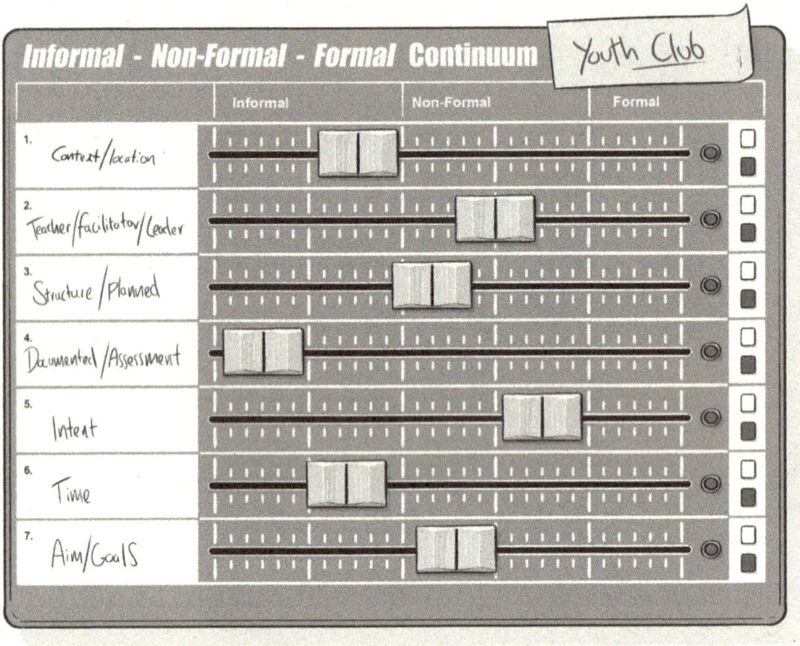

72    THINKING COMMUNITY MUSIC

Figure 3.2  Music making in a youth club.

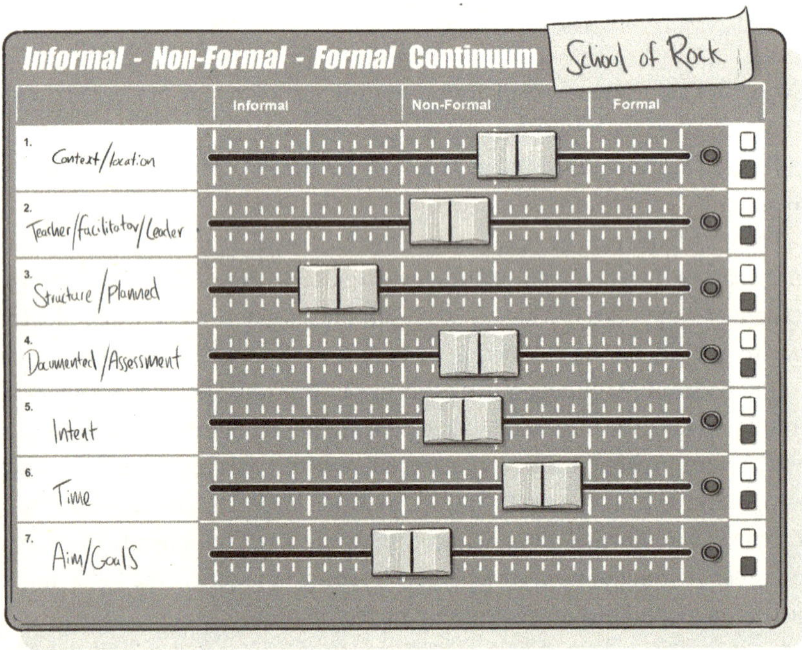

Figure 3.3  School of Rock.

PEDAGOGY 73

## Rock 'n' Roll After-School Club for Girls

*In a similar vein to the School of Rock and making music in a youth club programs discussed previously, singer-songwriter and BRIT Award[19] winner Kate Nash started her Rock 'n' Roll for Girls After-School Music Club placing an overt emphasis on addressing the underrepresentation of female songwriters in British Music. in.[20] Through collaboration with several schools across the United Kingdom, Nash and her band began running songwriting workshops in 2011. The motivation to begin the enterprise at that time was that only 14% of the 75,000 members of the Performing Rights Society, which collects and pays songwriting royalties in Britain, were female. In Nash's words, "A lot of women in pop aren't writing their own songs, and there is this preconception that women are meant mainly as performers" (Sharp, 2011). Employing nonformal music learning strategies, the workshops were designed to support female songwriters in finding confidence in their identity as musicians.*

*Esme, who was 15 then, was known in her school as a singer/songwriter and was invited to be involved in Nash's project. She was asked what she played and how she would like to work with the professional musicians from Nash's band. Choosing to work with the drummer, Esme discussed with her how the music should sound. Conversation between the two of them revolved around the types of artists that were currently influential on Esme's compositions and the musical possibilities for the songs she had written. Esme recalls that "the project was about not going with the crowd, to feel self-confident about what you do, to know that everyone is different and special." Esme felt that the project contradicted her school's formal music education: "Music in school was never about self-expression. It's too structured." The impact of the project helped Esme move forward as a performer playing in local venues around the city and continuing her music education at a community college where nonformal strategies were being used in a formal setting. From Esme's perspective, nonformal approaches to music making have "allowed" her to make the music she wants and to express the person she is. Esme completed a degree in music at Leeds College of Music and continues as a performer and a community musician.[21]*

Figure 3.4 presents a visualization for the Rock 'n' Roll After-School Club for Girls.

---

[19] The BRIT Awards are the British Phonographic Industry's annual pop music awards, similar to the American Grammy Awards. On February 20, 2008, Kate Nash received a BRIT Award for Best Female Artist.

[20] See http://www.youtube.com/watch?v=4-RLVciwbaA.

[21] https://www.esmebridie.com/

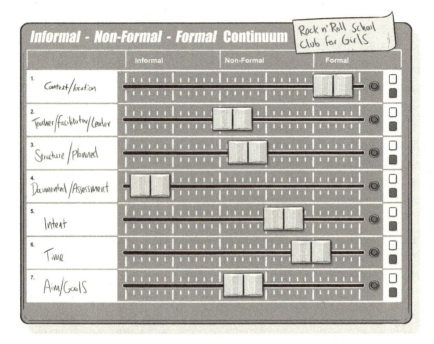

**Figure 3.4** Rock 'n' Roll After-School Club for Girls.

## Facilitating Musical Learning

As an approach to participatory music making, nonformal music learning provides opportunities to develop skills such as trust, respect, empathy, and creativity while intentionally intertwining social and personal aspects with music making. If notions of nonformal learning serve as the strategy for community musicians, then the technical deployment of *facilitation* acts as the mechanism through which things happen. Derivative from the French *faciliter* (to render easy) and the Latin *facilis* (easy), *facilitation* is concerned with encouraging open dialogue among different individuals with differing perspectives (Benson, 2010; Hogan, 2002, 2003; Preston, 2016). As self-reflective practitioners who have a variety of technical skills and knowledge together with a wide range of experiences to assist groups of people to journey together to reach their goals, community musicians as facilitators act as conduits who help participants' creative energy to flow, develop, and grow through pathways specific to individuals and the groups in which they are active. From this perspective, facilitation enables an intervention to happen (see Think Piece 1) and for community musicians to work strategically to generate music-making environments that are accessible and inviting for those who wish to participate. To generate such opportunities, community musicians have understood the approaches they use as flexible and responsive and seen these in opposition to a singular prescriptive methodology.

Being a facilitator does not mean the musician surrenders responsibility for music leadership; instead, their sense of control within the musical learning process is relinquished. In other words, the musical facilitators purposefully enable the learners to co-construct their learning, and through this indirect approach, deeper learning happens. Within any group setting, there is a fine line between leading and controlling, but the two processes are very different and provide contrasting results to the group experience. For example, in controlling the group journey, there is a strong sense of the beginning, middle, and end and the expectations and needs to be met. In facilitating the group experience, however, there may be a starting point, but the rest remains uncertain. Nonformal music educators offer routes toward suggested destinations. They are ready to assist if the group journey needs to be clarified. However, they are always open to the possibility of the unexpected that comes from individuals interacting with the group. These possibilities cannot be predicted, and that is the excitement of facilitated music that grows from the group, be they a group of young children, an older adults' choir, or members of a youth rock band, or, like Esme, a singer-songwriter. Anything can happen when musical events are proposed and facilitated but not directed in the top-down conductors/directors' tradition. Nonformal approaches were undoubtedly tested during the pandemic but appear to have proved robust during this challenging time, both for those leading projects and for those trying to participate in them. The special issue of the *International Journal of Community Music* presents 11 accounts of this. As editor Stephen Clift (2021) recounts, there is a "renewed thinking about the social function of music and its role in communities, leading to new theoretical insights" (p. 125).

Skillful facilitators move in and out of roles as the group dictates, necessitating trust in the ability of others as well as submission to the inventiveness of others. As nonformal music educators, community musicians develop trust as they listen to participants while maintaining cooperative participation. By establishing a secure but flexible framework from the outset, community musicians often give over control to the group and trust in the direction it takes. In giving up control, possibilities emerge for unpredictable musical outcomes; music becomes an invention personal to the participants, owned by and meaningful to them, with the potential to generate an experience that can shape, create, and impact identity formation (Green, 2011). From experience, participants look to the facilitator for reassurance, clarity, direction, encouragement, guidance, or help in shaping their music material. In this sense, there is a constant negotiation of power that the skilled facilitator reflects upon both within and outside their music sessions. Music facilitators who are tuned into the effects of this are often able to find a comfortable balance between being a "friend" and taking on the responsibility that comes with working with young people, such as being asked for advice on a diverse range of topics that might include sexual health, bullying, careers, and parents.[22] The ability to find comfort between being prepared and letting go bleeds into approaches to music making that emphasize enabling the group or individuals to discover the journey of musical invention.

Although the following illustration of practice is based within a formal school setting and has components quite at odds with other examples within this book—for instance, aspects of this work are compulsory and have credits associated with attendance—it is included because it is a project that works across the continuum and finds its most potent agency within a nonformal strategy. In this sense, it deepens an understanding of the fluidity that takes place across formal, nonformal, and informal learning.

---

[22] For further exploration of friendship within nonformal encounters, see Higgins (2012c).

# Samba at FDA

*In 2002, music classes at the Frederick Douglass Academy (FDA) in New York City's Harlem neighborhood were unpopular.[23] The band program had been in steady decline for years, and in order to get it back on its feet, the school administration hired Dana Monteiro,[24] a trumpet player and music educator from Providence, Rhode Island. After trying to develop the program for 4 years, Dana felt that he needed to make more progress and was faced with significant increases in class sizes and a transient student population.[25] While on vacation in Brazil, Dana met some local Pagode musicians, and they encouraged him to visit an escolar de samba in the Quadra da Villa Isabel favela in Rio. During this trip, Dana thought that this form of musicking, with 250 drummers playing Batucada, might resonate with his students back in the United States. As he reflected on the school environment he was working in, he recalled that many students had been vocal in expressing that they wanted to play drums rather than brass or wind instruments. Upon returning to New York City, he decided to join a community samba group, Samba New York, and experience how the music was performed as a participant. Dana began with the cavaquinho, a small string instrument, and later explored the percussion instruments such as the surdo, tamborim, caixa, and repinique. After an initial purchase of 10 drums, an after-school club was started that eventually consumed the rest of the music program, forming what is known today as Harlem Samba.*

*Harlem Samba is a Brazilian percussion ensemble modeled after the samba school baterias of the Rio de Janeiro carnival. The group's members are students, alumni, and friends of the Frederick Douglass Academy, a public high school in Harlem, New York City. The group was founded in 2005 as a non-traditional after-school music ensemble. It has expanded to include over 300 students a year at the school and an evening community ensemble for*

---

[23] The Frederick Douglass Academy (FDA) offers a college preparatory education for grades 6 through 12. Located in the borough of Harlem in New York City, the school serves an urban population and seeks to educate young people within a diverse curriculum. Under the motto "without struggle, there is no progress," the FDA prides itself in giving its students the best chance to be competitive in college applications (https://www.fda1harlem.org/

[24] http://www.danamonteiro.com/

[25] There are 1,700 students in the school, and they all must do music to graduate. Until recently, only one music teacher was seeing up to 50 students at a time. Another key reason was that the population could be transient in an urban school such as the FDA, making it very difficult to cultivate a traditional U.S. band program.

# 78 THINKING COMMUNITY MUSIC

*adult players. Samba has become an important part of our community and the key ingredient in expanding active participation in music making. We believe that everyone should have the opportunity to make music.*[26]

At the FDA, over 200 students play samba every week on instruments imported from Brazil. Students learn traditional Rio-style samba and sing entire songs in Portuguese. The ensemble has now performed at Lincoln Center, the Museum of Modern Art, and the Brooklyn Academy of Music in New York City; the World Cafe Live in Philadelphia; and the Broward County Performing Arts Center in Fort Lauderdale. The samba program has also been featured in the documentary film Beyond Ipanema: Brazilian Waves in Global Music (Barra & Dranoff, 2009). The FDA's performing band, Harlem Samba, won the 2012 Brazilian International Press Award in the category of Best Institution for the Promotion of Brazilian Culture in the United States, and in 2007 and 2009, the Harlem Samba program traveled to Rio de Janeiro.

Since Dana decided to introduce samba to the school, his strategy has been to create an open environment where every student can participate in a meaningful musical experience. He reinforces this by asserting, "I have almost an entire school with someone who is playing an instrument," and he further notes, "What I have made here will, I think, get more kids playing later in life than a traditional program." The students knew the transferable nature of the skills they learned in the samba classes. One group of students said that learning music from a culture other than their own would help them get the most out of study-abroad programs. Others described informal music-making experiences they are currently having outside of school, such as playing bongos with a local street band. Many saw how their music-making experiences provided a sense of independence and a thirst for playing beyond the school gates.

Students at the FDA listen to hip-hop, R&B, gospel, and reggae. How has playing samba influenced the students' listening? As Stephen explained, "I actually have samba on my iPod, and that was actually the biggest thing for me. . . . I didn't have samba as a mind-state in my freshman year, but now it is like second nature to me now." Sarah explained, "Well . . . I've never listened to samba before," and Jay noted, "Yeah, it's like I hear more the beat and how things are played than the flow of the music—you hear different instruments inside." One of the students explained that when learning a Brazilian song in Portuguese, he listened to it 50 times a day to understand what they were

---

[26] http://www.harlemsamba.com/https://www.youtube.com/watch?v=sg8azF1JC1M

PEDAGOGY    79

*saying. This sort of commitment was common with those who had become what Dana named "true believers," meaning those for whom the samba program had become an essential part of their lives. Commenting on being given an opportunity to learn an instrument, Simon, a 16-year-old who considered himself a sambista now, said, "I think I'm the first person in my family to start with music so I'm probably the first one to start a generation. I'll just pass it on." Student experience as instrumentalists varied, but most had little or no experience formally learning an instrument.*

*Described as a "dynasty" by senior students, samba at the FDA encourages music learning and peer teaching. Reflecting on her music classes, Juno stated, "It's more of teamwork than competition," and Robert noted that it feels like a family: "You help each other out." Findings from studies into effective parent-child communication provide a helpful analogy to the facilitator-group relationship (Karofsky et al., 2000; Rogers, 1995; Steinberg, 2001). A young child needs explicit instruction and boundaries to feel safe and secure; this premise enhances the child's growth and development. As they become older, the parent needs to step back a little. The child must face some milestones alone but can always return to the security of the caring parent who is ready, waiting, and expecting to offer comfort, support, guidance, and perhaps redirection. As the child moves into adolescence, the parent needs to release the reigns further, enabling the young adult to overcome challenges, encounter new discoveries, and develop self-assurance. To enable the development of autonomy, the diligent parent will carefully consider when to sensitively step in with offers of support, guidance, advice, or comfort.*

*Although the samba band had a strong sense of family and peer teaching, competition between students became visible between some students when performing, with drummers trying to outwit each other with fast triplets and inventive improvisations. This aspect of music making was discussed among the group with friendly banter and was described as "a healthy competition. It's not like oh I'm definitely better than you. The competition is almost like friendship—it makes you better; we learn from each other." In this context, the competition was a type of playfulness between musicians rather than fierce rivalry brought about by the pressures of an all-state competition or jostling to get first position in an orchestra. This is a testament to how the music program has been organized, the spirit of which can be found in many community music projects. Dana embraces cultural democracy (see Think Piece 2), in which creative arts opportunities, enjoyment, and celebration become available to all. Samba was not a part of any student's cultural heritage; however,* as one student noted, "Not only do we have to play [the instruments, but also] we have to learn about the history of the songs." As a political idea, cultural democracy advocates that people must create culture rather than having it made for them: "Culture isn't something you can get. You've already got it" (Graves, 2005, p. 15). The availability of performance footage from YouTube cannot be underestimated and exemplifies what Schippers (2010) deems recontextualization. Dana goes as far as to suggest that without YouTube, the advancement of the program would not have been possible because the students have immediate access to both the context and music from within their homes.

One of the things most intriguing about any world music ensemble is how the sound and form of the music reflect the local context and those who perform it. In terms of samba, this can be woven into the band's ethos or sound, such as MacUmba (samba with bagpipes), Bloco Vomit (samba-punk) and Sambangra (samba and bhangra). It is more common, however, that community samba bands strive for a so-called "authentic" sound, generally understood as approximating what might be perceived as original and authentic to a Brazilian cultural setting. In the case of Harlem Samba, their sound does approximate the Rio style quite closely but not at all costs. Dana's strategy has been to empower students to feel ownership of the music they make and the various samba bands they inhabit, emphasizing what students can achieve with their abilities. This is reflected in the day-to-day running of the classes where students take leadership roles. Consequently, a considerable number of graduates return each year to play with the band. "I don't lose many," Dana says, "once we get past December 10 [end of fall semester], all those college kids will be here every day. They will play when we have a concert; there are always us and the kids who have finished college. There are kids who are 22 [years of age] who come and play." This was evident in my conversations with the budding sambistas, who all said, "I'm coming back after school!"

Some students in the Harlem Samba project perceived "Mr. Monteiro" (Dana) as a friend: "Oh I'm much more of a friend to Mr. Monteiro than my other teachers in my old school. . . . I could say that he is definitely more interested in the work." From Dana's perspective, the teaching is very challenging "because no matter what I throw at them they get it—there is a level of comprehension—I think they really get it." He also rather modestly feels that students overvalue his musicianship. The musicianship is not in doubt;

PEDAGOGY 81

*listening to the ensemble, one could not help but be impressed by the quality of the samba "groove," a unified sound that was well crafted and well understood. Energy drifts from the streets into the rehearsal space and through the drum, a performance full of New York teenage intensity.*

*The FDA samba program has developed from a nonformal after-school club to include almost every school community member. It seems a truism to state, as Dana did, that "if you were to go in the hallway, if you were to take a walk around the building and 40 kids were going by, and we dragged them all in, they could probably play: Almost every 9th to 12th grader in the building knows how to play." Initially supported by a principal who believed in the power of music, the program has attracted a private donor who has now given significant amounts of money to purchase instruments and aid travel, for example, a collection of Candombe drums from Uruguay, which offers an opportunity to expand the school musical and cultural experiences. The program has given some students a stronger identity, reflected in the number of students returning to play after graduation. Stephen wore a T-shirt spelling "Harlem Samba": "Yes I'm proud of it. I'm proud to be part of this." Other participants have a sense of responsibility that emulates Dana's teaching strategy, enabling students to take active roles in peer teaching and directorship. Jay stated, "I will never forget this class—I will never forget."*

*As a musician who has embraced ethnomusicological approaches to music learning, such as those described by Mark Bakan (1999), Tim Rice (1994), and John Miller Chernoff (1979), Dana has been visiting the Santa Marta favela and the São Clemente samba school since 2010. Before 2010, he visited every primary samba school in Rio and Sao Paulo and schools in Tokyo, Cape Verde, London, and the United States, honing his skills and consolidating relationships. Dana realizes now that music teachers do not have to teach trumpet and have a traditional marching band to consider their program successful: "We can give a concert, we can do parades, so suddenly we had a marching band, a concert band, and we can do parades— all these things that at one point [the FDA] did have before it collapsed. Suddenly, it was back in this form." Does a U.S. music program need choir, band, and orchestra to have a good and thriving music program? Dana is emphatic: "Not at all."*

*This collaborative spirit is reflected in the day-to-day running of the classes, where students take leadership roles and feel ownership of the classes and their learning, as two young boys told me following the question, Do you like*

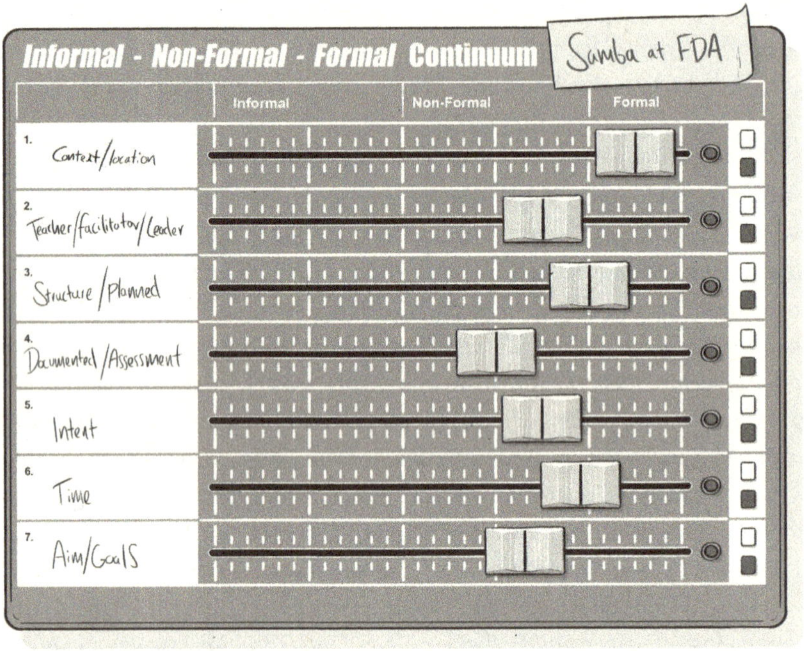

## 82 THINKING COMMUNITY MUSIC

**Figure 3.5** Samba at FDA.

*playing?*: "Yes, I'm leading the repinique section [small tenor drum], and he [pointing to his mate] is the leader for the caixa section [snare drum]. I'm pretty much the music director." The FDA samba program has developed to include almost every member of the school community, resulting in just about every year group in the building knowing how to play and partake in ensemble music making.*

*In resonance with those who work in applied ethnomusicology, in 2017, Harlem Samba set up A Life with Drums, a nonprofit organization that seeks to work with other schools and within other community settings throughout the United States. "Our organization is focused on expanding the role of non-traditional music education in our communities and improving access to the lifelong benefits of music participation."*[27]

Figure 3.5 presents an informal/nonformal/formal learning visualization for Samba at FDA.

---

[27] http://www.harlemsamba.com/

# Flight Lines

The following principles underline nonformal music engagement by drawing upon the ideas central to the illustrations of practice above.[28]

- Music learning can take place in any context and, as such, can play a crucial role in relationship and community building.
- Music learning is sensitive to local contexts and musical practices.
- Music learning is enriched by the ethos of inclusion and working with diverse and heterogeneous groups.

Drawing upon these principles, skilled facilitators approach music engagement in the following ways:

- Music engagement mainly takes place through group activities, focusing on playing, improvising, listening, and performing, with an emphasis on inclusivity and participation.
- Music engagement generates a dynamic creative process that involves participants co-constructing musical material.
- Music learning is embedded in planned activities that are not necessarily designated as "learning outcomes."

Key characteristics of nonformal music strategies can, therefore, be described as follows:

- Facilitators and participants actively engage in music making together.
- Music making often includes the creation of new ideas, arrangements, and/or compositions.
- Musical doing is through collaboration, and facilitators work toward engaging everybody in the process.

The field of community music is expanding and becoming more visible as part of the larger musical ecosystem (de Bruin & Southcott, 2023; Schippers & Grant, 2016). Consequently, its practices become more influential, opening opportunities for practitioners to be engaged in wider discussions that concern the growth and development of music teaching and

---

[28] Adapted from Singapore Teachers' Academy for the Arts (2020).

## 84 THINKING COMMUNITY MUSIC

learning more broadly. Is there a danger that the potential for influence has been weakened because of a lack of clear explanation regarding the processes that drive the work? Is a prevailing narrative regarding the community musician as presenting music teaching and learning approaches that are "alternative" and "radical" outdated? In concert with this, is it time for community musicians to shake off an entrenched sense of being in opposition to "traditional" and "formal" ways of engaging people in music? Can the notion of a continuum be embraced by those who work in the field? If approaches and processes are repeatable, is it time to consider these collective traits and name the approach in terms of community music pedagogy? On the other hand, is this too reductionist? Might framing approaches to community music practices this way place it inside the orthodoxy of school music education and, in so doing, limit complexity (see Think Piece 8)? Explicitly articulating working pedagogic practices, however, might push forward the change agenda that so often laces discussion surrounding the impact community music might have on music teaching and learning more generally.

# 4

# Social Justice

## The Soul of Hatay

*On February 6, 2023, a 7.8-magnitude earthquake struck southern and central Turkey and northern and western Syria, causing massive infrastructure devastation, the deaths of at least 55,000 people, and a humanitarian crisis with the displacement of almost 6 million people (IMC, 2023). Reflective of other disasters across the world, this event reveals inequalities between different strata of the population as indicated through the statistic that areas designated as poor suffered 3.5 times more damage (Bird, 2023) and points toward a series of construction scams (Osmaniye & Adiyaman, 2023). Huib Schippers and his partner Olcay Muslu had recently bought and restored a traditional house in the region. Huib is well known in the community music field and has a long and diverse history of engagement with music across various settings and cultures (Schippers, 2010, 2018; Schippers & Bartleet, 2013; Schippers & Grant, 2016). Olcay is a Turkish music educator working at the Mustafa Kemal Hatal University and, like Huib, has been involved in the sustainability of musical traditions with a specialty in music in the region of Sanlurfa, Turkey (Muslu Gargner, 2019).*

*In the heavy-hit capital of the Turkish province of Hatay, 85 miles from the earthquake's epicenter, Huib and Oclay's house and the surrounding neighborhood were all but destroyed. Many people they knew were killed or seriously injured, including music students and teachers whom Olcay worked with at the university. In a personal communication 5 days after the earthquake, Huib wrote, "Our biggest concern is what happens after the next harrowing stage of removing rubble and finding thousands more dead. We want to see if we can contribute meaningfully to rebuilding community through music and culture while the physical rebuilding takes place." As a response, Olcay and Huib immediately worked to set up the legal structure required to establish an association that could begin to mobilize support in saving the cultural "soul" of Hatay. Huib writes:*

*Thinking Community Music.* Lee Higgins, Oxford University Press. © Oxford University Press 2024.
DOI: 10.1093/9780190247027.003.0005

*It is easy to ignore this in a rush to build new and safe housing. However, we should never forget that rebuilding a traumatized community requires more than putting up dwellings: it needs people sensing the cultures around them, understanding how their history—both the good and the bad—make up who they are now, and seeing how this ancient city is the legacy of their ancestors, part of a present they help shape, and the cultural and spiritual basis for the future of their children (Schippers, 2023, para. 8).*

*Olcay and Huib established MİRAS in April 2023 as a nonprofit association in Istanbul. It will focus on working with communities to revitalize their intangible cultural heritage, referring to how people engage with music, dance, theater, poetry, culinary arts, histories, and built environments. The focus for MİRAS between 2023 and 2025 will be on assisting and restoring a sense of community, well-being, and connectedness for the people of Hatay and providing relief while rebuilding the ancient city of Antioch.[1]*

Community musicians focus on creating environments where, through musical interaction, individuals and communities can take charge of their self-expression and shape their futures. In this sense, community musicians set out as agents of change, often under the auspices of what might be described as a framework of social justice. Exploring a commonly expressed motivation that lies behind choices to become community musicians, namely an overarching perception that certain injustices are at work within the lives of many participants that frequent their projects, this think piece proposes the question: *How might social justice be understood as a framework for community music practices?* Briefly locating what social justice means, I explore the promise of justice through the lens of Jacques Derrida and connect the philosophical ideas to the other think pieces. With an orientation toward music making as a site for social justice, I use the two illustrations of practice, the Soul of Hatay and Empowering Song, to begin a discussion of what I will call "hospitable music making" characterized as a call, a response, and a welcome (see Think Piece 2) to the relational act of musicking alongside people brought about through a sense of injustice and a desire to intervene (see Think Piece 1).

[1] http://www.mirasheritage.org/

# Social Justice

Social justice is both a theoretical concept and a practical ideal.[2]

It is often characterized as social and economic equality within a democratic system, where equality refers to the concept that societal members have equal access to public goods, institutional resources, and life opportunities (Green, 1999; Miller, 1999; Miller & Walzer, 1995). The overall aim is, therefore, that all individuals within a society are treated equally. More recently, the notion of equity, a recognition that each person has different circumstances and therefore might need different resources and opportunities to reach an equal outcome, is being understood as more aligned with the social justice agenda and is reflected, for example, within discussions concerning education (Gorard, 2018), health (McKay & Taket, 2020), and research (Strunk & Locke, 2019).

As a nuanced expression of what constitutes justice, articulations of social justice are always in play with centuries of debate and contestation. For example, classic conceptions of justice have a long history from the ancient Greeks, Plato (2000), and Aristotle (2000) through to the scholastic interpretations of St. Thomas Aquinas (2002). In the modern era, Thomas Hobbes (1651/1968), John Locke (1963), Jean-Jacques Rousseau (1993), Immanuel Kant (1989), and John Stuart Mill (1859/1978) made significant contributions. From the 20th century, thinkers such as John Rawls (1999) and Jürgen Habermas (1984) have explored how justice might operate within modern industrialized nations. More specifically, philosophical thought that had social structures as an explicit aspect of the theories is included in the writings of Adam Smith (Solomon, 1999), Herbert Spencer (1946), Peter Kropotkin (1972), and Karl Marx and Friedrich Engels (Tucker, 1978). Historical analysis of the concept reveals that contemporary ideas about what social justice means are quite different from those of earlier times (Fleischacker, 2005). For example, political theorist David Miller (1999) has presented a pluralist account of social justice, arguing that there can be no single measure of justice. Orientated around need, desert,[3] and equality, Miller's proposal reflects how important the idea of social justice has been in the late 20th and early 21st century, embedding itself within Western community values and spreading across many domains and discourses.

---

[2] Extracts from this section have been adapted from Higgins (2015).
[3] A typical desert claim is a claim that someone—the "deserver"—deserves something.

As a "distinctly modern idea," law professor Brendan Edgeworth (2012) suggests that social justice can be seen as "emerging in tandem with the development of modern nation-states where for the first time in history it became possible to see communities as co-extensive with the states that governed them" (p. 418). Edgeworth continues by noting that the conventional notion of social justice as the principle of state-engineered redistribution has shifted toward a set of principles that now appear to hinge on the looser claims of "fairness" and "inclusion" (p. 418). With a focus on society as a whole rather than what is just for the lone individual, social justice has become an essential ideal for many institutions to aspire to; these include schools, hospitals, universities, and, in some cases, corporate businesses (Capeheart & Milovanovic, 2007). The breadth of issues being considered under the social justice mantle includes climate justice, sustainability, employment law, mental health and well-being, media and democracy, colonialism, being active in fair trade, research practices, and creating diversity, equality, and inclusion policies for a diverse workforce.[4] As noted in Think Piece 5, inclusion through the social justice lens emphasizes the human potential understood through fairness for all and opportunities to participate fully in society. Acts of community engagement and participation are therefore foregrounded (Gidley et al., 2010).

The growing concerns for what American political theorist Iris Young (2011) might call a "responsibility for justice" have impacted those working in music education (Benedict et al., 2015; Gould et al., 2009), music therapy (Webb & Swamy, 2020), and applied ethnomusicology (Pettan & Titon, 2015), all fields that intersect with community music. More specifically, those working in these fields have been concerned with the creation of plural and equitable musical curricula content (Benedict, 2021; Benedict & Schmidt, 2007; Gould, 2007; Hess, 2017), music teaching as a moral imperative to care (Allsup & Shieh, 2012; Allsup & Westerlund, 2012), leadership (Vaillancourt, 2012), ageism (Kruse, 2022), institution change (Vakeva et al., 2017), equitable representation of the musics of the world (Sands, 2007; Vaugeois, 2007), the development of equitable music policy and policymaking (Bradley, 2011; Schmidt, 2017), systematic racism (Quadros & Abrahams, 2022), preservice teacher training (Palmer, 2017), conflict resolution (Sweers, 2015), classical music (Bull

---

[4] See Conversations in Social Justice, a podcast series from the Institute of Social Justice, York St John University, United Kingdom. https://podcasters.spotify.com/pod/show/isj

et al., 2023), the socioculturally situatedness of music teaching and learning (Bowman, 2007), leisure and education (Mantie, 2022a; 2022c), activism in music education (Hess, 2018), and decolonization (Chávez & Skelchy, 2019; Mackinlay, 2015). Following music education scholars Lise Vaugeois (2009) and Juliet Hess (2017), working definitions of social justice are often enacted as a verb rather than a noun. Vaugeois contends that, as a verb, social justice is the work of undoing structures that produce raced, gendered, identity oppressions and systemic poverty, as well as challenging discourses that rationalize these structures. By employing this definition, social justice becomes the work of challenging structures that oppress. These structures might include, for example, government funding decisions that severely impact school resources.

From a community music perspective, a limited amount of literature deals explicitly with social justice. Marissa Silverman (2009; 2012), Andre de Quadros (2018), Naomi Sunderland (Sunderlund et al., 2016), and Nicola McAteer and Rory Wells (2024) are four examples of authors who do. Although this is surprising, it might reflect a general understanding that diversity, equality, and inclusivity are implicit within the practice and, therefore, acknowledgments of aspirations toward social justice. At the time of writing, the Creative Change Project has been investigating community music's role in addressing social inequity in Australia. With an orientation surrounding a "place-based" approach, this large-scale project has examined the social, cultural, physiological, and economic benefits of participating in music and how these might flow upstream to address inequitable and unjust systems.[5]

Although social justice has become one item in a list of generally endorsed public values, its import was only sometimes a comfortable fit within community politics. Described by the influential economist and neoliberal Friedrich Hayek (1976) as a mirage, idealistic, impractical, and vacuous,[6] social justice was part of an ideological struggle in the 1960s and 1970s and, as such, resonates with the history of community music as outlined in the opening chapter. However, it was during the 1980s that Ronald Reagan and Margaret Thatcher came to power in the United States and the United Kingdom, respectively, ushering in a political regime that resonated with

[5] See https://creativechange.org.au/ and Heard et al (2023) and Bartleet (2023).
[6] Hayek puts forth six claims: Social justice is (1) meaningless, (2) religious, (3) self-contradictory, (4) ideological, and (5) unfeasible, and to implement it, one must (6) destroy all liberty (Lukes, 1997). See also Lister (2011).

## 90 THINKING COMMUNITY MUSIC

Hayek's reasoning.[7] With policies that ate into the postwar welfare provision, the neoliberal political paradigm was marked by an abiding hostility to the notion of social justice. In some instances during the 1990s, there were policy shifts from issues of social justice to questions of social order. This promoted a dominant politics of community that valued self-reliance and individual enterprise in opposition to those human attributes that connect us to others (Everingham, 2001).

Against this political background and flowing from the ideas of the New Left,[8] postmodern and poststructural theories flourished. As a contribution to this worldview and in concert with this book's theoretical framework, the following section presents an overview of Jacques Derrida's account of justice. Derrida's detailed and insightful probing is helpful, not because it formulates a workable theory of social justice or provides a tight structure to follow, but because it invites us to return to the question of justice. The following section briefly sketches Derrida's conceptual thinking, unpacking the key ideas before moving them toward examples of community music practice.

### The Promise of Justice

Key to Derrida's analysis of justice is the distinction between justice and law. Law is constructed and constructible and is violent at its origin, in the sense of needing an aggressive and willful power to create and fix it: "Law cannot found itself lawfully, since the very question of legality obviously cannot be put until law has established itself" (Wortham, 2010, p. 80). Laws are also prescriptive and demand that those under their jurisdiction comply with a given authority. Although laws vary dramatically in degree from place to place and culture to culture, certain forms of law are deemed necessary for the lives we live. Some examples from the industrial nations include the age of consent, designated speed limits near schools, regulations on alcohol and drug consumption, and censorship classifications of films and

---

[7] According to the political and social theorist Steven Lukes (1997), Hayek's influence spawned one of Thatcher's most controversial statements: "There is no such thing as society."

[8] The New Left was a left-wing political movement operating mainly in the 1960s and 1970s. It consisted of activists campaigning for social issues, including civil rights, feminism, gay rights, and drug policy reforms.

SOCIAL JUSTICE    91

video games. Implementations of laws do, however, inevitably reduce individual and group decision-making and, consequently, may be said to limit responsibility.

In contrast, simply following or applying set laws cannot be said to provide justice as the truly "just" decision. Justice, if there is such a thing, "must stem from a fundamental responsibility that cannot prop itself up through mere reference to statutory or case law" (Wortham, 2010, p. 80). Justice can, therefore, come about through the force of law, and although there is reciprocity between both, justice needs laws to be justice. Following mathematician and Christian philosopher Blaise Pascal (1958, p. 144), who writes, "Justice without might is helpless," Derrida (2002a) concludes, "Justice is not justice, it is not achieved if it does not have the force to be 'enforced'; a powerless justice is not justice, in the sense of law" (p. 238). One might say that justice cannot be constructed and is beyond any legal system and is, therefore, unable to be calculated in terms of an exchange value within an economy of the law. Laws have their purpose toward this type of unconditional justice: "Justice is what gives us the impulse, the drive, or the movement to improve the law" (Derrida, 1997b, p. 16). As an affirmative gesture, justice is more than simply a response; it is an invitation toward that which is unforeseeable.

Justice thought this way should not be confused with the Platonic forms[9] (as this would indicate that we could describe the future situation of justice today) or Kantian regulative ideas[10] (which would imply a description of what justice is, although with the implication that the ideal is not expected to be ever present in some future; Biesta, 2001, p. 48). Why? Because experienced as an invitation, justice is structured toward an unforeseeable future, calling us to constantly rethink and reinvent the conditional forms suggested by the law because what might constitute "justice" today might not tomorrow. Justice solicits us from afar rather than presenting something we could accurately describe and know. Justice is not, therefore, a foreseeable idealization, something that is always within a horizon of guarantee. Following theologian and philosopher John Caputo (1997a), justice is always to come and will never fully arrive. Justice is a call toward something never fully knowable but

---

[9] Plato's theory of Forms is that they are ideas of things that exist. They suggest that the physical world is not as real as the timeless, absolute, unchangeable ideas that exist as nonphysical essences of all things.

[10] Kant's regulative ideas are brought about by pure reason alone and transcend possible experience.

always worth striving for. Through this way, justice is inhabited by a *memory* of those who have died in its name, those who are and who continue to be oppressed, and those who have been liberated under its call. Justice is also inscribed by *hope*, an appeal to others that can never be fully delivered. As a hopeful enterprise, humans who have a heart for justice make promises to each other. It is this power of the "promise," an affirmation or giving, that structurally opens the possibility of the Other as Other,[11] a conscious focus toward individuals as individuals. How can such a promise to justice help us think about community music practice?

As a field of practice, community music attracts musicians who have a heart for justice.[12] Considering the work with those at risk, in youth detention centers, or marginalized through disability, poverty, gender, or ethnicity, a common feature of those working in community music has been an outstretched hand toward those excluded. Through a Derridian lens, justice is a vocation, a positive response to the stranger in the shape of a call rather than a matter of knowledge. Justice is therefore ignited through the encounter and, as such, lies at the heart of any community music experience. Structured as an unforeseeable future, justice thought this way invites community musicians to question what it means to respond to those whom we know wish to be involved in active music making. Importantly, and perhaps crucially, justice thought this way turns our head toward those we do not yet know, those whose voices have been suppressed, or those we have yet to meet. For a community music experience to resist being unjust, there needs to be a recognition of all those in the space, participants, and those leading the work. Derrida's conception of justice helps us understand what this might mean both in a theoretical way and in a very practical sense. The following illustration of practice demonstrates this.

## Empowering Song

*Andre de Quadros is a choral conductor who has, over many years, been deeply committed to justice and equity, peace building, and reconciliation. Working through a framework of social justice and human rights activism, Andre believes that access to music and participation in music is a "basic*

---

[11] The Other with a capital "O" refers to a condition of difference (alterity) that is genuinely alien or impossible to understand.

[12] It is worth remembering Cathy Benedict's (2021) question: Social justice for whom?

*human right"; it is not to be given to you as everybody already has it (21c, 2014). I first encountered Andre's work when he worked with Jamie Hillman at a Massachusetts correctional institute for men. Within this setting, Jamie and Andre draw upon facilitatory techniques honed by the Brazilian dramatist August Boal (2002), seeking to generate a "safe" environment where musical risks could be taken (de Quadros, 2015). These included singing solo and reciting self-penned poetry and song lyrics. Jamie and Andre could not take any instruments into the prison, so developing a choir seemed the most obvious way forward. Noting that many choral programs in prisons are repertoire focused, skill centered, or performance oriented, they were not convinced that this approach was the ideal fit for their program, so they developed the Empowering Song approach. As Andre describes it, "Empowering Song has its provenance in improvisational approaches such as the Orff Schulwerk.[13] Rooted in improvised song, poetry, bodywork, and imagery, this approach is designed to enable individual and community transformation" (de Quadros, 2018, p. 266).*

*Developing this pedagogical approach while deepening a commitment to music making within a social justice framework, Andre leads the Common Ground Voices project. Under this umbrella, Andre leads choral groups in Jerusalem, Israel, and Tijuana, a border city in Mexico. These projects host residential workshops, and their broad aim has been to utilize music as a springboard for a meaningful discussion about social and political change within the group and society in general (de Quadros & Amrein, 2023).[14] Although these choirs are located in very different contexts, both operate as peace-building projects to bring together a diverse group of musicians and artists to transcend political and demographic borders "to expand perspectives and open hearts."[15]*

## Hospitable Music Making

The illustrations above are driven by musicians who feel that certain injustices are at work within the world. Huib and Oclay are musicians who have been profoundly affected by a natural disaster and have responded through the creation of an international nongovernmental organization.

[13] Andre was a student at the Orff-Institut of the Universität Mozarteum Salzburg in 1979–1980 and was struck by the Orff approach's open-ended and multidimensional qualities. He explored this approach in general classroom music in Australian elementary and secondary schools and in several community music initiatives in the Australian state of Victoria.

[14] https://www.commongroundvoices.com/

[15] https://www.cgvlafrontera.org/english

94 THINKING COMMUNITY MUSIC

They have brought to bear their history of professional commitment toward cultural sustainability and music ecosystems. Through the lens of human rights activism and arts education, Andre has developed and led choirs with a vision of peace building toward individual and community transformation. The projects run by Huib, Oclay, and Andre illustrate *hospitable* music making—musicking that is a response from the participant's call and sparked into life through an encounter of a promise toward justice. At the heart of hospitable music making lie the decision, thought, and action that operate as an interface between what is known and what is unknown. This might appear somewhat counterintuitive: to make a ruling or decision based on a law that sets out to be equal for all while respecting and responding to how each case is different. Derrida (2002a) would say that "each case is other, each decision is different and requires an absolutely unique interpretation" (p. 251). The result of such challenges would suggest that to decide on that which is already decidable is, in some ways, no decision at all.

Huib, Oclay, and Andre's modus operandi means they regularly step into the unknown—at least partially. Of course, there are always specific calculations, certain laws, and rules to consider and adhere to. However, to respond to an unjust situation, all three musicians moved toward something they could not fully know. The radical decision, a gesture that cannot be based solely on reason or knowledge, enabled the musicians and the participations now and in the future to find positions that prepare them for the possible experience of hospitable music making—that is, music making primed for the possibility of responding to issues of social justice. Making these types of decisions can provide the opportunity to energize citizenship and make political action responsible (Sokoloff, 2005). In the context of this think piece, decisions are made in the name of people, participation, places, equity, and diversity. When contextualized this way, decisions are continuously made despite not having all the evidence. A decision to intervene, to respond to a call for musical participation, is always made in a context that is not fully calculable. Huib and Oclay decided that the cultural life of the Hatay province was in serious jeopardy of being extinguished through rebuilding after the earthquake. A legal structure was needed to exert a vision for a cultural sustainability project to mobilize funds and people to ensure that precious heritages were not lost. Andre decided to use his privilege as a choral director and university professor to support the growth and development of education within a Massachusetts correctional institute and engage the men in creative music making rather than teach a course on music appreciation. He also regularly contributes to music workshops and events that unite singers across racial and political divides, enacting events with a strong message of peace and reconciliation. All three musicians were active in the process of decision making that led to a promise toward creating environments for hospitable music making, music making with justice as a significant feature in terms of the conception and the action itself. However, none of the musicians knew what to expect; their willingness to embrace the unknowable led to the musical interactions that eventually took place.

Human encounters connected through a call, a response, and a welcome bind these examples. In some cases, the call is direct, with people vocalizing a desire to be included in music making, while other cases require the musicians to make themselves and their resources available just in case something might happen. Whatever the context, there is, at some point, a moment of decision, a moment to affirm, a moment to utter "yes." The two illustrations of musicians working this way are single cases, each project offering nonrepeatable events ignited through a decision and a desire for justice.[16] It would, however, be wrong to assume that this type of justice, a justice that is to come, a justice residing in an unforeseeable future, is politically impotent. Quite the opposite—it is an urgent and nonprogrammable justice. Marked by justice beyond the law, this is not a question of utopia but a promise. This urgent and passionate justice is always in a heterogenic relation to the stranger. To some extent, it resides in what Sophia Parker (2023), director of Emerging Futures at the Joseph Rowntree Foundation,[17] describes as a relationship between "radical imagination" and social action, a way to inspire activism that seeks to foster radical new ways of imagining the world.

## Flight Lines

Like community music, social justice can be considered a vocation, ignited through relational experiences and manifesting through a decision to

---

[16] The music projects and those that run them are not to be understood as "just" because justice never fully arrives, and this is its power. Although responding within a different theoretical framework, Elizabeth Gould's (2007) notion of "stretching the boundaries of power" resonates with this idea (p. 235).

[17] The Joseph Rowntree Foundation is an independent social change organization working to support and speed up the transition to a more equitable and just future, free from poverty, where people and the planet can flourish. See https://www.jrf.org.uk/.

96 THINKING COMMUNITY MUSIC

say "yes." The work of the musicians featured as illustrations of practice throughout this book supports this. There are, of course, many more examples; whether working with those at risk; those in prisons and detention centers, health care settings, or youth centers; or people marginalized through disability, sexuality, poverty, gender, or ethnicity, it is a common feature of those working in community music to have an outstretched hand toward those who have been historically excluded from participation.

This think piece revolved around the provocation: *How might social justice be understood as a framework for community music practice?* Community music practice as a site of social justice would rely on those working in it to make radical decisions constantly. These decisions, which have an unknown fate, fuel an aspiration for justice by engaging participants as individuals. In this formulation, the Other is treated as the Other, so musical interactions begin as a site for justice. The decisions made by Huib, Oclay, and Andre were made not knowing what the precise outcomes would be. However, each person had a deep sense that something needed to be done. This combination—a sense of a current injustice and a desire to intervene—ignited their actions toward what I have called hospitable music making. Let us be clear: Hospitable music making can never truly *be* but can come to us through decisive moments of justice, an open embrace toward those who wish to participate in active music making, and those who just might. In a broader sense, educating within a context that celebrates people's differences, or at least thinking about it, might encourage a greater sensitivity toward social justice issues and, as such, locate community music as a vital field.

# 5

# Inclusion and Excellence

## Connect Project

*Experienced through a nonformal learning context, the Connect project, as Peter Renshaw (2005) reported, offered rich opportunities for the "voices" of its musicians to be heard and acknowledged. The Connect project sought to identify the leadership skills necessary for inclusive creative workshop practice to demonstrate how excellent music making can be achieved through collaborative composition and performance. These included:*

- *Knowing how to work musically in a group that incorporates any instrument brought to an ensemble*
- *Knowing how to work effectively in mixed groups varying in size, age, technical ability, and musical experience*
- *Knowing how to make music in a genre-free ensemble, where its musical material reflects the shared interests of the leaders and participants*
- *Knowing how to engage in music making virtually without notation*
- *Knowing how to create music collaboratively*

*With these aims in mind, musicians collaboratively engaged with participants to create, shape, and perform new music. As skilled facilitators, the musicians worked with processes and strategies that sought to enable participants to embrace their music potential while connecting it to the world in which they live. The participants I spoke to emphasized the collaborative nature of the work. For example, Jim, who played the trumpet, said, "I really like the creative tasks [the facilitators] have been very helpful . . . you get along with them [and] that is what makes it different." Shawn and Jane reinforced this by saying, "Yeah the [Connect] people are really helpful . . . they [the facilitators] like the ideas you come up with [and] encourage you." A group of five 11-year-olds told me during their lunch break that the approaches employed by the facilitators had enabled their ideas to be heard and that they felt that the "teachers" were always listening to them: "We like it" they said, "as it is a challenge."*

*Thinking Community Music.* Lee Higgins, Oxford University Press. © Oxford University Press 2024.
DOI: 10.1093/9780190247027.003.0006

## 98 THINKING COMMUNITY MUSIC

*Through a relational structure, the facilitators and the participants worked together, collaboratively negotiating the musical journey. There was an emphasis on engaging in "quality" learning experiences rather than making just "good" music. Context becomes all-important for those working with young people within nonformal music learning. In this case, the activities are "judged" by the appropriateness of the participants' learning goals and the way they make meaningful connections to the environment they are operating in: "the criteria used for evaluating a creative project in a non-formal setting are determined as much by the workshop/performance context (e.g. school classroom, hospital ward, prison, youth club, shopping mall) as by the shared values and expectations of the participants and their leader" (Renshaw, 2005, p. 21).*

When music participants work alongside community musicians in nonformal musical contexts, they are typically in groups co-constructing the types of music to be created, identifying specific tasks and goals, and emphasizing learning within the participants' life context (see Think Piece 3). Inclusion is central to this and a cornerstone of community music practices. Often associated with what is described as an "open-door policy," inclusion evokes an agency through which community musicians might welcome potential participants regardless of musical experience (Balsnes, 2016; Chadwick, 2011). Yerichuk and Krar (2019) suggest that many scholars have used "the concept of hospitality to underpin how the facilitator adopts an inclusive stance for welcoming in participants" and, as such, have provided a "framework for inclusion" (p. 173). These ideas were highlighted within the chapter "Inclusive and Empathetic Practices" in *Engaging in Community Music* (Higgins & Willingham, 2017), which foregrounded practitioners who work with children and young people in challenging circumstances (Mullen, 2022), adaptive and diverse learning contexts (DeVito & Gill, 2013), and inclusive activism (Laurila, 2021). Deriving from the word *include*, from the Latin *includere*, meaning "enclose" or to "shut in," inclusion is the act of making something a part of a larger whole,[1] the action or state of including or being included within a group or structure. As an active process, the notion of inclusion has been important for music educators more generally, as explored through literature reviews focused on special educational needs and disability (Jellison & Draper, 2015; Jellison & Taylor, 2007; Van Weelden & Whipple, 2014).

---

[1] https://www.etymonline.com/search?q=Inclusion

In terms of community music scholarship, inclusion is often understood as "musical access," as Yerichuk and Krar (2019) note in their scoping review. If inclusion is thought of in terms of degrees within political policy, the notion of access can be attributed to the ideology of neoliberalism (Gidley et al., 2010).[2] From this perspective, social inclusion is orientated around human capital investment, providing skills for economic growth within a nation's agenda to compete in global markets (Holborow, 2012). Providing access becomes a response to perceived ideas of exclusion and thus works from a deficiency model. With synergy to a social justice agenda (see Think Piece 4), inclusion with community music might be better understood as beginning with access but always focused on participation. Through a social justice lens, increasing inclusion becomes a call for human rights, equality, and social responsibility. As a prerequisite, this idea is not necessarily linked to economic interests; "its primary aim is to enable all human beings to participate fully in society with respect to their human dignity" (Gidley et al., 2010, p. 4). Through this framework, engagement and participation are foregrounded and, in so doing, create greater opportunities to maximize human potential. Consequently, this can embed models of possibility rather than deficiently placing human potential at the center, creating transformative potentials through individual and community empowerment.

## Johnny's Place

*While in South Africa, I made an acquaintance with a charismatic jazz trumpeter from Johannesburg. His name was Johnny Mekoa (1945–2017), and he directed a music academy located in Benoni, Gauteng, a large township near Johannesburg.[3] Johnny's project provided opportunities for local young people to learn instruments typically found in a South African jazz big band: brass,*

---

[2] See Steger and Roy (2010) and Cahill and Konings (2017) for an exploration of neoliberalism as a concept and political compass.

[3] Established in 1994, it has become a center of jazz excellence, with luminaries such as Malcolm Jiyane, Mthunzi Mvubu, Mpho Mabogoane (female trombonist), and Nthabiseng Mokoena and Linda Tshabalala (both female saxophonists), to mention but a few. The center has also focused on teaching jazz music to children from impoverished backgrounds. Mekoa identified their talents and nurtured them to become the jazz musicians they are today. This is a story of hope that South African society should pride itself on. Mekoa's excellent work has seen his center being awarded the prestigious International Jazz Education Network Award for 5 consecutive years. The University of Pretoria and the University of South Africa have respectively bestowed Mekoa with two honorary doctorates for his excellence in music and contribution to society (). See https://www.youtube.com/watch?v=x1lIqb36Fpk -https://www.youtube.com/watch?v=C-k1x4Xa2_4.

woodwind, drums, keyboard, guitar, etc. It also provided lessons on general musicianship and Western notation. I had been in South Africa attending a community music seminar, and Johnny had presented an overview of his project. A number of us were interested in visiting what became known as "Johnny's place." In response to this enthusiasm, Johnny asked a few delegates if we would like to visit his project, meet the participants, and listen to some of their music. We were all thrilled to be asked, and a date and time were set for the following day.

Johnny picked us up in his large old Mercedes at the prearranged place. About a quarter of the way into our 70-minute journey it became apparent that a large coach was following us; Johnny kept slowing down with his eyes constantly fixed on the rearview mirror. After we inquired about the coach behind us, Johnny announced that he had also invited a college jazz band from the East Coast of America. The band was due to play in Pretoria during the following week. The group traveling in Johnny's car exchanged glances that signaled a little disappointment regarding this news. I think we wanted to feel special, a kind of elite group of community musicians on their way to experience something new, not perceiving ourselves as the cultural tourists we now appeared to be.

It was always clear that Johnny's project was run on a shoestring budget. We had, after all, heard him talk about funding issues the previous week. We had been told that instruments were acquired through donations, as were the rehearsal rooms and all general resources. On arrival, we drove into a compound, a hot, dry, dusty environment dominated by a couple of buildings roofed with corrugated steel and a few crumbling outhouses to the rear. In fact, Johnny had told us that the building had been condemned and had only recently been deemed safe to use. From the car, the seminar delegates approached the largest of the buildings, and we could see through the windows that Johnny's youth jazz band appeared to be getting ready to play. Instruments were out of their cases, and there was the general hubbub of musicians on the verge of playing together. Most people not playing in the band looked attentively through the windows of the cracked white building. In some cases, the "audience," made up of mainly young people, was holding onto the upper window ledges, balancing precariously between the roof and window frame.

The coach carrying the college jazz band pulled into the compound, generating a dust cloud as its wheels ground to a halt on the sandy surface. One by one, its inhabitants leapt from the vehicle carrying various instruments in

INCLUSION AND EXCELLENCE    101

*black cases. With this arrival, a chain of events was set in motion, resulting in
one of my most profound musical experiences.*

*To my amazement, the guest band, seemingly unannounced, spilled into
the "rehearsal" room occupied by the South African youth, removed their
instruments from the cases, and began to take control of the space. It was not
long before the guest band was instructing the hosts on instrumental technique.
For example, I witnessed an American saxophonist demonstrate fast modal
passages to a somewhat bemused South African lad. He clearly had a secure
technical grasp of the instrument as he moved rapidly from one octave to another and from one mode to another. The South African lad tried in vain to
imitate this show of virtuosity on his dented tenor, eventually giving up and
resorting to listening politely.*

*The hosts, in typical South African style, were very hospitable and
welcoming and allowed their guests the space to "flex their musical muscles."
The guest band eventually gathered and began to play through a rather long set
of standard jazz tunes. Their sound was good, demonstrating a solid grasp of
big band tradition; they were technically proficient and self-assured. Because
the rehearsal room was small, many of the host band players had to watch their
guests through the outside windows. Frustrated at the events, I approached
Johnny: "When is your band going to play, Johnny?" I asked. Johnny appeared
relaxed, calmly saying, "Soon, just wait."*

*I left the rehearsal room to play djembe with some local children, and it
wasn't long before one of the local youths came to me and said, "Come, the
bands are going to play now." I squeezed into the rehearsal room and found a
space near Johnny's front-facing band. The guest band had now stepped away
from the performing space and was standing along the room's edges. As Johnny
assembled his band, he called for Richie. Richie shuffled into the room from the
back of the venue. He was small, barefoot, and wearing disheveled clothing. He
carried his alto saxophone under his arm and took his place, somewhat reluc-
tantly, in the heart of Johnny's band. Nothing could prepare me for the musical
experience I was about to encounter.*

*As the band got into its groove, I was overwhelmed by the sound: It was sen-
sational. The communication between the players and the audience was like
nothing I had witnessed before. From discussions that followed, all the seminar
delegates felt this. These young people from South Africa were playing "out of
their skin"; it felt like they were playing as if their lives depended on it. It was
mesmerizing. Johnny's rationalization supported this instinctive feeling when*

102   THINKING COMMUNITY MUSIC

*he explained that for many young people in his program, music was one of the only escape routes from the poverty of the townships. Through artists such as Hugh Masekela, Jonas Gwangwa, and Abdullah Ibrahim, South African jazz had gained popularity and value throughout the Western world. Participants who had grown through the project now viewed music as a possible and legitimate escape from poverty and little opportunity.*

*In short, Johnny's youth jazz ensemble, a group grown from an inclusive and open-door policy, had significantly upstaged the college band from the East Coast of America. As the host band continued to perform, I looked around the room at the guest instrumentalists. There was certainly a sense of respect, and I detected a real feeling of humility. I hope that the college band began to understand that their flawless technical ability was, in fact, deeply flawed as an a priori of musicianship. From my perspective, the host band was a far superior musical ensemble. They touched me very deeply, and I shall never forget the day when a group of South African youth took my breath away.*

The story above engages us with notions of excellence. It is not to be thought of as presenting a competitive statement—one band is better than another—but as a way of describing perceptions of what constitutes musical and communicative power. Paradigms of how excellence is conceived are often derived from the aesthetics of European art music. In this sense, excellence is housed within notions of virtuosity. At Johnny's place, I was confronted with two very different versions of excellence in quick succession, and this is what was so startling and, ultimately, why I can recall the event so vividly. As a musician, rethinking excellence can be challenging if you have grown through traditional routes of music education, for example, schools of music, conservatories, and private instrumental lessons. Excellence is also wrapped up in notions of virtuosity, even if you have not followed traditional routes. To some extent, we are enculturated into this through the media, recordings, and live events. Initially drawing upon summative ideas hailing from a collaborative research project, this think piece places the notion of inclusion alongside that of excellence and asks, *How might notions of inclusion and excellence exist as a balanced pairing?* This provocation begins by wondering whether excellence is better articulated as a process and inclusion better expressed as an outcome of this process. Following this, the flight line amplifies the ideas before encouraging some reflective thought to encourage those working in the field to find a greater nuance in their language.

## Provocation

Within certain cultures, music teaching and learning has a history of rigid expectations of performance skills, submission to higher "expert" authority, suppression of individual expression in favor of the collective, and comparison alongside competition among participants (Bucura, 2020; Williamon, 2004). In these environments, musical excellence is often defined in terms of a strict set of performance norms and heralded as the most important outcome. For those working in or advocating for community music, this becomes a problem. In response, an interventionist approach to community music (see Think Piece 1), understood through the theoretical lens of cultural democracy and hospitality (see Think Piece 2), can be seen to adopt a more encompassing definition of musical excellence, one that ethnomusicologist Thomas Turino (2008) argues has more in common with non-Western musical traditions, where music making is understood as a social and relational practice, and where its meaning lies within these relationships. Music education philosopher David Lines (2013) supports this position, noting that "an over-reliance on 'excellence' at the expense of 'significance' can have a weakening and disowning effect on those involved" (p. 27).

Following a research seminar[4] at the Royal College of Music, United Kingdom, in 2016, a predominantly U.K.-based network emerged named the Music and Social Intervention Network (MUSOC) in 2018. The network was made possible through funding by the Arts and Humanities Research Council[5] and was led by Jennie Henley and me. The network focused on issues concerning inclusion and excellence (Henley & Higgins, 2020a). Its core group consisted of musicians who provided active interventions in music therapy, community music therapy, music education, music and health, music and well-being, music and rehabilitation, and community music. Discussions resulted in the group noticing that contemporary rhetoric surrounding musicians' working practices often centered on the notions of "inclusion" and/or "excellence." For example, Youth Music's Musical Inclusion Programme invests in "music-making projects for children and young people in challenging circumstances,"[6] funding "high quality" projects that

---

[4] The seminar was Music Education and Community Music: Natural Bedfellows or Merely Exchanging Pleasantries?"

[5] https://www.ukri.org/councils/ahrc/

[6] https://youthmusic.org.uk/

contribute to Youth Music's vision of a "musically inclusive England."[7] In parallel, professional development programs for musicians working in different educational contexts focus on excellence; for example, Music Excellence London aims to offer professional development opportunities to "support excellent musical teaching and learning at Key Stage 3 (7–8 Grade) in London schools."[8] In many other organizations and charities, inclusivity and excellence sit side by side. For example, inclusive practice is embedded within the Spitalfields Music Professional Development program.[9] Its trainees have gone on to work for organizations such as the London Symphony Orchestra, Royal Academy of Music, and London Music Masters, all of which describe "excellence" as a prime quality of their work. There are also the awards that include the Music Teacher Awards for Excellence[10] and the National Association of Music Merchants (NANMM) best communities for music education.[11]

Those in the network felt that community musicians would have different understandings of what constitutes "excellence" and "inclusion" because of their work contexts. Understandings of "musical excellence" may vary between contexts such as prisons, schools, youth orchestras, pupil referral units, special education, and settings for older people. Similarly, "inclusion" may be interpreted differently depending on the social environment. For example, a program for children with specific disabilities may have very different aims from one in a pupil referral unit. There was a feeling among the discussion group that this is often problematic for practitioners who need to navigate between different settings. For example, tensions arise when a musician's conceptual understanding of "excellent inclusive practice" differs from that of the employer. Drawing from the work of the network (Kirstin & Willingham, 2020; Ansdell et al., 2020; Camlin et al., 2020; Currie et al., 2020), the group identified three underlying issues that affect the way these concepts manifest and are used.

---

[7] http://network.youthmusic.org.uk/Funding/about-youth-musics-grants-programme
[8] https://www.musicmark.org.uk/resources/providers/music-excellence-london/
[9] https://www.spitalfieldsmusic.org.uk
[10] https://www.musicteachermagazine.co.uk/news/article/winners-announced-for-music-drama-education-awards-2023
[11] https://www.nammfoundation.org/what-we-do/best-communities-music-education

## Pedagogy

There needs to be more understanding of inclusive practice attained through focusing on the content of the practice (what music) rather than the form the practice takes (how the music is made). Treating excellence as a product led to pedagogies centered on instructional strategies, and this is seen across the formal, nonformal, and informal spectrum. Considering an intervention as nonformal is not enough to claim inclusivity. Analyzing pedagogy rather than materials and content provides a better understanding of inclusion and excellence.

## Power

The effectiveness of the interventions can be understood by analyzing the power relations within the intervention itself and between the intervention and the broader context. Recognizing that power exists in any relationship and is always part of a facilitator/participant or teacher/student interaction is vital. Offering empowering opportunities requires understanding that relationships are built on inequality, which means acknowledging the responsibilities inherent within such interactions.

## Impact and Measurement

The need to measure impact to evidence the inclusivity and excellence of funded projects is problematic. Identifying outcomes before the participants have been identified and then measuring the success of a project against those outcomes is contrary to inclusive pedagogical approaches.[12] Often, the most impactful outcomes are either unseen or unmeasurable in the ordinary sense of the word, and the culture of future funding being reliant on reporting positive findings clouds the reporting of those things that did not work well.

With community music practices in mind, the research network considered using a figure to redefine excellence and inclusion (Figure 5.1;

[12] For an earlier iteration of these ideas see Henley (2015).

**Figure 5.1** Inclusion as a process.

Henley & Higgins, 2020b). It is common to understand excellence and inclusion in the following way:

- Excellence as a product
- Inclusion as a process

If intervention is understood as an active process and there is a desire for excellence in intervention, then excellence is better articulated as a process. The key ingredients often associated with excellence might be better understood in terms of engagement with the activity. This idea reinforces the

INCLUSION AND EXCELLENCE    107

premise that excellence might be a process rather than a product. Alongside this, the group suggested that inclusion might be more closely related to the outcome of engagement rather than engagement in and of itself. Moving toward a more inclusive society requires a process of change.[13] The success of the change process is determined by how we enact that change. If we flipped the common-place interpretations of what excellence and inclusion are, the formation would read:

1. Excellence, as a process, leads to;
2. Inclusion as an outcome.

With this figure in mind, how might this manifest in community music practices? How might the idea be operationalized through creative music workshops? Following this, how might this idea influence applications for funding where evaluation is an essential requirement? Is there an implication for arts policy? The Connect project attempted to create multiple access points for diverse musical doing. These aspirations are overtly paired with a notion of excellence in the music-making and/or the musical experience, creating an emphasis on engaging in "quality" learning experiences rather than focusing on making just "good" music.[14] Is this an example of inclusion as an outcome, as illustrated in Figure 5.2? Does the Connect project address the system or merely reinforce it? If community music should be inclusive, what practices is it contesting, what shared values is it advocating, and by what criteria should its successes be judged?

## Flight Lines

In his editorial for the inclusion-themed special issue of the *International Journal of Community Music*, Roger Mantie (2022b). writes,

Inclusion will undoubtedly continue to be a central principle of community music. As Yerichuk and Krar's study points out, however, we need

---

[13] The idea of exploring the change process rather than the impact (or the product) was posed as an alternative to attempting to measure impact. The theory of change is a comprehensive description and illustration of how and why a desired change is expected to happen in a particular context. See https://www.theoryofchange.org/what-is-theory-of-change/.
[14] For other considerations of what might constitute quality community music and arts experiences, see Moriarty (2004) and Renshaw (2010).

Figure 5.2 Inclusion as the outcome.

to be mindful of simplistic, Pollyanna notions of inclusion. It is easy to be *for* inclusion.... It is more difficult to acknowledge the limits of inclusion. (p. 320)[15]

As I have worked reflectively through this think piece, I wonder whether the MUSOC project and, consequently, the provocation would benefit from a closer inspection of the differences between the ideas inherent within the terms *inclusion* and *inclusivity*. As an idea, inclusivity has a different inflection, referring more often to the practice or policy of providing access to opportunities and resources for people who might otherwise be excluded or marginalized based on gender, ethnicity, class, sexuality, and disability.[16] In this sense, the notion of inclusivity is much broader than the practice of musical access, seeking to highlight the need for social equality instead. As a term, it signals "the deliberate, active, ongoing process necessary for inclusive community music" (Yerichuk & Krar, 2019, p. 184). Inclusivity becomes an active process of encouraging full participation by creating equitable spaces.

---

[15] See Hansen (2012 and Pozo-Armentia et al. (2020) for explorations regarding the theoretical limits of inclusion.
[16] See Smith (2020).

INCLUSION AND EXCELLENCE 109

Social inclusion is now a significant focus for many governments, and reform in the education system often acts as a critical driver for understanding the success of any given social integration and cohesion policy (Armstrong et al., 2009). Assumptions surrounding what constitutes inclusion can be a contested area—after all, who requires inclusion and why (Allan, 2014; Biesta, 2009; Graham & Slee, 2008; Liasidou, 2012)? Following the work of Finnish music educator Tuulikki Laes (2017), those working in community music might stop to think that the promotion of inclusion within familiar norms and structures may be "individually empowering, but will not necessarily change the socio-cultural reality" (p. 65).[17] Drawing upon public education scholar Gert Biesta's (2007) notion of democratic inclusion,[18] which considers the educational, social, and political spheres, inclusion remains an ongoing process rather than just becoming goal oriented. As an idea, democratic inclusion seeks a transformation from the private to the public interest and, in so doing, attempts to sharpen the point of inclusive policy by resisting action that is "carried forward through processes of socialization or normalization, but through individual *subjectification* towards political agency" (Laes, 2017, p. 75). If we consider that musical excellence in community music interventions can refer to the quality of the social experience, the bonds formed, the meaning and enjoyment derived, and the sense of agency that emerges for individuals and the group, can the formulation proposed in the provocation help community musicians articulate what they do and as a consequence provide an apt and nuanced language through which to argue for the right resources to support their work? In short, can we think of inclusivity as an outcome—albeit never complete and always on the horizon—in the music-making processes?

In the light of Think Piece 4, we might consider if social justice provides a more robust frame to argue for the values of community music. Is the idea of "hospitable music making" better reflected through social justice and thus does it more closely reflect the processes of those community musicians who are challenging discriminatory social norms while working to overcome barriers that block musical access? Yerichuk and Krar (2019) also ask community musicians to question the idea of inclusion, particularly in the light of scholarship relating to music in the criminal justice system (Cohen

[17] See Tuulikki talk about music as a tool to create a more inclusive society (https://www.rockhubs.com/post/our-tedx-talk-where-tuulikki-talks-about-how-musical-performance-reshapes-identities).
[18] See also Zilla (2022 and Baubӧck (2017) for application in political sciences.

& Henley, 2018; Dickie-Johnson & Meek, 2022), work with asylum seekers (Doherty, 2022; Vougioukalou et al., 2019; Weston & Lenette, 2016), and work within postcolonial contexts that considers Indigenous communities and their relationship to history and land (Bartleet et al., 2018; Sunderland et al., 2021). We might also wonder if the concept only really exists from inside a particular orthodoxy and, as such, has traces of what can be termed music *outreach*. If community music is rhizomatic and, as a consequence, participation is, at times, on the terms of the participants, maybe there is no need to reference inclusion. In saying this, inclusion and/or inclusivity are a "pervasive" albeit "complex" idea within community musicians' work. One of the common tensions in inclusive education has been attempts to show that it is a "multifaceted concept" and, therefore, "a much broader framework or perspective for action than developing proposals in reaction to particular learning problems owing to deprivation or deficits" (Pozo-Armentia et al., 2020, p. 1064).[19]

Inclusion has been an idea that has helped ensure that the potential of community musicians' shared values, beliefs, and ethical commitments remains a possibility. With four considerations in mind—purpose, leadership, musical processes, and social structures—the usefulness of this think piece might be to home in on the relationship between inclusivity and excellence, seemingly two ideas at odds.[20] It is a worthwhile thought experiment to try and reconcile the notions but remain cognitive of the thought journey. This conscious process of thinking, reflecting, and questioning may help reveal specific nuances that could respond to the call for more profound engagement in what constitutes community music practices and thus create the potential for the work to be more effective for more diverse populations and in more meaningful ways.

---

[19] See also Mitchell (2015).

[20] A conceptual limitation of inclusive education is that it "does not generally consider the term excellence" (Pozo-Armentia et al., 2020, p. 1068).

# 6

# Music

The purpose of this think piece is to respond to the question: How might we understand the "music" in community music? The question's construction seeks to address possible ways that those working in the field might describe the "music," or "musics," being made by the participants they work with and, to some extent, why it might be deemed valuable. In my previous work, I have explored the question, How can we understand the "community" in community music? This has led to statements regarding participation, access, inclusion (see Think Piece 5), and an articulation that the "community" in community music can be understood as an act of hospitality (see Think Piece 2). Alongside my efforts, many other community music scholars have also focused on the social-cultural aspect of the practice and/or the pedagogical dimension of the work. Less time has been spent exploring the music generated through the practice. This may be because it is the wrong question. I am happy to think this might be so. It certainly comes with complexity, and I must confess that I am experiencing some anxiety about attempting it myself.[1] Prior to its publication in 2012, music therapist Gary Ansdell read the final draft of *Community Music: In Theory and Practice.* I remember very clearly that in his email to me, he commented that I had yet to spend any time exploring the phenomena of music. He was right. At the time, I was more concerned with the facilitative processes and the contextual elements associated with the work. I felt that these things gave the practice its distinction— its identity, you might say. I had also begun to move away from thinking of the term "community music" as two separate words, rather conceiving it as a stand-alone phrase that had been given meaning and, consequently, agency. I do not recall many debates, discussion, or writing that has had a particular

---

[1] Dave Camlin (2023) has published *Music and the Civic Imagination*, outlining the idea of music as a complex adaptive system (CAS). As an idea, CAS suggests that music achieves its effects in many ways and through complementary traditions, aesthetic, participatory, and paramusical. This is an overarching "holistic philosophy" with different aims to mine as it is situated within human evolution, particularly addressing the "global existential threats to human flourishing" (p. 44). It is, however, noteworthy because Dave is a community musician, and his thoughts are deeply connected to many of the issues community music practitioners care about.

*Thinking Community Music.* Lee Higgins, Oxford University Press. © Oxford University Press 2024.
DOI: 10.1093/9780190247027.003.0007

112 THINKING COMMUNITY MUSIC

focus on the music(s) of community music when thought of as an intervention (see Think Piece 1). This may point toward an emphasis on scholarship that has explored questions surrounding what community music *does* rather than what it *is*. It may also point toward that those working in community music resist separating the "music" from the experience because there is an acute sense that the music is inescapably a part of the event and not separate from it. Whatever it may be, there does appear to be a blind spot in the literature. With this in mind, I am hopeful that the contents of this think piece might open a space for discussion.

I have drawn upon my practical experience as a community musician to approach this question. In this way, this think piece represents a piece of reflective practice-as-research. Through memories of three significant community music moments, I have wrestled with how music has presented itself to me as a facilitator and an audience member. Following these reflections, I outline three conceptual ideas to simulate thoughts surrounding the music made through community music projects.

## Orchestral Outreach

*During my time as a freelance community musician, I worked on several projects that involved the education departments of professional orchestras. Orchestral outreach, as it was often labeled, had a mixed reputation from those who understood their work as identifying with notions of community music. There was a concern that programs of this nature could appear far more focused on audience development than on the people they professed to engage. Orchestral outreach programs were often seen as "parachute" projects, for example, landing in a school for a quick musical "treat" and immediately departing, leaving little by way of practical and sustainable resources. Although the orchestral musicians were highly skilled in instrumental performance, legitimate concerns surrounded their suitability and skills to facilitate meaningful music participation.[2] Orchestras began responding to these criticisms, and this project had a training strand written into the initial funding proposal. As the*

[2] Things in the United Kingdom have undoubtedly changed since my story. The Association of British Orchestras reported in 2019 that almost 700,000 people attended education and outreach programs, including 11,570 sessions and 1,293 performances and events for, by, or with children and young people. https://abo.org.uk/assets/files/News-and-Press/ABO-The-State-of-UKs-Orchestras-in-2019.pdf

*community musician on the project, I was pleased to accept the challenge of leading three professional instrumentalists from a well-established orchestra; the instrumentalists included a French horn, a violin, and a viola player. As the music team, we worked with adult users of a special needs daycare center for 4 whole days. The days were long for this type of group, and as such, we had plenty of breaks and respites. During the breaks, other members of the daycare community were offered the chance of a music-making experience. These short sessions were not ideal but nevertheless did allow the project to have a wider impact, giving music experience to most of those who accessed the center.*

*As the project evolved, members of the orchestra and the participants began to form discrete groups; unsurprisingly, certain participants were drawn toward certain sounds and personalities. As encounters, these "face-to-face" interactions provided opportunities for invention, exploration, and finding ways of self-expression through active music making. Throughout the week, and with a giant drum on loan to us from the Remo drum company, the whole group, both participants and music leaders, could "play" together using one sonic source. These moments were reminders of our togetherness and offered an excellent way to start and finish the sessions.*

*The combination of the week's work was to be shared as a prelude to the orchestra's evening concert performance. As a prerequisite of the funding, this was important because it profiled the orchestra's wider remit. Alongside the music we had made together, I structured the showing to reveal the framework through which we had worked. The final piece made use of recorded sounds and live playing. A refrain made from many of the ideas generated by the wider community of daycare attendees introduced the live musical units. By now, these units consisted of one professional player and one or two participants. Each duet or trio performed one at a time, punctuated by the recorded refrain. The ending had an extraordinary vocalization by a participant who had no verbal language and was often told in her daily life to be quiet. Contrary to how she was often instructed to behave, her "singing" was amplified with full "permission." Although visibly uncomfortable for some of the audience, her vocals made musical connections in ways I had not experienced before.*

## Praxis

I want to begin by highlighting the detailed philosophical account of "music" made by David Elliott and Marissa Silverman in the second edition of *Music*

*Matters* (2015), a work dedicated to articulating a praxial philosophy of music education. Unlike the first edition (Elliott, 1995), community music facilitators (sometimes named "CM educators" in the book) are located alongside music educators as the potential beneficiaries of the ideas. To my knowledge, it has been the only source that has attempted to describe ways community musicians might think of music. Elliott's history with community music begins with participation in the 1996 International Society of Music Education (ISME) Commission for Community Music Activity (CMA)[3] in Liverpool, just after the first edition of *Music Matters* was published. I first met David in 1998 in South Africa, where he presented *Community Music and Postmodernity*[4] (Elliott, 1998). Through discussions at this event and later in New York, it became apparent that the types of music-making experiences discussed and demonstrated resonated closely with his articulation of a praxial philosophy. These experiences were formative in influencing subsequent work and, alongside Silverman's engagement in music making outside the school settings, resulted in the integration of community music within the second iteration of the book. As one of the anchors in articulating their praxial philosophy of music education, Elliott and Silverman uncover a meaning of what constitutes music that they believe aligns with the work of community musicians.

Although complex and detailed, the praxial philosophy of music education presents what the authors describe as "an integrated sociocultural, artistic, participatory, and ethics-based concept of," including other things, "community music"[5] (Elliott & Silverman, 2015, back page). In short, a praxial philosophy of music education emphasizes that music should be an "*active reflection and critically reflective action* dedicated to supporting and advancing *human flourishing and well-being,* the *ethical care* of others and the positive *transformation* of peoples' everyday lives," and "that each instance of music should be conceived, taught, and learned as a *social praxis*—as a fusion of people, processes, products, and ethical 'goods' in specific sociocultural contexts" (p. 52, emphasis in original). As part of their case, Elliott and Silverman build a normative[6] answer to the question, What is music? They construct their argument from a wide array of concepts from multiple

---

[3] The ISME has eight commissions. The CMA was established in 1986. Alongside Kari Veblen, David Elliott chaired the CMA seminar held in Toronto in 2000.

[4] See ISME CMA publications archive: https://isme-commissions.weebly.com/.

[5] See also the blog https://www.musicmatters2.com/.

[6] That is, a statement or judgment that makes claims of how music should be conceived.

MUSIC 115

fields, notably Christopher Small's (1987, 1998) sociological observations highlighting that music is a process (verb) rather than an object (noun);[7] Thomas Turino's (2008) articulations of what constitutes participatory performance and presentational performance; John Dewey's (1934) pragmatic philosophy, which argues that art enhances how people experience life; and the Aristotelian (2000) notion of *eudaimonia*, commonly translated as human flourishing or well-being.[8] Through this, Elliott and Silverman reject the concept of "music itself," an understanding that music somehow exists "out there" away from human agency. Instead, they show that music is, in fact, intersubjective,[9] and therefore a "socially situated human endeavor" (Elliott & Silverman, 2015, p. 84). Following Turino's (2008, p. 2) anthropological argument that states that music "can articulate the collective identities that are fundamental to forming and sustaining social groups, which are, in turn, basic to survival," Elliott and Silverman suggest that music experiences are both socially constructed and socially shared.

Responding to the scholarship of ethnomusicologist Bruno Nettl (1983) and musicologist Ian Cross (2003), Elliott and Silverman qualify the multiplicity of musics (with an "s"), stating that the praxial philosophy of musics embraces all dimensions of music, connecting musics with people's social worlds while resisting an aesthetic reduction to specific works and musical elements. By adding the "s," there is recognition that music only makes sense in relation to cultural context and can therefore be "optimal for the management of situations of social uncertainty [and] . . . collaboratively establishing a degree of social equilibrium" (Elliott & Silverman, 2015, p. 81). Important to this conception is an understanding of the ethical value of music. This refers to music made for the "'goods' of well-being, flourishing, democratic engagement, educative teaching and learning, or positive social transformation" and does, therefore, speak to the relational aspect of musical doing (Elliott & Silverman, 2015, p. 102). Following music education philosopher Thomas Regelski's (2011) exploration of the Aristotelian term *phronesis*,[10] praxis "invokes ethical criteria," whereas the term *practice* does not necessarily do

---

[7] Small (1987, p. 50) uses the neologism *musicking* as the present participle, or gerund, of the verb *to music*. The added *k* has historical antecedents (1998, p. 9). Music is not a thing but an activity, a personal-social encounter (p. 2). Elliott and Silverman (2015) employ the term *musicing*, which has a different function to Small's musicking by referring to praxis-specific forms of all music making (p. 16).

[8] Eudaimonia is an idea that has had a recent surge within music teaching and learning, see Smith (Smith et al., 2021).

[9] Intersubjectivity is the relation or intersection between people's cognitive perspectives.

[10] For an explanation of Greek philosophical language and meanings, see Peters (1967/1970).

116 THINKING COMMUNITY MUSIC

so (p. 81). Underlining the ethical values of music resonates with contemporary scholarship in issues relating to music and social justice (Benedict et al., 2015) and artistic citizenship (Elliott et al., 2017), both of which have strong connections for those working in community music. The authors summarize that a praxial understanding of music "supports the many kinds of music making contexts that community music facilitators create with people of all ages in joyful music making and transformational individual and group experiences" (Elliott & Silverman, 2015, p. 82).

From this perspective, music is always pluralistic and fluid, forever dictated by the situated circumstances of those who engage in its doing. The music made by those attending the daycare center, illustrated above, is best understood from the situation from whence it was made. During the participatory process, various musical forms were engaged, such as free improvisation, drumming, call and response, and leitmotifs. The final vocalization had no words but communicated through gesture and "spirit." Musicality was demonstrated through the ability to track the harmony that was supporting the improvisation and responding instrumentally through mimicry and individual musical contributions. A transformation took place for the participants and the facilitators; there was a sense of working in ways not thought of before, figuring out musical ideas together, finding different ways to communicate, and supporting emotional needs through musicking. The social-cultural context of the final performance was the concert hall, which at first appears at odds with this type of music making. As a "praxial" project, there was thought given to its ethical value. A preperformance talk appropriately framed the work to maximize audience engagement, promoting educative teaching and learning and consequently moving toward positive social transformations. Therefore, praxial notions of music were inherent within the processes of musical invention and the dissemination of the final work.

## Wind Quintet

*In the city where I was employed as a music development worker, a well-established wind quintet had been booked to perform at its prestigious music festival. As part of the concert sponsorship, the wind quintet was contracted to provide some educational work in the local community. As this was where my place of work resided, I was asked if I could suggest and organize some masterclasses between professional musicians and instrumentalists from local*

MUSIC 117

*schools and orchestras. In this instance, masterclasses meant one-to-one tuition between a professional musician and up-and-coming young instrumentalists. I declined this offer because although masterclasses have been an important and necessary part of music education, my interest as a community musician did not lie in the sponsor's particular vision of virtuosity. Of course, I wanted to take advantage of an opportunity for a funded community music project, so I presented the sponsors with an alternative course of action, which was far more fitting for my work. The project I suggested had three main threads: (1) I would capitalize on existing relationships by working in an adult daycare center for 12 weeks—one 2-hour session per week; (2) I would work with the "members"[11] of the daycare center toward the creation of a new piece of music—this would be organized in such a way that it could be rehearsed by the wind quintet within the designated hours assigned to the educational aspect of the project (this was somewhat limited, so an economy of time was essential); and (3) the piece was to be "premiered" in the daycare center, but serious consideration should be given to its inclusion within the main concert program.*

*This idea was communicated to the management of the wind quintet, and with some negotiation, a schedule was agreed upon. This type of project was outside of the musicians' comfort zone, and they expressed some anxiety over not knowing what to expect. They needed to be more sure about the inclusion of a new composition into their evening program. This was perfectly understandable as concert programs are carefully balanced months, if not years, before. During a meeting with the quintet, I assured them that the project would be rewarding and, much to my delight, persuaded them to include the work in the evening concert.*

*Throughout the 12 weeks leading up to the performance, I worked with six to 10 adults with varying learning and physical difficulties. Alongside their care workers, I worked with the group to generate their own music material through an open, playful approach to musical doing. This included free and structured improvisation using assorted percussion, keyboards, and guitars. I also utilized a Soundbeam, which could be described as an invisible keyboard in space.[12] This electronic device enabled the participants to explore sound and composition using their bodies; the Soundbeam was also used in conjunction with the instrument playing. Funding constraints and touring schedules meant*

---

[11] Following discussion, those who used the daycare center decided to be collectively called "members."

[12] Soundbeam is a touch-free musical device that uses sensor technology to translate movement into music and sound. See https://www.soundbeam.co.uk/.

## 118 THINKING COMMUNITY MUSIC

*that time was limited, so the quintet could not spend any time with the project participants. This restriction led to a decision to provide the musicians with a traditional Western notated score. In short, there was no time to induct the quintet into a personalized graphic notation that may have been more suited to the participants I had been working with.*

*The decision to use Western musical notation now required that I find an inclusive strategy to interpret the participant's invention. I did this in the following way: Each week, the music material was recorded onto a computer hard drive. By connecting the Soundbeam to a sampler and then through a laptop computer, I could "record" the music made through movement using sequencing software. The sampler could emulate the sounds of the wind quintet, flute, oboe, French horn, bassoon, and clarinet. Over the weeks, the participants became familiar with the various sound qualities, tones, and textures. Individually, the participants began to vocalize or signal their favorite sounds. As each session finished, I would work on the material at home, "transcribing" it into a notation that would be familiar to the professional musicians who would eventually be performing it. To involve the participants in the decision-making process, I would take my transcriptions back to the group and play them through a sequencer. I would ask the participants: Do you recognize your tune? Do you like your tune in this register with this sound? If not, would you prefer this register with this sound? Through an ongoing feedback loop between the participants, their care workers, and the facilitator, we included the participants in the many choices available when composing, arranging, and orchestrating a piece of music.*

*After the creative process was finished, the piece was sent to the wind quintet for rehearsal. They performed the "Kingfisher Suite," named after the daycare center, both at the venue where the workshops had taken place and in the concert hall. How fantastic it was to hear Freddy, Gwen, Dave, Joan, Ali, Peter, Barbara, and Constantine's pieces performed between Mozart and Haydn. The composer's faces expressed sheer delight as they heard and experienced their pieces being fed back to them.*

## Always-Already

Following from my experiences as a community music practitioner, I often felt that my work was given less credence than other forms of music making. The feeling was always less than: less than "professional" music, less than those focused on performing, and less than those with "'excellent virtuosic" instrumental technique. Equally within my roles as a lecturer or assistant/ associate professor within higher education institutions, community music as a subject of study has often appeared to be less than: less than the music degree and less than those studying performance, no matter what art form. As many of my community music colleagues can attest, there have been, and continue to be, constant struggles for visibility, resources, status, and, ultimately, value. My PhD work (Higgins, 2006) reflected these frustrations and presented an argument that the identity of community music might be understood as a primordial component within any conception of music.

To recall David Elliott's work in the last section, he assigned a visual look to the multidimensional concept of music understood in his praxial philosophy. Elliott (1995) alters the look of the word *music*[13] and offers three related senses of what the word might mean (pp. 39–45). First, "MUSIC" represents a diverse human practice consisting of many different musical practices, genres, and music cultures. Second, "Music" (with a capital "M") indicates different genres of musical practice, for instance, rock, jazz, and classical, where each genre is conceived as a musical practice within an artistic social community or music culture. Third, each contextualized practice-specific action is termed "music" (all lowercase) in the product sense of musical works that embody values, standards, and traditions of any given practice of culture. Although rather unwieldy, I rather liked it and took the visual form of MUSIC and its subsequent meaning, all music in the world, and made a case for community music being always-already housed within any understanding of it. The argument went something like this: As a process of music making that emphasizes people, participation, places, equity, and diversity, community music comes before Music (different genres) and before music (pieces or works) and, therefore, has its traits of practice situated within any notion of MUSIC as a diverse human practice. Employing some conceptual language from Derrida, community music is a trace,[14] a musical practice that disrupts ordinary notions of music while constituting its very existence. In one sense, it is an ethical gesture, alerting each domain to face each

---

[13] This also appears in the 2nd edition (Elliott & Silverman, 2015, p. 105).

[14] As a crucial notion for Derridean thought, the trace refuses the possibility that an element can be present in and of itself, thus referring only to itself. By interrogating Saussure's semiotics, Derrida states, "No element can function as a sign without referring to another element which itself is not simply present" (Derrida, 1981b, p. 26). The trace is "the alterity of the past that never was and can never be lived in the ordinary or modified form of presence" (Derrida, 1976, p. 70).

# 120 THINKING COMMUNITY MUSIC

other with a willingness to acknowledge how interdependent they actually are. To present this graphically, the name "community music" was written *Community* MUSIC.[15] The word *community* was altered to indicate that it is under erasure,[16] both necessary and unnecessary, a constantly dissolving entity both essential and unessential. In this instance the "community" in *Community* MUSIC is a "community-to-come," beckoning generosity to be washed upon the shoreline and calling for "community without unity," which involves hospitality (see Think Piece 2), promise (see Think Piece 4), cultural democracy (see Think Piece 1), and an opportunity to say "yes" (see Think Piece 3).

Ever so slightly off the wall, granted, but I always bought the Sunday newspaper for the color magazines tucked inside its folds. The so-called Sunday supplements constituted the condition of what was considered the main item—the black-and-white newspaper. Put another way, without the supplement, there was no Sunday newspaper. In Derrida's thought, the supplement attests to an inbuilt paradox, a dilemma that sees the supplement as both an add-on and a means to take the place of. The logic of the supplement divides and repeats, both adding to and replacing:

> The supplement adds to itself, it is a surplus, a plenitude enriching another plenitude, *the fullest measure of presence*. . . . [B]ut the supplement supplements. It adds only to replace. It intervenes or insinuates itself *in-the-place-of*; if it fills, it is as if one fills a void. (Derrida, 1997a, pp. 144–145)

Following this, without the pathways, openings, tracks, and marks generated through participatory music-making experiences, there would be no "professional" music, virtuosic technicians, or music degree courses. Community music is thus conceived as a future to come, a trace always-already constituted within MUSIC. Community music is MUSIC's condition of possibility, its primordial Other always haunting[17] musical practice and thought. Within this matrix, community music refuses repression,

---

[15] The question of identity begins with "What is Community Music?" and this question is returned to the past, positioned behind the question that asks, "What is MUSIC?" This movement of memory follows Derrida's interrogation of Heidegger's question of Being and seeks to disclose community music's identity away from a system of thinking that relies on essences and origins. For a detailed discussion on Derrida's perspective of the origin and genesis, see Marrati (2005).

[16] Derrida occasionally used a Heideggerian strategy of putting terms under erasure (*sous rature*). See Derrida (1982).

[17] For Derrida's work on the logic of haunting, see Derrida (1994b).

resisting opposition while sliding across MUSIC's intertextuality[18] in a play of possibility. In attempts to sideline community music from the interior of more traditional understandings, music educators, policymakers, professional musicians, and music business executives have all played a role in its exclusion. Community music has been understood as an outsider led away from the traditional interior, its amateurness, methodologies, eclecticism, and political voice poisoning the purity of other music making.[19] For community music to have been led outside traditional views of music making, it must have been already within traditional views of music making.

Traditional perspectives of music and music making have created a polarized reality, with some forms of music dominating other forms. This has led to higher value placed on specific aspects of music and music making and consequently is seen as sending everything else off to the periphery. This form of binary thinking[20] manifests itself in the marginalization of community music. This type of exclusion creates a hierarchical situation, one idea privileging the other, a center "ruling" over the margins (see Think Piece 7). Community music is positioned within this binary system and overwhelmed by the fixity of a dominant center or discourse. This freezes any sense of play by raising the domination of specific ideas of music and music making and the values bestowed upon them and relegating community music to a second-order activity. Even contemporary attempts to reverse hierarchical oppositions perpetuate other binary positions; I am thinking particularly of the trend in music education to privilege popular or world music over Western classical music or vice versa.

---

[18] First introduced by Julia Kristeva (1980), intertextuality was defined as "the transposition of one or more systems of sign into another, accompanied by a new articulation of the enunciative and denotative position."

[19] The aporia of inside/outside is analyzed in some detail within Derrida's major work on aesthetics, *The Truth in Painting* (Derrida, 1987a). The "Parergon" is a lengthy essay emphasizing the nature of the frame as it appears in Kant's *Critique of Judgment* and is particularly useful in unpacking the nature of the supplement. See also Plato's Pharmacy, where the scapegoat is used as a metaphor (Derrida, 1981a, pp. 128–134).

[20] Jacque Derrida's philosophical strategy of "deconstruction" engages a thinking of the force of noncenter, attempting to overturn hierarchical polarities and create a space for the play of differences. As a gesture that works against the ideas of self-sufficiency and absolute completion, play is "the disruption of presence." It is reminiscent of the Nietzschean thought of joyous affirmation in the play of the world and the innocence of becoming (Derrida, 1963/1978, p. 369). See also Derrida (1988, pp. 115–116) and Derrida (1985, p. 69). Derrida's attack on binary thinking was crucial to his philosophy: Binary thinking "is not just *one* metaphysical gesture among others, it is *the* metaphysical exigency, that which has been the most constant, most profound and most potent" (Derrida, 1988, p. 93).

## 122 THINKING COMMUNITY MUSIC

Logocentrism,[21] a fundamental or privileged predisposition toward particular things, such as music, promotes binary thinking and reduces the second term in each polar pair as the negative, corrupt, and undesirable versions of the first. The second term, in this case community music, represents a falling away, a less than. It therefore follows that community music is the fall from "professional musical-doing" and that the extramusical is the lack of the aesthetic, while informal or nonformal music learning is less than formal music learning (see Think Piece 3). Centuries of musical thought have bestowed privilege upon such things as Western classical music, staff notation, and concert hall performance (and, one might argue, a reversal that can now favor popular culture). Identifying community music within MUSIC's formulation begins the process of undoing this tightly knitted web. Musical aspects such as those listed above forcibly reveal themselves within MUSIC's textuality, repressing community music beneath the surface and marginalizing its primordial character. The hope here is to resist any self-satisfying completeness, enabling the work of the community musician to slip across the surface while refusing repression. In this way, community music as a practice has no essence; it cannot be assigned a fixed spot. Music is always contextual, and its value is determined by those who engage in it.[22]

Music making from within a community music context is therefore always on the horizon, a trace that is always-already within the modality of MUSIC itself. Community music will not appear under the sign of the possible, what I know and what I am familiar with, but under the sign of the *im*possible,[23] what will surprise me, challenge me, and perhaps even distress me.[24] This effect ruptures the surfaces and opens the way for new experiences within any notion of MUSIC, both as a diverse human practice and as an important aspect of how humans come to know themselves and understand the world in which they live. We can see this playing out through the wind quintet project illustrated above. The initial proposition was one-to-one

---

[21] The etymon of logocentrism is derived from the ancient Greek for "word," *logos*. John 1:1 ff. "In the beginning was the Word [*Logos*], and the Word was with God, and the Word was God" (Life Application Bible, 1992, p. 1861). Derrida (1994a) states that "deconstruction starts with the deconstruction of logocentrism" (p. 15). Derrida's explorations of the logocentric initially oscillated around metaphysical inquiry with its aspirations to seek an ultimate origin and drive to ground truth in a single ultimate point.

[22] Sociologist Tia DeNora (2000) highlights this in Chapter 2 of *Music in Everyday Life*.

[23] I explore this idea more fully in "*The Impossible* Future" (Higgins, 2007b).

[24] Derrida's later work on religion and the commentaries that follow plays host to this idea in terms of a call to the Messiah; see Derrida (1995), Hart (2004, pp. 87–128), and Caputo (1997b).

lessons. What transpired was the creation of new music. The weight given to the music possibilities between master and student dominated the suggestion that a group of adults with learning disabilities could create music for a programmed evening concert. The very idea was initially sidelined, pushed to the periphery, perhaps not consciously, but decisions were certainly made through a specific socially constructed experience. The music eventually was performed at the main concert event in a hall known for "excellence" in music. This certainly was different from the funder's original proposition and took a lot of politicking and negotiation with the wind quintet and the concert promotor. The "Kingfisher Suite" was finally sandwiched between two of the great "masters" and served to shine a light on what is regularly missing at these types of events: accessible, inclusive music making. I am not saying this is always appropriate and/or necessary—that would be ridiculous—but the fact that it can happen reveals that traits of community music practice are always-already internal to any music-making possibility. Music, as often conceived, is never fully present; it always carries traces of other music possibilities. These possibilities haunt any given moment of music, ready to disrupt, refusing to assert that music is a closed system, and always-already prepared for fresh interpretations.

## The Music Collective

*With a small grant, space made possible by the local governing body, and support from surrounding neighbors, youth workers joined forces with hip hop artists to create an open space to make and create music. Initially operating informally—as a "hang" where young people could come and go as they pleased—the venture began to organically organize itself with structured sessions that both passed on skills associated with the music genre and facilitated spaces that encouraged self-expression. Young people from across the age range told any adult prepared to listen about issues important to the world they were currently negotiating. Themes included typical concerns such as relationships, schooling, parents, drugs, and alcohol. There were many insights into young people's anxieties and stresses, issues surrounding body image, sexual identity, depression, street violence, and future employment. Their rhymes and lyrics capture their worries about racial tension, the rise of Far Right politics, concerns for sustainable living, the planet's ecology, and social inequalities brought about by poverty and lack of opportunity.*

# 124 THINKING COMMUNITY MUSIC

*Now regularly facilitating music workshops, the Music Collective, as it is now called, has crafted a space where youth from the locality can feel safe at home and express who they are. Musical structures familiar to hip hop provided the initial framework to voice thoughts, opinions, and anger. This has extended now, including a more comprehensive array of songwriting styles, which is evident at their weekly open mic nights. With continued support from both those in a position of power and the local community, the Music Collective offers young people in the area a safe space through which they can be empowered to "have their say" while learning ways to harness a craft. As I have experienced this project, it is this combination that has provided the context for such powerful music making.*

## Expression

Musical encounters can host the values and ideas that are at the heart of how we articulate contemporary urgencies and possibilities. Expressions of hopes and fears, ideas of how things might be, internal dilemmas, and moments of celebration can be revealed through musical doings. The work of the community musician can disrupt the ordinary and everyday, enabling participants to ask questions about where they are, who they are, and how they might be accountable to one another.[25] In this section, I will present some thoughts about music from a perspective of *expression* and consider how this Deleuzian concept might enable access to a meaningful understanding of music in community music.

Flowing from his worldview where immanence is the first requirement in thinking of an ontology[26] of difference,[27] the concept of expression refers to the coming into existence. To advance an ontology of difference, French philosopher Gilles Deleuze abandons transcendence[28] in favor of

---

[25] Sally Tallant asks these questions surrounding the Liverpool biennial art show. See Tallant (2012).

[26] Ontology is a branch of philosophy that deals with questions relating to existence, being, becoming, and reality. In the analytic tradition, ontology is orientated around questions of what there is. In continental philosophy, ontology has its focus on the study of Being.

[27] Baruch Spinoza (1632–1677) is influential in this aspect of Deleuze's thinking. Spinoza was a subversive thinker for his time, one who acknowledged no God except nature, who rejected any distinction between mind and body, and who demanded an absolute freedom of conscience in matters of religious belief (Norris, 1991). He paid a great personal price and was excommunicated by the Amsterdam synagogue in 1656 (Jarrett, 2007).

[28] In synergy with other poststructural thinkers, Deleuze understands a philosophy of transcendence as a disrupted process that wishes to capture the vital differences that perpetrate all thought and thus submit thinking to the judgment of a single perspective. To get beyond the transcendental,

# MUSIC   125

immanence.[29] From a Deleuzian vantage point, "transcendence freezes living, makes it coagulate and lose its flow" (May, 2005, p. 27); put another way, transcendence suggests a relation "to" something, while immanence suggests a relation "in" something. For the sharing of music to come into existence, it requires a "force,"[30] which refers to any capacity to produce a change.[31] To give expression its force, it relies on time, or "duration."[32] Synonymous with existence, duration means life as perpetual change and invention, "continual elaboration of the absolutely new" (Guerlac, 2006, p. 6). A philosophy of immanence, therefore, places emphasis on connections and connectivity rather than forms of separation and fixed identities. The individual figure expresses itself in the many, but through an openness toward multiple connections, it does not become lost.

Following this, musical expression heard in the context of those engaged with community music should not be thought of within a structure of repetition or as canonical or fixed identities. Instead, they are conceived and heard as singular, creative, inventive musical happenings that are always open to future potentials. Music has an infinite moldable plasticity, and it can be folded, unfolded, and refolded like an origami lotus flower.[33] As material to be worked with, sounds await a breath of life through the mechanics

Deleuze turns to the notion of univocity. Univocity, rather than equivocity (one being truly is, while other beings are dependent or secondary), is a position that understands that no event or phenomenon is more real than any other. In line with Spinoza, Deleuze claims there cannot be a supreme creator outside of its creation (morphogenesis). In other words, there is only one being or substance (core concept of ontology and metaphysics) through which everything comes into existence.

[29] Immanence is pitted against transcendence. These are terms that describe the relations of things within metaphysical inquiry. In short, transcendence has its relation "to" and immanence "in." Transcendence is rejected because of its need to collapse into concepts of identity, eventually leading to conformism. Contrary to Deleuze's project, transcendence favors knowledge over thought. Immanence sets out to overcome transcendence, which is, according to Deleuze, an "illusion" (Deleuze & Guattari, 1994, p. 49).

[30] Deleuze draws upon French philosopher Henri Bergson (1859–1941); see Deleuze (1988). Bergson uses the term *elan vital*, meaning the vital force or impulse of life: a creative principle held by Bergson to be immanent in all organisms and responsible for evolution (Bergson, 1911/2022).

[31] The notion of "force" has close associations with the work of Nietzsche and can be understood in its relation to (1) speed and movement and (2) a power that effects social order (Stivale, 2005, pp. 19–30).

[32] Bergson's concept of temporality as duration is as unusual to time as Spinoza's conception of God as nature and helps deepen Deleuze's thought of differences. Bergson makes an argument for freedom against determinist thinking. He does this through an appeal to time that celebrates the immediate experience. Susan Guerlac (2006) makes the point that both Merleau-Ponty and Satre were also steeped in Bergsonism.

[33] Through the Japanese art of origami, everything happens as an expression of one sheet of paper. Origami is the substance, the paper is its attribute, and the figures are the modes of expression. If we can imagine the paper folding and unfolding itself, we can get near to Deleuze's concept of expression (May, 2005)

126 THINKING COMMUNITY MUSIC

of process and facilitation. Engaged in musical doing, community music participants generate music that is both singular and individual and their music should not be reduced to what Emmanuel Levinas would call "the same,"[34] an identity that insists on category, genre, and stylistic certainty. As audience members listening to a community music event, we might focus our attention and bear witness to the person making the sounds. The music is not to be understood as separate from the person but rather integral to the person from whom it flows. Because a philosophy of immanence emphasizes connections rather than forms of separation, the music participant is, during these moments, *becoming-musician* as they seek to make connections through their musical doing.[35] In this way, participants are sensing the world as musicians.

Within this system of thought, there is no predisposed music identity, no transcendental force external to the participant that provides an innate musical ability—or, equally, *no* musical ability. As a person open to the possibility of becoming-musician, developing ever-increasing capacities in music making is contingent on the connections one makes, for example, inspiring music professionals, local music clubs, meaningful music education, access to music resources, and attentive listeners. There is not a preplanned musician identity with an outlined destiny but only the connections made when interacting in the world at large, which is constantly becoming, unfolding, and in motion. There will always be conflict because although a participant and/or an audience might not identify with standard ideals of what music should sound like, these "standards" still impact any musical existence. For example, the vocal improvisation during the orchestral outreach project and the music produced by those attending the adult daycare center, illustrated above, were all subject to judgments based on particular value systems.

The creation of music understood through a plane[36] of musical happening enables us to think of all music making as belonging to a connected organism. Mindful of the origami metaphor, the music of Beethoven, Miles Davis, and Hugh Masekela is considered as being made from the same music sensations as those young jazz musicians performing at Johnny's place. They

---

[34] Levinas's ethics conceives that the relationships between people are separate, thus resisting a reduction of the "other" to the "same" (Levinas, 1969).

[35] Gould utilizes this idea by explaining that becoming is best understood in terms of becoming-*alongside* rather than becoming-as (Gould, 2012).

[36] The image of a "plane" is used by Deleuze to evoke a type of thinking that mediates between the chaos of chance and the structure of orderly thinking (Parr, 2005, p. 204).

are all "in" relation to one another; each person's musical encounter does not just relate "to" each other but evolves "in" and through their engagements (Richerme, 2020, p. 104). If we were able to interact with participants' music from within their expression, entering their milieu[37] let's say, our respective musical experiences could intermingle and form new experiences. We might say, in Deleuze's terms, that our respective multiplicities may mingle to form new multiplicities[38] (Buchanan & Swiboda, 2004, p. 10). To resist hierarchy and division, the idea of musical "expression" challenges the view of musical creation that affirms the creator as privileged regarding its creation. As dynamic and active potentialities, community music expressions can be understood as expressions of those who made them, singular moments reaching out for connective opportunities. The music made by those engaged in my three "memories" is best understood through an encounter of who they were. Their expressions unfold from their situated bodies. Each person generates sounds that travel through time, seeking to connect with fellow performers and those listening. Music spoken here refuses to be fixed as an identity but rather understood within an infinite conception of musics, a multiple pathway of connective possibilities.

## Flight Lines

When starting this think piece, as I have already noted, I was still determining whether the question set was really the right one: *How might we understand the "music" in community music?* I was unaware of any literature or conference conversations that had previously explored the notion. I did know that it had been on my mind for quite some time—since Gary Ansdell raised the point back in 2012. After sitting with the question and trying to figure out what it might entail, I was reassured that the sentiments behind it were indeed worthy of some interrogation, not just as a personal enterprise but one the field should engage with. I found the task challenging, and I hope my thoughts here provide springboards for further discussion. My

---

[37] Distinct articulations within particular contexts (Stivale, 2005, p. 78).

[38] Resisting the binary one/many, multiplicities are complex structures that have a form of their own rather than being multiples of something else (Deleuze, 2006, pp. 23–24). For our discussions, the multiplicity is an important idea. In the most basic sense, a multiplicity is a complex structure that does not reference a prior unity. Multiplicities that are continuous and intensive will always be affected by encounters with others.

128 THINKING COMMUNITY MUSIC

process began by initially engaging in reflective thinking concerning some of the past experiences that had impacted me musically. After writing the autoethnographic memories, I used them to explore three philosophical lenses predominantly expressed by Elliott and Silverman, Derrida, and Deleuze. As singular responses, they might be summarized in the following way:

1. Music is intersubjective, socially situated, and socially shared. It is deeply contextual, and value must be given to its multiplicity.
2. The traits of community music practice are always-already inherent in any case of musical doing. No music has full presence, but the possibility of meaningful music-making experiences is continually on the horizon and challenges any privilege given over to one style, genre, or historical period.
3. Music is an expression of those who make it, each performance seeking to make connections integral to the person from whom it flows. Existing on a plane of musical happenings, those that engage through participation are becoming-musicians, opening future potentials.

Intersections between these three ideas can be found, for example:

- Music made within the framework of community music can be multiple, contextual, and socially situated.
- Music can provide moments of profound self-expression, connecting participants to who they are and where they may want to go.
- Music often responds to various genre characteristics but is not bound by any particular style, which means that across the gamut of projects globally, there is a wide and diverse spectrum of styles and forms.

From my experience, the music people make within community music projects is the least talked about and discussed aspect of the work. Why has this been so? Is the music of lesser importance to the social-cultural aspect of the work, or is it that it is always inescapably part of the overall experience? Following this, should there be a move toward more explicit discussions surrounding the phenomenon of music within projects? Do you hear any distinctive music characteristics that suggest a community music project is happening or has happened? On the flip side, might discussions surrounding the music fall into the trap of disembodied de-socialized aesthetic experiences and, as such, pull community music into an existing historical debate? Because of my initial doubts surrounding the guiding question, the field might discuss whether there might be a different framing. Did my central question have the right orientation? If so, what other ways might there be to respond to it? If not, how might a question concerning the music within community music be articulated?

# 7

# Research

## Making Music Together

*Jo Gibson is a community music practitioner-researcher with a history of working in the East End of London, United Kingdom. Through a methodology guided by community music, she employs long-term practice-research within educational, community center, and adult recovery programs. Jo's central question, how do we make music together, explores approaches to cocreative music making to deepen understanding of (1) how community musicians and participants conceptualize working together and (2) strategies of research through community music making. In Jo's words: "Using my practice as both evidence and methodology, I explore the intricacies and tensions of facilitated music making, unpacking the community musician's dual collaborator/facilitator status by zooming in on the starting points for material generation with participants" (Gibson, 2020, p. 4). Her PhD project was understood as "evidence" and "methodology" and appears in two parts: an exegesis and a website.[1] Videos of the work in each situated setting are found on the website. Key themes, such as voice, visibility, vulnerability, collaboration, and becoming-a-band, are articulated through "critical incidents": "revelatory or significant moments in practice that highlight deviations (either positive or negative) from what is 'normal' or 'expected.'"[2]*

*One of the important things to this work is the discussion surrounding ethics within community music practice-research:*

> *The enactment of ethical practice has been a motivator, guide, and concern throughout my research. By ethical, at its most straightforward, I mean attempting to do what is "good" or "right" as a community musician music-making with participants. This leads to the question, what is "good" or*

---

[1] https://www.jogibson.org/. The exegesis is available on this site.
[2] https://www.jogibson.org/critical-incidents. The critical incident literature is drawn from diverse fields such as nursing, airline breakdowns, and teaching.

*Thinking Community Music.* Lee Higgins, Oxford University Press. © Oxford University Press 2024.
DOI: 10.1093/9780190247027.003.0008

# RESEARCH 131

*"right"? What does, for example, "good" or "right" look, feel, or sound like in community music practice? How can that be known? And who decides?[3]*

*As a "situated process of interrelation," practice-research is a research approach whereby the practice is a central method of the inquiry. Theory is, therefore, imbricated within the doing, and Jo's work teases out the community musicians' doing-knowing.[4] This extends the idea of reflective practice, which has been central to the community musicians' work,[5] and, in so doing, offers challenges to possible entrenchment in orthodoxy underpinned by well-worn evaluation and project output tropes. Jo continues to explore practice-research with communities of music makers to critically consider cocreation as enacted in contemporary practice by cocreating with others. This approach locates practice as the central method of inquiry, building on the assertion that creative practice can constitute knowing.*

In 2010, the Commission for Community Music Activity (CMA) met in Hangzhou, China. During this meeting, I encouraged those with research supervision status to actively promote and support methodological approaches that resonated with the practice.[6] I used arts-based research as an example and suggested that as a research strategy, it might provide an opportunity to merge the *scholar-self* and the *community musician-self.* Putting the research tools in the hands of those invested in the practice would ensure that practice and scholarship do not drift apart. Responding to this call would mean that questions appropriate to the work would be "answered" by those closest to it, resulting in research pertinent to the "field."

The purpose of this think piece is to revisit this thought, reflect on what has followed, and build upon its agency toward evoking research approaches that are resonant with community music's ethos and practice. After contextualizing questions that have driven my project, I engage with the figure of the margin and present some ideas of how this may be useful when considering community music research. Following this, I use my tenure as the editor of the *International Journal of Community Music* (IJCM) as a case

---

[3] https://www.jogibson.org/ethics

[4] See a video on YouTube that discusses these ideas: https://www.youtube.com/watch?v=vZmVegiIUHE.

[5] I'm thinking particularly of Donald Schön (1991), who identifies two types: reflective-in-action and reflective-on-action. Practice-research also responds to other models of reflective practice. See Rolfe (Rolfe et al., 2011), Gibbs (1998), and Kolb (1983).

[6] See Higgins (2010).

132 THINKING COMMUNITY MUSIC

to explore Gianni Vattimo's notion of weak thought, suggesting ways those in positions of power might model community musics ethos for the next generation of scholars. Next, I interact with two illustrations of practice, Making Music Together and Noise Solution, and use these to discuss the representation of community music practice within a research frame. Finally, I advocate for future community music scholars and researchers to have sensitivity and understanding of the practices and the issues inherent within the work to generate a conducive environment through which powerful critique can be made.

## Critique Not Criticism

My engagement in the field of community music has been a response to the following questions: What makes community music distinctive? Where is community music happening? What do the practices look like? Is community music important, and if so, how? These questions have their roots in the encounters I had with music teachers and professors in my youth. I experienced first-hand an abuse of power between teacher and student within a formal institution. I can recount the following example that took place in a college. After leaving a U.K. comprehensive school and in an attempt to pursue a music education, I applied for a place at the local technical college. Unlike the myriad music courses available now, opportunities in music education were limited in towns and cities across Britain in the early 1980s. In short, the head of music ridiculed my application and left no doubt that I was entirely unsuited for the "serious" study of music. My experience as a rock musician interested in jazz was not deemed acceptable within this music department: the head of the department did not even ask to hear me play my guitar. Books that I "should" have read were piled up in front of me, one by one, each one on the stack confirming the deficits in my upbringing and education. I was given an essay and told to read it. The music teacher left the room only to return 5 minutes later to emphasize that these were the expected "standards." I was stunned and humiliated, and I doubted both my musical capabilities and my self-worth.

My musical education came to fruition through informal musical learning set against a musical background of punk, new wave, and heavy metal. Reflective of Lucy Green's (2002) accounts in *How Popular Musicians Learn*, I began teaching myself guitar and later found refuge with a good

RESEARCH    133

guitar teacher. Although my musical preferences emerged from the new wave of British heavy metal,[7] the spirit of the punk movement affected my attitude toward music participation. Those who have commented on Britain's musical subcultures, such as Jon Savage (1991) and Roger Sabin (1999), have described the *mentalité*, or cultural consciousness, that permeated youth culture during this period. From the perspective of a 16-year-old, the punk *zeitgeist* created positive energies. The spirit of the punk movement cleared the baggage that had prevented young people from having the opportunities to turn aspirations of musical performance into reality. My orientation toward community music initially sprang from the ghost of the punk mentalité.

One of the important tropes for community music is that of the "margin." I have highlighted this before using the phrase *boundary walkers*,[8] suggesting that from such a vantage point, music educators can take stock of the center, understand its construction, and "dream" of going beyond its limits.[9] This idea can be operationalized in several ways, for example, a musician's response to those who have limited or no access to music education, a challenge to hierarchical structures within the delivery of music education, a critique toward cultural policy and the distribution of government monies and funding opportunities, public perception, and value to what constitutes "good" music.

I want to recall the figure of the margin and consider how it might be used to interrogate understandings of community music practices. In the first instance, community music researchers might carefully reflect on their positionality and what power this affords. Avoiding an overreliance on the notion of the center rather than the margin could avoid creating a hierarchy of those who know and those who do not. This can reduce possible instances where the researcher's knowledge is placed above others. Power is always at work, and it is always worth acknowledging this. However, privilege in its many forms is often not recognized, and a sense of entitlement is brought to

---

[7] The new wave of British heavy metal was a musical movement that started in the United Kingdom in the late 1970s.

[8] *Boundary walkers* was a term Kushner et al. (2001) used to describe community musicians' uncertainty toward their professional status. This idea was reinterpreted as a positive trope by suggesting that being at the boundaries or margins provided clear sight lines of those central structures that can dominate music practice. From a position of "seeing" and recognizing the forces at work, opportunities for change may become more concrete. See Higgins (2012b, p. 6).

[9] The notion of dream evokes the work of John Caputo (1997b). Dreaming here points toward an affirmative opportunity to see in between over and beyond. See Higgins (2012b, pp. 171–172).

## 134  THINKING COMMUNITY MUSIC

bear upon the work. In these instances, researchers might posit themselves before those they are working with and thus work within a deficit model (see Think Piece 1).

Inherent within notions of the margin are challenges to what constitutes scholarly "standards" and/or currently accepted ways of presenting research. As a practice, community music has provided a fulcrum through which to consider music making, but what if it was considered a critical lens or perhaps a methodology? Might it help untangle notions of scholarly standards as a universal, one-size-fits-all measure or norm and enable scholars to be more in sync with ideas connected to cultural democracy, inclusion, and social justice? (See Think Pieces 1, 3, and 5). Binary thinking can be ubiquitous but often resides in "speaking" for other people and placing the researcher in a position of dominance over potential cocreators or collaborators. I would stress that privilege, power plays, and a sense of entitlement are out of resonance with community music scholarship and are in direct tension with contemporary epistemological diversity and discourses surrounding, for example, feminist thought and decolonization. Community music research and scholarship need to open constructive dialogue rather than close it down. As researchers, our positionality should allow two-way traffic, not hostile conversations. The margins of our work point both inward, toward the "text" we create, and outward, beyond the text's structural limits. I want to advocate for carefully considering the imposition of "our knowledge" and think how it might be decentered. Let us consider notes in an academic book or article as forming the margin, and we allow these edges to melt away and disseminate throughout the whole. They reveal our orientation and the substance of what we stand for, who we are, and how our work might be considered both now and in the future. The figure of the margin, or *parergon*,[10] can be a powerful way to take a step back and reflect on how we, as researchers and scholars, might want to be thought of as academics, community musicians, or simply human beings.[11]

---

[10] *Parergon* means "outside the work" or a supplement to a larger piece. It is also the title of an essay written by Derrida (1987a), which emphasizes the nature of the frame as it appears in Kant's *Critique of Judgment*.

[11] For an example of an analysis using the figure of the margin, see Higgins (2020a). I consider the article "Daring to Question: A Philosophical Critique of Community Music" (Kertz-Welzel, 2016).

RESEARCH    135

## On Being a (Weak) Editor

First appearing in 2004, the IJCM began as a peer-reviewed online journal.[12] In this form, the journal was free of charge and was run as a nonprofit venture. In 2007, I joined David Elliott and Kari Veblen, the founders of the online journal, as an editor. A decision was made to work alongside a professional publisher and an inaugural issue was published in 2008. I became the senior editor in 2009 and remained in the position until 2021. I never had ambitions of being an editor of a journal. However, when the opportunity presented itself, I wondered whether the format could be mobilized to "work" for the good of community music. There was a disquiet, an apprehension, regarding my new "gatekeeping" status. Journals, as part of the broader education machinery, play an important role in individuals' careers, vital in factors relating to tenure portfolios, grant awards, and promotions. The name "editor" carries prestige within academia, conjuring up images of power, status, and hierarchy. After all, the editor's vision and leadership craft the directive regarding what gets published and what does not.[13] Of course, this is an oversimplification as many factors are at play, including the all-important editorial board and external reviewers who play a vital and significant role in any decision-making process. Editors also coordinate journal administration and liaise with the publisher, among other responsibilities. However, for a potential contributor, the editor can be seen as the final word in whether their work gets published. Community music practices oscillate around ideals such as access, inclusivity, participation, equality, and diversity; how could the editor's role and the journal respond to this ethos while seeking to establish the reputation needed to attract would-be contributors? The question I pondered was, How might a community musician curate an academic journal that is in keeping with the tenets of the practice while adhering to the responsibilities of a professional journal? Engaging with Italian philosopher Gianni Vattimo's notion of weak thought helped to respond to this question, furthering the discussion surrounding the central question of this think piece: *How might I do community music research?*

---

[12] Edited by David Elliott and Kari Veblen, four issues were published drawing papers from the Special Research Interest Group on Adult and Community Music Education, part of a national conference held in the United States.

[13] For an interesting article and blog, see Rachel Toor (2009).

136 THINKING COMMUNITY MUSIC

What is weak thought? Weak thought is a turn of phrase that originates in Gianni Vattimo's response to the terrorist interpretation of the Italian Democratic Left during the 1970s.[14] An Italian philosopher, newspaper columnist, and social democratic politician, Vattimo worked through an ethical interpretation of Nietzsche's and Heidegger's critique of Western metaphysical values. With a focus on Nietzsche's nihilism and Heidegger's ontological difference, Vattimo concludes that philosophy can only now be an "adventure of difference," suggesting that difference and multiplicity imply that we accept the disintegration of unity (Vattimo, 1993). Through the Nietzschean problematic of the "eternal return"[15] and Heideggerian problem concerning the "overcoming of metaphysics,"[16] Vattimo moves toward the liberation of philosophy from its Platonic metaphysical explanations. In sympathy with Heidegger's history of Western metaphysics, he suggests that accounts of how things are have found stability by reducing everything to a single ideological principle. Emmanuel Levinas (1969) might say that the "same" has been emphasized at the expense of the "other."[17] Following the trajectory of

---

[14] The Red Brigades were formed in 1970 (Brigate Rosse in Italian, often abbreviated as the BR). They were a Marxist-Leninist militant group based in Italy and actively involved in several political assassinations. They sought to create a revolutionary state through armed struggle and to extract Italy from the North Atlantic Treaty Organization (NATO; Meade, 1990). During this time (1974), Vattimo published a book that was supposed to be a political-philosophical manifesto for those who wanted to change the power relationships within the country. Unfortunately, after some of Vattimo's students were arrested and imprisoned, he felt that his ideas had been misunderstood and sought other ways to express his political and ideological justifications (Zabala, 2007b, pp. 12–13). Vattimo (1999, p. 34) also notes that the term *weak thought* is an expression used in an essay from the early 1980s that became the introductory text to a volume of essays edited with Pier Aldo Rovatti.

[15] The eternal return stresses the significance of our present actions: Whatever we do now will return to us repeatedly. It is a circulating passage of history and the future that moves in all directions. It underlines the fact that we have responsibility for our actions and implies an exhortation: Strive to be greater than you are, to overcome yourself; the present moment is all, so let's make the best use of it and of ourselves (Nietzsche, 1969, pp. 176–180). See also Think Piece 8, note 46.

[16] Heidegger challenged 2,500 years of Western metaphysics by "reinstating" Being as the central question of philosophy. Heidegger draws distinctions between questions of beings (ontic) and Being (ontological). Conceding that if humans remain the "animal rational" there is no chance of ridding ourselves of metaphysics, Heidegger creates a groundwork through which to transform the essence of humans and, in doing so, push toward a "transformation of metaphysics" (Inwood, 1999, p. 128). Later, Heidegger speaks of "getting over" rather than "overcoming." Vattimo considered this outlook "nihilistic" because it is not a positive doctrine but a series of negations.

[17] As a philosophic enterprise, Levinas's thought reprimands the Western philosophy tradition for its emphases on the "same" at the expense of the "other." The use of the terms the *same* and the *other* can be found in Plato, especially in the *Sophist* and the *Parmenides*, where he proceeds to show that the separation of the spheres of the absolute and the relative cannot be maintained and grabbles with his own ideas of the forms (Plato, 1999, pp. 79–89, pp. 1152–1168). From this perspective, the whole history of metaphysics is a search for foundations, certainty, presence-to-self, and unity. As a result of this obsession for absolute truth, the celebration of different has been subsumed into the black hole of the same; as Levinas puts it, "We call it 'the same' because in representation, the I precisely loses its opposition to its object; the opposition fades" (Levinas, 1969, p. 126).

RESEARCH 137

continental philosophy, Vattimo (1988) insists that postmodernity acquires philosophical credibility by interrogating stable and universal concepts. During the waning of modernity, our experience of unlimited interpretability weakens the cogent force of reality; what might have been considered facts are now taken for interpretations (Zabala & Vattimo, 2002).

Described by Michel Foucault as the three masters of suspicion,[18] Marx (critique of ideology), Freud (unconscious), and Nietzsche (the thing in itself)[19] laid pathways that cast doubt on what appears most apparent. Vattimo adds Heidegger (deconstruction of ontology)[20] to the mix and in resonance with Jean-François Lyotard (Lyotard & Thébaud, 1985) suggests that postmodernity is not to be understood just as a radical rupture with modernity but rather grasped as a new attitude toward the modern, a critique of the objectivist conditions of Enlightenment philosophy.[21] We are postmodern, Vattimo (2004) exclaims, because the logic of linear time as a continuous and unitary process that moves toward betterment no longer has meaning for us (p. 50). Weak thinking is an "attitude" and approach to modernity, a way of thinking that has its head turned toward new purposes, surpassing and twisting free a future through liberation.[22] We might describe this as a Great Getting Loose,[23] a refusal to surround ourselves with unyielding margins and static domesticity. Vattimo emphasizes that the relationship between the predecessor and the successor would be a gentler relation of "turning to new purposes" rather than as "the power-laden notion of overcoming" (Zabala, 2007b, p. 15).

[18] See Foucault (1998).

[19] In *Human, All Too Human*, Nietzsche suggests that our picture of the world has been founded on errors. Science cannot lead us beyond the phenomenal realm to the "thing in itself": "so that what appears in appearance is precisely *not* the thing in itself . . . that which we humans call life and experience—has gradually *become,* is indeed still fully in course of *becoming,* and should not be regarded as a fixed object" (Nietzsche, 1996, pp. 19–20). For Vattimo's account of how to read Nietzsche, see Vattimo (2002).

[20] Traditional interpretations of Aristotle emphasized his "categories" of beings. Heidegger "destroyed" these through a deconstruction and reread Aristotle as a practical philosopher. See Heidegger (2002, pp. 41–51).

[21] Jean-François Lyotard proposed that postmodernism is not to be taken in a periodizing sense; it is instead an intensification of modernity through technology and freedom (Lyotard & Thébaud, 1985, p. 16n). Postmodernity is not a new age but a rewriting of some of the features claimed by modernity. Postmodernity is ultimately understood as an *event* that disrupts the possibility of thinking of history as a succession of moments (Lyotard, 1991, p. 34).

[22] Through a confrontation with Heidegger's use of the German word *verwindung* ("overcoming") *überwindung* ("going beyond"), Vattimo suggests that the former has no notion of a "leaving behind," which characterizes the connection we have with a past that no longer has anything to say to us. A postmodern attitude that moves toward overcoming modernity must encounter these terms to define the "post" in postmodernism (Vattimo, 1987). However, Vattimo does not want us to understand weak thought as just a mode of "overcoming." Instead, it relates to dialectics and differences (Vattimo, 1984).

[23] For a discussion on the Great Getting Loose within Nietzsche, see McCumber (2000).

# 138 THINKING COMMUNITY MUSIC

Weak thought, as a philosophical appeal, is a responsible ethical announcement rather than a claim,[24] a conversational charity rather than objective truth. In short, it is a philosophy that places its proponents in a position to always listen to others. Weak thought produces "a desirable humility about our moral intuitions and the social institutions to which we have become accustomed" (Vattimo, 2004, pp. xviii–xix). Through this humility, tolerance for other intuitions can be encouraged with a willingness to experiment with different ways of refashioning or replacing static and tired institutions. It is not a term of derision but a positive term of praise that can be used as a tool for political emancipation and a democratic philosophy (Robbins, 2004). Without claiming any rights in the name of universal principles or·ideal truths, weak thought maintains dialogue through edifying consensus and encouraging a reach toward a plurality of information.[25] For Vattimo, hermeneutics becomes the philosophical stance that most faithfully reflects the pluralism of modern Western democratic society.[26] Hermeneutics is, therefore, the philosophical tool of weak thought because it celebrates a plurality of interpretations. With a resonance toward the Nietzschean thesis that suggests that "there are no facts, only interpretations,"[27] weak thought emphasizes interpretation as weakening the weight of objective structures. Institutions such as the church, empire, or media define truth through artificial preaching, ideological propaganda, and selected news. Postmodern philosophy has attempted to show that "truth" is a game of interpretations and is always marked by the interests that inspire them. Interpretation might be understood as a "virus" or "pharmakon"[28] loosening and weakening the weight of static structures. This is a call for transformation, a look in the direction of Nietzsche's nihilism (the dissolution of any ultimate foundations) as an "active" emancipatory agent (the process in which constraints are shed), "the

---

[24] "God is dead!" is an announcement, not a claim. It means not that God does not exist but that our experience has been transformed such that we no longer conceive ultimate objective truths and now respond only to appeals and announcements. See Zabala (2007b, pp. 453–454).

[25] In a conversation with Zabala, Vattimo is quoted as stating that "philosophy is more an edifying discourse than a demonstrative one, more oriented toward the edification of humanity than toward the development of knowledge and progress" (Vattimo & Zabala, 2002, p.452).

[26] With a history in biblical texts, hermeneutics is a theory and method of interpreting verbal and nonverbal texts. See Zimmermann (2015).

[27] "Facts are precisely what is lacking, all that exists consists of *interpretations*. We cannot establish any facts 'in itself': it may even be nonsense to desire to do such a thing" (Nietzsche, 1974, §481 at p.412).

[28] *Pharmakon* is a Greek word that has no proper or determinate character. It can be translated to mean either remedy or poison. For an exposition of this idea concerning Vattimo's work, see Zabala (2007a). Derrida explores this idea in Plato's Pharmacy (Derrida, 1981a).

chance to begin a different history" (Vattimo, 2004, p. 40). As an idea, weak thought undermines and shakes a sense of an all-prevailing being. American philosopher John Caputo states that weak thinking illuminates "the gradual weakening of being that has transformed contemporary philosophy from its former obsession with the metaphysic of truth to its current understanding of itself as sticky and interpretative exercise" (Caputo & Vattimo, 2007, p. 16). As a positive affirmation, one might suggest that within a robust theory of weakness, "the philosopher's role would not derive from the world 'as it is,' but from the world viewed as the product of a history of interpretation throughout the history of human cultures" (Vattimo & Zabala, 2002, p. 453).

As the editor for the IJCM, or put another way, a temporary gatekeeper in the world of community music research, keeping the ideas associated with Vattimo's weak thinking close to my chest helped me recognize my privilege and, where possible, enabled action in a manner that was in concert with the ethos of the field. As a "weak editor,"[29] I sought anarchic deliberations to disturb the ideal of an editor, thus igniting possibilities of behaving differently. I used the editorial position to galvanize a discourse that was as wide and inclusive as I could make it within the tight borders inherent within academic journals. I am still determining how successful I was; recipients of the journal would need to comment on this. One of the tangible outcomes I can talk to, however, was creating an open space to promote themes of contemporary importance, such as work in ritual, chant, and song;[30] prison and probation service;[31] life-long learning;[32] the field of leisure studies;[33] community music therapy;[34] online participation;[35] early childhood;[36] parents and the child;[37] peace, empathy, and conciliation;[38] musical life course;[39] and Covid-19.[40] Two issues were geographically located, Germany[41] and Norway;[42] these were thought to encourage national discussions to support visibility and policy change.

---

[29] It was first proposed at the U.S. National Conference in Music Education in Baltimore in 2012.
[30] Volume 2, Issue 1, guest editor Helen Phelan.
[31] Volume 3, Issue 1, guest editor Mary Cohen.
[32] Volume 5, Issue 3, guest editor William Dabback; Volume 11, Issue 2, guest editor Susan Avery.
[33] Volume 6, Issue 2, guest editor Roger Mantie.
[34] Volume 7, Issue 1, guest editor Giorgos Tsiris.
[35] Volume 8, Issue 1, guest editor Janice Waldron.
[36] Volume 10, Issue 3, guest editors Diana Dansereau and Beatriz Iiari.
[37] Volume 12, Issue 1, guest editor Susan Conkling.
[38] Volume 12, Issue 3, guest editors Samantha Dieckman and Jane Davidson.
[39] Volume 14, Issue March 2021, guest editors Andrea Creech and Roger Mantie.
[40] Volume 10, Issue November 2021, guest editor Stephen Clift.
[41] Volume 9, Issue 1, guest editors Alicia de Banffy-Hall, Theo Hartogh, and Burkhard Hill.
[42] Volume 10, Issue 1, guest editors Kim Boeskov and Brit Agot Broske.

# 140 THINKING COMMUNITY MUSIC

As an idea, the weak editor is an open-ended concept refusing to be trapped within the confines of its name. Actively resisting categorization as a determined entity, a weak editor would appeal to the call rather than a causality rejecting outright strength and power. As a particular attitude toward the job in hand, there is an intensification toward the subject matter, an acceptance that there are boundaries that would require negotiations to maintain an openness toward the critical ideas of the field; in the IJCM case, this would include access, equality, and inclusion. Following the ideas laid out here, I would like to suggest that those in positions that support community music research, academic supervisors, journal and book editors, conference organizers, and review panels might reflect on the notion of "weak thought" and respond hospitably and as such model nurturing leadership that has a chance to be embodied by the next generation of community music researchers.

## Noise Solution

*We take people who have probably not had a successful experience of education and give them one. We make them good at something quickly, whether that's making Trance or Dubstep or playing the piano or drums, and we share that success with the people important to them using a secure social media-based platform that we have built. We have found that this fairly simple experience of success combined with recognition goes a long way to building young people's self-confidence, which was often the thing that was holding them back.[43]*

*Noise Solution[44] is a social enterprise using music technology with disengaged people from mainstream schooling. As an intervention, Noise Solution is designed to improve the well-being of its young participants referred to the organization by schools and mental health and social work teams.[45] Sessions occur over 20 hours and often focus on beat making, digitally capturing the activities and personal reflections, and posting weekly feeds to those people the participants see as important in their lives, for example, family and key*

[43] Personnel communication

[44] http://www.noisesolution.org/; https://linktr.ee/NoiseSolutionUK

[45] Referrals to Noise Solution predominantly come from statutory organizations in mental health, education, or U.K. local government authorities.

workers. *The first five 2-hour sessions occur at participants' homes, with the remaining five at commercial recording studios local to the young person. The focus is on musicians encouraging competence and supportive behaviors, where the participant gains a quick mastery in whatever music-making process they have decided to follow (Glenister, 2024).*

*With a background in working with young offenders and as a professional musician, Simon Glenister established Noise Solution to work musically with marginalized people across the East of England. By engaging music creation through predominantly music technology and working one to one, Simon and his team of facilitators focus on unlocking confidence and self-belief in the people they work alongside. Situating themselves in whatever location is appropriate, often in the home, their nonformal education approach provides some fundamental steps toward providing positive pathways to improving young people's lives who have battled with mental health problems, drug addictions, and offending behavior.*

*Simon explains that he does not think of Noise Solution as a "music" project per se: "I didn't start this as I think most music projects start as a musician—thinking I really love playing music and I've got this hunch this it will be great for kids so I'll set this up for kids. . . . I come at this from a very different angle." From a background in working with challenging young people, he saw much frustration with the services being provided. After 15 years of professional practice, Simon understood what young people need, believing that a nonthreatening approach through music could inspire them to reconnect and move positively forward with their lives. Simon believed that issues of self-confidence were at the root of the chaotic lives of those he was regularly seeing: "If you can make them feel they are good at something—if you can do that, then you are much more likely to have an impact to get them to take a risk and try a new avenue."*

*Although Simon has a background in social work, he also has substantial experience as a professional musician, having had four recording contracts and playing from Iceland to Australia as a drummer in various bands, most recently in the internationally acclaimed Tunng.[46] Because Simon sees his project as something other than a music project, his focus is never just on the "quality" of the music being created (see Think Piece 5). His emphasis resides on the intervention (see Think Piece 1). Noise Solution is a project based on developing self-confidence and motivation, building positive progressions into voluntary*

[46] http://www.tunng.co.uk/

## 142 THINKING COMMUNITY MUSIC

placements and education in the hopes of creating successful pathways into community integration and well-being. Therefore, music is employed as an engagement tool to reach these ends. For example, one young man had just been released from prison. He needed to find some purpose, a positive direction that would help him stay out of trouble. Simon suspected he would not be able to sustain a mainstream college course, an opportunity open to him and one through which he would gain valuable and positive experiences. By engaging him in the creation of music he was interested in, Simon created a situation where the young man's achievements were reflected back at him and, over a short period, generated a sense of confidence that transpired into attending further education. As Simon notes, "You can get fantastic results really quickly!" The notion of "quickly" is surprisingly essential here. In Simon's words:

> Quick is vital. When I walk into a situation and I meet someone for the first time they would have had all sorts of shitty experiences and normally they meet this professional who asks them to tell their story—again—and you have to go through the process of winning trust which can be really tedious—they have been through the situation lots of times. . . . I want to walk in and say, "hello, my name's Simon and I don't give a toss what has gone on before. I'm not interested in the back story—I'm not a mental health worker or youth offing worker; I'm a musician and here to help you make music—what are you into what do you want to do?"

There is no sense here in dictating the outcomes; Simon will not tell the people he works with what to do. The relationship orientates around the client stating their interest and the Noise Solution worker facilitating the activity through a mentoring process. Quick is essential, and within 20 minutes, a music track has been created that the young person feels they own, and it has been Bluetoothed to their phone where an hour later, they can play to their mates or family and say, "I made that!"

Perceived as high quality but expensive, it has meant that providing evidence to demonstrate the effectiveness of Noise Solution's pedagogic strategies is vital. The challenge has been to find "data collection" methods that resonate with the organization's mission. Simon and his facilitators have been capturing the processes through blogs, videos and artifical intellegence.[47] This approach has been folded into the process, so the "evidence" is seamlessly woven with

[47] https://youtu.be/qydtDCcTCJA

*the music making. Simon says this does three key things: (1) Reflect the client's successes. They can directly see and hear what they have achieved. (2) They are then encouraged to write it down in blog form to consolidate their feelings. (3) The collection of data can then be used as evidence for Arts Awards.*[48] *To date, Noise Solution has gathered "evidence" of the work's effectiveness from everybody engaged in their processes. It has shared strength-based narratives that has helped build and strengthen relationships for the young people while also capturing and analysing outcomes.*

## Representing Practices

Previously, I have sung the praises of ethnographic approaches to studying community music because they enable direct access to what is happening on the ground. Through narratives of those who participate, ethnography as a strategy and participant observation as an associated data collection method can unmask the traits of community music in action. Intertextual webs of significance provide portals to know community music as active musical-doing. Beyond sound and musical genre, these explorations unearth a rich and complex connectivity between context, community, participation, and pedagogy. Examining the body of community music research reveals a host of other methodological approaches, including, for example, case study (Grodd & Lines, 2018), philosophical (Krönig, 2019), historical (Gunther, 2022), survey (Matthews et al., 2022), narrative (Rohwer, 2017), biographical (Zeserson, 2021), content analysis (Rowher, 2018), phenomenological (Lee et al., 2022), autoethnographic (Turner, 2017), and arts-based research (Gouzouasis & Bakan, 2018); practice as research (Swijghuisen Reigersberg & Lloyd, 2019); and action research (de Banffy-Hall, 2019). Maybe unsurprisingly, the nature of the practice has meant that quantitative research strategies and methods have not been common within community music research. The work of Douglas Lonie (2018) on evaluation design and implementation is interesting in how it blends quantitative and qualitative approaches, focusing on communicating impact to funders and the public at large.[49] However, as illustrated above, Simon Glenister's work presents

---

[48] http://www.artsaward.org.uk/site/?id=64

[49] Lonie's work was essential to developing the Youth Music (https://network.youthmusic.org.uk/) outcomes framework, which sought to measure impact—discussed more recently in terms of a quality framework.

an innovative mixed-method approach through a bespoke customer relationship management (CRM) system used to capture and share participant stories. Through the lens of self-determination theory (Ryan & Deci, 2017), Simon and his company, Noise Solution, a digital "data-driven organization," use the CRM system as a one-stop shop that acts as a website through which everything happens. For example, it is the referral point connecting people across the network; it captures stories as case studies simultaneously measuring participants' subjective understanding of their well-being; it is an analytical tool producing statistical significance and comparing the data against national averages; it tracks engagement and analyzes video content in terms of sentiment and linguists; it enables musicians to book sessions, report on attendance, and report any safeguarding issues; and it can anonymize and track data protection compliance.

Thought of as a "digital community of relatedness," the Noise Solution CRM brings the participant together with musicians, family, friends, care coordinators, and social workers, providing each with the information relevant to their needs. Using the National Health Service's Short Warwick-Edinburgh Mental Well-being Scale,[50] Noise Solution seeks to demonstrate changes in participant well-being and can compare their results with thousands of other users nationwide. Alongside the stories told by the participants, the statistical data helps Noise Solution make the case that the service improves well-being outcomes for the participants and is economically effective in tackling soaring health care costs related to a rise in young people's struggles regarding their mental health. Noise Solution presents community music research with a comprehensive approach to "evidencing" in terms of concepts and methodological rigor. It is visionary but also challenging as it sets out to "prove" its effectiveness, beginning its methodological journey from a positivist standpoint following a comment leveled at Simon when he was first presenting the idea: "But it's all snake oil unless you can prove it" (Glenister, 2021, n.p.). The problem with this position is that it suggests that there is only one way to achieve something, as proof suggests an absolute. A consequence of this language may also inadvertently undermine other approaches to exploring questions concerning community music. The work of Noise Solution is impressive, providing a growing program of inclusive music-making opportunities for young

---

[50] There are two versions of the Warwick-Edinburgh Mental Well-being Scale. Both scales are considered robust and valid when applied in population, community, educational, occupational, and clinical settings. See https://warwick.ac.uk/fac/sci/med/research/platform/wemwbs/about/wemwbsvsswemwbs/.

RESEARCH 145

people that contribute to their well-being while simultaneously generating an economy of employment for musicians. It appears very effective at operating within a metrics system and thus responds to the neoliberal political and economic environment that dominates so much of what we do. It is part of what Deane (2018) describes when discussing the policy and politics imbued in the instrumentalization of music.

On the other hand, the illustration at the beginning of this think piece flows from a different conceptual lens. Jo Gibson names her research approach as practice-research and is broadly part of a strategy referred to in various ways, for example, practice-led research, practice-based research, research as practice, and/or arts-based practice. All are employed to make two arguments regarding practice, which often overlap and are interlinked: (1) creative work is a form of research that generates detectable research outputs, and (2) specialized research insights can be generalized and written up as research (Smith & Dean, 2009). The first emphasizes the creative artwork itself, and the second highlights the insights, conceptualizations, and theorizations that can arise through a profound reflection on the creative process. By using these terms, Smith and Dean (2009) refer to the work of art as a form of research and the creation of the work as generating research insights that can be documented and theorized. Practice-research points toward a way of knowing with a trajectory rooted in a history of qualitative research (Denzin & Lincoln, 2018). Simon is clear that the importance of his work lies in the relationships it builds, and Jo is equally emphatic, noting in a personal communication that "community music is a relational practice." For Jo and practice-researchers like her, the epistemological considerations that practice-research foregrounds enable a more profound understanding. In a personal communication, she states, "The work is often understood and engaged with via terms that are not its own. It is in that sense that community music is Othered. *How can we better understand community music on its own terms?* That's the question I think community music practice research can speak to."

With foresight from Elliot Eisner (1981), who illustrated differences in scientific and artistic approaches to qualitative research, practice-research emerges through what Norman Denzin and Yvonne Lincoln (2005) might describe as the fourth moment of qualitative research or the "crisis of representation" (pp. 18–19).[51] Accordingly, this moment occurred in the

---

[51] Denzin and Lincoln (2018) expand and discuss their historical timeline in the fifth edition of their book.

## 146 THINKING COMMUNITY MUSIC

mid-1980s and has a propensity with the reflexive turn of anthropologists James Clifford (1988) and Victor Turner (1988), among others. As a movement toward a fifth moment or the "postmodern period of experimental ethnographic writing" (Denzin & Lincoln, 2005, p. 20), the crisis of representation also included concerns over legitimation and praxis (Ellis & Bochner, 1996). Situated within a postmodern framework, practice-research is one of a group of research approaches that offers a radical challenge to the epistemological foundations of thinking promoted by the Enlightenment and can therefore be closely linked to the work of Vattimo discussed above.

As a "product" of postmodernity, practice-research offers direct challenges to assumptions found in modernity, for example, the universality of reason, the premise that external reality can be detected through scientific modes of investigation and that rationality allows humans to agree on what is "real," "right," "just," and "inhumane."[52] Consequently, practice-research can destabilize our multidisciplinary reliance on objective, detached, and neutral research inquiry. It can call into dispute our facts about the social world and the disinterested language of representation while stressing that there is contingency, temporality, and situational logic for any definition of the world out there. As theater practitioner Baz Kershaw (2009) suggests, "Placing creativity at the heart of research implied a paradigm shift, through which established ontologies and epistemologies of research in arts-related disciplines, potentially, could be radically undone" (p. 105).[53] Using the American Education Research Association's (AERA) "Standards for Reporting on Humanities-Oriented Research,"[54] Denzin (2009) distinguishes between two strands of what he describes as arts-based research: first, the humanistic or traditional as presented in the AERA report, and second, the work done by activists through the lens of critical pedagogy. Susan Finley's (2005; 2018) work is rooted firmly in the latter, and it is here that community music and practice as research share a common heritage: the activist art making of the late 1960s and 1970s. Finley (2005) suggests that researchers should seek to "construct action-oriented processes for inquiry that are useful within

---

[52] Many books discuss postmodernism. These are a few that I have found helpful (Docherty, 1993; Butler, 2002; Jameson, 1991; Lyotard, 1984).

[53] Arts-based research is, therefore, to be understood as a methodological approach rather than a type of knowledge and can be defined in the following way: "The systematic use of the artistic process, the actual making of artistic expressions in all of the different forms of the arts, as a primary way of understanding and examining experience by both researchers and the people that they involve in their studies" (McNiff, 2008, p. 29).

[54] See American Education Research Association (2009).

the local community where the research originates" (p. 682). This marks a clear distinction between the arts as a data collection mechanism and the arts as research. Practice-research is a research approach whereby practice becomes the primary method of inquiry, the theory is embedded within the practice, and therefore, creative practice can constitute knowing (Kershaw, 2009; Nelson, 2013). As Robin Nelson (2013) states, "We 'do' knowledge, we don't just think it" (p. 66). Gibson (2020) furthers this and provides a clear rationale for the relationship between practice-research and community music, asserting that the community musician's knowing is in their doing (pp. 42–64). Following Nelson's "know how—know what—know that," Gibson moves toward cocreative music making as a research method.

Community music emerged from the counterculture prevalent throughout the Western industrialized nations during the later 1960s and early 1970s with direct links to the endeavors of those working in community arts and community cultural development (see "Arrival": 1984). New activist cultural practice, as described by contemporary art curator Nina Felshin (1995), has strong ties to this tradition and contains innovative use of public space to address sociopolitical and cultural significance issues. Characteristics include community participation as a means of empowerment and social change, emphasis on process rather than object or product oriented, temporal interventions, and an emphasis on collaboration. It is through a commitment to these types of attributes that Finley (2003) articulates the dispositions of what she calls arts-based research, describing them as (1) relational to the community—to dialogical, nurturing, caring, and democratic relationships between researchers and participants who share their commitments to the understanding of social life; (2) to action within the community, engaging with research that is local, useable, and responsive to cultural and political issues and that takes a stand against social injustice, and (3) to visionary critical discourses—to research efforts that examine how things are but also how things could be otherwise (p. 293). As an approach that celebrates the art-making process, practice-research can put the method of inquiry back into the hands of the community musician. This would enable the *scholar-self* and the *community musician-self* to merge, blurring the distinction between traditionally understood "professional" and "academic" practices. As Australian academic and artist Barbara Bolt asserts, "Theorizing out of practice is . . . a very different way of thinking than applying theory to practice" (Smith & Dean, 2009, p. 7). Through such assertions, one can recognize a clarification between what constitutes "just" practice and "practice-research." This

# 148 THINKING COMMUNITY MUSIC

difference lies within notions of "praxial knowledge," distinguished through "the particular form of knowledge that arises from our handling of materials and processes" (Bolt, 2006, p. 6). Derived from Heidegger's (2002) argument that we do not come to "know" the world theoretically through contemplative knowledge in the first instance but rather through an understanding of our experience of "handling" it, Bolt argues that there can arise out of creative practice a particular sort of knowing through handling materials in practice. Sociologist and novelist Patricia Leavy (2009) adds to this, commenting that practice-research may "allow research questions to be posed in new ways, entirely new questions to be asked, and new non-academic audiences to be reached" (p. 12).

Those working as researchers in the field of community music might ponder Leavy's comments beyond the specific methodology referred to and think of research as striving to create critical awareness and consciousness, enabling subjugated voices to be heard through the promotion of dialogue, evoking rather than denoting meaning, and through inductive research design seeking to present multiple meanings and interpretations. To quote Gibson at length:

> To "re-search," to search anew, could suggest fresh inquiry, breaking from the patterns of professional practitioner reflective practice, which may be entrenched in established approaches underpinned by specified output aims—be that funder evaluation, high profile performance or the freelancer's repeat booking. Moreover, research through creative practice, or rather re-search through the musical doing of community musician(s) and participant(s), focuses the lens of inquiry to active musical doing as it is undertaken in contemporary practice. This, therefore, has the potential to reduce any haze (for example, entrenchment in established approaches or output aims) that may cloud professional practitioner reflective practice by zooming in on music-making processes as they are enacted in current practice rather than how they are discussed. (Gibson, 2020, pp. 45–46)

From this position, research directed through a practice-research strategy offers an advantageous framework for the community music scholar as it taps into the knowledge-producing potential of the active doings of community music. As community musician Dave Camlin (2023) states, "Making practice the focus of the research ensures that the tacit knowledge that is generated through innovative and creative practices is not lost" (p. 33).

## Flight Lines

In 2020, the International Centre for Community Music[55] hosted a symposium titled Critique Not Criticism: Why We Ask the Questions We Ask. Kathleen Turner, a community musician, songwriter, and storyteller, was the keynote speaker and performed her response. Deeply autoethnographic, Kathleen sings her "data" and, in so doing, questions her assumptions about the value of music making and her motivations for doing the work. Wider implications for community music research might be that thoughtful, critical questions can lead to a richer understanding when asked with care, with compassion, and without judgment. Turner (2020) poses, "As a result of critical questions, I now look for evidence of fearlessness, kindness, consideration, commitment, enthusiasm and joy. I seek out agency, reflexivity, solidarity, shared spaces and experiences, empathy, imagination, vulnerability and gratitude" (p. 13). Creating what Lee Willingham and I termed a "culture of inquiry," community music research must involve diverse viewpoints and a multitude of perspectives (Higgins & Willingham, 2017, pp. 129–144). An excellent example of this flows from those working with Indigenous knowledges in Australia (Bartleet, 2021, 2023; Sunderland et al., 2021; Swijghuisen Reigersberg & Lloyd, 2019), Aotearoa New Zealand (Rakena, 2018), and Canada (Laurila, 2021). Projects like these bring Indigenous traditions and knowledge systems to the fore, rooting research in specific Indigenous methods emerging from language, culture, and worldview. In this sense, the work presents both a system of knowledge creation and a response to colonial practices (Evans et al., 2014).[56]

In resonance with concerns of our age, decolonization, and ecology, for example, the research landscape has changed dramatically. It is reflected in the types of "evidence" demanded by funding councils such as the United Kingdom's Research Excellence Framework (REF), a "system for assessing the quality of research in U.K. higher education Institutions" through what is described as a process of "expert review."[57] Governmental emphasis has changed from a domination of disciplinary-specific subject areas to a significant increase in multidisciplinary, interdisciplinary, and now transdisciplinary approaches to knowledge creation (Leavy, 2014, p. 725).

---

[55] https://www.yorksj.ac.uk/research/international-centre-for-community-music/

[56] For further discussions, see the work within critical development studies, for example, Stewart-Harawira (2022).

[57] https://www.ref.ac.uk/about-the-ref/

The notion of transdisciplinary is well within the purview of community music research as the practice has collaboration and cocreation as one of its mantras. Of course, these orientations are responses to themes of our times; issues of social justice such as LGBTQ+ rights, women's rights, the Black Lives Matter movement, state oppression, and displaced peoples through war and natural disasters all reveal the inequalities in our society (see Think Piece 4). Fueled by public interest to tackle some of these problems, Leavy (2014) points to the widespread move toward public scholarship, highlighting the need for research to be more widely accessible to larger audiences, noting that "the effects of the social justice movements shed light on the importance of inclusion within knowledge building and dissemination" (p. 727).[58] How might community music researchers effectively work in these spaces? Where are the examples of those already doing this, what can we learn from them, and how might we increase its visibility?[59]

As community music scholarship moves forward and with it an increasing range of research strategies and data collection approaches and methods, consideration must be given to how the field positions itself to the challenge and development of knowledge production, critique, review, and dissemination in an environment where there is a growing ethical responsibility to do so. Publishing academic writings in established and "traditional" venues can be influential acts that enable community music research to sit alongside, and thus interact with, other fields. Albeit in a limited context, this will raise the visibility of the work, opening it up to new ideas and reminding community music researchers that there is a lot to learn in areas such as theory building and methodological approaches. Working collaboratively within the academy alongside nonacademic partnerships becomes vital in a world where public scholarship carries significant weight. Recent experiences have illuminated the need for robust dialogue with funders and nonacademic partners regarding the difference between research and advocacy, critique, evaluation, and criticism.[60] Such things may make for challenging conversations but might prevent compromising the findings through interference and censorship.[61] Rather than a direct challenge, community music researchers

---

[58] Within their revised timeline, Denzin and Lincoln (2018) note "an uncertain, utopian future, where critical inquiry finds its voice in the public arena (2016–)" (p. 9).

[59] See Bartleet (2023) for a presentation of a conceptual framework that works toward a way to understand and articulate social impact. These ideas edge us toward some responses to the questions posed within the above text.

[60] The Centre for Cultural Value is a good starting point to explore discussions regarding the relationship between these domains: https://www.culturalvalue.org.uk.

[61] For a discussion on contemporary challenges with research, see Mantie (2022d).

might see this as an opportunity to flex our proverbial welcoming muscles and think hospitably within the character of weak thought. With historical roots in social activism, I hope the *scholar-self* and the *community musician-self* can organize around a power of the powerless and sustain sensitivity for the exceptional and singular, for the different and left out.

# 8

# Becoming

### Charlie Keil

*Despite being a professor in American studies at SUNY-Buffalo for most of his academic life, Charles (Charlie) Keil's career was dominated by an interest in music and music education.* [1] *His scholarly contributions took many forms, such as ethnographic fieldwork that resulted in wide-ranging books* (Urban Blues, Tiv Song: The Sociology of Art in a Classless Society, Polka Happiness, My Music, Bright Balkan Morning: Romani Lives and the Power of Music in Greek Macedonia, Music Grooves), *many essays and papers on music and music education, and efforts in promoting music education in the Buffalo area through his organization, MUSE (Musicians United for Superior Education).*[2] *When Roger Mantie and myself reviewed the Keil Collection at the Boston University archive center, it became clear that Keil's commitments to social causes were not just empty words for show. Before social justice issues became fashionable, Keil was a devoted pacifist, environmentalist, equal rights crusader, Green Party mobilizer, and defender of those without advantage. Roger and I suspected that, along with musical motivations, Keil's social commitments contributed to his interest in studying the Tiv of Nigeria during the tumultuous period of civil unrest in the 1960s. Tiv Song (Keil, 1979), the book based on his fieldwork of the period, is a tour de force of scholarship but also reveals insights into experiences that may have contributed to his worldview. In the introduction, for example, Keil describes leaving Nigeria prematurely due to the bloodshed, he and his wife, Angeliki, "counting the disemboweled and bloated corpses along the roadside, crying from the smell and from the shame." The experience, he writes, "was numbing and demoralizing" (Keil, 1979, p. 3).*

*Viewed in this light, Keil's convictions are certainly understandable. He has never been an armchair activist; he walks the talk. While some may fault him for what might be considered unrealistic idealism, Charlie has religiously*

---

[1] Adapted from a paper written in 2015. See Mantie and Higgins (2015).
[2] https://www.youtube.com/watch?v=WZp--jLIRBQ

*Thinking Community Music*. Lee Higgins, Oxford University Press. © Oxford University Press 2024.
DOI: 10.1093/9780190247027.003.0009

BECOMING 153

*pursued a utopian vision of American society, emulating what he described as the world's classless societies: "With Colin Turnbull's version of the Mbuti or with Bob Dentan's version of the Semai or with anybody who's gone out there and celebrated the harmless people, the forest people, the peaceful people—you could say the romanticization of classless society that anthropologists at their best have done—is my deep reference point for what could happen in Lakeville, Salisbury, Canaan, Connecticut, my nearby environs."[3] Asked about what he would do to foster such a vision, he replied:*

> *I really want to restore that sense of a bopi [i.e., playground] where kids are autonomous and unsupervised and can mimic their elders in drumming and singing and dancing and not be interfered with. That, to me, is a little Eden that classless societies help to create for their children and that we don't have. It's just disappeared. We don't have a clue to how that could work anymore. Keeping that lone flame alive is, to me, crucial.*

*In the 1980s, Keil described his grassroots publishing company, 12/8 Path Publishers, as not just nonprofit but "anti-profit and devoted to the fusion of matter-energy-spirit in directions of diversity and equality," further evidence of Keil's complete fidelity to his social values. Unsurprisingly, his late 1980s and early 1990s newsletters, such as* Echology *and the* Muse Letter, *were always printed on "Minimum Impact 100% recycled paper."[4] In his personal life, Keil has refused to pay federal taxes since 2008 based on his reading of the Constitution. His objection to some of the government's priorities has, he says, "made me want to take every bit of income that I have and put it into 501c3s,[5] charitable organizations, anything that I can find that is trying to affirm the principles of children's liberation, family liberation."*

*Roger and I were reminded during our interview with him of the genuineness of his resolve to foster forms of harmonious living from childhood through adulthood, stemming from his deep-seated resolve that society needed to be saved from its imminent demise.*

---

[3] See, for example, Dentan (1968). Colin Turnbull (1961) published numerous works on the Mbuti Pygmies of Zaire. Keil suggests that John Blacking highly regarded both authors. Keil takes issue with those who claim that classless societies are a myth and submits that examples of nonviolent, "gentle" peoples should serve as models for how to live, not as examples of naïve primitivism. Such examples, for Keil, demonstrate that it is possible to educate young people differently.

[4] These type of declarations are to be found printed on the inside cover of every issue of Echology and the Muse Letter.

[5] A 501(c)3 organization is a U.S. corporation, trust, incorporated association, or other type of organization exempt from federal income tax.

154 THINKING COMMUNITY MUSIC

*All the bad stuff is moving with integrated momentum in the wrong direction. And here we sit, are we going to go for sainthood or not? Are we going to try to be as helpful as possible to little kids as they get born, or are we just going to let it slide? So, to me, it's a crusade or a religious mission to get the word out. Pass the word with a capital W. Can we get the word out in time to save humanity? Save the planet? Roll back the capitalist nastiness that seems to be guiding policy and guiding people toward more altruism, more war, more nationalism? We're the antidote to that. We're the cure for that. That's my hope, and that's been a pretty constant thing in my life since I was a teenager and got into conscience objection to war.*

Keil's values help partly explain his approach to music learning and teaching, which he has described not in terms of music education but as "applied sociomusicology." Both Echology and the Muse Letter contain editorial commentary revealing the concerns that have animated his work: How can we get more participatory practices into our lives and those around us? What problems are we solving (or stumbling over) in making live, life-affirming music? What problems are we solving in assisting children toward fully expressive lives? How can we further empower all people musically?

What becomes clear in reading Keil's books and essays is his overriding concern with how "working class" music and dance—musics "of the people"—help create a sense of community and belonging. His studies of Tiv song, urban blues, and polka share this probing interest in wanting to "get to the core" of how and why everyday people engage with music.[6] As he explained, Keil felt his 1984 essay, "Paideia con Salsa," best summarizes his beliefs about how music must reclaim its connection with dance. In brief, Keil posits that coupling the ancient, pre-Platonic conception of paideia with New York Afro-Cuban dance music is the best way of overcoming the loss of rhythm and harmony in our lives and of reviving classical conception of education as music and movement (embodied in the "3 Ms" of music, motion, and morality).[7] As he stated in our interview:

---

[6] One inconsistency in his thought, in our reading at least, lies at the intersection of vernacular music making and popular culture. Keil's egalitarian commitments sometimes seem to butt up against the commercial interests of popular music, which he views as a product of capitalist society.

[7] Paideia was a reference to the practical and academic education of the aristocratic members of ancient Greek society. As a concept, *paideia* points toward the shaping of the Greek character, a socialization of individuals that embraced intellectual, moral, and physical refinements; this included music and movement. See Jaeger (1986). In his essay, Keil acknowledges the problematic aspects of slavery and patriarchy but suggests that *paideia* could still serve as an ideal.

*Physical education and musical education was all of education for those ancient Greek kids that gave us Socrates and Plato and Aristotle and all the famous names in sculpture and in tragedy and so on and so forth. They were all brought up on sports competition, recitation of poetry, music lessons on the kithara and the aulos.[8] All that stuff was crucial for that little city of Athens. Thirty thousand people produced an awful lot of geniuses per capita with nothing but sports and music education!*

*In reading Keil's books and essays, what is unmistakable is not just his commitment to music and dance, peace and harmony, but the rigorous grounding in all his work. Keil truly embodies the ideal of the musician-teacher-scholar.[9] Keil's high personal ethical standards may be challenging for some of us to emulate (though he might counter that we just are not trying hard enough). However, his scholarly contributions and continued work as a practitioner deserve serious reflection from those working in community music and music education more generally. In the face of viral neoliberal market rationality that continues to threaten so many facets of our lives, community musicians continue to work toward creating a more musical society. Keil's idealistic conception of music, dance, and education may not provide a cure. However, it might help to alleviate some of the symptoms, helping us to live happier, healthier lives along the way.*

How *might* community music become? This question is, I hope, an encouragement for those involved in community music practice to pause ⌢ for a moment and reflect upon its current status, both within its terms of reference and also within the broader parameters of music making, teaching, and learning. The question is open and exploratory, containing a "might" rather than an "ought" or a "should," and thus points toward opportunities to explore its challenge either as an individual practitioner or collaboratively as a group, as an ensemble, at a conference, at a symposium, or as part of an academic course. It is a chance to wonder or imagine community music's future

---

[8] The kithara was a two-stringed lyre. The aulos, or double aulos, was a double reed instrument. As Keil joked with us, "Plato disliked the aulos; too Dionysian, especially in the Phrygian mode, and hated the John Coltrane of the day, Timotheus of Miletus, for his 'shrill squealings in the uppermost tetrachord'" (Keil, personal communication).

[9] A more detailed description of Keil's ideas about music and music learning and teaching can be found in his many books and published articles. Another excellent resource for those interested in learning more about Keil's work, especially his ideas about "groovology," is the website https://borntogroove.com/.

## 156   THINKING COMMUNITY MUSIC

regarding impact, policy, pedagogy, musicking, and research. In part, it is an extension of questions regarding definition. Over many years, the "what is" question has been problematized and challenged. These discussions have culminated in a general proposition suggesting that community music activities are too diverse, complex, multifaceted, and contextual to be captured in one universal statement of meaning. The act of defining "community music" can therefore be understood as a violation of its "project," a practice often responding to context, whether environmentally, geographically, or demographically (see "Arrival": A Field of Practice). Questions of definition, and consequently identity, are often now oriented around what community music *does* rather than what it is.[10]

So why ask how *might* community music become, and why ask it now? It is time to expand the collective thinking beyond notions of what community music is and what it does to create opportunities for discussion surrounding its future trajectory. The question is timely because, as a practice, community music has grown significantly in its practical and theoretical appeal. In 2018, the introduction to *The Oxford Handbook of Community Music* suggested that the "emerging voices, agendas, and contexts" pertinent to the book's 57 authors were an indication that the field is "continuing to expand, diversify, and mature" (Bartleet & Higgins, 2018b, p. 2). Deemed as a field that had "come of age," this assumption acknowledged the convergence of decades of practical activity with the growth in research and scholarship. Since the book's publication, the field has remained on a trajectory of growth, evidenced by articles, chapters, PhD theses, and books in English but, importantly, other languages as well, for example, German (Hill & Banffy-Hall, 2017; Richter, 2020), Italian (Coppi, 2017, 2020; van der Sandt, 2019), and translations of *Community Music: In Theory and in Practice* into Korean[11] and Chinese.[12] There has also been continued interest in supporting courses within institutes of higher education, as discussed in the "Arrival" chapter.

---

[10] In 1995, the board of the national development organization for the United Kingdom, Sound Sense, produced a short document that asked not what community music *is* but instead what community music *does* (Macdonald, 1995). The question of what community music does was much more productive than questions associated with what community music is. This orientation was influential beyond the United Kingdom. Plenty of examples illustrate international community music practice and a growing evidence base underpinning claims of what it does (See the *International Journal of Community Music*).

[11] Published by Hakjisa Publisher in 2019.

[12] Published as part of the New Horizons in Higher Musical Education Translated Series by Shanghai Music Publishing House in 2020 (http://product.dangdang.com/28971164.html).

BECOMING 157

At its most potent, the practice has provided a critical response to issues such as music inclusivity (Camlin, 2015; Gunther, 2022; Henley & Higgins, 2020b; Yerichuk, 2015; Yerichuk & Krar, 2019), diversity (Bird, 2017; Daria, 2018), cultural democracy (Broeske, 2017; Gibson, 2020b), and nonformal music learning (Bonshur, 2016; Higgins, 2016; Veblen, 2012; West & Cremata, 2016). It has also played an important role in offering illustrations of practice and conceptual interrogation within the areas of social justice (de Quadros, 2018; Higgins, 2015; Howell et al., 2019; Silverman, 2012; Sunderland et al., 2016), popular music pedagogies (Powell, 2022), life-long musical learning (Coffman, 2018; Lee et al., 2016; Myers, 2018; Pitts et al., 2015), music and leisure (Mantie, 2018, 2022b), artistic citizenship (Silverman & Elliott, 2018), trauma-informed practice (Birch, 2022), music and well-being (Hallam et al., 2014; Lee et al., 2018; Matherne, 2022), and music in prisons (Cohen, 2012; Dickie-Johnson & Meek, 2022; Ze'evi et al., 2022). Offering illustrations of practice and conceptual interrogations, the work in these areas has contributed to a broader understanding of music and its role in society. Notably, there have been fruitful intersections between music therapy, applied ethnomusicology, and music education.

Considering all this, rather than an emergent field, might community music be better described as having arrived? If this is so, what does it mean to have arrived? Problematizing the notion of "arrival" provides an opportunity for those working in the field to consider the destination or, better put, the various journeys and pathways being either followed or plowed. It also allows for reconsidering notions of the field's "identity." As the confidence in work grows, will the field's identity be solidified? It might be reasonable to presume this will be the case. What, then, are the pros and cons of a heightened sense of identity? By bringing this question forward, my purpose is to start a conversation. I do not intend to offer precise answers or solutions but rather get the "party" started by providing a framework and some creative thinking strategies. To do this, I intend to draw from the oeuvre of French philosopher Gilles Deleuze and his collaborator psychoanalyst Felix Guattari. By doing so, I aim to create a continuity to previous thought and that of others working in music and music education (Bogue, 2003; Buchanan & Swiboda, 2004; Gould, 2007b; 2011; Hess, 2018; Hulse & Nesbitt, 2016; Jorgensen & Yob, 2013; Leppänen, 2011; Lines, 2013; Richerme, 2019; Szekely, 2012).[13]

---

[13] Richerme (2020) observes that only some music education scholars "have undertaken sustained engagement with Deleuze and Guattari's work" (p. 11).

# 158 THINKING COMMUNITY MUSIC

This think piece is organized in the following way: first, a brief context of why Deleuze and Guattari's ideas are helpful for a task that seeks to think about what community music might look like in the future (see "Arrival": Theoretical Framework for further context); second, an outline of four domains of thought through which to consider the guiding question. These four parts, difference, becoming, machine, and rhizome, are laced with comments and questions referring to the opening illustration and community music more generally. It is worth reiterating that the illustrations of practice are to be seen as embodiments of the ideals and ideas to be discussed; I finish with a reflection on why the question is important and offer a further four questions for discussion.

## Context

Thinking in Deleuzian terms can provide radical freedom, offering possibilities of how to change the world in ways that do not always seem possible—as music educator Lauren Kapalka Richerme (2020) puts it, a commitment to "an unceasing welcoming of diverging potentialities, including those that may initially seem unfeasible" (p. 96). Deleuze's work draws upon a wide gamut of disciplines. It has many references to science, biology, geology, and evolution and has been used extensively in areas such as film and media studies, art, ecology, anthropology, archaeology, and literature, among other things.[14] The application of Deleuze's concepts across a wide variety of fields is a testament to their agility and, as a process of thinking, has the potential to push current thought and understanding in new and unforeseeable directions.[15] Below, I offer three reasons Deleuze and Guattari's ideas help respond to questions associated with community music's possible future:

1. In previous work, I have considered community music as an act of hospitality, friendship, intervention, facilitation, event, boundary walking, safe space, nonformal music learning, and improvisation. These investigations have predominantly engaged with ideas that fall under

---

[14] Edinburgh University Press has published a series of books that explore Deleuze in relation to different fields, including music (see Buchanan & Swiboda, 2004). See also the journal *Deleuze and Guattari Studies* (https://www.euppublishing.com/loi/dlgs).
[15] Deleuze and Guattari's work has its critiques. See the concluding chapter in Marks (1998).

the purview of poststructuralism and have a lineage that resonates with Deleuze and Guattari. Their ideas offer a way of thinking about community music that is already somewhat in sync with my own (see also "Arrival": Theoretical Lens).

2. Deleuze and Guattari challenge the possibility that there are foundational knowledges. The revolutionary aspect of their work resonates with a history of community music as social activism.

3. For Deleuze and Guattari, concepts are there to move us beyond our current experiences toward the thinking of new possibilities. Concepts are understood as creative or active acts "rather than representative, descriptive, or simplifying" (Parr, 2005, p. 51).[16] Community music seeks to provide springboards for creative expression, and Deleuze and Guattari's notion of concepts as invention provides, for me at least, tangible links between community music and theoretical interrogation.

In the following section, I will introduce a number of concepts that provide the conceptual apparatus to respond to this think piece's guiding question; I have thematized them as difference, becoming, machine, and rhizome. Although I have created and ordered these sections, please be mindful that Deleuze and Guattari's philosophy emphasizes connections, so their ideas and concepts continually collide.

## Difference

Deleuze can be understood as a philosopher of *difference* and *becoming*. His thought is a rigorous attempt to think of process and metamorphosis not as a transition or transformation from one substance to another but rather as an articulation of experiential reality as always in a perpetual state of continual change. The two terms, difference and becoming, resist what Deleuze sees as the dominance of "identity" and "being" within Western philosophy. Why? Because the notions of identity and being are understood as giving precedence to an ontology[17] of what there *is*. Deleuze is challenging two

---

[16] Deleuze and Guattari (1994) isolate three central features of concepts: relatedness to other concepts, internal consistency, and condensation of its internal components (pp. 19–21).

[17] Ontology is a branch of philosophy that deals with questions relating to existence, being, becoming, and reality. In the analytic tradition, ontology is orientated around questions of what there is. In continental philosophy, ontology has its focus on the study of Being.

## 160 THINKING COMMUNITY MUSIC

assumptions often used to reject an ontological approach: (1) *Ontology involves discovery rather than creation*. Deleuze suggests that it is possible to create an ontology that presents limitless visions of how we might see the world rather than one dictated by its limits. (2) *Ontology involves an emphasis on identity rather than difference*. Deleuze suggests that overthrowing discovery as an ontological prerequisite gives way to an ontology that must abandon the search for essences and conceptual stability and begin with difference.

For Deleuze, Western philosophical thought from Plato onward attempts to articulate stable categories of thought housed within the notions of identity and being looking to capture understandings of the world in terms of unity, resemblance, and repetition.[18] As an emphasis toward that which is stable and eternal, these ideas are in tension with Deleuze's thinking that maintains that the world might be better understood in terms of movement and flux. Deleuze does not necessarily see anything wrong with perspectives that seek stability; after all, humans need to navigate and predict things, and these approaches to understanding human life have been very important and continue to be valuable. The problem for Deleuze is that if this is our only perspective, the way we see and engage with the world is severely limited. If we only focus on things that are "essential," we will always have a blind spot for potentialities; we will miss both how things change and the possibility of an evolution toward the new. Deleuze wants to focus on the spaces between things, the difference that creates the possibilities of newness. It is not that the other perspectives should be dismissed but that they limit our horizons of possibilities. Deleuze's philosophy involves "thinking outside of representation" and, by focusing on difference and becoming, enables an exploration of how things change over time. From a Deleuzian perspective, thinking can be considered an "antidote" to the Western tradition that has given precedence and focus to "identity" and "being" (Parr, 2005, p. 21).[19] Identity and being are an ontology of what there *is* rather than Deleuze's ontology of *difference* that seeks to describe "difference in itself" rather than

---

[18] For example, Plato's forms, which seek to define essences surrounding the good, the just, and the beautiful; Aristotle's metaphysics, which is described as the discipline that addresses the problems of the essential attributes of things; Kant's rational judgments in the *Critiques of Pure Reason*; and Hegel's *The Phenomenology of the Spirit*, where he argued that the becoming and difference of life and history could be understood as one movement of spirit (absolutes).

[19] Discussions surrounding what is now framed as "being" and "becoming" have a long history going back to the pre-Socratic philosophers. Parmenides of Elea (early to mid-5th century BCE) saw change as an illusion, conveying "opinions of mortals," while Heraclitus of Ephesus's (c. 540–c. 480 BCE) thesis states that "everything is in flux," like the flowing of a river.

"difference from the same." As Deleuze (1968/2004) states, "Difference is behind everything, but behind difference there is nothing" (p. 57).

Difference from the same, our usual ways of encountering the idea, refers to a variation between two states, and this implies "managing" difference by picking out and grouping qualities or things through similarity. The problem is not only that the notion of difference is understood as a function of the concept of identity, and thus not "in itself," but that this model is based on recalling essences and consequently may exclude other types of differences, for example, those that are accidental, that are contingent, or that "fall outside of the general purview of the concept or limits of its division" (Stivale, 2005, p. 44). In this sense, difference names the process of change but is always inclusive of the product (Boundas, 2006). As two intertwining flows,[20] referred to as the virtual[21] and the actual,[22] Deleuze argues for an existence that is vibrant and affirming.[23]

Deleuze sees the world as "swarms of differences" that come together to create forms of identities rather than a world composed of fixed identities that form and re-form themselves (May, 2005, p. 114). He wants us to seek connections away from stable identities, "to reach, not the point where one no longer says I, but the point where it is no longer of any importance whether one says I" (Deleuze & Guattari, 1988, p. 3). From a Deleuzian perspective, these "swarms" are not outside the world but *of* the world operating on a plane of immanence,[24] a field of becoming, a place where possible events are brought together where new connections between them

---

[20] The concept of flow is sometimes translated as flux to underline that the world is always in motion (Young et al., 2013, p. 125). Flows form rhizomatic networks and become part of identities. Following Deleuze and Guattari, flow is a term frequently used in anthropological discussions of globalization. See Rockefeller (2011).

[21] Following Bergson's use of the word to describe the past distinct from the presence of duration and succession, Deleuze's "virtual" signals a past that can never be fully present but is, nevertheless, capable of bringing about actualization. Concepts, then, are ways "of articulating the hidden virtual reality out of which the actually experienced reality emerges" (May, 2005, p. 19). In Deleuzian thought, the virtue precedes possibilities—it creates the condition for it. The virtue is the surplus of the present moment—of any fixed incident and grounded in the spaces of differences.

[22] Colebrook describes Deleuze's use of the term *actual* as an unfolding from potentiality (Parr, 2005, p. 10). Intertwined, the actual can only be fully understood if we have an instinct for the virtual. In this way, real-life experiences cannot be presupposed by the actual. To understand community music now, for example, we must go beyond its current context and engage with the conditions that gave it potentiality.

[23] Deleuze draws from Nietzsche's thought that emphasizes human will, the taking of action to affirm life as an ongoing creative act, to exert a will to power.

[24] "It is the plane that secures conceptual linkages with ever increasing connection, and it is the concepts that secure the populating of the plane on an always renewed and variable curve" (Deleuze & Guattari, 1994, p.37). See Expression in Think Piece 6.

162 THINKING COMMUNITY MUSIC

are continually made and "continually dissolved"[25] (Parr, 2005, p. 205). For Deleuze, then, it is the spaces between things that give rise to the possibility of newness. If we just focus on the essence of things, what is essential to the thing itself, then we might be hard pressed to account for how things change. As a thought experiment, how might the "essences" of school music education be described? A mixture of a curriculum, a qualified teacher, a building, a standardized test, listening to great "works," history, and systematic lessons on melody, harmony, and rhythm? If, for example, we just focused on these things, it might be hard for us to think about why nonformal approaches to music making can play a significant role within this environment (see Think Piece 3). Suppose we reflected on changes outside "our" description of the essences of school music education, for example, developments in technology and music media platforms; independent learning through YouTube; increasing sales of instruments such as guitars, drums, and keyboards; changes in how young people communicate; and contemporary political and ethical values. In that case, we might see how these contextual interactions lead us toward new possibilities. Thinking of school music education as a stable identity rather than in movement or flux reduces the potential of conceiving how things could be different. In this instance, an approach to school music teaching and learning responds to the multiple ways young people currently engage in music and contemporary ways of living. Difference is not a thing, therefore—it is a process continually unfolding. It is that which makes possible the ordinary ways we have of representing the world.[26]

Leaving the concept of community music open to individual interpretation has been a strategy used throughout the field's history. As mentioned above, a general proposition suggests that community music activities are too diverse, complex, multifaceted, and contextual to be captured in one universal statement of meaning. Definitions, however, do exist. I used the following to orientate my work: "an active intervention between a music

---

[25] A plane of immanence, sometimes referred to as a plane of consistency, serves as a field for concepts. It is a field of becoming a surface upon which all events occur. Employing the term *immanence* shows Deleuze's commitment to "transcendental empiricism," empiricism that does not have any foundations outside of experience and "cannot be grounded on man, the subject, culture of language" (Colebrook, 2002, p. 89). Deleuze built upon his exploration of Baruch Spinoza (1632–1677) and Scottish philosopher David Hume (1711–1776).

[26] Deleuze draws many ideas from art, film, music, and literature. Artistic mediums offer different ways of relating to the world, having the capacity to evoke and question through nonrepresentative means. See (O'Sullivan, 2007).

BECOMING    163

leader or facilitator and participants" (see Think Piece 1). Following the International Society for Music Education's Commission for Community Music Activity meeting in Toronto in 2000, community musicians started articulating its distinctive traits to help capture the significant principles that constitute the practice.[27] It was understood that these vary from musician to musician and offer "ideals" rather than guarantees but help explain what community music purports to do. We might rethink community music as a field of difference by utilizing Deleuzian thinking strategies. The argument goes like this:

> Difference is presented as a way to resist claiming an identity that rests on stable categories such as essences, unity, and resemblance. Difference speaks to "that which eludes capture" (May, 2005, p. 82) and challenges an ontology of what *is*. The "is" becomes problematic within a Deleuzian framework, for in a world of becoming, what something "is" is always open to what it is yet to be. As a *minority*[28] field, community music draws from its past and is productive in the present to create a new future. Rather than replicating itself as a model to repeat or advocating for methodological compliance in pedagogy, for example, community music might be better understood as a practice that repeats the power of difference. In this way, community music as a practice would be understood to always be in flux, constantly adapting to change, and always seeking new potentialities. From this perspective, community music would not represent anything abso- lutely identifiable but instead seek to palpate and gesture toward what we cannot grasp; "difference is the overflowing character of things themselves, their inability to be wrestled into categories of representation" (May, 2005, p. 82).

How many community musicians use games, exercises, or approaches that they "know" are replicable because they have been using them for years? How many community musicians utilize these across multiple contexts, employing tried-and-tested strategies known to bring about the desired outcomes (see Think Piece 3)? Although many understandable

---

[27] See also (Veblen, 2008; Veblen & Olsson, 2002, p. 731).
[28] For Deleuze, minority, or minoritarian, is not defined by numbers but rather by its capacity to become. In this way, majority is linked to state power and domination. Deleuze uses these ideas concerning cinema, music, and particular literature. See Parr (2005, pp. 164–170), Colebrook (2002, pp. 103–123), and Stivale (2005, pp. 110–120).

reasons exist for working this way, should this be challenged? Should community music seek to articulate stable categories to capture how it does what it does? There are very good reasons for stable and repeatable approaches to engaging people in active music making, but what are the dangers of unthinkingly doing this? Might it limit growth and development and contradict a history that advocated social activism through creative endeavor? By focusing on difference, Deleuze's philosophy involves thinking outside of representation, exploring instead how things change over time. He does not dismiss perspectives that seek stability but notes that they limit our horizons of possibilities. Deleuze's notion of difference is a resistance to developing a model that would advocate for methodological compliance. Community music, as a field of difference, would seek an emphasis on process but not at the expense of end results or product (see Think Piece 5). Conceived as a field of difference, community music would always retain its emphasis on creative and transformative movement. In this sense, the field would not seek an understanding of what it is by comparing its traits to that of music education, ethnomusicology, or music therapy, for example, but rather offer itself as a field always open to change and evolution. The Deleuzian concept of difference could act as a reminder that within every repetition, something different takes place, and it is here that dynamic invention can flourish.

## Becoming

Western philosophy has, according to Deleuze, consistently privileged being over becoming. Being endures; it underscores that which remains constant; it is a source, a foundation, and real. On the other hand, becoming is a passing illusion; it is ephemeral, changing, and inconsistent. From a Deleuzian perspective, appearances of being are only available because of becoming. Deleuze does not value becoming over being but challenges the opposition altogether (Colebrook, 2002). The concept of becoming is entwined with difference-in-itself, which means "becoming-different." From this perspective, the stability encapsulated within understandings of "beings" does not lie behind the real world; "there 'is' nothing other than the flow of becoming. All 'beings' are relatively stable moments in a flow of becoming-life" (Colebrook, 2002, p. 125). Becoming is not understood as comparing a start and end point and ascertaining the difference. Following

BECOMING 165

Nietzsche's[29] idea of the "eternal return,"[30] the very production of each instance is in a continual flow of change.[31] It is unlimited and unending with no true point of origin or destination and occurs between the past and the future.[32]

Crucial to an understanding of becoming is the notion of singularities. Against a background of cartography and discovery, where maps were always open to change and revision, Deleuze embraces the idea of virtual travel, infinite trajectories "that lead the thinker anywhere about the world" (Parr, 2005, p. 252). Singularities can be seen as "turning points determining an actual thing as a process but resistant to identity" (Williams, 2008, p. 91).[33] These tensions exist in the opening illustration of Charlie Kiel's work; actual events such as the 12/8 pathway bands,[34] video groove-along,[35] and the *Echology* newsletter can be understood as turning points, a series of becoming something other than it currently is. Each singularity exerts an intensity toward a change process, a turning point that houses a potential to become "the locus of an inflection or change" (p. 91). Connected through lines of flight,[36] the "turning points" become an "expression"[37] of the singular

---

[29] Deleuze's project is indelibly marked by Friedrich Nietzsche's (1844–1900) life-affirming philosophy. See Deleuze (2006). Like Nietzsche, Deleuze moves beyond the human reliance on transcendence—"the ascription of ideas beyond life that determine the goal and value of life" (Parr, 2005, p. 179).

[30] The eternal return is one of Nietzsche's enduring ideas. Open to a range of interpretations, the idea initially prompts us to think what it would be like if we knew we would have to live the same life repeatedly. See *The Gay Science* aphorism 341. Reworked in *Thus Spoke Zarathustra*, the eternal return alerts us that there are no future guarantees. It teaches us that all creativity is an experiment. "To affirm our creativity is to open ourselves to the experimentation that the future offers us rather than clinging to the illusory identity that the present places before us" (May, 2005, p. 68).

[31] "If the world had a goal, it must have been reached. . . . If it were capable of pausing and becoming fixed of 'being,' if in the whole course of its becoming it possessed even for a moment this capability of 'being,' then all becoming would long since have come to an end, along with all thinking and 'spirit'" (Nietzsche, 1968, p. 546).

[32] This is discussed in relation to Lewis Carol and Plato in the opening pages of *The Logic of Sense* (Deleuze, 1969/1990).

[33] The concept of singularity comes from the mathematical theory of differential relations, and Deleuze applies this to ontology. See Zourabichvili (2012, pp. 112–134).

[34] https://www.youtube.com/watch?v=oy1NRve34UQ&t=3s

[35] https://borntogroove.com/video/

[36] Lines of flight suggest movement. As May suggests, it is not to be understood as a leap from one realm to another "but productions within the realm of that from which it takes flight" (May, 2005, p. 128). Deleuze and Guattari discuss three types of lines: (1) segmentary (molar)—forming a binary root-like system of segments, (2) segmentation (molecular)—more supple but still segmentary, and (3) lines of flight (velocity)—rupturing the other two (Deleuze & Guattari, 1988, pp. 204–205). Lines of flight can, therefore, be creative or destructive. They are changes enabled through the connections between bodies that were previously only implicit. The connections formed "can release new power in the capacities of those bodies to act and respond" (Parr, 2005, p. 145).

[37] The notion of expression is reworked through Nietzsche's take on Spinoza's idea of "expressionism" and part of his approach to immanence, whereas "what is 'expressed' exists only by virtue of

166 THINKING COMMUNITY MUSIC

qualities of every event (see Think Piece 6: Expression). The present is then always a productive moment of becoming a constantly changing assemblage of forces.[38] Inextricably linked to the notion of becoming is Deleuzian ethical thought. Ethics, for Deleuze, "involves a creative commitment to maximizing connections and maximizing the powers that will expand the possibilities of life" (Parr, 2005, p. 85).[39] Kiel's work asks us to consider the Deleuzian ethical question of "What *might* we do?" or "What *could* we do?" (Jun & Smith, 2011). His thinking and his practical pursuits show a commitment to a community of inquiry that affirms and evaluates through creative and active actions.[40]

In the introduction to this book, I claimed that community music had shifted from an emergent to an established field (see Arrival). Connected to this thought, and as part of my "announcement," I wondered what the implications of this assertion might be. From a Deleuzian perspective, community music as becoming helps us think through some of the problematics inherent in a field that might argue that it has arrived. Entwined within community music as difference, and therefore a resistance to thinking grounded through identity and being, becoming would signal community music's contingent form. It reflects a commitment to fluid working practices that are responsive, person centered, or, better put, world centered.[41] Again, this is not a philosophy that seeks to replace or deny the importance of stable moments but rather conceives these as situated within an unlimited flow of change. Through the notion of becoming, community music has no true

---

its expression" (Young et al., 2013, p. 118). "It is not that we have a world of set terms and relations—rather life is an expressive and open whole, nothing more than the possibility for the creation of new relations" (Parr, 2005, p. 93). Expression is also linked to the idea of concepts as creativity—concepts must try and grasp movements and potentials.

[38] From Deleuze's perspective, force is not to be understood as aggressive or pressure. Force is the capacity to produce a change or becoming. Following Nietzsche, force suggests a world comprising a chaotic web of natural and biological forces that never come to rest. Interacting ceaselessly, this constitutes a dynamic world in flux.

[39] Deleuze draws a clear distinction between ethics and morality. Morality is a way of judging life, whereas ethics is a way of assessing what we do in relation to how we exist in the world. See Deleuze (1995, p. 100).

[40] Marks highlights that Deleuze admired the American pragmatist's model that substitutes experimentation for salvation (Parr, 2005, pp. 85–86). To cross-reference this with the philosophy of music education, music educators such as Randell Allsup, Heidi Westerlund, and Paul Woodford have engaged in pragmatist ideas, particularly in the form of John Dewey. Elizabeth Gould (2007) critiques notions of Deweyan democracy as it relates to social justice and music education through Deleuze's thought. Richerme (2020) discusses Deleuzian ethics in relation to school music education (pp. 67–83).

[41] To explore this concept, see Biesta (2022).

point of origin or destination. It stands that any arrival is to be experienced as a fleeting moment. So, should the field continue thinking of itself as emergent? Through this perspective, we would affirm that "yes," community music is always to be understood as an emergent field—not because it is academically young but because it is always in process, a turning point through which practitioners map new trajectories with those they work alongside rather than tracing what has gone before. Consider a community group that meets weekly to sing a mixed repertoire. As a singularity, the group consists of people from many walks of life, a meeting space, a time period, a facilitator, music material, and an atmosphere of togetherness. New members wanting to join, a last-minute change of venue, a revised set list for the performance in 2 weeks' time, and an ill facilitator are all turning points. Every aspect of the workshop can be thought of as a singularity, and each is a potential site for change. Through the notion of becoming, these qualities can be productively connected through lines of flight, realizing new power in the capacities of both the people and the context. Rather than being conceived as an identity with robust concepts and rational stability changing here and there but principally remaining the same, a Deleuzian perspective would conceive community music as a constantly changing assemblage. Engaging with the Deleuzian concept of becoming might provide community music with an alternative framework to consider the question of identity. Using the lens of becoming would affirm that community music is always in a state of emergence. From this perspective, community music is always "becoming-different," always in flux, and constantly changing.

Related to this is the concept of assemblage,[42] used by Deleuze and Guattari to explore the play between contingency and structure, organization and change. It is not a static term and does not signify predetermined parts or a random collection of things, but rather, it denotes "a process of arranging, organizing, fitting together" (Stivale, 2005, p. 77). As complex constellations, assemblages come together to create new functioning ways. As a set of forces, assemblages apply to all structures, "from the behavior patterns of an individual, the organization of institutions, an arrangement of spaces, to the functioning of ecologies" (Parr, 2010, p. 18). Charlie Kiel's body of work can be understood this way: His ethnographic monologues, activism in the form of political protest, newsletters, and groove-along

---

[42] From the French word *agencement*, meaning putting together, laying out, arrangement, fitting, or fixing.

# 168 THINKING COMMUNITY MUSIC

music-making events are all emerging singularities that create an assemblage of diverse heterogeneous elements. The 60 or so boxes of archive material Roger and I trawled through can be understood as expressing identity and claiming territory from the milieus.[43] Territories have a stake or claim of being more than just spaces but a "malleable site of passage" (Parr, 2005, p. 275). They are not fixed but rather always made and unmade. They are, therefore, always open to deterritorialization, "the movement by which one leaves the territory," and reterritorialization, the claiming or organizing of the space[44] (Deleuze & Guattari, 1988, p. 508). Deterritorialization offers potential movements framed as a "line of flight," productive opportunities to carry us away "across our thresholds, towards a destination which is unknown, not foreseeable, not pre-existent" (Deleuze & Parnet, 1996, p. 125).[45] This idea underscores how things connect rather than how things are. As the creative potential of an assemblage, deterritorialization offers the opportunity to free up any given fixed relations while exposing it to new organizations—it is a movement producing change. "The territory is the first assemblage, the first thing to constitute an assemblage; the assemblage is fundamentally territorial" (Deleuze & Guattari, 1988, p. 323). Assemblages are then always territorial and multiple. Resisting the binary one/many, multiplicities are complex structures with a form of their own rather than multiples of something else.[46] Deleuze and Guattari consider things multiplicities rather than substances;[47] they are not to be thought of as part of a greater whole that has been fragmented but rather are reflective of the world as a cognitive organism. As such, the concept of multiplicities resists any sense of the transcendental realm and places human beings as actors within a world of flux,

---

[43] *Milieu* is a French term meaning environment or surrounding context but also carries connotations of "middle." Having a spatial and temporal dimension, a milieu is something that you are living in. A milieu is something you are in the process of experiencing (Young et al., 2013, p. 193).

[44] As Deleuze and Guattari are concerned with overcoming a dualistic philosophical framework, territorialization and deterritorialization are not to be understood as opposites.

[45] Deleuze and Guattari use Olivier Messiaen's (1908–1992) composition *Catalogue d'oiseaux*, which uses bird song in its compositional material, as an example. They describe Messiaen transcribing birdsong into compositions for the piano and, as such, transforming the territory of the instrument. The compositional style also changes because of the relation with the bird song. The composition could be described as becoming-bird. See Deleuze and Guattari (1988).

[46] Deleuze's work on multiplicities extends from the thinking of the German mathematician Georg Riemann (1826–1866) and the French philosopher Henri Bergson. Riemann uses the notion of patchworks, articulating that situations are composed of multiplicities that form an ensemble without becoming a whole. Bergson places this idea in terms of both space and time.

[47] The general understanding of the substances in any given philosophical system is that they are those things that, according to the system, are the foundational or fundamental entities of reality. See https://plato.stanford.edu/entries/substance.

BECOMING 169

thus offering endless potential configurations; "there is no being beyond becoming nothing beyond multiplicity" (Deleuze, 2006, pp. 23–24). From this perspective, Kiel's corpus represents a collection of entities, an assemblage that has a productive force through which change might happen and, in so doing, produce effects and affects.[48] As a multiplicity, Kiel's work seeks to shine a light on ways of living that embrace a cultural democracy and freedom of self-expression (see Think Piece 2). The body of thought does not have a beginning or end but flows from the middle, interrogating existence through music engagement. It looks at ways people connect and utilize music to create meaningful interactions.

As a field of difference, the expressive and intensive territories that community music operates through collectively form an assemblage. A complex constellation of facilitation, musical content, social interaction, contextual considerations, funding dilemmas, and political activism intersects as a set of forces to create new and interesting productive experiences. From a Deleuzian perspective, the community music assemblage claims territory from its milieu—a workshop, a weekly activity, or an extensive residency inhabits a space. The site—a prison, a youth center, an opera house, a geographical region, or a country—becomes a malleable site of passage, a place where the intensive moments of a becoming community music pass through. Always in a state of flux, the affect and effect of community music practice are deterritorialized through its lines of flight that seek to rupture and disrupt any sense of the segmentary.

## Machine

Closely connected to the notion of assemblages is that of the machine: "Everywhere *it* is machines—real ones, not figurative ones: machines driving other machines, machines being driven by other machines, with all the necessary coupling and connections . . . we are all handymen: each with his little machines" (Deleuze & Guattari, 2013, p. 11). For Deleuze and Guattari, a machine is defined as "a system of interruptions and breaks," interventions between the flow and flux as machine connects to other machines (p. 50). Take a musical instrument like a guitar, for example. In and of itself, it does

---

[48] Affect is the change or variation that occurs when bodies collide or come into contact (Parr, 2005, p. 11). Deleuze uses it to refer to the focus, powers, and expression of change.

not do anything; however, when it is connected to another machine, the human body, the combination brought about through connections enables something to happen. The obvious and most common way of actualizing the guitar would be to play chords, a melody, or a blues riff. The human body becomes a "guitarist" or a "musician." Different connections, however, would produce different machines. The guitar could be reimagined as a work of art by painting it and mounting it on the wall. The human body would then become an artist. The guitar could become a heat source by using the wood on a bonfire, or it could be stripped of its raw materials, the strings refashioned as hand and neck jewelry. The potential of the guitar can be actualized in many different ways. "There is no aspect of life that isn't mechanic; all life only works and *is* insofar as it connects to some other machine" (Colebrook, 2002, p. 56).[49] A machine has no fixed identity and can connect in many different ways with other machines to actualize themselves. From the perspective of Deleuze and Guattari, "Becoming is like a machine: present in a different way in every assemblage, passing from one to the other, opening one onto the other, outside and fixed order or determined sequence" (Deleuze & Guattari, 1988, p. 347). When machines connect, they are always productive.

As a system of connectives that seek to interrupt, how might we conceive of community music as a machine? Machines intervene between the flow and flux of other machines (see Think Piece 2). Might we conceive of community music as a potential to create new and exciting possibilities that are always open for conversation and negotiation? Community music is only operationalized through those things that connect with it. If opened to its potentialities as a field of difference, its impact can be more productive than is now thought possible. Deleuze and Guattari might have framed community music as a desiring machine, an expression of an engagement with processes of production.[50] In this way, community music would always seek opportunities to connect—it would be a portal of intensity. The concept of the machine might be one approach to discussing how community music potentials might be realized.

---

[49] Colebrook offers the following categorization: An *organism* is a bounded whole with an identity and end; a *mechanism* is a closed machine with a specific function; a *machine* is nothing more than its connections.

[50] Deleuze and Guattari use the term "desiring-machines" that express an engagement with processes of production. Their critique of Freud's "desire" and Marx's "production" frames these ideas. Recasting desire as the driving force for machines to connect, Deleuze and Guattari edge away from the notion that desire signals a lack or a need. As a productive force, desire is inherent to life itself.

BECOMING    171

## Rhizome

Describing connections that occur between things, the philosophical figuration[51] of the rhizome is possibly Deleuze and Guattari's most referenced concept. It is a concept that maps[52] a process of networked, relational, and traversal thoughts and a way of being without "tracing" the construction of a fixed identity (Deleuze & Guattari, 1988, p. 12). Drawing upon its etymological meaning, *rhiza*, meaning "root,"[53] and its botanical use to describe a plant stem system that sends out roots and shoots from its nodes, rhizomatic thinking challenges that which is grounded through a fixed and individual base in a tree-like fashion.[54] "There are no points or positions in a rhizome, such as those found in a structure, tree, or root." (Deleuze & Guattari, 1988 p. 8). As a metaphor, the tree is rooted in one place with clear lines of demarcation; there is a clear beginning, middle, and end. The different parts of its hierarchy work well together, and it is a static system with well-defined roles. Deleuze and Guattari believe that this "arborescent" thinking, self-contained or closed systems of thought, has mirrored much of philosophical life since Plato. As an idea, rhizome puts forth a concept that resists rigid categories and, in turn, might enable us to challenge previous ways of thinking. As an organic matrix that does not grow in uniform directions, rhizomes are anti-genealogy, and one of its most important characteristics is that "it always has multiple entryways" (Deleuze & Guattari, 1988, p. 12). Forming a decentered milieu, rhizomatic connections can be chaotic[55] with no distinctive end or entry points. Acting in a rhizomatic way is "not simply a process that assimilates things, rather it is a milieu of perpetual transformation" (Parr, 2005, p. 233), ceaselessly establishing new connections.

Within a Deleuzian frame, community music, understood as a rhizomatic practice, would challenge those who wish to stand behind ring-fenced

---

[51] For Deleuze, philosophical figurations are used to complicate rather than explicate (St. Pierre, 1997).

[52] Contrary to "tracing," which has reproducible principles and can be understood as arborescent "mapping," is a process of creation. The rhizome is "a *map and not a tracing*" (Deleuze & Guattari, 1988, p. 12).

[53] Modern Latin *rhizome*, "mass of trees roots" (https://www.etymonline.com/word/rhizome).

[54] Deleuze and Guattari (1988) note, "It is odd how the tree has dominated Western reality and all of Western thought from botany to biology and anatomy, but also gnoseology, theology, ontology, all of philosophy" (p. 18).

[55] Following Nietzsche, chaos is a "play of forces" (Young et al., 2013, p. 59). "In fact, chaos is characterized less by the absence of determination than by the infinite speed with which they take shape and vanish" (Deleuze & Guattari, 1994, p. 42).

## 172 THINKING COMMUNITY MUSIC

structures. Conceiving community music in this way would resist arborescent thinking and might help open the field to the construction of relational networking and challenge thought processes that resisted change and/or erected disciplinary borders (see Think Piece 1). As an organic matrix, community music, understood as a rhizomatic gesture, develops and transforms in multiple directions. Conceived this way, the field may be more open to create connections not previously imagined, social and cultural geography, neuroscience, anthropology, social work, linguistics, etc. Understood through a rhizomatic lens, community music might be in a better place to respond to Huib Schippers's (2018) call for musical ecosystems that aim to increase sustainable futures. Rhizomatic notions of community music suggest a decentered milieu, a nod toward the diversity it claims to champion, a chance to grabble with its possible histories as virtual networks illuminating themselves in multiple guises and within many territories.

### Flight Lines

How *might* community music become? This question was brought to the metaphoric table for the following reason: Through an experience of both participating in and observing a marked increase in community music activity, there is a strong sense of arrival, a field growing in confidence with a global increase in practices, research, scholarship, and education. With this comes a clearer sense of identity, a sharper appearance of what community is and what community music does. To some extent, this is very welcome, and it represents the work of many people over many years who have believed in the potential of community music in the realms of education, cultural policy, and creative community development. I have wondered whether an "arrival" might lead to a crystallization of community music's identity. A consequence of this might be a reduction of its potentialities, achieving the opposite of what many people have worked toward.

The purpose of this think piece has been to both offer the provocation and provide a framework through which one can problematize the proposed questions. For Deleuze and Guattari, concepts are there to move us beyond our current experiences toward the thinking of new possibilities. In pursuing productive connections, "concepts are creative or active rather than representative, descriptive, or simplifying" (Parr, 2005, p. 51). The concept has "no *reference*: it is self-referential" (Deleuze

BECOMING 173

& Guattari, 1994, p. 22) and, as such, has not been employed as a way to use experiences to deduct abstract ideas for categorizing phenomena. As political philosopher Todd May (2003) says, "These concepts do not ask of us our epistemic consent; indeed they ask nothing of us. Rather, they are offerings, offerings of ways to think, and ultimately to act, in a world that oppresses us with its identities" (p. 151). The fact that I have brought a Deleuzian perspective to the proceedings indicates my thoughts on the matter and is, of course, not a neutral gesture. I hope the concepts "work" for the task at hand. This will be the marker of their success by shifting community musicians in the direction of thinking of new potentials and possibilities and thus exposing others "to the interesting, the remarkable, and the important" (May, 2003, p. 151). So how does one conclude something never set up to be concluded?

Community music has seen tremendous global growth supported by a healthy engagement with research and scholarship. The increase in national and international conversations, a growth of learning and research opportunities in schools of music and university, and a steady flow of scholarly writing have all nourished the practice. Examples of this include those working on the Creative Change Project[56] (2022–2025), which focuses on community music's role in addressing entrenched social inequity in Australian communities (Bartleet, 2023). The project team is working with a wide range of community music and social sector organizations, as well as a diverse group of emerging researchers who bring to this topic a wide range of creative skills, community music experiences, and lived experiences. Joel Spence focuses on collective songwriting as a form of community healing and activism in communities where there have been collective trauma and long-standing social injustices. Flora Wong examines how grassroots community music practices intersect with cultural tourism to address regional and remote location inequities. Pearly Black focuses on how shared singing, particularly in improvisatory contexts, can promote social connection and trust and enhance collective well-being and social equity in communities where there has been division. Emma Heard (Heard et al., 2023) is examining the role that grassroots community music making can play in building community identity and resilience in urban places where there is rapid gentrification, social service provision, and escalating social inequities. Another longitudinal project was Ethno Research, a 4-year project (2018–2022)

[56] http://creativechange.org.au

## 174 THINKING COMMUNITY MUSIC

considering intercultural music making through nonformal processes.[57] Sarah-Jane Gibson was the postdoctoral researcher who collaboratively developed the final report and the chapter book Gibson et al., 2022; Higgins & Gibson, 2024;). New research flowing from the United Kingdom includes that of Ryan Humphrey (2023), whose research explores common language used within community music, focusing on the terms *ownership, empowerment,* and *transformation*; Catherine Birch (2022; 2021), who is exploring a trauma-informed framework of community music practice; Chiying Lam (2023), whose doctoral thesis explores the development of community music practice as a heterodox praxis of becoming in the context of Hong Kong; Ruth Currie (2020), who explored the roles and responsibilities of being a cultural leader within the U.K. arts and cultural sector; and Rory Wells (2021), an activist musician exploring asset-based community development and alongside Nicola McAteer the political imperative of community music (McAteer & Wells, 2024). In response to issues associated with the pandemic, McAteer explores digital poverty through critical participatory action research and intersectionality (McAteer, 2022). New work from Canada includes Laura Curtis's (2022) work with choirs of involuntarily childless women; Fiona Evison's (2022) explorations of what it means to be a composer within community music settings; Cynthia Kinnunen's proposed inquiry surrounding the musical identities of adults in midlife; Dion Flores's work with the Filipino diaspora and the popular and Indigenous music of the Philippines; and festival manager Nathan Stretch's practice-as-research, which investigates the ethical significance of nonrepresentational art in public spaces. New ideas and new voices in community music can be read in *Transform*, an open-access, online, peer-refereed journal for emerging scholars working in community music.[58]

As I argued in the book's introduction, community music can now be named a field of practice, a domain of definable activity with accountable histories, and a bona fide body of scholarship. This is an achievement and can be celebrated, but what are the implications of this for a field that engages

---

[57] https://www.yorksj.ac.uk/research/international-centre-for-community-music/projects/ethno-research/

[58] *Transform* flows from the student research symposiums organized and curated by the International Centre for Community Music at York St. John University, United Kingdom. Students and early career researchers make up the editorial and production team. *Transform* aims to provide its collaborators with a 360-degree experience of the publication process. See http://transformiccm.co.uk/

with ideas related to cultural democracy, diversity, inclusivity, and issues related to social justice? Some questions follow:

1. Can community music be described as always in a state of emergence? What are the dangers, and what are the possibilities?
2. Should community musicians seek to develop pedagogic strategies responsive in multiple and complex contexts while resisting methodological crystallization? If so, what might this look like? If not, what are the alternatives?
3. What are the potentials of community music? How might these be realized?
4. Where are the opportunities for community music to intersect with other fields? Can the field of community music demonstrate what "openness" means? If so, how?

A Deleuzian frame might help the collective "us" reflect on issues of the future of community music while acknowledging the significant achievements to date. Understood through this lens, community music would resist a fixed identity. As a practice that affirms the power of difference, community music would be conceived as always in flux, constantly adapting to change while actively seeking creative potentialities. With an emphasis on productive processes, community music's evolution would be open to possibilities yet unknown. Situated in the flow of becoming, those working in and advocating for community music would commit to fluid working practices that were contextually responsive, person or world centered, and ethical. Community music would affirm its emergent character, mapping its histories and actualizations as multiple connectives unfolding through an immanent plane. As a complex assemblage community music claims territory, but fleetingly, its lines of flight deterritorializing occupied environments and, in its wake, providing opportunities for vibrant negotiation through disruption and critique. As a rhizomatic practice, community music would transform in multiple ways, a desiring-machine that craves other domains through which connection might result in expressive processes of production. Community music, a practice of difference and becoming, a rhizomatic desiring-machine.

Finally, in the wake of this discussion, Figure 8.1 takes on a visual form reflective of the ideas presented throughout this think piece. Kaleidoscopic in character, community music appears as a group of distinct yet interconnected practices that intersect in, through, and around other

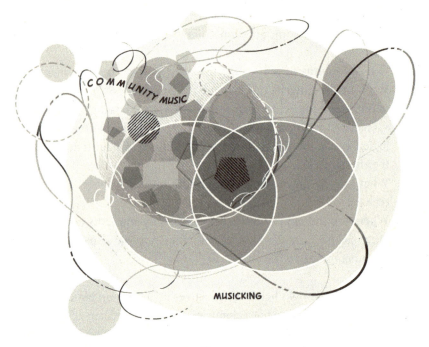

**Figure 8.1** Community music assemblage.

musical "disciplines" and/or domains. Unlike Figure A.1, which builds from a drawing that appeared in a previous text (Higgins & Willingham, 2017, p. 172) and purposely names music education, ethnomusicology, and music therapy as interdisciplinary crossfields, Figure 8.1 leaves the domains open for interpretation. From this vantage point, community music is a multiplicity, an assemblage that seeks connections and, with it, a multitude of potential configurations.

# Departure

In the "Arrival" chapter, I explained that the impetus of this book began with eight questions. The questions were:

1. *Is the notion of intervention apt for a growing global field?*
2. *What makes the idea of community music as an act of hospitality important?*
3. *Can community music have a pedagogy?*
4. *How might social justice be understood as a framework for community music practices?*
5. *How might notions of excellence and inclusion exist as a balanced pairing?*
6. *How might we understand the "music" in community music?*
7. *How might I do community music research?*
8. *How might community music become?*

These questions, shaped as provocations, were designed to get those invested in community music to think about the practice and explore avenues that required discussion. To kickstart the conversations, I created a "think piece" for each and presented some ways I have been reflecting on these questions. Each think piece ends with a flight line, a springboard for discussion and critical reflection.

In keeping with the notion of connections, networks, and assemblages, the "final" chapter, named "Departure," offers five different statements, each representing an arrangement of the ideas found within the flight lines. I have called these statements "constellations" because, as a group, each one forms a particular pattern or outline and, in so doing, presents a particular perspective. As springboards for thought, I encourage you to review the flight lines and assemble your own constellations in accord with the things that most strongly resonate with your practice. My constellations began by creating a mind map of the ideas from the book (Figure D.1), followed by a process of looking for interconnecting patterns. I have indicated in

*Thinking Community Music.* Lee Higgins, Oxford University Press. © Oxford University Press 2024.
DOI: 10.1093/9780190247027.003.0010

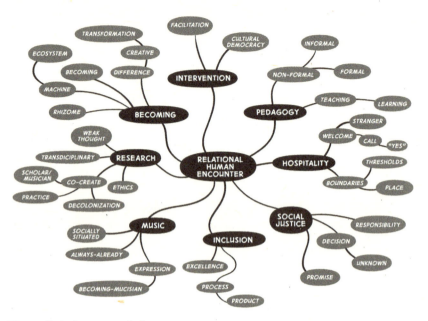

**Figure D.1** Concept mind map.

parentheses which think piece houses the specific idea as it appears in the sentences. For example (2) indicates Think Piece 2 and (5) corresponds to Think Piece 5 etc.

Recalling the kaleidoscopic nature of the text, the constellations and their components can be arranged and rearranged to produce countless optics. Each constellation orbits through "relational human encounters," underscoring community music's resolve as a hospitable collaborative enterprise. The constellations may be helpful as soundbites, each loaded with intentionality and conceptual weight but always open for discursive dialogue and challenge.

## Constellations

Community musicians look toward creating environments where individuals and communities can take charge of their *expression* (6) and shape their futures. Ignited through relationships, often structured as a *call*, a *welcome* (2), and a *decision* (4) to say "yes" (2), community musicians attempt to work with *inclusive processes* (5) and, as such, respond to societal structures that marginalize (4). Inherent within this work is a *promise* (4) of something different, an opportunity for participants to be heard and the potential to have an experience of *becoming-musician* (6).

Those who interrogate and explore community music practices are often practitioners themselves (7). In trying to reflect music making as it is experienced, contextually driven, and *socially situated* (6), community music researchers *cocreate* (7) alongside participants in attempts to *decolonize* (7) knowledge and redistribute power to those who often feel powerless. Research in this field has the opportunity to be *ethically responsive* (7) to issues concerning access, equality, and *inclusion* (5), key ideas that resonate deep within the practice. As lines of flight, *deterritorializing* (8) research can occupy traditional and nontraditional spaces, providing opportunities for vibrant disruption and critique.

In trying to shape pedagogic processes that are in keeping with the notion of community music as an *act of hospitality* (2), facilitators often work dynamically through a fluid continuum that, while it predominantly revolves around *nonformal music* approaches to learning (3), often includes a mixture of both formal and informal characteristics. Under the political banner of *cultural democracy*, (1) initiatives to redress inequalities of cultural participation might require such *intervention processes* (1). Approaching such action with *hospitality* (2), a *promise* (4) to each other, and a *weak* "attitude" toward a future process of liberation (7), strategies of intervention can *inhabit spaces* (8) and open *expressive* (6) opportunities both musically and in terms of *opening doors* (2) toward greater understandings of who we are singularly and as part of wider community networks (4 and 8).

Although community music is a relational practice (2), many participants are drawn to projects because of the music-making possibilities. *Rhizomatic* (8) in character, the music made through hospitable approaches to learning (3) are diverse and multiple and are continually on the horizon. They are, however, *intersubjective, socially situated*, and *socially shared* (6) and at their best *expressions* (6) of those that make it, each performance seeking to make connections integral to the person from whom it flows.

By consciously recognizing and acknowledging *difference* (8), the field of community music has a greater chance of remaining emergent and, in so doing, will *always-already* (6) be open for conversation and negotiation, keeping a buoyancy toward productive *connections* (8) throughout the

180    THINKING COMMUNITY MUSIC

music ecosystem. Alongside a practice that strives to welcome the *stranger* (2), powerful *critique* (7) is needed that opens debate and discussion that will, in turn, create pathways through which those engaged with the practice can learn and develop.

## Boarding

As a diverse rhizomatic network of practices, community music takes place within the criminal justice system, health settings, youth centers, schools, pupil referral units, foster care homes, rural settings, and inner-city metropolises, to name but a few. Featured illustrations used throughout this book include work in community centers, youth clubs, high schools, prisons, areas of natural disasters, adult daycare centers, concert halls, music academies, recovery program centers, recording studios, areas of conflict, and people's private homes. As a collective, these examples took place in the continents of Europe, North America, Asia, Africa, and Australia and spanned a wide variety of styles and genres, including samba drumming, percussion, improvisation, songwriting, hip hop, rock pop ensembles, orchestral and chamber music, new composition involving adapted musical instruments, 12/8 pathway bands, singing in choirs, traditional music of Indigenous peoples, jazz, and singing. Binding these diverse practices is an ethos from its historical roots, oriented around cultural democracy and spilling out as deeply concerned with being together with others.

As a kaleidoscopic constellation of concepts articulated here, community music can be understood as hospitable music making, a relational music practice vibrating to the tune of the politics of cultural democracy and responding to contemporary and historical forms of cultural and social inequality. This characterization affords community music a distinctive position in any music ecosystem. Community music can provide a useful critical lens through which to view other musical practices and the various political and cultural policies that frame them. Constantly emerging, community musicians look to create opportunities for open dialogue, conversation, and negotiation, seeking connection with people and places. With an emphasis on processes that reflect the tensions inherent within any act of hospitality, community musicians consciously create opportunities for musicking. Pedagogic strategies that operate in, around, and through a continuum of music facilitation styles generate spaces where the music made is intersubjective, socially situated, and socially shared and, at its most powerful, an expression of those who make it. Grounded in the anthropological argument that music is fundamental to humanity, the field of community music is an assemblage, a complex, and multiple constellations of social interaction, facilitation, musical content, context, funding dilemmas, and political activism. Understood this way, those who ignite the field's becoming set forth the potential to create productive experiences that are impactful and, at times, transformative for those who wish to engage.

# References

21c. (2014). *Documentary trailer, music and community transformation*. Documenting 21c. https://documenting21c.com/medias/videos/?lang=en

64 Million Artists with Arts Council England. (2018). *Cultural democracy in practice*. Arts Council England.

Adams, D., & Goldbard, A. (2001). *Creative community, the art of cultural development*. Rockefeller Foundation.

Allan, J. (2014). Waiting for inclusive education? An exploration of conceptual confusions and political struggles. In F. Kiuppis & R. Sarromaa Hausstätter (Eds.), *Inclusive education twenty years after Salamanca* (pp. 181–190). Peter Lang.

Allsup, R. E., & Shieh, E. (2012). Social justice and music education: The call for a public pedagogy. *Music Educators Journal, 98*(4), 47–51. https://doi.org/10.1177/002743211244

Allsup, R. E., & Westerlund, H. (2012). Methods and situational ethics in music education. *Action, Criticism, and Theory for Music Education, 11*(1), 124–148.

American Education Research Association. (2009). Standards for reporting on humanities-oriented research. *Educational Researcher, 38*(6), 481–486.

Anderson, K., & Willingham, L. (2020). Environment, intention and intergenerational music making: Facilitating participatory music making in diverse contexts of community music. *International Journal of Community Music, 13*(2), 173–185. https://doi.org/https://doi.org/10.1386/ijcm_00018_1

Ansdell, G., Brøske, B. Å., Black, P., & Lee, S. (2020). Showing the way, or getting in the way? Discussing power, influence and intervention in contemporary musical-social practices. *International Journal of Community Music, 13*(2), 135–155.

Ansdell, G., & Denora, T. (2016). *Musical pathways in recovery: Community music therapy and mental health*. Routledge.

Apter, E., Baker, J., Houston A., Benhabib, S., Bennington, G., Cadava, E., Culler, J., Dailey, P., Ricciardi, A., Freccero, C., Hartman, G. H., Kamuf, P., McDonald, C. V., Miller, J. H., Parker, A., Rabaté, J.-M., Redfield, M., Ronell, A., Rowlinson, M., & Spivak, G. C. (2005). Forum: The legacy of Jacques Derrida. *Modern Language Association, 120*(2), 464–494. http://www.jstor.org/stable/25486172

Aquinas, T. (2002). *Shorter Summa: Saint Thomas's own concise version of his Summa Theologica* (C. Vollert, Trans.). Sophia Institute Press.

Arendt, H. (1958). *The origins of totalitarianism*. Meridian Books.

Aristarkhova, I. (2012a). Hospitality and the maternal. *Hypatia, 27*(1), 163–181.

Aristarkhova, I. (2012b). *Hospitality of the matrix: Philosophy, biomedicine, and culture*. Columbia University Press.

Aristotle. (2000). *Nicomachean ethics* (E. b. R. Crisp, Trans.). Cambridge University Press.

Armstrong, A. C., Armstrong, D., & Spandagou, I. (2009). *Inclusive education: International policy and practice*. Sage.

Ashley, L., & Lines, D. (Eds.). (2016). *Intersecting cultures in music and dance education: An oceanic perspective*. Springer.

Bakan, M. B. (1999). *Music of death and new creation*. University of Chicago Press.

Baker, F., & Krout, R. (2012). Turning experience into learning: Educational contributions of collaborative peer songwriting during music therapy training. *International Journal of Music Education, 30*(2), 133–147.

## 184 REFERENCES

Balsnes, A. H. (2016). Hospitality in multicultural choir singing. *International Journal of Community Music, 9*(3), 171–189.

Barra, G., & Dranoff, B. (2009). *Beyond Ipanema: Brazilian waves in global music* [Film].

Bartleet, B.-L. (2019). How concepts of love can inform empathy and conciliation in intercultural community music contexts. *International Journal of Community Music, 12*(3), 317–330.

Bartleet, B.-L. (2021). What the experiences of working alongside First Peoples can bring to our understandings of community music. In L. Willingham (Ed.), *Community music at the boundaries* (pp. 249–259). Wilfrid Laurier University Press.

Bartleet, B.-L. (2023). A conceptual framework for understanding and articulating the social impact of community music. *International Journal of Community Music, 16*(1), 31–49.

Bartleet, B.-L., Bennett, D., Power, A., & Sunderland, N. (2018). Community service learning with First Peoples. In B.-L. Bartleet & L. Higgins (Eds.), *The Oxford handbook of community music* (pp. 653–669). Oxford University Press.

Bartleet, B.-L., & Carfoot, G. (2016). Arts-based service learning with Indigenous communities: Engendering artistic citizenship. In D. J. Elliott, M. Silverman, & W. D. Bowman (Eds.), *Artistic citizenship: Artistry, social responsibility, and ethical praxis* (pp. 339–358). Oxford University Press.

Bartleet, B.-L., & Higgins, L. (2018a). Introduction: An overview of community music in the twenty-first century. In B.-L. Bartleet & L. Higgins (Eds.), *The Oxford handbook of community music* (pp. 1–20). Oxford University Press.

Bartleet, B.-L., & Higgins, L. (Eds.). (2018b). *The Oxford handbook of community music.* Oxford University Press.

Barz, G., & Cohen, J. M. (Eds.). (2011). *The culture of AIDS of Africa: Hope and healing through music and the arts.* Oxford University Press.

Bauböck, R. (2017). *Democratic inclusion: Rainer Bauböck in dialogue.* Manchester University Press.

Bearn, G. C. F. (2000). Differentiating Derrida and Deleuze. *Continental Philosophy Review, 33,* 441–465.

Belsey, C. (2002). *Poststructuralism: A very short introduction.* Oxford University Press.

Benedict, C. (2021). *Music and social justice: A guide for elementary educators.* Oxford University Press.

Benedict, C., & Schmidt, P. K. (2007). From whence justice? Interrogating the improbable in music education. *Action, Criticism, and Theory for Music Education, 6*(4), 21–42.

Benedict, C., Schmidt, P., Spruce, G., & Woodford, P. G. (Eds.). (2015). *The Oxford handbook of social justice and music education.* Oxford University Press.

Benson, J. F. (2010). *Working more creatively with groups* (3rd ed.). Routledge.

Bergh, A. (2010). *I'd like to teach the world to sing: Music and conflict transformation.* University Exeter.

Bergson, H. (2022). *Creative evolution.* Routledge.

Bhabha, H. K. (1994). *The location of culture.* Routledge.

Bhatia, M. V. (2003). *War and intervention: Issues for contemporary peace operations.* Kumarian Press.

Biesta, G. (2007). Democracy, education and the question of inclusion. *Nordisk Pedagogikk, 27*(1), 18–29.

Biesta, G. (2009). Sporadic democracy: Education, democracy, and the question of inclusion. In M. Katz, S. Verducci, & G. Biesta (Eds.), *Education, democracy, and the moral life* (pp. 101–112). Springer.

Biesta, G. (2015). Resisting the seduction of the global education measurement industry: Notes on the social psychology of PISA. *Ethics and Education, 10*(3), 348–360. https://doi.org/10.1080/17449642.2015.1106030

Biesta, G. (2022). *World-centred education: A view for the present.* Routledge.

## REFERENCES 185

Biesta, G., Takayama, K., Kettle, M., & Heimans, S. (2020). Teacher education between principle, politics, and practice: A statement from the new editors of the Asia-Pacific Journal of Teacher Education. *Asia-Pacific Journal of Teacher Education*, *48*(5), 455–459. https://doi.org/10.1080/1359866X.2020.1818485

Biesta, G. J. J. (2001). "Preparing for the incalculable": Deconstruction, justice, and the question of education. In G. J. J. Biesta & D. Egea-Kuehne (Eds.), *Derrida and education* (pp. 32–54). Routledge.

Biesta, G. J. J. (2004). The community of those who have nothing in common. Education and the language of responsibility. *Interchange*, *35*(3), 307–324. https://link.springer.com/article/10.1007/BF02698880

Biesta, G. J. J. (2006). *Beyond learning: Democratic education for a human future.* Routledge.

Birch, C. (2021). Voices from the inside: Working with the hidden trauma narratives of women in custody. In D. Bradley & J. Hess (Eds.), *Trauma and resilience in music education* (pp. 141–156). Routledge.

Birch, C. (2022). Hidden voices: Towards a trauma-informed framework of community music practice. *International Journal of Community Music*, *15*(1), 143–164. https://doi.org/DOI:10.1386/ijcm_00055_1

Bird, F. (2017). Singing out: The function and benefits of an LGBTQI community choir in New Zealand in the 2010s. *International Journal of Community Music*, *10*(2), 193–206.

Bird, P. (2023, February 16). Poor areas suffered 3.5 times more damage in Turkey's earthquake. *The Economist.* https://www.economist.com/graphic-detail/2023/02/16/poor-areas-suffered-35-times-more-damage-in-turkeys-earthquake

Blacking, J. (1973). *How musical is man?* Faber and Faber.

Boal, A. (2002). *Games for actors and non-actors* (A. Jackson, Trans.; 2nd ed.). Routledge.

Boas, F. (1887). A year among the Eskimo. *Journal of the American Geographical Society of New York*, *19*, 383–402.

Bogue, R. (2003). *Deleuze on music, painting, and the arts.* Routledge.

Bolger, L. (2012). Music therapy and international development in action and reflection: A case study of a woman's music group in rural Bangladesh. *Australian Journal of Music Therapy*, *23*, 22–41.

Bolt, B. (2006). A non standard deviation: handlability, praxical knowledge and practice led research. *RealTime Arts:* Special issue: *Speculation and Innovation: Applying Practice Led Research in the Creative Industries Conference*, *74*(August–September).

Bonshur, M. (2016). Sharing knowledge and power in adult amateur choral communities: The impact of communal learning on the experience of musical participation. *International Journal of Community Music*, *9*(3), 291–305. https://doi.org/doi:10.1386/ijcm.9.3.291_1

Boundas, C. V. (2006). *Deleuze and philosophy.* Edinburgh University Press.

Bowman, W. (2007). Who's asking? (Who's answering?) Theorizing social justice in music education. *Action, Criticism, and Theory for Music Education*, *6*(4), 1–20.

Bowman, W. D. (1998). *Philosophical perspectives on music.* Oxford University Press.

Bradley, D. (2011). In the space between the rock and the hard place: State teacher certification guidelines and music education for social justice. *Journal of Aesthetic Education*, *45*(4), 79–96.

Broeske, B. A. (2017). The Norwegian Academy of Music and the Lebanon Project: The challenges of establishing a community music project when working with Palestinian refugees in South Lebanon. *International Journal of Community Music*, *10*(1), 71–83.

Brookfield, S. (1986). *Understanding and facilitating adult learning.* Josey-Bass.

Brown, T., Higham, B., & Rimmer, M. (2014). *Whatever happened to community music?* AHRC Research Network Report.

Buchanan, I., & Swiboda, M. (Eds.). (2004). *Deleuze and music.* Edinburgh University Press.

Bucura, E. (2020). Rethinking excellence in music education. *Visions of Research in Music Education*, *36*, Article 6. https://opencommons.uconn.edu/vrme/vol36/iss1/6

## 186 REFERENCES

Bugos, J. A. (Ed.). (2017). *Contemporary research in music learning across the lifespan: Music education and human development*. Routledge.

Bull, A., Scharff, C., & Nooshin, L. (Eds.). (2023). *Voices for change in the classical music profession: New ideas for tackling inequalities and exclusions*. Oxford University Press.

Butler, C. (2002). *Postmodernism: A very short introduction*. Oxford University Press.

Cahill, D., & Konings, M. (2017). *Neoliberalism*. Polity Press.

Camlin, D. (2015). This is my truth, now tell me yours. *International Journal of Community Music, 8*(3), 233–257.

Camlin, D. A. (2016, July 19–23). *Whatever you say I am, that's what I'm not: Developing dialogical and dissensual ways of conceiving of and talking about community music*. Commission on Community Music Activity Edinburgh.

Camlin, D. A. (2020). Response to: Reappraising community music as intervention: A provocation for discussion. In *MUSOC Discussion Forum*. Royal College of Music.

Camlin, D. A. (2023). *Music making and civil imagination*. Intellect.

Camlin, D., Caulfield, L., & Perkins, R. (2020). Capturing the magic: A three-way dialogue on the impact of music on people and society. *International Journal of Community Music, 13*(2), 157–172.

Campbell, P. S. (1996). Music, education, and community in a multicultural society. In M. McCarthy (Ed.), *Cross currents: Setting an agenda for music education in community culture* (pp. 4–33). University of Maryland.

Candea, M., & da Col, G. (2012). The return to hospitality. *Journal of the Royal Anthropological Institute, 18*, S1–S19.

Capeheart, L., & Milovanovic, D. (2007). *Social justice theories, issues, and movements*. Rutgers University Press. http://site.ebrary.com.ezproxy.bu.edu/lib/bostonuniv/Doc?id=10202539

Caputo, J. D. (1997a). Justice, if such a thing exists. In J. D. Caputo (Ed.), *Deconstruction in a nutshell: A conversation with Jacques Derrida* (pp. 125–155). Fordham University Press.

Caputo, J. D. (1997b). *The prayers and tears of Jacques Derrida: Religion without religion*. Indiana University Press.

Caputo, J. D., & Vattimo, G. (2007). *After the death of God*. Columbia University Press.

Carroll, C. L. (2020). Seeing the invisible: Theorising connections between informal and formal musical knowledge. *Research Studies in Music Education, 42*(1), 37–55.

Casey, E. S. (2011). Strangers at the edge of hospitality. In R. Kearney & K. Semonovitch (Eds.), *Phenomenologies of the stranger: Between hostility and hospitality* (pp. 39–48). Fordham University Press.

Chadwick, S. (2011). Lift every voice and sing: Constructing community through culturally relevant pedagogy in the University of Illinois Black Chorus. *International Journal of Community Music, 4*(2), 147–162.

Chávez, L., & Skelchy, R. P. (2019). Decolonization for ethnomusicology and music studies in higher education. *Action, Criticism & Theory for Music Education, 18*(3), 115–143.

Cheah, P. (2013). To open: Hospitality and alienation. In T. Claviez (Ed.), *The conditions of hospitality: Ethics, politics, and aesthetics on the threshold of the possible* (pp. 57–80). Fordham University Press.

Chernoff, J. M. (1979). *African rhythm and African sensibility*. University of Chicago Press.

Cisney, V. W. (2018). *Deleuze and Derrida: Difference and the power of the negative*. Edinburgh University Press.

Clifford, J. (1988). *The predicament of culture: Twentieth-century ethnography, literature, and art*. Harvard University Press.

Clift, S. (2021). Editorial. *International Journal of Community Music, 14*(2&3), 125–128.

Coffman, D. (2018). Community music with adults. In B.-L. Bartleet & L. Higgins (Eds.), *The Oxford handbook of community music* (pp. 693–709). Oxford University Press.

Cohen, M. L. (2012). Harmony within the walls: Perceptions of worthiness and competence in a community prison choir. *International Journal of Music Education, 30*(1), 46–56.

## REFERENCES  187

Cohen, M. L., & Henley, J. (2018). Music-making behind bars: The many dimensions of community music in prisons. In B.-L. Bartleet & L. Higgins (Eds.), *The Oxford handbook of community music* (pp. 153–171). Oxford University Press.

Cohen, M. L., Silber, L. H., Sangiorgio, A., & Iadeluca, V. (2012). At-risk youth: Music-making as a means to promote positive relationships. In G. McPherson & G. F. Welch (Eds.), *The Oxford handbook of music education* (Vol. 2, pp. 185–202). Oxford University Press.

Colardyn, D. (Ed.). (2001). *Lifelong learning: Which ways forward?* Lemma.

Colebrook, C. (2002). *Giles Deleuze.* Routledge.

Colwell, R. (Ed.). (1992). *Handbook of research on music teaching and learning.* Schirmer Books.

Colwell, R., & Richardson, C. P. (2002). *The new handbook of research on music teaching and learning.* Oxford University Press.

Coombs, P. (1968). *The world educational crisis.* Oxford University Press.

Coombs, P. H., & Ahmed, M. (1974). *Attacking rural poverty: How nonformal education can help.* John Hopkins University Press.

Coppi, A. (2017). *Community music: Nuovi orientamenti pedagogici.* FrancoAngeli.

Coppi, A. (Ed.). (2020). *Musica e inclusione sociale: proposte di ricerca.* Libreria Musicale Italiana.

Council of Europe. (2011). *Pathway 2.0 towards recognition of non-formal learning/education and of youth work in Europe.*

Creech, A., Varvarigou, M., & Hallam, S. (2020). *Contexts for music learning and participation: Developing and sustaining musical possible selves.* Springer.

Critchley, S. (2005). Derrida's influence on philosophy . . . and on my work. *German Law Journal, 6*(1), 25–29. https://doi.org/10.1017/S2071832200013420

Critchley, S. (2014). *The ethics of deconstruction: Derrida and Levinas* (3rd ed.). Edinburgh University Press.

Cross, I. (2003). Music and biocultural evolution. In M. Clayton, T. Herbert, & R. Middleton (Eds.), *The cultural study of music* (pp. 19–30). Routledge.

Currie, R. (2020). *Been, being and becoming more music: A critical ethnographic case study of the role and responsibility of a community music organisation in the UK* [Doctoral thesis]. York St. John University.

Currie, R., Gibson, J., & Lam, C. Y. (2020). Community music as intervention: Three doctoral researchers consider intervention from their different contexts. *International Journal of Community Music, 13*(2), 187–206.

Curtis, L. (2022). Singing my story too: Navigating positionality from the "inside." *Transform: New Voices in Community Music, (4),* 92–105. http://79.170.44.82/transformiccm.co.uk/?page_id=915

Cutting, G. (2011). *Thinking the impossible.* Oxford University Press.

D'Amore, A. (2009). *Musical futures: An approach to teaching and learning.* https://www.musicalfutures.org.uk

Daria, J. (2018). Community music on campus: Collaborative research, activist methods and critical pedagogy in a fandango-based participatory music programme. *International Journal of Community Music, 11*(1), 91–108. https://doi.org/doi:10.1386/ijcm.11.1.91_1

Davis, S. A. (2011). *Acts of hospitality: A case study of the University of South Carolina String Project.* New York University.

de Banffy-Hall, A. (2019). *The development of community music in Munich.* Waxmann.

de Bruin, L. R., & Southcott, J. (2023). *Musical ecologies: Instrumental music ensembles around the world.* Routledge.

de Quadros, A. (2015). Rescuing choral music from the realm of the elite: Models for twenty-first-century music making—Two case studies. In C. Benedict, P. Schmidt, G. Spruce, & P. G. Woodford (Eds.), *The Oxford handbook of social justice and music education* (pp. 501–512). Oxford University Press.

188 REFERENCES

de Quadros, A. (2018). Community music portraits of struggle, identity, and togetherness. In B.-L. Bartleet & L. Higgins (Eds.), *The Oxford handbook of community music* (pp. 265–279). Oxford University Press.

de Quadros, A., & Abrahams, F. (2022). No justice, no peace: An arts-based project with a college choir. *Music Education Research, 24*(5), 533–548. https://doi.org/DOI:10.1080/14613 808.2022.2134330

de Quadros, A., & Amrein, E. (2023). *Empowering song: Music education from the margins.* Routledge.

de Quadros, A., & Dorstewitz, P. (2011). Community, communication, social change: Music in dispossessed Indian communities. *International Journal of Community, 4*(1), 59–70.

Deane, K. (2018). Community music in the United Kingdom: Politics or policies? In B.-L. Bartleet & L. Higgins (Eds.), *The Oxford handbook of community music* (pp. 323–342). Oxford University Press.

Deleuze, G. (1988). *Bergsonism.* Zone Books.

Deleuze, G. (1990). *The logic of sense* (M. Lester & C. Stivale, Trans.). Columbia University Press. (Original work published 1969)

Deleuze, G. (1995). *Negotiations, 1972–1990.* Columbia University Press.

Deleuze, G. (2004). *Difference and repetition.* Continuum. (Original work published 1968)

Deleuze, G. (2006). *Nietzsche and philosophy.* Columbia University Press.

Deleuze, G., & Guattari, F. (1988). *A thousand plateaus: Capitalism and schizophrenia.* Continuum.

Deleuze, G., & Guattari, F. (1994). *What is philosophy?* (G. Burchell & H. Tomlinson, Trans.). Verso.

Deleuze, G., & Guattari, F. (2013). *Anti-Oedipus: Capitalism and schizophrenia.* Bloomsbury.

Deleuze, G., & Parnet, C. (1996). *Dialogues* (Nouv. éd.). Flammarion.

Deleuze, G., & Parnet, C. (2002). *Dialogues II.* Continuum. http://www.loc.gov/catdir/toc/ ecip071/2006031862.html

DeNora, T. (2000). *Music in everyday life.* Cambridge University Press.

Dentan, R. K. (1968). *The Semai: A nonviolent people of Malaya.* Holt, Rinehart and Winston.

Denzin, N. K. (2009). *Qualitative inquiry under fire: Toward a new paradigm dialogue.* Left Coast Press.

Denzin, N. K., & Lincoln, Y. S. (Eds.). (2005). *The Sage handbook of qualitative research* (3rd ed.). Sage.

Denzin, N. K., & Lincoln, Y. S. (Eds.). (2018). *The Sage handbook of qualitative research* (5th ed.). Sage.

Derrida, J. (1976). *Of grammatology* (1st American ed.). Johns Hopkins University Press.

Derrida, J. (1978). Structure, sign, and play in the discourse of the human sciences (A. Bass, Trans.). In *Writing and difference* (pp. 351–370). Routledge. (Original work published 1963)

Derrida, J. (1981a). Plato's pharmacy (B. Johnson, Trans.). In *Dissemination* (pp. 61–171). Athlone Press.

Derrida, J. (1981b). *Positions* (A. Bass, Trans.). Athlone Press.

Derrida, J. (1982). Différance (A. Bass, Trans.). In *Margins of philosophy* (pp. 1–27). Harvester Press.

Derrida, J. (1985). *The ear of the other: Otobiography, transference, translation* (P. Kamuf, Trans.). Schocken Books.

Derrida, J. (1987a). Parergon (G. Bennington & I. McLeod, Trans.). In *The truth in painting* (pp. 15–147). University of Chicago Press.

Derrida, J. (1987b). *The truth in painting* (G. Bennington & I. McLeod, Trans.). University of Chicago Press.

Derrida, J. (1988). *Limited Inc.* Northwestern University Press.

Derrida, J. (1991). Letter to a Japanese friend (D. Woods & A. Benjamin, Trans.). In P. Kamuf (Ed.), *A Derrida reader: Between the blinds* (pp. 269–276). Columbia University Press.

REFERENCES    189

Derrida, J. (1994a). The spatial arts: An interview with Jacques Derrida. In P. Brunette & D. Wills (Eds.), *Deconstruction and the visual arts: Art, media, architecture* (pp. 9–32). University of Cambridge.

Derrida, J. (1994b). *Specters of Marx: The state of the debt, the work of mourning, and the new international* (P. Kamuf, Trans.). Routledge.

Derrida, J. (1995). *The gift of death* (D. Wills, Trans.). University of Chicago Press.

Derrida, J. (1997a). *Of grammatology* (G. C. Spivak, Trans.). John Hopkins University Press.

Derrida, J. (1997b). The Villanova roundtable. In J. D. Caputo (Ed.), *Deconstruction in a nutshell: A conversation with Jacques Derrida* (pp. 1–28). Fordham University Press.

Derrida, J. (1999). *Adieu: To Emmanuel Levinas* (P.-A. B. a. M. Naas, P-A. Brault & M. Naas, Trans.). Stanford University Press.

Derrida, J. (2000a). Hostipitality. *Angelaki: Journal of Theoretical Humanities, 5*(3), 3–18.

Derrida, J. (2000b). *Of hospitality* (R. Bowlby, Trans.). Stanford University Press.

Derrida, J. (2001). *On cosmopolitanism and forgiveness* (M. Dooley & M. Hughes, Trans.). Routledge.

Derrida, J. (2002a). Force of law: The "mystical foundation of authority." In G. Anidjar (Ed.), *Acts of religion* (pp. 230–298). Routledge.

Derrida, J. (2002b). Hostipitality. In G. Anidjar (Ed.), *Acts of religion* (pp. 356–420). Routledge.

Derrida, J., Brault, P.-A., & Naas, M. (2001). *The work of mourning.* University of Chicago Press.

DeVito, D., & Bingham, S. (2014). Hospitality and facilitation at the Notre Maison Orphanage in Haiti: A community music approach to inclusion in Port a Prince. In Mary L. Cohen (Ed.), *CMA XIV: Listening to the world: Experincing and Connecting the Knowledge from Community Music Proceedings from the ISME 2014 Seminar of the Commission for Community Music Activity.* (pp 59–64). ISME.

DeVito, D., & Gill, A. (2013). Reaching out to participants who are challenged. In K. Veblen, S. J. Messenger, M. Silverman, & D. J. Elliott (Eds.), *Community music today* (pp. 217–230). Rowman and Littlefield.

Dewey, J. (1934). *Art as experience.* Capricorn Books.

Diamond, J. (2014). *The third chimpanzee: On the evolution and future of the human animal.* Oneworld Publications.

Dickie-Johnson, A., & Meek, R. (2022). A qualitative study of the rehabilitative potential of music in prisons and immigration removal centers. *Journal of Creativity in Mental Health, 17*(2), 140–153. https://doi.org/10.1080/15401383.2020.1848673

Dikeç, M., Clark, N., & Barnett, C. (2009). Extending hospitality: Giving space. Taking time. *Paragraph, 32*(1), 1–14.

Diprose, R. (2009). Women's bodies giving time for hospitality. *Hypatia, 24*(2), 142–163. https://doi.org/10.1111/j.1527-2001.2009.01036.x

Docherty, T. (Ed.). (1993). *Postmodernism: A reader.* Harvester Wheatsheaf.

Doeser, J. (2014). *Step by step: Arts policy and young people 1944–2014.* King's College London.

Doherty, S. (2022). "I am because you are": A critical reflection on composing choral music to promote social inclusion for asylum seekers in Ireland. *International Journal of Community Music, 15*(3), 341–353. https://doi.org/https://doi-org.yorksj.idm.oclc.org/10.1386/ijcm_00067_1

Dooley, M. (1999). The politics of Exodus: Hospitality in Derrida, Kierkegaard, and Levinas In R. L. Perkins (Ed.), *International Kierkegaard Commentary: Works of love* (pp. 167–192). Mercer University Press.

Dore, R. (1997). *The diploma disease: Education qualification and development* (2nd ed.). Institute of Education.

Due, R. (2007). *Deleuze.* Polity Press.

Dufourmantelle, A. (2013). Hospitality—Under compassion and violence. In T. Claviez (Ed.), *The conditions of hospitality: Ethics, politics, and aesthetics on the threshold of the possible* (pp. 13–23). Fordham University Press.

Dunbar, R. (2021). *Friends: Understanding the power of our most important relationships.* Little Brown.

## 190 REFERENCES

Eckstrom, E. (2008). Ukrainian youth development: Music and creativity, a route to youth betterment. *International Journal of Community Music, 1*(1), 105–115.

Edgeworth, B. (2012). From Plato to NATO: Law and social justice in historical context. *UNSW Law Journal, 35*(2), 417–448.

Eisner, E. W. (1981). On the difference between scientific and artistic approaches to qualitative research. *Educational Researcher, 10*(4), 5–9.

Elliott, D., Silverman, M., & Bowman, W. (Eds.). (2017). *Artistic citizenship: Artistry, social responsibility, and ethical praxis.* Oxford University Press.

Elliott, D. J. (1995). *Music matters: A new philosophy of music education.* Oxford University Press.

Elliott, D. J. (1998). *Community music and postmodernity.* Commission for Community Music Activity: Many Musics-One Circle.

Elliott, D. J. (Ed.). (2005). *Praxial music education: Reflections and dialogues.* Oxford University Press.

Elliott, D. J., & Silverman, M. (2015). *Music matters: A philosophy of music education* (2nd ed.). Oxford University Press.

Ellis, C., & Bochner, A. P. (Eds.). (1996). *Composing ethnography: Alternative forms of qualitative writing.* AltaMira Press.

Eraut, M. (2004). Informal learning in the workplace. *Studies in Continuing Education, 26*(2), 247–273.

Evans, M., Millar, A., Hutchinson, P., & Dingwell, C. (2014). Decolonizing research practice: Indigenous methodologies, Aboriginal methods, and knowledge/knowing. In P. Leavy (Ed.), *The Oxford handbook of qualitative research* (pp. 179–191). Oxford University Press.

Everingham, C. (2001). Reconstituting community: Social justice, social order and the politics of community. *Australian Journal of Social Issues, 36*(2), 105–122.

Evison, F. (2022). Inside, outside, upside, downside: Navigating positionality as a composer in community music *Transform: New Voices in Community Music,* (4), 5–25. http://79.170.44.82/transformiccm.co.uk/?page_id=915

Fagan, M., Glorieux, L., Hašimbegović, I., & Suetsugu, M. (2007). *Derrida: Negotiating the legacy.* Edinburgh University Press. http://www.jstor.org.yorksj.idm.oclc.org/stable/10.3366/j.ctv2f4vfg7

Felshin, N. (1995). *But is it art?: The spirit of art as activism.* Bay Press.

Finley, S. (2003). Arts-based inquiry in QI: Seven years from crisis to guerrilla warfare. *Qualitative Inquiry, 9*(2), 281–296. http://qix.sagepub.com/cgi/reprint/9/2/281

Finley, S. (2005). Arts-based inquiry: Performing revolutionary pedagogy. In N. K. Denzin & Y. S. Lincoln (Eds.), *The Sage handbook of qualitative research* (3rd ed., pp. 681–694). Sage.

Finley, S. (2018). Critical arts-based inquiry: Performances of resistance politics. In N. K. Denzin & Y. S. Lincoln (Eds.), *The Sage handbook of qualitative research* (5th ed., pp. 561–575). Sage.

Fleischacker, S. (2005). *A short history of distributive justice.* Harvard Univeristy Press.

Folkestad, G. (2005). The local and the global in musical learning: Considering the interaction between formal and informal settings. In P. S. Campbell, J. Drummond, P. Dunbar-Hall, K. Howard, H. Schippers, & T. Wiggins (Eds.), *Cultural diversity in music education: Directions and challenges for the 21st century* (pp. 23–28). Australian Academic Press.

Folkestad, G. (2006). Formal and informal learning situations or practices vs formal and informal ways of learning. *British Journal of Music Education, 23*(2), 135–145.

Foucault, M. (1980). *Power/knowledge: Selected interviews and other writings 1972–1977.* Pantheon Books.

Foucault, M. (1998). Nietzsche, Freud, Marx. In J. D. Faubion (Ed.), *Aesthetics, method, and epistemology* (pp. 269–278). New Press.

Freire, P. (2002). *Pedagogy of the oppressed.* Continuum. (Original work published 1970)

Friese, H. (2009). The limits of hospitality. *Paragraph, 32*(1), 51–68.

Fusi, L. (2012). Disappearing human beings, not problems. In S. Tallent & P. Domela (Eds.), *The unexpected guest: Art, writing and thinking on hospitality* (pp. 10–15). Art/Books.

## REFERENCES 191

Geertz, C. (1975). Deep play: Notes on the Balinese cockfight. In *The interpretation of cultures* (pp. 412–453). Hutchinson and Co.

Gibbs, G. (1998). *Learning by doing: A guide to teaching and learning methods*. Oxford Brooks University.

Gibson, J. (2020). *Making music together*. https://www.jogibson.org/

Gibson, S. J., Higgins, L., & Schippers, H. (2022). *Understanding the magic of ethno: Key findings of ethno research 2019–2022*. https://www.ethnoresearch.org/

Gidley, J., Hampson, G., Wheeler, L., & Bereded-Samuel, E. (2010). Social inclusion: Context, theory and practice. *Australasian Journal of University Community Engagement*, 5, 6–36. https://researchrepository.rmit.edu.au/esploro/outputs/journalArticle/Social-inclusion-Context-theory-and-practice/9921857731901341#file-0

Gillespie, D. (2010). The transformative power of democracy and human rights in nonformal education: The case of Tostan. *Adult Education Quarterly*, 60(5), 477–498.

Glenister, S. (2021). Why analyse the impact of making bleepy noises with kids in studios? *Sounding Board*, (3). https://www.soundsense.org/DB/sounding-board/sounding-board-2021-issue-3?ps=hDl3S_tVVSs3OldusHA8lTkEgVPyDE

Glenister, S. (2024). Evaluating well-being outcomes of the social enterprise "noise solution": Digital approaches to outcome capture. In P. Dale, P. Burnard, & R. Travis (Eds.), *Music for inclusion in school and beyond* (pp. 335–360). Oxford University Press.

Goh, I. (2020). Rethinking philosophical perspectives on community: Prepositional community. In B. Jansen (Ed.), *Rethinking community through transdisciplinary research* (pp. 85–96). Palgrave MacMillan.

Goldbard, A. (2006). *New creative community: The art of cultural development*. New Village Press.

Goldstein, R. (2014). Propaganda, protest, and poisonous vipers: The cinema war in Korea. *Daily Beast*. https://www.thedailybeast.com/white-house-official-floated-withdrawing-us-forces-to-please-putin?source=dictionary

Golec de Zavala, A., Guerra, R., & Simão, C. (2017). The relationship between the Brexit vote and individual predictors of prejudice: Collective narcissism, right wing authoritarianism, social dominance orientation. *Frontiers in Psychology*, 8. https://doi.org/10.3389/fpsyg.2017.02023

Goodrich, A. (2007). Peer mentoring in a high school jazz ensemble. *Journal of Research in Music Education*, 55(2), 94.

Gorard, S. (2018). *Education policy, equity and effectiveness: Evidence of equity and effectiveness*. Policy Press.

Gouk, P. (2000). *Musical healing in cultural contexts*. Ashgate.

Gould, E. (2007). Social justice in music education: The problematic of democracy. *Music Education Research*, 9(2), 229–240. https://doi.org/10.1080/14613800701384359

Gould, E. (2011). Writing Trojan horses and war machines: The creative political in music education research. *Educational Philosophy and Theory*, 43(8), 874–887.

Gould, E. (2012). Uprooting music education pedagogies and curricula: Becoming-musician and the Deleuzian refrain. *Discourse Studies in the Politics of Education*, 35(1), 75–86. https://doi.org/10.1080/01596306.2012.632168

Gould, E., Countryman, J., Morton, C., & Rose, L. S. (Eds.). (2009). *Exploring social justice: How music education might matter*. Canadian Music Educators' Association.

Gouzouasis, P., & Bakan, D. (2018). Arts-based educational research in community music. In B.-L. Bartleet & L. Higgins (Eds.), *The Oxford handbook of community music* (pp. 573–592). Oxford University Press.

Graça, J., & Rodrigues, H. (2021). *Different shades of community music in Portugal*. http://hdl.handle.net/10362/143597

Graeber, D., & Wengrow, D. (2021). *The dawn of everything: A new history of humanity*. Penguin.

Graham, L., & Slee, R. (2008). Inclusion? In S. L. Gabel & S. Danforth (Eds.), *Disability & the politics of education: An international reader* (pp. 81–100). Peter Lang.

## 192 REFERENCES

Graves, J. B. (2005). *Cultural democracy: The arts, community, and the public.* University of Ilinois Press.

Greaney, J. (2021). On the legacies of Derrida and deconstruction today: An interview with Jean-Michel Rabaté. *Derrida Today, 14,* 91–106. https://doi.org/10.3366/drt.2021.0254

Green, L. (2002). *How popular musicians learn.* Ashgate Publishing Company.

Green, L. (2005). The music curriculum as lived experience: Children's "natural" music learning processes. *Music Educators Journal, 94*(4), 27–32.

Green, L. (2008). *Music, informal learning and the school: A new classroom pedagogy.* Ashgate.

Green, L. (Ed.). (2011). *Learning, teaching, and musical identity: Voices across cultures.* Indiana University Press.

Green, L. (2014). *Hear, listen, play!: How to free your students' aural, improvisation, and performance skills.* Oxford University Press.

Green, P. (1999). *Equality and democracy.* New Press.

Grodd, U., & Lines, D. (2018). Manukau Symphony Orchestra: Reflections on a sustainable model for a community orchestra in Aotearoa New Zealand. *International Journal of Community Music, 11*(3), 325–336. https://doi.org/https://doi-org.yorksj.idm.oclc.org/10.1386/ijcm.11.3.325_1

Guerlac, S. (2006). *Thinking in time: An introduction to Henri Bergson.* Cornell University Press.

Gunther, K. (2022). Inclusion, auditions and American community choirs: A historical inquiry. *International Journal of Community Music, 15*(3), 405–424. https://doi.org/https://doi-org.yorksj.idm.oclc.org/10.1386/ijcm_00071_1

Habermas, J. (1984). *Reason and the rationalization of society: Vol. 1: The theory of communicative action.* Beacon Press.

Haggerty, D. (2010). Shame in feminine hospitality. In M. Hamington (Ed.), *Feminism and hospitality* (pp. 55–69). Rowman & Littlefield.

Hallam, S., Creech, A., & McQueen, H. (2015). Teachers' perceptions of the impact on students of the Musical Futures approach. *Music Education Research, 19*(3), 263–275. https://doi.org/https://doi.org/10.1080/14613808.2015.1108299

Hallam, S., Creech, A., Varvarigou, M., McQueen, H., & Gaunt, H. (2014). Does active engagement in community music support the well-being of older people? *Arts & Health, 6*(2), 101–116. https://doi.org/DOI:10.1080/17533015.2013.809369

Hamington, M. (2010). Toward a theory of feminist hospitality. *Feminist Formations, 22*(1), 21–38.

Hansen, J. H. (2012). Limits to inclusion. *International Journal of Inclusive Education, 16*(1), 89–98. https://doi.org/10.1080/13603111003671632

Hart, K. (2004). *Postmodernism: A beginner's guide.* Oneworld Publications.

Hayek, F. A. (1976). *Law, legislation and liberty, Vol. 2: The mirage of social justice.* University of Chicago Press.

Heard, E., Bartleet, B.-L., & Woolcock, G. (2023). Exploring the role of place-based arts initiatives in addressing social inequity in Australia: A systematic review. *Australian Journal of Social Issues, 58*(3), 1–23. https://doi.org/https://doi.org/10.1002/ajs4.257

Hebert, D. G., & Kertz-Welzel, A. (Eds.). (2016). *Patriotism and nationalism in music education.* Routledge.

Heidegger, M. (2001). *Poetry, language, thought* (A. Hofstadter, Trans.). Perennial Classics.

Heidegger, M. (2002). *Being and time* (J. Macquarrie & E. Robinson, Trans.). Blackwell Publishing.

Held, V. (2006). *The ethics of care: Personal, political, and global.* Oxford University Press.

Henley, J. (2015). Music: Naturally inclusive, potentially exclusive? In J. Deppeler, T. Loreman, R. Smith, & L. Florian (Eds.), *Inclusive pedagogy across the curriculum.* (pp. 161–186). http://dx.doi.org/10.1108/S1479-363620150000007015

Henley, J., & Higgins, L. (2020a). MUSOC: Music and Social Intervention Network excellence, inclusion and intervention in music: Navigating contexts and building sustainable working practices for musicians. *International Journal of Community Music, 13*(2), 127–134.

## REFERENCES    193

Henley, J., & Higgins, l. (2020b). Redefining excellence and inclusion. *International Journal of Community Music, 13*(2), 207–216.

Hess, J. (2017). Equity in music education: Why equity and social justice in music education? *Music Educators Journal, 104*(1), 71–73.

Hess, J. (2018). Revolutionary activism in striated spaces? Considering an activist music education in K-12 schooling. *Action, Criticism and Theory for Music Education, 17*(2), 22–49. https://doi.org/doi:10.22176/act17.2.22

Hess, J. (2020). Finding the "both/and": Balancing informal and formal music learning. *International Journal of Music Education, 38*(3), 441–455.

Hesser, B., & Bartleet, B. (Eds.). (2020). *Music as a global resource: Solution for cultural, social, health, educational, environmental, and economic issues* (5th ed.). Music as a Global Resource.

Higgins, L. (2006). *Boundary-walkers: Contexts and concepts of community music* University of Limerick.

Higgins, L. (2007a). Acts of hospitality: The community in Community Music. *Music Education Research, 9*(2), 281–291.

Higgins, L. (2007b). *The impossible* future. *Action, Criticism, and Theory for Music Education, 6*(3), 74–96. http://act.maydaygroup.org/articles/Higgins6_3.pdf

Higgins, L. (2010). Representing practice: Community music and arts-based research. In D. D. Coffman (Ed.), *CMA XII: Harmonizing the diversity that is community music activity: Proceedings from the International Society for Music Education 2010 Seminar of the Commission for Community Music Activity* (pp. 98–104). Open University of China.

Higgins, L. (2012a). The community in community music. In G. McPherson & G. F. Welch (Eds.), *The Oxford handbook of music education* (Vol. 2, pp. 104–119). Oxford University Press.

Higgins, L. (2012b). *Community music: In theory and in practice.* Oxford University Press.

Higgins, L. (2012c). One-to-one encounters: Facilitators, participants, and friendship. *Theory into Practice, 51*(3), 159–166. https://doi.org/10.1080/00405841.2012.690297

Higgins, L. (2015). Hospitable music making community music as a site for social justice. In C. Benedict, P. Schmidt, G. Spruce, & P. G. Woodford (Eds.), *The Oxford handbook of social justice and music education* (pp. 446–455). Oxford University Press.

Higgins, L. (2016). My voice is important too: Non-formal music experiences and young people. In G. McPherson (Ed.), *The child as musician* (2nd ed., pp. 594–605). Oxford University Press.

Higgins, L. (2020a). Note 57: Hospitable approaches to community music scholarship. *International Journal of Community Music, 13*(3), 223–233.

Higgins, L. (2020b). Rethinking community in community music: The call, the welcome, and the "yes." In B. Jansen (Ed.), *Rethinking community through transdisciplinary research* (pp. 231–246). Palgrave MacMillan.

Higgins, L., & Willingham, L. (2017). *Engaging in community music: An introduction.* Routledge.

Higgins, L., & S.J. Gibson (Eds.). (2024). *Ethno music gatherings: Pedagogy, experience, impact.* Intellect.

Hill, B., & Banffy-Hall, A. d. (Eds.). (2017). *Community music—Beiträge zur Theorie und Praxis aus internationaler und deutscher Perspektive.* Münster.

Hobbes, T. (1968). *Leviathan.* Pelican Books. (Original work published 1651)

Hogan, C. (2002). *Understanding facilitation: Theory and principles.* Kogan Page.

Hogan, C. (2003). *Practical facilitation: A toolkit of techniques.* Kogan Page.

Holborow, M. (2012). Neoliberalism, human capital and the skills agenda in higher education - The Irish case. *Journal for Critical Education Policy Studies, 10*(1), 93–111.

Homer. (2003). *The odyssey* (E. V. Rieu, Trans.). Penguin Classics.

Horden, P. (2000). *Music as medicine: The history of music therapy since antiquity.* Routledge.

Howell, G. (2013). Finding my place: Examining concepts of community music as a visiting artist in rural East Timor. *International Journal of Community Music, 6*(1), 65–78.

## 194 REFERENCES

Howell, G. (2015). Music interventions: Shaping music participation in the aftermath of conflict. In S. Schonmann (Ed.), *In the wisdom of the many: Key issues in arts education* (pp. 87–92). Waxmann.

Howell, G. (2018). Community music interventions in post-conflict contexts. In B.-L. Bartleet & L. Higgins (Eds.), *The Oxford handbook of community music* (pp. 43–70). Oxford University Press.

Howell, G., Pruitt, L., & Hassler, L. (2019). Making music in divided cities: Transforming the ethnoscape. *International Journal of Community Music, 12*(3), 331–348. https://doi.org/doi:10.1386/ijcm_00004_1

Hulse, B., & Nesbitt, N. (Eds.). (2016). *Sounding the virtual: Gilles Deleuze and the theory and philosophy of music.* Routledge.

Humphrey, R. (2023). *What we say and what we do: An examination into the discourse of community music and its interrelation with cultural policy.* York St. John University.

Hunter, J., Micklem, D., & Artists, M. (2016). *Everyday creativity.* http://64millionartists.com/everyday-creativity-2/.

Husserl, E. (1973). *Cartesian meditations: An introduction to phenomenology* (D. Cains, Trans.; 5th ed.). Martinus Nijhoff.

IMC. (2023). *Syria/Turkey earthquakes situation report #9, May 9, 2023.* International Medical Corp. https://reliefweb.int/report/syrian-arab-republic/syriaturkey-earthquakes-situation-report-9-may-9-2023

Inwood, M. (1999). *A Heidegger dictionary.* Blackwell.

Jaeger, W. (1986). *Paideia: The ideas of Greek culture: Vol. 1: Archaic Greek: The mind of Athens.* Oxford University Press.

Jameson, F. (1991). *Postmodernism, or, The cultural logic of late capitalism.* Verso.

Jarrett, C. (2007). *Spinoza: A guide for the perplexed.* Continuum.

Jeffers, A., & Moriarty, G. (Eds.). (2017). *Culture, democracy and the right to make art: The British community arts movement.* Bloomsbury Methuen Drama.

Jeffs, T., & Smith, M. K. (2005). *Informal education: Conversation, democracy and learning.* Educational Heretics Press.

Jellison, J. A., & Draper, E. A. (2015). Music research in inclusive school settings: 1975 to 2013. *Journal of Research in Music Education, 62*(4), 325–331. https://doi.org/DOI:10.1177/0022429414554808

Jellison, J. A., & Taylor, D. M. (2007). Attitudes toward inclusion and students with disabilities: A review of three decades of music research. *Bulletin of the Council for Research in Music Education, 172,* 9–23.

Jenkins, P. (2011). Formal and informal music educational practices. *Philosophy of Music Education Review, 19*(2), 179–197.

Jones, P., & Langston, T. W. (2012). Community music and social capital. In G. McPherson & G. F. Welch (Eds.), *The Oxford handbook of music education* (Vol. 2, pp. 120–137). Oxford University Press.

Jorgensen, E. R., & Yob, I. M. (2013). Deconstructing Deleuze and Guattari's *A Thousand Plateaus* for music education. *Journal of Aesthetic Education, 47*(3), 36–55.

Joss, T. (1993). A short history of community music. In T. Joss & D. Price (Eds.), *The first national directory of community music* (pp. 3–8). Sound Sense.

Juan-Morera, B., Nadal-García, I., & López-Casanova, B. (2022). Systematic review of inclusive musical practices in non-formal educational contexts. *Education Sciences, 13*(1). https://doi.org/https://doi.org/10.3390/educsci13010005

Jun, N., & Smith, D. W. (Eds.). (2011). *Deleuze and ethics.* Edinburgh University Press.

Kant, I. (1903). *Perpetual peace: A philosophical essay* (M. C. Smith, Trans.). Macmillan.

Kant, I. (1989). *Foundations of the metaphysics of morals/what is enlightenment?* Macmillan USA.

Kant, I. (1998). *Critique of pure reason* (P. Guyar & A.W. Wood, Trans.). Cambridge University Press.

## REFERENCES 195

Karofsky, P., Zeng, L., & Kosorok, M. R. (2000). Relationship between adolescent–parental communication and initiation of first intercourse by adolescents. *Journal of Adolescent Health, 28*(1), 41–45.

Kearney, R., & Semonovitch, K. (2011). *Phenomenologies of the stranger: Between hostility and hospitality.* Fordham University Press.

Keil, C. (1979). *Tiv song: The sociology of art in a classless society.* University of Chicago Press.

Kelly, O. (1984). *Community, art and the state.* Comedia.

Kelly, O. (2023). *Cultural democracy now: What it means and why we need it.* Routledge.

Kershaw, B. (2009). Practice as research through performance. In H. Smith & R. T. Dean (Eds.), *Practice-led research, research-led practice in the creative arts* (pp. 104–125). Edinburgh University Press.

Kertz-Welzel, A. (2016). Daring to question: A philosophical critique of community music. *Philosophy of Music Education Review, 24*(2), 113–130. https://doi.org/10.2979/philmusie ducrevi.24.2.01

Khaleel, M. (2017). The virtues and limits of hospitality. *CrossCurrents, 67*(3), 546–554.

Anderson, K., & Willingham, L. (2020). Environment, intention and intergenerational music making: Facilitating participatory music making in diverse contexts of community music. *International Journal of Community Music, 13*(2), 173–185.

Kitlinski, T. (2022). The powers and limits of hospitality: Lublin, Poland. *Social Research: An International Quarterly, 89*(1), 179–198.

Knowles, M. S., Holton, E. F., & Swanson, R. A. (2011). *The adult learner.* Elsevier.

Koen, B. D. (Ed.). (2008). *The Oxford handbook of medical ethnomusicology.* Oxford University Press.

Kolb, D. A. (1983). *Experiential learning: Experience as the source of learning and development* (7th ed.). Prentice Hall.

Kors, N. (2007). *Case studies of non-formal music education and informal learning in non-formal contexts.* Lectorate Lifelong Learning in Music.

Kristeva, J. (1980). *Desire in language: A semiotic approach to literature and art.* Basil Blackwell Ltd.

Krönig, F. K. (2019). Community music and the risks of affirmative thinking: A critical insight into the semantics of community music. *Philosophy of Music Education Review, 27*(1), 21–36. https://doi.org/https://www.muse.jhu.edu/article/720663.

Kropotkin, P. (1972). *Mutual aid: A factor of evolution.* New York University Press.

Kruse, N. B. (2022). Equity in music education: Disrupting ageist ideologies through inclusive music-making. *Music Educators Journal, 109*(2), 56–58.

Kuiken, K. (2005). Deleuze/Derrida: Towards an almost imperceptible difference. *Research in Phenomenology, 35*, 290–308.

Kushner, S., Walker, B., & Tarr, J. (2001). *Case studies and issues in community music.* University of the West of England.

Kyriakidou, M. (2021). Hierarchies of deservingness and the limits of hospitality in the "refugee crisis." *Media, Culture & Society, 43*(1), 133–149.

Laes, T. (2017). *The (im)possibility of inclusion: Reimagining the potentials of democratic inclusion in and through activist music education.* University of the Arts Helsinki.

Lam, C. (2023). *In the process of becoming: An ethnographic case study of the development of community music practice in Hong Kong* [Doctoral thesis]. Royal College of Music.

Lashley, C., Lynch, P., & Morrison, A. (Eds.). (2007). *Hospitality: A social lens.* Elsevier.

Laurila, K. (2021). Song as the catalyst that promotes envisioning ethical spaces. In L. Willingham (Ed.), *Community music at the boundaries* (pp. 260–273). Wilfrid Laurier University Press.

Leavy, P. (Ed.). (2009). *Method meets art: Arts based research practice.* Guilford Press.

Leavy, P. (Ed.). (2014). *The Oxford handbook of qualitative research.* Oxford University Press.

Lebler, D. (2008). Popular music pedagogy: Peer learning in practice. *Music Education Research, 10*(2), 193–213.

## 196 REFERENCES

Lee, J., Davidson, J.W., & Krause, A. E. (2016). Older people's motivations for participating in community singing in Australia. *International Journal of Community Music, 9*(2), 191–206. https://doi.org/doi:10.1386/ijcm.9.2.191_1

Lee, P., Stewart, D., & Clift, S. (2018). Group singing and quality of life. In B.-L. Bartleet & L. Higgins (Eds.), *The Oxford handbook of community music* (pp. 503–523). Oxford University Press.

Lee, S., O'Neill, D., & Moss, H. (2022). Promoting well-being among people with early-stage dementia and their family carers through community-based group singing: A phenomenological study. *Arts & Health, 14*(1), 85–101. https://doi.org/10.1080/17533 015.2020.1839776

Leppänen, T. (2011). Babies, music and gender: Music playschools in Finland as multimodal participatory spaces. *Policy Futures in Education, 9*(4), 474–484.

Levinas, E. (1969). *Totality and infinity: An essay on exteriority* (A. Lingis, Trans.). Duquesne University Press.

Levinas, E. (1987). *Time and the others* (R. A. Cohen, Trans.). Duquesne University.

Levinas, E. (2006). *Humanism of the other* (N. Poller, Trans.). University of Ilinois Press.

Liasidou, A. (2012). *Inclusive education, politics and policymaking*. Continuum.

*Life application bible: New international version*. (1992). Tyndale House.

Lines, D. (2013). Deleuze and music education: Machines for change. In D. Masny (Ed.), *Cartographies of becoming in education: A Deleuze-Guattari perspective* (pp. 23–33). Sense Publishers.

Lister, A. (2011, May 10). *The "mirage" of social justice: Hayek against (and for) Rawls*. Oliver Smithies Lecture, Trinity Term, Balliol College, Oxford.

Liu, Y., Yang, S., Ren, T., Li, H., Hogg, A., Shah, P., Li, J., Zhang, Y., & Chhetri, A. (2022). A hybrid and non-formal music education connecting China's local family communities and cultures with Nepal. *International Journal for Infonomics, 15*(1), 2088–2093. https://inf onomics-society.org/wp-content/uploads/A-Hybrid-and-Non-Formal-Music-Education-Connecting-Chinas-Local-Family-Communities.pdf

Locke, J. (1963). *Two treatises of government*. Mentor.

Lonie, D. (2018). Measuring outcomes and demonstrating impact. In B.-L. Bartleet & L. Higgins (Eds.), *The Oxford handbook of community music* (pp. 281–298). Oxford University Press.

Lonie, D., & Dickens, L. (2015). Becoming musicians: Situating young people's experiences of musical learning between formal, informal and non-formal spheres. *Cultural Geographies, 23*(1), 87–101.

Lopez, M. A. G. (2012). *Using e-learning in intercultural non-formal education activities*. http://www.coe.int/t/dg4/youth/Source/Training/Quality_NFE/2012_Mapping_Elearning_st udy.pdf

Lukes, S. (1997). Social justice: The Hayekian challenge. *Critical Review: A Journal of Politics and Society, 11*(1), 65–80.

Lynch, P., Molz, J. G., Mcintosh, A., Lugosi, P., & Lashley, C. (2011). Theorizing hospitality. *Hospitality and Society, 1*(1), 3–24.

Lyotard, J.-F. (1984). *The postmodern condition: A report on knowledge* (G. Bennington & B. Massumi, Trans.). Manchester University Press.

Lyotard, J.-F. (1991). *The inhuman: Reflections on time* (G. Bennington & R. Bowlby, Trans.). Polity Press.

Lyotard, J.-F., & Thébaud, J.-L. (1985). *Just gaming* (W. Godzich, Trans.). University of Minneapolis Press.

Macdonald, I. (1995). The Leiston statement. *Sounding Board*, Spring, 29.

MacDonald, R., Kreutz, G., & Mitchell, L. (Eds.). (2012). *Music, health, and wellbeing*. Oxford University Press.

MacDonald, R. A. R., Hargreaves, D. J., & Miell, D. (2002). *Musical identities*. Oxford University Press.

## REFERENCES 197

Mackinlay, E. (2015). Decolonization and applied ethnomusicology: "Story-ing" the personal-political-possible in our work. In S. Pettan & J. T. Titon (Eds.), *The Oxford handbook of applied ethnomusicology* (pp. 379–397). Oxford University Press.

Mak, P. (2007). *Learning music in formal, non-formal and informal contexts.* http://www.emc-imc.org/fileadmin/EFMET/article_Mak.pdf

Mak, P., Kors, N., & Renshaw, P. (2007). *Formal, non-formal and informal learning in music.* Groningen and Royal Conservatoire.

Malpas, S. (2003). *Jean-François Lyotard.* Routledge.

Mantie, R. (2012). Learners or participants? The pros and cons of "lifelong learning." *International Journal of Community Music, 5*(3), 217–236.

Mantie, R. (2018). Community music and rational recreation. In B.-L. Bartleet & L. Higgins (Eds.), *The Oxford handbook of community music* (pp. 543–554). Oxford University Press.

Mantie, R. (2022a, June 8). Conversations in social justice. *Music, Leisure, Education.* https://podcasters.spotify.com/pod/show/isj/episodes/Music--Leisure--Education-e1jlo7c

Mantie, R. (2022b). Inclusion for all; all for inclusion. *International Journal of Community Music, 15*(3), 317–321.

Mantie, R. (2022c). *Music, leisure, education: Historical and philosophical perspectives.* Oxforf University Press.

Mantie, R. (2022d). Struggling with good intentions: Music education research in a "post" world. *Research Studies in Music Education, 44*(1), 21–33.

Mantie, R., & Higgins, L. (2015). Paideia con salsa: Charles Keil, groovology, and the undergraduate music curriculum. *Symposium, 55.* https://symposium.music.org/55/item/10885-paideia-con-salsa-charles-keil-groovology-and-the-undergraduate-music-curriculum.html

Maragani, M. H., Pandaleke, S. M., & Wibowo, M. (2019). Strategy of non formal music education in disruptive era. *First International Conference on Christian and Inter Religious Studies*, Manado, Indonesia.

Marks, J. (1998). *Gilles Deleuze: Vitalism and multiplicity.* Pluto Press.

Marrati, P. (2005). *Genesis and trace: Derrida Reading Husserl and Heidegger.* Stanford University Press.

Massumi, B. (1992). *A user's guide to capitalism and schizophrenia: Deviations from Deleuze and Guattari.* MIT Press.

Matarasso, F. (1994). *Use or ornament? The social impact of participation.* Comedia.

Matarasso, F. (2019, November 5). Instrumentalisation: A convenient mask. *A Restless Art, Ethics, Where do you stand?* https://arestlessart.com/2019/11/05/instrumentalisation-a-convenient-mask/comment-page-1/

Matherne, N. (2022). Investigating well-being and participation in Florida New Horizons ensembles through the PERMA framework. *International Journal of Community Music, 15*(2), 283–311. https://doi.org/DOI:10.1386/ijcm_00064_1

Matthews, W. K., Bertleff, A., Dellmann-Jenkins, M., & Flory, M. (2022). Dimensions of Community Band Participation Scale (DCBP): Development of a survey. *International Journal of Community Music, 15*(2), 269–282. https://doi.org/https://doi-org.yorksj.idm.oclc.org/10.1386/ijcm_00063_1

Mauss, M. (1990). *The gift* (W. D. Hall, Trans.). Routledge. (Original work published 1924)

May, T. (2003). When is a Deleuzian becoming? *Continental Philosophy Review, 36*, 139–153. https://doi.org/https://doi.org/10.1023/A:1026036516963

May, T. (2005). *Gilles Deleuze: An introduction.* Cambridge University Press.

McAteer, N. (2022). "We're NOT all in this together". Transitioning from practice to research during the COVID-19 pandemic: A period of deep reflection, decentralisation and reframing of social justice. *Transform: New Voices in Community Music,* (4), 42–62. http://79.170.44.82/transformiccm.co.uk/?page_id=908

McAteer, N., & Wells, R. (2024). Community music and its political imperative: Music making and the struggle for social justice. In J. Nichols (Ed.), *The Sage handbook on school music education* (pp. 253–269). Sage.

198 REFERENCES

McCarthy, M. (2008). The Community Music Activity Commission of ISME 1982–2007: A forum for global dialogue and institutional formation. *International Journal of Community Music, 1*(1), 49–61.

McCumber, J. (2000). *Philosophy and freedom: Derrida, Rorty, Habermas, Foucault.* Indiana University Press.

McFerran, K., Derrington, P., & Saarikallio, S. (Eds.). (2019). *Handbook of music, adolescents, and wellbeing.* Oxford University Press.

McGuire, C. E. (2009). *Music and Victorian philanthropy: The tonic sol-fa movement.* Cambridge University Press.

McKay, F. H., & Taket, A. (2020). *Health equity, social justice and human rights* (2nd ed.). Routledge.

McKay, G., & Higham, B. (2012). *Community music: History and current practice, its construction of "community", digital turns and future soundings.* http://www.ahrc.ac.uk/

McNiff, S. (2008). Art-based research. In J. G. Knowles & A. L. Cole (Eds.), *Handbook of the arts in qualitative research* (pp. 29–40). Sage.

McPherson, G., & Welch, G. F. (Eds.). (2012a). *The Oxford handbook of music education* (Vol. 1). Oxford University Press.

McPherson, G., & Welch, G. F. (Eds.). (2012b). *The Oxford handbook of music education* (Vol. 2). Oxford University Press.

McPherson, G., & Welch, G. F. (Eds.). (2018). *Special needs, community music, and adult learning: An Oxford handbook of music education* (Vol. 4). Oxford University Press.

Meade, R. C. (1990). *Red Brigades: The story of Italian terrorism.* St. Martin's Press.

Merleau-Ponty, M. (1962). *Phenomenology of perception* (C. Smith, Trans.). Routledge and Kegan Paul.

Merriam, A. P. (1964). *The anthropology of music.* Northwestern University Press.

Mill, J. S. (1978). *On liberty.* Hackett Publishing. (Original work published 1859)

Miller, D. (1999). *Principles of social justice.* Harvard Univeristy Press.

Miller, D., & Walzer, M. (Eds.). (1995). *Pluralism, justice, and equality.* Oxford University Press.

Mitchell, D. (2015). Inclusive education is a multi-faceted concept. *Center for Educational Policy Studies Journal, 5*(1), 9–30.

Moiz, J. G., & Gibson, S. (2012). *Mobilizing hospitality: The ethics of social relations in a mobile world.* Ashgate.

Mok, O. N. A. (2011). Non-formal learning: Clarification of the concept and its application in music learning. *Australian Journal of Music Education*, (1), 11–15.

Moran, D. (2000). *Introduction to phenomenology.* Routledge.

Morgan, L. H. (2012). *Houses and house-life of the American Aborigines.* Public Domain. (Original work published 1881)

Moriarty, G. (2004). Community arts and the quality issue. In S. Fitzgerald (Ed.), *An outburst of frankness: Community arts in Ireland—A reader* (pp. 148–156). New Island.

Morrison, A., & O'Gorman, K. D. (2008). Hospitality studies and hospitality management: A symbiotic relationship. *International Journal of Hospitality Management, 27*(2), 214–221.

Mualuko, N. J. (2008). Empowering out of school youth through non-formal education in Kenya. *Educational Research and Review, 3*(2), 56–60. http://www.academicjournals.org/ERR

Mullen, P. (2022). *Challenging voices: Music making with children excluded from school.* Peter Lang.

Mullen, P., & Deane, K. (2018). Strategic working with children and young people in challenging circumstances. In B.-L. Bartleet & L. Higgins (Eds.), *The Oxford handbook of community music* (pp. 177–194). Oxford University Press.

Muslu Gardner, O. (2019). Sustaining vanishing cultures in domanic, Turkey In *The Nahrein Network Podcast.* https://www.ucl.ac.uk/nahrein/media/podcasts

Myers, D. E. (2018). Music education frontiers: Fulfilling legacies . . . breaking boundaries. *International Journal of Community Music, 11*(2), 127–129. https://doi.org/doi:10.1386/ijcm.11.2.131_7

## REFERENCES 199

Naidus, B. (2009). *Arts for change: Teaching outside the frame.* New Village Press.

Nelson, R. (2013). *Practice as research in the arts: Principles, protocols, pedagogies, resistances.* Palgrave MacMillan.

Nettl, B. (1983). *The study of ethnomusicology: Twenty-nine issues and concepts.* University of Illinois Press.

Ng, H. H. (2020). Towards a synthesis of formal, non-formal and informal pedagogies in popular music learning. *Research Studies in Music Education, 42*(1), 56–76.

Nietzsche, F. (1968). *The will to power* (W. Kaufmann & R. J. Hollingdale, Trans.). Vintage Books.

Nietzsche, F. (1969). *Thus spoke Zarathustra* (R. J. Hollingdale, Trans.). Penguin Books.

Nietzsche, F. (1996). *Human, all too human: A book for free spirits* (R. J. Hollingdale, Trans.). Cambridge University Press.

Nietzsche, F. W. (1974). The will to power: An attempted transvaluation of all values (A. M. Ludovici, Trans.). In O. Levy (Ed.), *The complete works of Friedrich Nietzsche: The first complete and authorised English translation* (p. 412). Gordon Press.

Noddings, N. (1984). *Caring, a feminine approach to ethics and moral education.* University of California Press.

Norris, C. (1991). *Spinoza and the origins of modern critical theory.* Blackwell.

O'Flynn, J. (2006). Vernacular music-making and education. *International Journal of Music Education, 24,* 140–147.

O'Gorman, K. D. (2007). Dimensions of hospitality: Exploring ancient and classical origins. In C. Lashley, P. Lynch, & A. Morrison (Eds.), *Hospitality: A social lens* (pp. 17–32). Elsevier.

Ortner, S. B. (1978). *Sherpas through their rituals.* Cambridge University Press.

Osmaniye, K., & Adiyaman. (2023, February 18). Turkey's earthquakes show the deadly extent of construction scams. *The Economist.* https://www.economist.com/europe/2023/02/12/turkeys-earthquakes-show-the-deadly-extent-of-construction-scams

O'Sullivan, S. (2007). *Art encounters Deleuze and Guattari.* Palgrave MacMillan.

Otero, M. S., McCoshan, A., & Junge, K. (2005). *European inventory on validation of non-formal and informal learning: A final report to DG Education & Culture of the European Commission.* E. R. a. C. Limited.

Palmer, E. S. (2017). Literature review of social justice in music education: Acknowledging oppression and privilege. *Music Education Research, 36*(2), 22–31.

Parent, D. (2022). Afghan refugees on the racism they've faced in their first year in Europe. *Open Democracy.* https://www.opendemocracy.net/en/afghanistan-europe-refugees-one-year-anniversary-taliban/

Parker, S. (2023, January 10). *Conversations in social justice.* Social Action and the Radical Imagination. https://podcasters.spotify.com/pod/show/isj/episodes/Music--Leisure--Education-e1jlo7c

Parr, A. (Ed.). (2005). *The Deleuze dictionary.* Edinburgh University Press.

Parr, A. (2010). *The Deleuze dictionary revised edition.* Edinburgh University Press.

Pascal, B. (1958). *Pascal's pensees.* E. P. Dutton and Co.

Patton, P., & Protevi, J. (Eds.). (2003). *Between Deleuze and Derrida.* Continuum.

Payne, M., & Schad, J. (Eds.). (2004). *life.after.theory.* Continuum.

Peace Corps. (2004). *Non formal education manual.* http://files.peacecorps.gov/multimedia/pdf/library/M0042_nfemanual1.pdf

Peters, F., E. (1970). *Greek philosophical terms: A historical lexicon.* New York University Press. (Original work published 1967)

Pettan, S., & Titon, J. T. (Eds.). (2015). *The Oxford handbook of applied ethnomusicology.* Oxford University Press.

Phelan, H. (2012). Sonic hospitality: Migration, community, and music. In G. McPherson & G. F. Welch (Eds.), *The Oxford handbook of music education* (Vol. 2, pp. 168–184). Oxford University Press.

Phillips, R., Brennan, M. A., & Li, T. (Eds.). (2020). *Culture, community, and development.* Routledge.

## 200  REFERENCES

Pitt-Rivers, J. (2012). The law of hospitality. *HAU: Journal of Ethnographic Theory, 2*(2), 501–517.

Pitts, S., Robinson, K., & Goh, K. (2015). Not playing any more: A qualitative investigation of why amateur musicians cease or continue membership of performing ensembles. *International Journal of Community Music, 8*(2), 129–147. https://doi.org/doi:10.1386/ijcm.8.2.129_1

Plato. (1977). *Timaeus and Critias* (H. D. P. Lee, Trans.). Penguin Classics.

Plato. (1999). *The essential Plato* (B. Jowett & M. J. Knight, Trans.). Quality Paperback Book Club.

Plato. (2000). *The republic* (T. Griffith, Trans.; G. R. F. Ferrari, Ed.). Cambridge University Press.

Polońska-Kimunguyi, E. (2022). War, resistance and refuge: Racism and double standards in western media coverage of Ukraine. *LSE.* https://blogs.lse.ac.uk/medialse/2022/05/10/war-resistance-and-refuge-racism-and-double-standards-in-western-media-coverage-of-ukraine/

Powell, B. (2021). Modern band: A review of literature. *Update: Application of Research in Music Education, 39*(3), 39–46.

Powell, B. (2022). Community music interventions, popular music education and eudaimonia. *International Journal of Community Music, 15*(1), 7–29. https://doi.org/DOI:10.1386/ijcm_00056_2

Pozo-Armentia, A. d., Reyero, D., & Gil Cantero, F. (2020). The pedagogical limitations of inclusive education. *Educational Philosophy and Theory, 52*(10), 1064–1076. https://doi.org/10.1080/00131857.2020.1723549

Preston, S. (2016). *Facilitation: Pedagogies, practices, resilience.* Bloomsbury Methuen Drama.

Price, D. (2013). *Open: How we'll work, live and learn in the future.* Crux Publishing.

Rakena, T. O. (2018). Community music in the South Pacific. In B.-L. Bartleet & L. Higgins (Eds.), *The Oxford handbook of community music* (pp. 71–88). Oxford University Press.

Rawls, J. (1999). *A theory of justice* (2nd ed.). Oxford University Press.

Readings, B. (1991). *Introducing Lyotard: Art and politics.* Routledge.

Regelski, T. (2011). Praxialism and "aesthetic this, aesthetic that, aesthetic whatever." *Action, Criticism, and Theory for Music Education, 10*(2), 61–99. http://act.maydaygroup.org/artic les/Regelski10_2.pdf

Regelski, T. A. (1998). The Aristotelian bases of praxis for music and music education as praxis. *Philosophy of Music Education Review, 6*(1), 22–59.

Renshaw, P. (2005). *Simply connect: "Next practice" in group music making and musical leadership.* Paul Hamlyn Foundation.

Renshaw, P. (2010). *Engaged passions: Searches for quality in community contexts.* Eburon Academic Publishers.

Reynolds, T. E. (2010). Toward a wider hospitality: Rethinking love of neighbour in religions of the book. *Irish Theological Quarterly, 75*(2), 175–187. https://doi.org/10.1177/00211 40009360497

Rice, T. (1994). *May it fill your soul: experiencing Bulgarian music.* University of Chicago Press.

Richerme, L. K. (2019). Could there be Deleuzian assessment in music education. In D. Elliott, M. Silverman, & G. McPherson (Eds.), *The Oxford handbook of philosophical and qualitative assessment in music education* (pp. 123–136). Oxford University Press.

Richerme, L. K. (2020). *Complicating, considering, and connecting music education.* Indiana University Press.

Richter, C. (2020). *Special Issue: Community Music Zeitschrift Diskussion Musikpädagogik* (87). Hildegard Krützfeldt-Junker. http://www.junker-verlag.de/de/Zeitschrift-DMP/Heft-87:-Community-Music

Ricoeur, P. (1992). *Oneself as another* (K. Blamey, Trans.). Univeristy of Chicago Press.

Ritzer, G. (2004). *The McDonaldization of society: Revised new century edition.* Sage.

Robbins, J. W. (2004). Weak theology. *Journal for Cultural and Religious Theory, 5*(2), 1–4. http://www.jcrt.org/pastissues.shtml

Rockefeller, S. A. (2011). Flow. *Current anthropology, 52,* 557–718.

REFERENCES 201

Rodriguez, C. X. (2009). Informal learning in music: Emerging roles of teachers and students. *Action, Criticism, and Theory for Music Education, 8*(2), 35–45. http://act.maydaygruop.org/articles/Rodriguez8_2.pdf

Rogers, A. (2004). *Non-formal education: Flexible schooling or participatory education?* Comparative Education Research Centre, the University of Hong Kong. http://link.library.utoronto.ca/eir/EIRdetail.cfm?Resources__ID=593596&T=F

Rogers, C. R. (1983). *Freedom to learn for the 80s.* Merrill.

Rogers, C. R. (1995). The implications of client-centered therapy for family life. In *On becoming a person: A therapist's view of psychotherapy* (pp. 314–328). Houghton Mifflin.

Rohwer, D. (2017). A narrative investigation of adult music engagement. *International Journal of Music Education, 35*(3), 369–380.

Rolfe, G., Melanie, J., & Freshwater, D. (2011). *Critical reflection in practice: generating knowledge for care* (2nd ed.). Palgrave, Macmillian.

Rousseau, J. J. (1993). *The social contract and discourses.* Everyman.

Rowher, D. (2018). A content analysis of the International Journal of Community Music, 2008–18. *International Journal of Community Music, 11*(3), 353–362. https://doi.org/https://doi-org.yorksj.idm.oclc.org/10.1386/ijcm.11.3.353_1

Ryan, R. M., & Deci, E. L. (2017). *Self-determination theory: Basic psychological needs in motivation, development, and wellness.* Guildford Press.

Sabin, R. (Ed.). (1999). *Punk rock: So what? The cultural legacy of punk.* Routledge.

Sakya, T. M. (2001). Innovation in literacy and non formal education. *Literacy Watch Bulletin,* No 17.

Salvador, K., Knapp, E. J., & Mayo, W. (2021). Reflecting on the "Community" in Community Music School after a transition to all-online instruction. *Music Education Research, 23*(2), 194–210. https://doi.org/10.1080/14613808.2021.1905623

Sander-Staudt, M. (2010). Su casa es mi casa? Hospitality, feminist care ethics, and reciprocity. In M. Hamington (Ed.), *Feminism and hospitality* (pp. 19–38). Rowman & Littlefield.

Sands, R. M. (2007). Social justice and equity: Doing the right thing in the music teacher education program. *Action, Criticism, and Theory for Music Education, 6*(4), 43–59.

Sarup, M. (1993). *An introductory guide to post-structuralism and postmodernism.* Harvester Wheatsheaf.

Saunders, J., & Welch, G. (2012). *Communities of education: A pilot study.* International Music Education Research Centre.

Savage, J. (1991). *England's dreaming: Sex Pistols and punk rock.* Faber and Faber.

Sawchuk, P. H. (2009). Informal learning and work: From genealogy and definitions to contemporary methods and findings. In R. Maclean & D. Wilson (Eds.), *International handbook of education for the changing world of work: Bridging academic and vocational education* (pp. 319–331). Springer.

Schift, A. D. (2019). Pluralism = monism. In D. Olkowski & E. Pirovolakis (Eds.), *Deleuze and Guattari's philosophy of freedom* (pp. 155–167). Routledge.

Schippers, H. (2010). *Facing the music: Shaping music education from a global perspective.* Oxford University Press.

Schippers, H. (2018). Community music contexts, dynamics, and sustainability. In B.-L. Bartleet & L. Higgins (Eds.), *The Oxford handbook of community music* (pp. 23–42). Oxford University Press.

Schippers, H. (2023). The heart of Antakya must be saved. *Folklife.* Smithsonian Center for Folklife and Cultural Heritage. https://folklife.si.edu/magazine/antakya-turkey-earthquake-restoration

Schippers, H., & Bartleet, B.-L. (2013). The nine domains of community music: Exploring the crossroads of formal and informal music education. *International Journal of Music Education, 31*(4), 454–471. https://doi.org/10.1177/0255761413502441

Schippers, H., & Grant, C. (Eds.). (2016). *Sustainable futures for music cultures: An ecological perspective.* Oxford University Press.

## 202 REFERENCES

Schmidt, P. (2017). *Policy and the political life of music education.* Oxford University Press.

Schön, D. A. (1991). *The reflective practitioner.* Basic Books.

Sharp, R. (2011, March 19). Kate Nash launches scheme to get girls into songwriting. *The Independent.* http://www.independent.co.uk/arts-entertainment/music/news/kate-nash-launches-scheme-to-get-girls-into-songwriting-2246422.html

Sheringham, C., & Daruwalla, P. (2007). Transgressing hospitality: Polarities and disordered relationships. In C. Lashley, P. Lynch, & A. Morrison (Eds.), *Hospitality: A social lens* (pp. 33–45). Elsevier.

Shryock, A. (2009). Hospitality lessons: Learning the shared language of Derrida and the Balga Bedouin. *Paragraph, 32*(1), 32–50.

Silverman, M. (2009). Sites of social justice: Community music in New York City. *Research Studies in Music Education, 31*(2), 178–192.

Silverman, M. (2012). Community music and social justice: Reclaiming love. In G. McPherson & G. F. Welch (Eds.), *The Oxford handbook of music education* (Vol. 2, pp. 155–167). Oxford University Press.

Silverman, M., & Elliott, D. (2018). Rethinking community music as artistic citizenship. In B.-L. Bartleet & L. Higgins (Eds.), *The Oxford handbook of community music* (pp. 155–167). Oxford University Press.

Simmel, G. (1950). *The sociology of Georg Simmel* (K. H. Wolff, Trans.). Free Press.

Simmons, J. (Ed.). (1980). *The education dilemma: Policy issues for developing countries in the 1980s.* Pergamon Press.

Singapore Teachers' Academy for the Arts. (2020). *Providing a rich music learning experience.* Ministry of Education.

Singh, M. (2015). *Global perspectives on recognising non-formal and informal learning.* Springer Open.

Small, C. (1977). *Music, society, education: A radical examination of the prophetic function of music in Western, Eastern and African cultures with its impact on society and its use in education.* Calder.

Small, C. (1987). *Music of the common tongue: Survival and celebration in Afro-American music.* J. Calder; Riverrun Press.

Small, C. (1998). *Musicking: The meanings of performance and listening.* Wesleyan University Press.

Smilde, R. (2008). Lifelong learners in music: Research into musicians' biographical learning. *International Journal of Community Music, 1*(2), 243–252.

Smilde, R. (2021). *Journeys of lifelong learning in music.* Eburon.

Smith, A. M. (1996). To intervene or not to intervene: A biased decision. *Journal of Conflict Resolution, 40*(1), 16–40. https://doi.org/https://doi.org/10.1177/0022002796040001003

Smith, C. A. (2020). *Inclusivity, inclusive and inclusion: The paradoxical framework of simultaneous reality and fantasy.* Misson to Educate. https://www.calease-writer.com/post/inclusivity-inclusive-and-inclusion-the-paradoxical-framework-of-simultaneous-reality-and-fantasy

Smith, D. W. (2003). Deleuze and Derrida, immanence and transcendence: Two directions in recent French thought. In P. Patton & J. Protevi (Eds.), *Between Deleuze and Derrida* (pp. 46–66). Continuum.

Smith, G. D. (2013). *I drum, therefore I am: Being and becoming a drummer.* Ashgate.

Smith, G. D., Silverman, M., & Schyff, D. v. d. (2021). Eudaimonia and music learning. *Frontiers in Psychology, 12.* https://doi.org/10.3389/fpsyg.2021.735393

Smith, H., & Dean, R. T. (Eds.). (2009). *Practice-led research, research-led practice in the creative arts.* Edinburgh University Press.

Snow, M. (2013). Community music perspectives: Case studies from the United States. *International Journal of Community Music, 6*(1), 93–111.

Snow, N. E. (2010). Hospitableness: A neglected virtue. In M. Hamington (Ed.), *Feminism and hospitality* (pp. 3–17). Rowman & Littlefield.

## REFERENCES 203

Söderman, J., & Folkestad, G. (2004). How hip-hop musicians learn: Strategies in informal creative music making. *Music Education Research, 6*(3), 313–326.

Sokoloff, W. W. (2005). Between justice and legality: Derrida on decision. *Political Research Quarterly, 58*(2), 341–352. http://www.jstor.org/stable/3595634

Solomon, R. C. (Ed.). (1999). *What is justice?: Classic and contemporary readings* (2nd ed.). Oxford University Press.

Spencer, H. (·1946). *First principles.* Watts and Co.

Stewart-Harawira, M. (2022). Colonialism's miasmas. In H. Veltmeyer & P. Bowles (Eds.), *The essential guide to critical development studies* (2nd ed, pp. 358–365). Routledge.

St. Pierre, E. A. (1997). Guest Editorial: An introduction to figurations—A poststructural practice of inquiry. *International Journal of Qualitative Research in Education, 10*(3), 279–284.

Steger, M. B., & Roy, R. K. (2010). *Neoliberalism: A very short introduction.* Oxford University Press.

Steinberg, L. (2001). We know some things: Parent–adolescent relationships in retrospect and prospect. *Journal of Research on Adolescence, 11*(1), 1–19.

Stige, B. (2012). Health musicking: A perspective on music and health as action and performance. In R. MacDonald, G. Kreutz, & L. Mitchell (Eds.), *Music, health, and wellbeing* (pp. 183–195). Oxford University Press.

Stige, B., Ansdell, G., Elefant, C.; & Pavlicevic, M. (2010). *Where music helps: Community music therapy in action and reflection.* Ashgate.

Stivale, C. J. (Ed.). (2005). *Giles Deleuze: Key concepts.* Acumen.

Stokes, M. (Ed.). (1994). *Ethnicity, identity and music: The musical construction of place.* Berg Publishers.

Straka, G. A. (2005). Informal learning: Genealogy, concepts, antagonisms and questions. In K. Künzel (Ed.), *International yearbook of adult education* (Vol. 31, pp. 93–126). Böhlau.

Strunk, K. K., & Locke, L. A. (Eds.). (2019). *Research methods for social justice and equity in education.* Palgrave MacMillan.

Sullivan, B. M. (2017). *Exploring a theory and ethic of hospitality through an instrumental case study of a middle school band room* University of Illinois at Urbana-Champaign.

Sunderland, N., Graham, P., & Lenette, C. (2016). Epistemic communities: Extending the social justice outcomes of community music for asylum seekers and refugees in Australia. *International Journal of Community Music, 9*(3), 223–241. https://doi.org/doi:10.1386/ijcm.9.3.223_1

Sunderland, N., Woodland, S., O'Sullivan, S., & Bartleet, B.-L. (2021). The role of Australian First Nations' knowledges and the arts in "inclusive" regional and remote development: A narrative review. *Journal of Rural Studies, 89*, 423–436. https://doi.org/https://doi.org/10.1016/j.jrurstud.2021.11.002

Sweers, B. (2015). Music and conflict resolution: The public display of migrants in national(ist) conflict situations in Europe: An analytical reflection on university-based ethnomusicological activism. In S. Pettan & J. T. Titon (Eds.), *The Oxford handbook of applied ethnomusicology* (pp. 511–550). Oxford University Press. https://doi.org/https://doi.org/10.1093/oxfordhb/9780199351701.013.18

Swijghuisen Reigersberg, M. E., & Lloyd, J. (2019). To write or not to write? That is the question: Practice as research, Indigenous methodologies, conciliation and the hegemony of academic authorship. *International Journal of Community Music, 12*(3), 383–400. https://doi.org/https://doi-org.yorksj.idm.oclc.org/10.1386/ijcm_00007_1

Szekely, M. (2012). Music education: From identity to becoming. In W. Bowman & A. L. Frega (Eds.), *The Oxford handbook of philosophy in music education* (pp. 163–179). Oxford University Press.

Tallent, S. (Ed.). (2012). *The unexpected guest: Art, writing and thinking on hospitality.* Art/Books.

Taylor, J. M., Gilligan, C., & Sullivan, A. M. (1995). *Between voice and silence: Women and girls, race and relationship.* Harvard University Press.

## 204 REFERENCES

Thomson, P. (2008). Field. In M. Grenfell (Ed.), *Pierre Bourdieu: Key concepts* (pp. 67–81). Acumen.

Thorleifsson, C. (2016). The limits of hospitality: Coping strategies among displaced Syrians in Lebanon. *Third World Quarterly, 37*(6), 1071–1082.

Toor, R. (2009). Your review was brutal. *Chronicle of Higher Education.* https://www.chronicle.com/article/your-review-was-brutal/

Torres, R.-M. (2001). *What works in education?: Facing the new century.* International Youth Foundation.

Treanor, B. (2011). Putting hospitality in its place. In R. Kearney & K. Semonovitch (Eds.), *Phenomenologies of the stranger: Between hostility and hospitality* (pp. 49–66). Fordham University Press.

Tucker, R. C. (Ed.). (1978). *The Marx-Engels reader* (2nd ed.). W. W. Norton and Company.

Turino, T. (2008). *Music as social life: The politics of participation.* University of Chicago Press.

Turnbull, C. M. (1961). *The forest people.* Chatto and Windus.

Turner, K. (2017). "The line between us": Exploring the identity of the community musician through an arts practice research approach. *Voices: A World Forum for Music Therapy, 17*(3). https://doi.org/https://doi.org/10.15845/voices.v17i3.941

Turner, K. (2020). Critique not criticism: Why we ask the questions we ask. *Transform: New Voices in Community Music,* (2), 4–14. http://79.170.44.82/transformiccm.co.uk/?page_id=448

Turner, V. (1988). *The anthropology of performance.* PAJ Publications.

Urie, A., McNeill, F., Fröden, L. C., Scott, J. C., Thomas, P. C., Escobar, O., Macleod, S., & McKerracher, G. (2019). Reintegration, hospitality and hostility song-writing and song-sharing in criminal justice. *Journal of Extreme Anthropology, 3*(1), 77–101. https://doi.org/http://dx.doi.org/10.5617/jea.6914

Vaillancourt, G. (2012). Music therapy: A community approach to social justice. *The Arts in Psychotherapy, 39*(3), 173–178.

Vakeva, L., Westerlund, H., & Ilmola-Sheppard, L. (2017). Social innovations in music education: Creating institutional resilience for increasing social justice. *Action, Criticism & Theory for Music Education, 16*(3), 129–147. https://doi.org/doi:10.22176/act16.3.129

van der Sandt, J. (Ed.). (2019). *La Community music in Italia: Cenni storici, modelli pedagogici contesti sociali.* Carocii editore.

Van Weelden, K., & Whipple, J. (2014). Music educators' perceived effectiveness of inclusion. *Journal of Research in Music Education, 62*(2), 148–160. https://doi.org/DOI:10.1177/0022429414530563

Váradi, J. (2022). A review of the literature on the relationship of music education to the development of socio-emotional learning. *SAGE Open, 12*(1), 1–11.

Vattimo, G. (1984). Dialectics, difference, and weak thought. *Graduate Faculty Philosophy Journal, 10*(1), 151–164.

Vattimo, G. (1987). "Verwindung": Nihilism and the postmodern in philosophy. *SubStance, 16*(2), 7–17. http://www.jstor.org/stable/3685157

Vattimo, G. (1988). *The end of modernity: Nihilism and hermeneutics in postmodern culture.* Johns Hopkins University Press.

Vattimo, G. (1993). *The adventure of difference: Philosophy after Nietzsche and Heidegger.* Johns Hopkins University Press.

Vattimo, G. (1999). *Belief* (L. D'Isanto & D. Webb, Trans.). Polity Press.

Vattimo, G. (2002). *Nietzsche: An introduction* (N. Martin, Trans.). Athlone Press.

Vattimo, G. (2004). *Nihilism and emancipation: Ethics, politics, and law* (W. McCuaig, Trans.). Columbia University Press.

Vattimo, G., & Zabala, S. (2002). "Weak thought" and the reduction of violence. *Common Knowledge 8*(3), 452–463. https://doi.org/10.1215/0961754X-8-3-452

Vaugeois, L. (2007). Social justice and music education: Claiming the space of music education as a site of postcolonial contestation. *Action, Criticism, and Theory for Music Education, 6*(4), 163–200. http://act.maydaygroup.org/articles/Vaugeois6_4.pdf

Vaugeois, L. (2009). Music education as a *practice* of social justice. In E. Gould, J. Countryman, C. Morton, & L. S. Rose (Eds.), *Exploring social justice: How music education might matter* (pp. 2–22). Canadian Music Educators' Association.

Veblen, K. (2008). The many ways of community music. *International Journal of Community Music*, *1*(1), 5–21.

Veblen, K. (2012). Adult music learning in formal, nonformal, and informal contexts. In G. McPherson & G. F. Welch (Eds.), *The Oxford handbook of music education* (Vol. 2, pp. 243–256). Oxford University Press.

Veblen, K., Messenger, S. J., Silverman, M., & Elliott, D. J. (Eds.). (2013). *Community music today*. Rowman and Littlefield.

Veblen, K., & Olsson, B. (2002). Community music: Toward an international overview. In R. Colwell & C. P. Richardson (Eds.), *The new handbook of research on music teaching and learning* (pp. 730–753). Oxford University Press.

von Trier, L. (2003). *Dogville* [Film]. V. Windeløv; Lions Gate.

Vougioukalou, S., Dow, R., Bradshaw, L., & Pallant, T. (2019). Wellbeing and integration through community music: The role of improvisation in a music group of refugees, asylum seekers and local community members. *Contemporary Music Review*, *38*(5), 533–548. https://doi.org/10.1080/07494467.2019.1684075

Wallace, S. (Ed.). (2009). *A dictionary of education*. Oxford University Press. https://www.oxfordreference.com/display/10.1093/oi/authority.20110803095707115;jsessionid=00B290CD499298DA90866B8B5B2BE47B

Webb, A., & Swamy, S. (2020). Introduction to the focus on social justice. *Music Therapy Perspectives*, *38*(2), 100–101. https://doi.org/https://doi.org/10.1093/mtp/miaa013

Wells, R. (2021). Activist music education: Where is the community? *Transform: New Voices in Community Music*, (3), 4–24. http://79.170.44.82/transformiccm.co.uk/?page_id=715

Werquin, P. (2010). Recognizing non-formal and informal learning outcomes, policies and practices: Outcomes, policies and practices. OECD Publishing. https://doi.org/10.1787/9789264063853-en

West, C., & Cremata, R. (2016). Bringing the outside in blending formal and informal through acts of hospitality. *Journal of Research in Music Education*, *64*(1), 71–87.

Westerlund, H. (2006). Garage rock bands: A future model for developing musical expertise? *International Journal of Music Education*, *24*(2), 119–125. http://ijm.sagepub.com/cgi/reprint/24/2/119

Weston, D., & Lenette, C. (2016). Performing freedom: The role of music-making in creating a community in asylum seeker detention centres. *International Journal of Community Music*, *9*(2), 121–132.

Williamon, A. (Ed.). (2004). *Musical excellence: Strategies and techniques to enhance performance*. Oxford University Press.

Williams, J. (2008). *Gilles Deleuze's logic of sense: A critical introduction and guide*. Edinburgh University Press.

Willingham, L. (Ed.). (2021). *Community music at the boundaries*. Wilfrid Laurier University Press.

Willson, R. B. (2011). Music teachers as missionaries: Understanding Europe's recent dispatches to Ramallah. *Ethnomusicology Forum*, *20*(3), 301–325. https://doi.org/10.1080/17411912.2011.641370

Wilson, N., Gross, J., & Bull, A. (2017). *Towards cultural democracy: Promoting cultural capabilities for everyone*. http://www.kcl.ac.uk/Cultural/culturalenquiries/Towards-cultural-democracy/Towards-Cultural-Democracy-2017-KCL.pdf

Wortham, S. M. (2010). *The Derrida dictionary*. Continuum.

Wright, R., & Kanellopoulos, P. (2010). Informal music learning, improvisation and teacher education. *British Journal of Educational Studies*, *27*(1), 71–87.

Wright, R., Younker, B. A., & Beynon, C. (2016). *21st Century music education: Informal learning and non-formal teaching approaches in school and community contexts*. CMEA/ACME National Office.

## 206 REFERENCES

Wrobleski, J. (2012). *The limits of hospitality*. Liturgical Press.

Yerichuk, D. (2015). Grappling with inclusion: Ethnocultural diversity and socio-musical experiences in Common Thread Community Chorus of Toronto. *International Journal of Community Music, 8*(3), 217–231. https://doi.org/https://doi-org.yorksj.idm.oclc.org/10.1386/ijcm.8.3.217_1

Yerichuk, D., & Krar, J. (2019). From inclusion to inclusivity: A scoping review of community music scholarship. *International Journal of Community Music, 12*(2), 169–188. https://doi.org/https://doi-org.yorksj.idm.oclc.org/10.1386/ijcm.12.2.169_1

Yoon, M. Y. (1997). Explaining U.S. intervention in third world internal wars, 1945–1989. *Explaining U.S. Intervention in Third World Internal Wars, 1945–1989, 41*(4), 580–602. https://doi.org/10.1177/0022002797041004005

Young, E. B., Genosko, G., & Watson, J. (2013). *The Deleuze and Guattari dictionary*. Bloomsbury.

Young, I. M. (2011). *Responsibility for justice*. Oxford University Press.

Zabala, S. (2007a). Pharmakons of onto-theology. In S. Zabala (Ed.), *Weakening philosophy: Essays in honour of Gianni Vattimo* (pp. 231–249). McGill-Queen's University Press.

Zabala, S. (2007b). *Weakening philosophy: Essays in honour of Gianni Vattimo*. McGill-Queen's University Press.

Zabala, S., & Vattimo, G. (2002). "Weak thought" and the reduction of violence: A dialogue with Gianni Vattimo. *Common Knowledge, 8*(3), 452–463.

Ze'evi, N., Bensimon, M., & Gilboa, A. (2022). Into the groove of an alternative masculinity: Drumming groups for incarcerated individuals in a maximum-security facility. *International Journal of Community Music, 15*(2), 245–267. https://doi.org/DOI:10.1386/ijcm_00062_1

Zeserson, K. (2021). The magnificent territory: Pausing to reflect on a lifetime of working with people and music. *International Journal of Community Music. 14*(March), 9–19. https://doi.org/https://doi-org.yorksj.idm.oclc.org/10.1386/ijcm_00035_1

Zilla, C. (2022). Defining democratic inclusion from the perspective of democracy and citizenship theory. *Democratization, 29*(8), 1518–1538. https://doi.org/10.1080/13510347.2022.2090929

Zimmermann, J. (2015). *Hermeneutics: A very short introduction*. Oxford University Press.

Zourabichvili, F. (2012). *Deleuze: A philosophy of the event: Together with The Vocabulary of Deleuze*. Edinburgh University Press.

Zürcher, R. (2010). Teaching-learning processes between informality and formalization. In *Encyclopaedia of Pedagogy and Informal Education*. www.infed.org/informal_education/informality_and_formalization.htm

# Index

*For the benefit of digital users, indexed terms that span two pages (e.g., 52–53) may, on occasion, appear on only one of those pages.*

Tables are indicated by an italic *t* following the page number.

activism, social, 9, 150–51, 159, 163–64
activist, 29–30, 146–48, 152–53, 173–74
adults with learning disabilities, 122–23
affect, 169n.48, 169
always-already, 22, 118–23
Anderson, Kristin, 31–32
animateur, 5n.6
Ansdell, Gary, 111–12, 127–28
anthropological, 6, 48–49, 114–15,
    161n.20, 180–81
Arendt, Hannah, 57
Aristarkhova, Irina, 49–50
Aristotle, 54, 87, 137n.20, 160n.18
assemblage, 165–69
asylum seekers, 109–10
audience, 67–68, 101–2, 112–13, 125–26

Bartleet, Brydie-Leigh, 32
becoming-musicians, 125–26, 128, 178–79
Being, 17n.41, 43, 120, 136n.16, 159–61, 164–
    65, 165n.31. *See also* identity
belonging, 20–21, 41–42, 50–51, 57, 126–27, 154
Bergson, Henri, 125n.30, 168n.46
Biesta, Gert, 33–34, 66, 109
binary thinking, 121n.20, 122, 134
boundary walker, 13, 133, 133n.8
Brexit, 52

Camlin, Dave, 9n.12, 33–34, 111n.1, 148
Caputo, John, 91–92, 133n.9, 138–39
care ethics, 50
censorship, 90–91, 150–51
certification, 67
choirs, 28–29, 93–94, 173–74
CMA (Commission for Community Music
    Activity), 4–5, 113–14, 131, 162–63
collaboration, 37–38, 83, 130, 147–48, 149–50
colonialism, 29–30, 88
community
    arts, 27, 29, 37, 147–48

cultural development, 4–5, 147–48
    etymology of, 42
    without unity, 40, 119–20
competition, 79–80, 103
conductor, choral, 92–93
*conscientization*, 6
context, 16
Coombs, Philip, 64–65
counterculture, 27, 147–48
Covid-19 30–31, 69–70
    pandemic, 10–11, 75–76, 173–74
creativity, 6, 34, 54, 74–75, 146–47, 165n.30,
    165–66n.37
Critchley, Simon, 16–17
cultural
    consciousness, 132–33
    context, 37–38, 115–16
    democracy, 34–35
    development (*see* community: cultural
        development)
    policy, 34, 133, 172
    tourism, 173–74
    inequality, 23–24, 180–81
curriculum, 27, 64–65, 66–67, 70, 77n.23, 161–62

daycare center, 43, 180
decision, 93–95
decolonization, 33–34, 134, 149–50
    indigenous knowledges, 149
deconstruction, 15–16, 121n.20, 122n.21
deficit model, 34, 133–34
definitions, community music, 12–13
Deleuze, Gilles, 17–19
    arborescent, 171–72
    cartography, 165–66
    contingency, 167–69
    essences, 159–60, 161–62
    ethics, 165–66
    force, 124–25
    Guattari, and, 17

## 208 INDEX

Deleuze, Gilles (*cont.*)
  materialism, 18n.44
  monism, 18n.45
  ontology, 124–25, 159–61, 163
  plane of consistency, 162n.25
  segmentary, 165n.36, 169
  Spinoza, and, 124n.27
  transcendence, 124–25
  virtual, 161nn.21–22, 165–66
  *See also* assemblage; desire;
    deterritorialization; difference;
    expression; folding; immanence; lines of
    flight; milieu; multiplicities; rhizome
democracy, 57–58, 166n.40
  *to* come, 34–35, 36
  John Dewey, and, 166n.40
  *See also* cultural democracy
de Quadros, Andre, 92–93
Derrida, Jacques, 15–17
  aesthetics, 121n.19
  essences, 120n.15
  ethics, and, 16–17
  haunting, 120–21
  Heidegger, 15, 19, 120nn.15–16
  parergon, 121n.19, 134
  *See also* always-already; deconstruction;
    context; democracy: *to* come; logocentrism;
    justice; promise; supplement; trace; "yes"
desert, 87
desire, 36, 170n.50
deterritorialization, 167–69
Dewey, John, 166n.40. *See also* democracy
difference, 19, 124–25, 159–64
disability activists, 48n.12
dreaming, 133
drumming, 4–5, 116, 153, 180

editor, 12–13, 131–32, 135, 139. *See also* weak
  thought
education, online, 69–70
Elliott, David, 7–9, 22, 113–14, 119–20, 135.
  *See also* praxis
empathy, 74–75, 149
empowerment, 27, 37, 99, 147–48
enculturated, 102
Enlightenment, 137, 145–46
equality, 6, 41, 66, 87, 99
  diversity, and, 89, 153
  economics, and, 87
  social, and, 108
equity, 87, 92–93, 173–74
essence, and community music, 122
ethno research, 69–70, 173–74

ethnomusicology, applied, 82, 88–89, 157
*eudaimonia,* 114–15
evaluation, 107, 131, 143–44, 148, 150–51
event, the, 137n.21
exclusion, 48, 55, 99, 120–21
expression, 67, 124–27

face to face, 43
facilitation, 36, 63–64, 74–75, 169, 180–81.
  *See also* learning, non-formal.
  co-constructing, 83, 98
  etymology of, 74–75
  responsibility, and, 35–36, 45–46, 73, 75–76
  workshops, 37–38, 39, 45–46, 73, 93, 94–95,
    107, 118, 124
feminist critique, 49–50
field, of practice, 10, 11–13
folding, 125n.33
Foucault, Michel, 57, 137
  genealogy, 17–18
  ontology, 18n.42
freedom, 43, 51–52, 57, 137n.21, 158
  absolute, 124n.27
freelancer, 9
Freire, Paulo, 6, 37, 66–67. *See also*
  *conscientization*
friendship, 26, 67–68, 76n.22, 79–80, 158

Gibson, Jo, 130, 145. *See also* research, practice
Glenister, Simon, 141. *See also* Noise Solution
globalization, 50–51, 64–65, 161n.20
Goh, Irving, 43
government, 27, 48, 109, 149–50, 153
  decentralization, 64–65
  funding, 88–89, 133
  policy, 66
Guattari, Felix, 14–15, 17, 157. *See also* Deleuze

Hayek, Fredrich, 89–90
health, 4–5, 27–28, 30–31
  care settings, 4–5, 95–96, 180
  education, 27, 30–31
  mental, 45–46, 88, 140–41, 144–45
  sexual, 30–31, 76
  well-being, and, 27–28
Heidegger, Martin, 15
  Being, 136n.16, 137n.20
  experience, 14n.35
  metaphysics, 136–37
Henley, Jennie, 22, 103–4
hermeneutics, 123–24, 138–39
higher education, 4–5, 9, 10–11, 118–19,
  149–50, 156

INDEX 209

hip hop, 78–79
hospitality, 39–51. *See also,* democracy: *to* come
  gift, as, 49–50
  inauthentic, 48, 57
  Kant, and, 49n.13
  Levinas, and, 43–44, 48–49
  limits, of, 58–60
  visitations, 56–57
human capital, 66, 99
  flourishing, 111n.1, 114–16
  rights, 3–4, 29–30, 44–45, 90n.8, 92–94,
    99, 149–50

ICCM (International Centre for Community
  Music) 149
idealism, 18n.44, 152–53
identity
  community music, and, 118–19, 155–56, 157,
    166–67, 172, 175
  difference, and, 159–53, 171
  musicians, 126
  Nietzsche, and, 165n.30
  transcendence, 125n.29
IJCM (International Journal for Community
  Music), 63–64, 75–76, 131–32
immanence, 124–25, 161–62
*im*possible, 122–23
improvisation, 36, 45–46, 79–80, 92–93, 116,
  117–18, 126, 158, 180
inclusivity, 44, 58, 83, 89, 103–4, 105, 108–10, 157
industrial nations, 90–91
  revolution, 28–29
inequality, 105
  social, 23–24, 180–81
intercultural, 33–34, 173–74
intertextuality, 120–21
intervention, 29–31
  etymology of, 29, 36

justice, 90–92
  climate, and, 88

Kant, Immanuel, 87
  absolute, 43–44, 45–46
  reason, 91–92, 146–47, 160n.18
Kapalka Richerme, Lauren, 158
Keil, Charlie, 152, 165–66
khôra, 49–50

Laes, Tuulikki, 109
learning
  continuum, 70–71
  formal, 21, 70–71

  informal, 66, 68–69, 70–71, 122, 132–33
  lifelong, 7–9, 39, 66, 69–70, 71, 139, 157
  nonformal, 37–38, 63–76, 97, 122, 158, 179
  Youtube, 79–80, 161–62
Leavy, Patricia, 147–48
Levinas, Emmanuel, 26, 40, 43–44. *See also* face
  to face
  ethics, on, 48–49
  same, the, 125–26, 136–37
lines of flight, 165–66, 175, 179
logocentrism, 122

machine, 169–70
Matarasso, François, 29
milieu, 168n.43, 171
multiplicities, 18n.45, 126–27, 167–69
music
  aesthetic, and, 29, 111n.1, 115–16,
    122, 128–29
  business, 120–21
  classical, 4–5, 68–69, 88–89, 119–20, 121–22
  classroom, in the, 55–56, 68–69, 98
  commercial, 140–41, 154n.6
  composition, 4–5, 97, 117–18, 168n.45, 180
  conflict, and, 27–28
  conservatoire, 4–5, 10–11, 25, 68–69
  ecosystem, 3–4, 21, 83–84, 179–81
  infinite, as an, 125–27
  notation, 97, 99–100, 117–18, 122
  pop and rock, 4–5, 68–69, 70–71, 73,
    157, 173–74
  prisons, in, 92–93
  repertoire, and, 92–93, 166–67
  standards, 25, 119–20, 126, 132
  teaching, 55–56, 57–58, 68–69, 83–84, 88–89,
    103, 161–62
  therapy, 27–28, 39, 103–4, 139, 157,
    163–64, 175–76
musical
  identities, 173–74
  instruments – adapted, 180
musician-self, 150–51
musicking, 3–4, 6, 51–52, 57–58, 77, 86, 93–94,
  115n.7, 155–56, 180–81

neoliberalism, 99
Nietzsche, 15, 137
  creativity, and, 165n.30
  eternal return, and the, 136n.15
  God is dead, 138n.24
  interpretations, 138n.27
  nihilism, and, 138–39
  will to power, and the, 161n.23

# 210 INDEX

Noise Solution, 140–43

ontology, 17n.41, 124n.26, 159–60
origami, 125–26
Other, the, 92n.11
outreach, 109–10, 112–13, 126
ownership, 41, 80, 81–82, 173–74

parents, 25–26, 39, 76, 123, 139
peace and reconciliation, 94–95
performance, 62–63, 67–68, 80–81, 92–93, 97, 103, 112–16, 118–19, 122, 133, 166–67
phenomenology, 14–15, 51
*phronesis*, 54, 115–16
Plato, 49–50, 136–37
    forms, 91–92
political activism, 169, 180–81
postcolonial, 109–10
postmodernism, 137nn.21–22
postmodernity, 136–37, 146–47
poststructuralism, 14–15, 158
poverty, 37, 88–89, 92, 95–96, 101–2, 123
    digital, 173–74
praxis, 54n.19, 113–16
prepositional, 43
professionalization, 29
promise, 20–21, 34–35, 60–61, 91–92, 119–20, 178–79
punk rock, 132–33

qualifications, 66, 70

recontextualization, 79–80
refugee crisis, 58–59
research
    arts-based, 131, 143–44, 145, 146–48
    autoethnographic, 127–28, 143–44, 149
    crisis of representation, 145–46
    dissemination, 149–51
    ethical, 130–31, 150–51, 155, 173–74
    ethnography, 143–44
    practice– 130–31
    practice as, 130, 131, 143–44, 146–47, 173–74
    relationships, and, 145
resilience, 173–74
rhizome, 171–72
rural communities, 25

samba, 77–82

Schippers, Huib, 85, 171–72
schooling, 63–65, 123, 140–41
school music education, 55–56, 83–84, 161–62, 166n.40
Silverman, Marissa, 22, 89, 113–14
singing, 27–28, 63–64, 92–93, 113, 153, 173–74, 180
songwriting, 73, 76, 173–74, 180
soundbeam, 117–18
Spinoza, Baruch, 124nn.27–28
stranger, 44–45, 46–47, 51–53, 55, 92
    immigration, 48, 52
subcultures, 132–33
supplement, 120, 134n.10
sustainability, cultural, 85, 93–95

temporality, 125n.32, 146–47
togetherness, 34–35, 113, 166–67
tourism, 47–48
trace, 119–20
transdisciplinary, 149–50
transformation, 37
trauma, 173–74
    informed practice, 157
Turino, Thomas, 103, 114–15
Turner, Kathleen, 149

unconditionality, 43–44
UNESCO, 4–5, 66

Vattimo, Gianvani, 14–15, 136–37. *See also,* weak thought
Veblen, Kari, 4–5, 6, 7–9, 69–70, 114n.3, 135
virtuosity, 101, 102, 116–17
vulnerability, 57–58, 130, 149

Warwick-Edinburgh Mental Well-being Scale, 144–45
weak thought, 131–32, 135–39
welcome, the, 35–36, 41–45
    etymology, 36
wellbeing, 7–9, 28–29, 86, 88, 103–4, 114–16, 140–41, 144–45, 157, 173–74
Willingham, Lee, 149
Wrobleski, Jessica, 54

"yes", 20–21, 40–41, 54, 58, 60–40, 95–96, 119–20, 166–67, 178–79
Youth workers, 62, 123
    centres, 95–96, 180